THE CULL

Tony Park was born in 1964 and grew up in the western suburbs of Sydney. He has worked as a newspaper reporter, a press secretary, a PR consultant and a freelance writer. He also served thirty-four years in the Australian Army Reserve, including six months as a public affairs officer in Afghanistan in 2002. He and his wife, Nicola, divide their time equally between Australia and southern Africa. He is the author of thirteen other African novels.

THE CULL
TONY PARK

PAN BOOKS

First published 2017 by Pan Macmillan Australia Pty Ltd

First published in the UK in 2017 by Pan Books
an imprint of Pan Macmillan
20 New Wharf Road, London N1 9RR
Associated companies throughout the world
www.panmacmillan.com

ISBN   978-1-5098-7529-0

Cartographic art by Laurie Whiddon, Map Illustrations

1 3 5 7 9 8 6 4 2

A CIP catalogue record for this book is available from the British Library.

Printed and bound by CPI Group (UK) Ltd, Croydon, CR0 4YY

Visit **www.panmacmillan.com** to read more about all our books
and to buy them. You will also find features, author interviews and
news of any author events, and you can sign up for e-newsletters
so that you're always first to hear about our new releases.

For Nicola

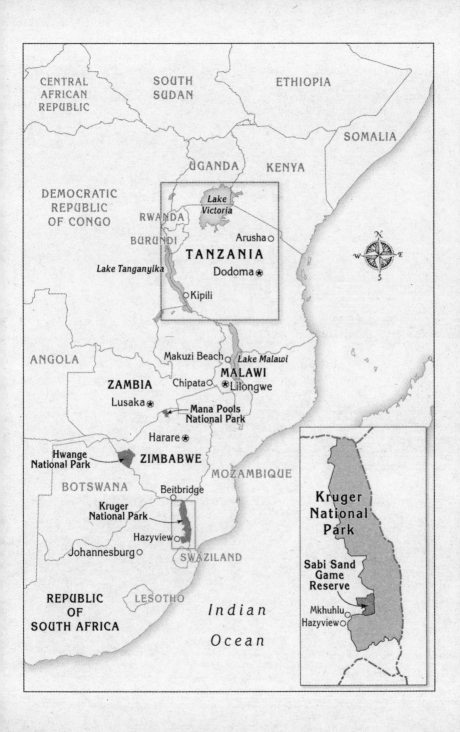

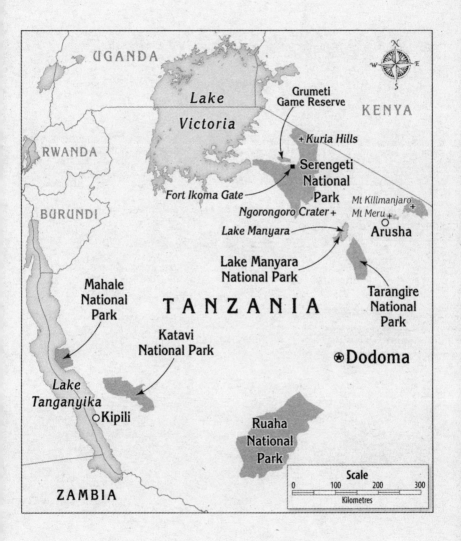

PART 1

The Night

S he killed quietly, strangling the life out of her victim.

It was her special skill, the ability to take a life in the darkness, without making a sound. She was a single mother and she did what she did for the sake of her daughter, and herself, and she thought nothing of the act.

She had stalked her quarry carefully, creeping through the dry African bush under the bright light of a full, clear moon. She had paused in the shadow of a giant jackalberry tree and watched him. He cut a handsome figure, silhouetted against the silvery waters of the Sabie River. He was watchful, alert, looking around him and sniffing the wind for danger.

She had dropped to her belly and, with even more care than before, crept until she was within striking distance. He'd gone back to eating – one of the two things males usually had on their minds – and it was then that she had launched herself from the darkness.

It was quick, it was clean, it was necessary. It was what she had been designed for, what she had spent her life perfecting. Killing.

She needed to go about her business in silence because she,

too, was being hunted. She had enemies, male and female, who were bigger, stronger than her, and some were far better armed than her.

The whispered voices of women were carried on the cool night breeze through the South African bush. In their language, xiTsonga, they called the killer *Ingwe*, and they were acutely aware of the danger she posed to them. They may all have been females – Ingwe and the women who patrolled the bush around her – but they were still enemies.

Ingwe listened, all her senses alert, as the life ebbed from the victim in her grasp. When at last he was still she laid him at her feet.

She lifted her head and sniffed the wind. The women were getting closer.

'Be quiet,' a voice hissed.

A lion called, mercifully far off, but a baboon barked its *wa-hoo* warning call. The baboon hadn't seen her, but it might have seen the women, or possibly a spotted hyena.

Ingwe sensed imminent danger.

The women were getting closer and, as she had feared, a hyena lent its eerie whooping call to the cacophony of chattering baboons. Her enemies were closing in on her, but she would survive. She had to, for the sake of her daughter.

Ingwe grasped the neck of the impala ram firmly in her strong jaws, lifted him and climbed up the jackalberry tree, out of reach and sight of the women who passed below her.

Chapter 1

Sonja Kurtz was unsure of herself. It might have been an acceptable feeling for most people, but not for her.

She heard whispering ahead of her, and tittering laughter. The sounds multiplied her annoyance. 'Be quiet.'

The women in front of her stopped making their noise. It would be Patience and Goodness, whose names belied their characters.

Sonja didn't fear the bush, with its myriad deadly creatures, nor the armed poachers she was training the six Shangaan women with her to hunt. She was more worried about a lovely house on the banks of the Sabie River, just a few kilometres away, and a handsome man who was there right now, cooking dinner for her.

That picture of domestic bliss under an African moon worried her more than anything.

Tema Matsebula, the woman immediately in front of her, stopped and held up a hand. Tema clicked her fingers so that Patience and Goodness, the Mdluli sisters, looked back and also halted.

Sonja closed the gap between her and Tema. Tall, pretty and intelligent, Tema was the most serious and capable of her recruits to the Leopards Anti-Poaching Unit in the Sabi Sand Game Reserve. The Leopards were an all-female unit, based on the success of the first such outfit, the Black Mambas, in the Balule Reserve, north of where they were operating now.

'What is it?' Sonja whispered.

Tema pointed the barrel of her LM5 assault rifle, the semi-automatic version of the South African millitary's R5, to the ground. There was a game trail, a dirt path made by the regular passing of animals towards the Sabie River. Across the path was a drag mark. Tema dropped to one knee, touched a muddy spot and raised her fingers to sniff them. 'Kill.'

Sonja saw the compact pugmarks on either side of the drag trail; there had been an unseasonal shower of rain that morning so the tracks stood out clearly in the soil, which had retained some moisture beneath the surface. '*Ingwe.*'

'Yes,' Tema said quietly. 'Leopard.'

The two women looked at each other, then down again, following the trail of blood and flattened grass that led right to the base of the trunk of the huge jackalberry tree under which they were standing.

Sonja saw, as no doubt her trainee did, the fresh pale scars that the leopard's claws had carved into the tree's bark. They both looked up. Sonja searched the high branches.

'What is it now?' Patience said. Her tone was typically surly. She would have been smarting from Sonja's sharp command for her to be quiet. Patience took every order as an insult.

'*Ingwe,*' said Tema.

Patience's eyes widened and her jaw dropped as Tema pointed upwards.

Sonja finally located the sleek silhouette, though the big cat was expertly camouflaged. It raised its head. 'Nobody move.'

'*Eish,*' said Patience. She brushed past Sonja and Tema, waddling quickly back the way they had come.

'Patience, I said don't move.'

'I don't care.' Patience spoke in her normal voice, not bothering to whisper. 'Stop telling me what to do. I'm going home.'

There was a rustle in the branches above and a dappled blur as the leopard ran halfway down the tree trunk then launched itself into mid-air above Sonja's head. Goodness screamed as the leopard hit the ground. Patience looked back, changed direction and ran.

'Don't run,' Sonja called. The leopard seemed as startled and confused as the women around it. Sonja thought it might chase down the fleeing Patience. She raised her LM5 to her shoulder and took aim.

A burst of gunfire sent the women diving for the ground, but Sonja hadn't fired the bullets. Panic spread through the women like a veld fire. Sonja took in Patience, yelling in pain this time, and crumpling to the ground. The leopard bounded away into the night, away from them all. Goodness screamed her sister's name.

Tema returned fire, two shots. 'By the big leadwood, towards the river.'

Good girl, Sonja thought. Tema had seen where the shots had come from and given a target indication, as per her training. Sonja got up. 'Tema, with me.' She looked to the other women in the patrol. They looked justifiably terrified. 'Mavis, Lungile, Lucy, give us covering fire. And for fuck's sake don't shoot us in the back.'

Sonja stood and fired two rounds to the right and the left of the leadwood. 'Where's Goodness?'

'She's run away,' Tema said, not bothering to hide the disgust in her voice.

Patience was a pain in the butt, but Goodness was her sister. Tema set off and Sonja, a couple of decades older but just as fit, ran to catch up with her. Patience was crying out to them for help. The three women behind them fired sporadic shots in the direction from which the first burst had come.

Tema arrived at Patience first and dropped to her knees. She checked the other woman and by the time Sonja reached them Tema had her first aid kit out and was placing a field dressing over a wound in Patience's belly.

'Keep the pressure on the wound,' Sonja advised.

Tema looked up at her, and swallowed hard to control her fear. 'She's hurt badly.'

Sonja took her handheld radio from the pouch on her belt. 'Sabi Sand warden, this is call-sign Leopard Niner, we're in a contact with one woman wounded, request immediate casualty evacuation . . .'

A storm of fire erupted from the bushes ahead of them. Tema lay across Patience to protect her. Sonja dropped to her belly, brought her LM5 to bear and returned fire.

'We can't stay here, we're exposed,' Sonja said as bullets whizzed around them. 'Covering fire!' she called to the others.

Sonja willed herself to stand, and fired two more bursts towards her still unseen enemies. 'Help me get Patience on my shoulders.'

Tema ignored the order, slung her rifle and bent and hoisted Patience, much heavier than herself, in a fireman's carry. 'I'm younger than you.'

Sonja shook her head. She put herself between her girls and the people shooting at them and kept firing while walking backwards, as they fell back to the others.

Lucy, Lungile and Mavis had moved to a position of cover, behind a fallen tree trunk. Tema, panting, lay Patience on her back behind the other women. Lucy dropped her rifle, put a hand over her mouth and started to sob when she saw how badly Patience was hit.

Tema grabbed her by a shoulder. 'Stop that. Stop your crying. You must be strong.'

Sonja repeated her call for assistance and was told by the reserve's warden that he had contacted the Mission Area Joint

Operations Command at Skukuza Airport, inside the neighbouring Kruger National Park. An evacuation helicopter and armed response team were being scrambled. The headquarters for the anti-poaching effort in the Kruger Park and surrounding game reserves was only twelve kilometres away and the reinforcements would be with them in minutes.

Sonja shrugged off her daypack. From inside it she took her first aid kit and handed it to Tema, to replace the dressing on Patience's wound, which was already soaked through with blood. She also fished out a pair of night vision goggles. She had planned to give each of the women in the Leopard patrol a chance to try out the device. However, their night-time movement and navigation training exercise had suddenly turned very real.

Sonja put on the goggles and scanned the bush ahead of them.

'I hear movement,' Lungile said.

Sonja nodded and held up a hand for silence. About fifty metres ahead of them she saw a man. A second then moved forward and dropped to one knee behind a tree.

They were moving like soldiers, Sonja observed. One stayed still and looked for targets, ready to give covering fire, while the other moved. These men were disciplined, trained. And they were not running away, which was unusual for poachers, who tended to flee the scene once they were observed or ambushed. Also out of the ordinary for poachers was that these men had fired first.

Sonja scanned the frightened faces around her. Only Tema looked calm as she finished changing Patience's dressing. 'Ladies, listen to me. We have to hold on until the helicopter gets here, but these men, they are coming for us.'

'No!' Lucy cried.

'Shut up,' said Tema. 'Listen to the commander.'

Lucy shook her head. 'This woman wants to get us all killed.' She started to stand but Tema slapped her face. Lucy, taken aback, sat down, rubbing her cheek.

Sonja was their mentor, not their commander, but now was not the time for semantics. If these men were not running away it meant they were intent on bringing the fight to them. If her Leopards would not, or could not fight, they might not survive until the cavalry arrived.

'Listen up. I'm going to try to outflank them, draw their fire and keep them busy. When the shooting starts, carry Patience further back, towards Lion Sands. You know the way to the lodge, Tema?'

'I do, madam. But I am coming with you. Lungile knows the way, she used to be a chef in the lodge there, right, sisi?'

Lungile nodded.

Sonja got back on the radio and updated the warden so he could relay the news to the inbound helicopter. Sonja didn't want armed rangers in the sky firing on the girls as they moved towards the luxurious safari lodge on the banks of the Sabie River. 'And tell the chopper there are at least two men armed with AK-47s, probably more, looking for a fight.'

'Roger,' said the warden over the radio. 'Security's advice is for you to retreat, as well.'

'Whatever. Out,' Sonja said. 'Go with the others, Tema.'

'No, madam.'

'You're not my maid, Tema, call me Sonja, and do as I tell you.'

Tema shook her head. 'You are right, Sonja, I am not a maid, not any more, but you are our trainer, not our commander. I am a Leopard and I am coming with you. My job is to hunt poachers.'

Sonja wasn't given to public displays of affection, not with her daughter, Emma, who she loved, nor her boyfriend or lover or friend with benefits or whatever Hudson Brand, who waited in his house along the river cooking dinner for her, liked to think of himself as. But she reached out her free hand and squeezed Tema's arm. 'All right. Let's go.'

Lungile and Lucy picked up Patience, and Mavis carried her weapon and the first aid kits. Sonja and Tema retreated with them, and when Sonja was sure they were out of sight of anyone watching them, she and Tema broke off to the left. 'Keep going until you get to Lion Sands or the chopper finds you,' she said to the others in parting.

Sonja had expected the poachers to open fire on them as soon as they started moving, but quiet had returned to the bush, with the exception of the baboons, who were still unsettled by the firefight and the leopard.

The poachers may have retreated, but Sonja had not heard any movement in the dry bush, nor seen anyone through the night vision goggles. The men had advanced on the patrol, but then seemingly gone to ground. None of it made sense. She tried to process the events as she and Tema moved quietly through the thorny dry bushveld.

This was supposed to have been a training exercise only, to get the Leopards used to working and navigating at night. The property they were on, Lion Plains, had been hard hit by rhino poachers, but a combination of increased anti-poaching patrols and a recent scarcity of rhino sightings in the area had meant that poaching activity had been quiet for the past four weeks. It had seemed an acceptable risk to conduct the night exercise, but now they were in a very real fight with an enemy who was not acting in a way that passed for normal for illegal hunters.

Sonja was still wearing the goggles, and taking point, moving in the lead, but she stopped when Tema clicked her fingers.

Tema moved to Sonja and brought her lips close to her ear. 'Men talking.'

Tema pointed ahead and to the right. The women slowly lowered themselves to one knee, behind a wickedly barbed buffalo thorn tree. Sonja had the benefit of modern technology, but her ears had suffered an adult lifetime spent around guns and explosives; Tema had a twenty-two-year-old's hearing.

They waited and watched. Sonja saw movement and brought up her rifle. There were two men. One carried an AK-47 and the other a longer weapon. At first Sonja thought it was a hunting rifle, but it looked bulkier.

'What is that gun?' Tema whispered.

The men stopped and the man with the odd weapon said something to his comrade.

From across the Sabie River, inside the Kruger Park, came the whine of a turbine engine and the *thwap* of rotor blades cleaving the cool night air.

Sonja looked at the men. They had heard the helicopter approaching, because they, too, scanned the sky, but they did not run for cover. Instead the big man reached to the front of the weapon, under the barrel, and unfolded a spring-loaded bipod.

'Shit.'

'What is it?' Tema asked.

'That's an RPD light machine gun. Russian made. They're not just hunting rhinos with that bloody thing.' Sonja scrabbled for her handheld radio.

'National parks helo, national parks helo, this is Leopard Niner, anti-poaching call-sign. If you read me, break away, do not, I repeat, do not come to this location. There are armed tangos with a machine gun waiting for you. Abort mission, fly to Lion Sands.'

Sonja waited for a reply. The warden she had been speaking to earlier called and said he had heard her and would try to relay the message. In the meantime the helicopter bore down on them, low and fast, its nose-mounted searchlight tracing a path towards them.

The man with the AK-47 aimed his weapon skywards. The

gunner, however, had moved behind a leadwood tree and Sonja could not get a bead on him.

'They're going to shoot down the helicopter,' Sonja said. 'They used us to draw it in, to set an ambush.'

Tema looked scared for the first time that night. 'What are we going to do?'

Sonja had turned her back on wars, on fighting and dying, and had agreed to this job on the basis that she was a trainer, not a fighter. All that had changed in a few short minutes.

'We're going to kill them.'

'Shouldn't we try to warn the helicopter again, wait for the police?'

Sonja raised her LM5 and took aim at the man who was about to help the RPD gunner take on the helicopter. He wasn't pointing a gun at her or threatening anyone right now, but in about five seconds both gunmen would have a clean line of sight to the helicopter.

She drew a breath, watched the tip of the barrel of her rifle rise, then exhaled half a lungful of air. She squeezed the trigger.

The man with the AK-47 staggered and fell and the machine gunner let off a long burst, prematurely, Sonja hoped.

From the bush on either side of the gunner two other AK-47s started firing on full automatic. Their combined fire and a warning from the reserve's warden, which Sonja heard squawking through her radio, made the helicopter pilot bank sharply and peel away.

The machine gunner stepped from behind his tree and saw Sonja. He let loose a twenty-round burst and she and Tema split and sprinted for cover.

Tema flattened herself behind a tree and looked, wide-eyed, to Sonja. 'What do we do?'

The machine gun had stopped firing. 'We advance.'

Sonja looked around her tree, fired at the gunner who had also ducked back behind cover, then ran forward. She had the satisfaction of hearing Tema laying down covering fire. When Sonja had closed the distance between her and the men she dropped down behind a granite boulder and started firing. 'Move, Tema!'

The other woman started running. Off to her right Sonja saw a fifth poacher break cover and raise his AK-47.

'It's a woman,' the man yelled.

Sonja took aim at him and fired twice. The man fell before he could get a shot off. 'Damn straight it's a woman.'

Sonja searched for targets but couldn't see any more men. She fired a few shots into the bushes where she'd last seen the machine gunner. Tema came abreast of her. 'Stop, Tema, get down.'

Tema did as ordered but looked to her, panting. Sonja thought she could almost see disappointment, maybe anger, on the younger woman's face. 'Why? We have them on the run, let us finish them.'

'They've got an RPD machine gun. If they find good cover and reload we'll be tickets. You have to learn when to break contact, when to retreat.'

Tema's lips were pressed firmly together. 'I don't want to retreat. I don't ever want a man to think he can hurt me again just because I'm a woman.'

Sonja nodded. 'I don't think that will happen to you again, Tema.'

Tema scanned the bush, searching for targets, while Sonja checked in on her radio. She listened to conversations between several men.

'What now?' Tema asked.

'The national parks helicopter was hit by ground fire. The pilot reported a fuel leak and turned back to Skukuza. Patience is in luck, though, there's another chopper coming from one of the lodges and they're going to take her to the hospital in Nelspruit.'

'Thank the Lord,' Tema said.

Sonja listened into her earpiece again. 'Yes, and thank that British billionaire and bunny hugger Julianne Clyde-Smith who owns Khaya Ngala Safari Lodge. It's her helicopter. Now, let's get back to the girls.'

They stood and Tema looked over her shoulder to where the remaining men had disappeared. 'I don't want them to get away.'

'Neither do I,' Sonja said. 'It makes me sick. But that's what happens in war; sometimes you have to retreat.'

Tema was coming down from the adrenaline high of her first combat and Sonja knew what that was like.

Tema sniffed and wiped her eyes, the resentment gone from her voice, which was softer now. 'This is a war.'

Chapter 2

Julianne Clyde-Smith was waiting at the entrance to Lion Sands Game Reserve when Sonja Kurtz and an African woman in the same camouflage uniform, also carrying a rifle, jogged down the access road.

A male staff member held up a platter to Sonja as she arrived. 'A hot towel, madam?'

Sonja just stared at the man for a second. He turned to the African woman, who greeted him in xiTsonga and accepted a towel.

'Sonja, hello, I've heard what happened,' Julianne said.

'How's my woman?' Sonja said to Julianne. No nonsense, just as she'd expected. 'I just saw your helicopter take off.'

'She's serious, but my head of security, James Paterson, is on board, and he'll make sure she's well looked after. Both he and my pilot, Doug Pearse, are ex-military. James has replaced her dressings and put in an IV.'

Sonja nodded. 'And my other operators?'

'That's a special forces term, I believe?'

'Well, they started the night as trainees, but their shit just got real, as the Americans would say.'

'Quite. Can I stand you a drink? Your ladies . . . er, operators, are also at the bar,' Julianne said.

Sonja frowned, but seemed to bite back the retort that was forming. 'With me, Tema. We need to talk about what happened tonight, all of us. Any sign of Goodness?'

'No, she's still missing,' the girl called Tema said.

'Miss Clyde-Smith,' Sonja began.

'Jules to my friends. Please.'

'Julianne, thank you for the use of your helicopter. We really appreciate it, and I know of the work and the money you've put into conservation issues.'

'If you have a woman missing I can task my helicopter to help in a search as soon as it returns from the hospital.'

'Thank you,' Sonja said. 'She's a local woman so I'm hoping she will head here or to the reserve gate.'

'How about that drink?'

Julianne led the way through the white rendered open reception area to the bar on the left. A log fire burned in the fireplace, more for ambience than necessity as it was a mild evening. Sonja's other three women got to their feet as she entered.

'Sit,' Sonja said. 'What are you drinking, Lungile?'

'Coke. We assumed we were still on duty.'

Sonja gave a small nod. 'It's no time for celebration.' She turned to Julianne. 'Will you excuse us, Julianne?'

'Can I have ten minutes of your time, first?' Julianne asked. 'I'd like to speak to you privately.'

'I really need to talk to my people.' Sonja turned away from her.

'Yes, I understand completely, but I have some information about the poaching gang behind tonight's terrible business.' Julianne beckoned to a waiter and ordered a large bottle of sparkling water and two glasses.

Sonja looked back. 'They were way better armed than the average bunch of ragtag poachers from Mozambique, but OK, I'm listening.'

'I know who's bankrolling that gang, and I know about their machine gun, the RPD.'

'How did you know about that?'

Julianne gestured to a couch in the corner of the bar. She led the way and Sonja followed. Sonja set her LM5 assault rifle down on a side table and sat down. The waiter brought their water and poured for them.

'You look exhausted.'

'Don't worry about me. Talk to me,' Sonja said.

'You're very direct,' Julianne said.

'You knew my name, just now, when I arrived, but we've never met. Did one of my girls tell you?'

'Google's a wonderful thing,' Julianne said. 'I know you need to get back to your troops so I'll cut to the chase. I want to offer you a job.'

Sonja looked her in the eye. 'I'm not in the market.'

'Then what are you doing here, with these women?'

'It's a voluntary position. An old army friend who runs a charity that pairs military veterans with anti-poaching units asked me to work with the Leopards, to mentor them. He thought having a woman with some military experience train them for a few months might be better for them than just another male ex-soldier. Not that it's any of your business, but I have a personal connection to the property next to this one, where the Leopards are based.'

Julianne had not only googled Sonja, she'd had James, the head of security for her global IT, tourism and online media company, conduct a thorough check into Sonja's background. 'Yes, your partner was killed at Lion Plains while filming a documentary on the plight of South Africa's rhinos.'

Sonja took a sip of water. 'Good old Google.'

'You're experienced enough to realise, I hope, that training a few women from the local townships to shoot and navigate in the bush at night won't stop rhino poaching.'

Sonja finished her drink and set it down on the carved wooden table.

'I realise, Julianne, that anything that helps lift women out of the drudgery of being forced to take a job as a domestic servant because of rampant unemployment when they've attained a respectable matriculation mark at high school is a good thing. I also realise, through my experience, that a female recruit is as good as any man, and probably better because she's not burdened by an overdose of testosterone or her own self-importance.' Sonja stood and turned her back on her.

'Drink up, girls,' she called to the women.

Julianne Clyde-Smith wasn't used to people walking out on her, but Sonja Kurtz was everything she'd thought she would be – tough, outspoken, fearless in combat, and dedicated to the people under her command. 'How would you like to stop rhino poaching, or reduce it to near zero?'

Sonja looked back at her. 'You're right about one thing. Boots on the ground, male or female, here in the Sabi Sand, isn't enough to stop poaching here. We're barely holding the line.'

Julianne lowered her voice. 'How would you like to get the men who trained and commanded the poaching team you encountered tonight, who shot your operator?'

'They're probably in Mozambique, across the border from Kruger. They're out of our jurisdiction, and the fact is the Mozambican government has neither the will nor the expertise to capture the ringleaders, the middlemen, nor the buyers from Asia who come looking for rhino horn and elephant ivory.'

'Yes, you're correct on all counts, but would you like to get them?'

Sonja raised an eyebrow. Her face was streaked where her sweat had cut through her camouflage cream. She patted the breast pocket of her uniform as though she was instinctively reaching for a cigarette. Her fingers were caked with dried blood. 'You want me to train the Mozambican police, work with them? They don't take kindly to strangers telling them what to do.'

'No. What I mean is that you could do it yourself, you and a hand-picked team, operating undercover in Mozambique and wherever the poaching kingpins are living with impunity.'

She scoffed. 'An anti-poaching black ops unit? It's the stuff of fiction. No one's got the balls or the money or the political will to go through with it.'

'I've got the money, plenty of it, and the will. Helicopters, drones, weapons, thermal imaging gear, night vision kit. Anything you want. You name it, you get it. You can even hire some balls if you need them.'

'It's a nice fantasy, but it's nothing without hard intelligence and proper targeting. Plus, who's going to take the risk of being caught in a foreign country illegally, and why? Not for money alone.'

Julianne had anticipated her questions. She didn't want someone who was motivated by money, nor some radical animal rights campaigner. 'As for intelligence, I can give you the name of the person who sold the poachers that RPD machine gun you saw tonight, and the name of the man who bought it and financed tonight's mission. I can give you his address, the make of his car and its licence plate, and the names of his wife and children.'

Sonja looked over her shoulder to the members of her team, her Leopards. She seemed to be weighing it up, and then she called to them, 'Have another drink, girls.'

Sonja came back to Julianne and resumed her seat. 'How did you know about the RPD?'

'My intelligence is better than the South African government's. I warned them about a machine gun attack on the military or an anti-poaching team, or maybe one of the security forces' helicopters. They thought I was mad.'

'How do you know so much more than the people at the Joint Operations Command?'

Julianne smiled. 'I've got more money than them.'

'I know. I read the newspapers.'

Julianne's phone was set to silent, but it vibrated in her pocket. She took it out. 'Excuse me, this is James, my head of security. Hello?'

Julianne listened to James's report; he was at the hospital in Nelspruit. She realised Sonja must have been able to read the look on her face.

'Bad news?'

Julianne nodded. 'I'm so very sorry. Your woman . . .'

'Patience.'

'There was nothing my men could do to save her. They did their very best. She died in my helicopter on the way to the hospital.'

Sonja called the waiter over, her face like stone, and said to him, 'Bring us a bottle of Klipdrift.'

'Sonja,' Julianne said.

'What? I need to be with my team now.'

'I really am very sorry for your loss. I think you, of all people, someone who has lost so much, knows that we're in a war here, and I can tell you that it's escalating. Tonight proved that. I could be wrong, but I don't think you're the sort of person to be training people when you could be making a real difference on the front line. Will you please just come to my lodge and at least hear what I have to say? I believe it's in your best interests. We have to do more, Sonja.'

Sonja stood. 'I'll think about it.'

*

Hudson Brand stirred at the sound of a diesel engine.

He had fallen asleep in the comfy green canvas and brown leather designer camping chair in front of the fireplace. The house

21

in the Hippo Rock Private Nature Reserve, on the banks of the Sabie River just outside the Kruger Park, wasn't his, but he'd come to think of it as home over the past few years. Hippo Rock was popular with South Africans and foreigners alike, a place where people could live side by side with wildlife.

Hudson rubbed his eyes. Headlights shone through the curtain and then the engine was cut. He heard footsteps, and swearing in German. He'd learned the hard way that Sonja lapsed into German when she was angry. He went to the door.

'Well, good morning.' He checked his watch. She should have been home from the training patrol by nine pm, but it was after midnight.

'Don't get smart with me.'

She was on the defensive already, which for Sonja meant being on the attack.

'I've had a shit evening,' she said.

Hudson smelled the booze on her breath. She brushed past him and dumped her webbing gear and LM5 on the floor. 'I heard gunfire from the Sabi Sand side. I guess that was you.'

She glared at him, rocking a little. 'Of course it was us.'

He ran a hand through his hair and took a deep breath. He told himself not to get angry. 'Want to talk?'

'I want a fucking drink.'

She went past him, across the flagstone floor to the dark hardwood drinks cabinet where the home's owners, Cameron and Kylie, who lived in Australia and kept the Hippo Rock house as a holiday home, stored their booze. Hudson's arrangement with the couple was that he could use whatever food and alcohol he wanted as long as he replaced it. Sonja took out a bottle of brandy; she was drinking up most of the money he received in tips as a safari guide.

'Klippies and Coke Zero?'

'*Ja*,' she said. She dropped into an armchair, and opened the bottle.

He went to the kitchen and organised half a glass of ice and cola. She added the brandy to the brim.

'What happened?'

'One of my girls was shot and died of wounds on an evac chopper. Another, the dead one's sister, is missing somewhere in the bush after running from the firefight like a scared rabbit, but I got two poachers. Shit.' She sagged deeper into the armchair.

He reached out from the chair next to hers and took her hand and squeezed it. 'I'm so sorry, Sonja.'

She shrugged off his touch. 'They had an RPD, for fuck's sake.'

'A machine gun for *rhino*? That's overkill.'

'For a helicopter.'

He whistled. 'That's what I call escalation.'

She looked at him. 'This is a war, Hudson. A real, live, shooting war, and we're losing.'

He shrugged. 'The parks guys, the police and army do OK. Think of all the rhinos that would have been killed if they did nothing, which is pretty much what's happened in most of Africa over the last forty years.'

She leaned towards him and once again he could smell the booze on her breath. 'Yes, but we're not winning. We have to do more.'

'Sure. Are you hungry?' He wanted to try to take her mind off the evening's traumatic events.

Sonja reclined in her chair again and raised her glass. 'Eating's cheating, that's what the Australians say. Did I tell you about these Aussie guys I got drunk with in Afghanistan? All illegal, of course. They weren't allowed to have alcohol.'

'Dinner's in the oven, but it's as dry as biltong now. I saved you some.'

'What?'

She sat up, like a cat with its hair raised. His first impression of her, when he'd met her in Etosha National Park in Namibia two years earlier, was of a feral animal. She had that look about her again now. 'Nothing.'

'You're pissed off at me because I wasn't home right on the dot? Is that it? Well, let me tell you, while you were here playing MasterChef, I was out fighting the fucking war.'

'It's OK, Sonja.'

She drained her drink, in only her second mouthful. She went into the kitchen. He heard the tinkle of more ice in her glass. 'I'll take a beer, if you're offering,' he called after her.

Sonja said nothing. He waited a minute then got up. She was standing by the refrigerator, her glass in her hand, staring at the sink and the two wineglasses, two plates, and the empty bottle of La Motte Shiraz that were in it.

'Sannie van Rensburg came over for a sundowner. You remember, I told you she might drop by?'

She blinked at him a couple of times. 'You mentioned a police captain named van Rensburg, not that she was a she.'

'I met her working a case. I was a murder suspect – not guilty. Long story. She and her husband had a banana farm, but sold up and bought a house here at Hippo Rock a while ago. She's the officer in charge of the anti-rhino poaching squad at Skukuza Police Station now. I've been meaning to get her over for dinner for some time and I thought as you were in anti-poaching she'd be a good person for you to meet.'

Sonja poured Coke into her glass until it was half full. Hudson stepped aside as she walked back into the lounge room.

When he wasn't working as a safari guide, driving tourists around the Kruger Park in his open-sided Land Rover, he did private investigation work. He knew how interrogations worked – sometimes the best way to get someone talking was to be quiet and let them fill the void. He had nothing to feel guilty about so he was happy to talk while Sonja added more brandy to her drink.

'Sannie's husband's away. Tom's an ex-cop. He was a protection officer, a bodyguard, and he got a gig doing some UN work in Iraq. He flies over there for a few weeks at a time. Money's good.'

Sonja sipped her drink and walked to the sliding door that led out to the balcony, overlooking the Sabie River and the national park on the other side. Hippo Rock Private Nature Reserve took its name from a pair of granite boulders that shone in the moonlight, in the middle of the rushing river. Hudson followed her out. There was a chill in the air and the floorboards were cool under his feet. He cracked the beer he'd taken for himself.

'I asked Sannie to stay for dinner. Her kids are in boarding school now, at Uplands, during the week. I thought the three of us could have a nice night.'

She looked from the river back to him.

'Sonja.'

'It's OK. I know you have a lot of female friends. There's that detective in Zimbabwe; the Cuban doctor, Elena; the woman who runs the bar in Hazyview . . . I forget her name.'

'Hannah.'

'Yes, she's an ex, right?'

He nodded. 'I told you, when we went for a drink there.'

Sonja walked back inside, draining her drink as she went. She put her glass down on the bar as she passed it, nearly spilling the ice out, and went to the room they'd been sharing for going on eight weeks now.

Hudson waited in the lounge room, wondering if she'd gone to use the en suite bathroom. The resident wood owl asked *who, who, who are you* from the weeping boer bean tree out by the deck. *Good question*, he thought.

When Sonja came back she was carrying her camouflage rucksack and green vinyl dive bag. It was everything she'd brought with her to Africa.

'Sonja, where are you going?'

'I'll check in to the Protea Hotel, by the Kruger Gate, for tonight. I got a call from the owners of Lion Plains on the way here; the Leopards' training program has been indefinitely suspended, so I'm not sure if my gig will continue there. The experiment to arm the women seems to have failed at its first hurdle.'

The Leopards, Hudson knew, had originally been formed as an unarmed anti-poaching unit to walk the western boundary of the Lion Plains Game Reserve in daytime to look for overnight breaks in the electric fence, and to search vehicles coming into and out of the area. Sonja had been brought in to convert them to a gun-toting paramilitary force.

He reached out a hand to take her bag. 'You can stay here as long as you like. Listen, nothing happened between Sannie and me. We're friends and she's happily married.'

Sonja looked over her shoulder, down the hallway to the open door of the master bedroom and the rumpled, turned-back sheets.

She shrugged his hand off her. 'I've been offered a job that will take me away. Julianne Clyde-Smith wants me to train her anti-poaching people.'

'Sonja, please, nothing happened. Let's sit down and talk. We can chat about what happened tonight if you like. And I've got a good therapist in Nelspruit. She's really nice.' Hudson knew enough to recognise that Sonja had issues, but her reaction to him having dinner with Sannie was off the Richter scale.

'She?'

'Yes. Look, Sonja, you're tired. You're reading too much into all of this. I . . . I want you around. We have fun, don't we?'

She stood there, by the front door, a little unsteady on her feet. 'You think that's what life is all about? Fun?'

'For crying in a bucket, Sonja, no, it's not all fun. I know that as well as you. We've both served, both lost friends, but doesn't

26

that make it all the more important to enjoy life when we can?'

'I need to sleep, but not here. Bye, Hudson. Have *fun*.'

She closed the door slightly harder than was necessary and he stood there, listening to her start up the Toyota Hilux that had been donated to the anti-poaching patrol. It wasn't good that she was driving in her state, but at least the hotel was only a couple of kilometres down the road and there would be little or no traffic at this time of night.

Brand took his beer outside to clear his head and thought about what had just happened and how he had handled the situation. He had never read the instruction book on relationships and hadn't had one yet that had worked. He and Sonja had slept together when they met in Namibia two years earlier, and while there had been chemistry, she had returned to where she had been living in the States. They had been in touch, off and on, and when the volunteer position with the Leopards had come up, Hudson had been looking forward to seeing her again.

Theirs had turned out to be one of those friendships that survived long absences, with the pair of them falling straight back into conversations as if they had been apart for days, not years. The sex had come back easily as well, but try as she might to be happy, Hudson knew she was still smarting from the death of her partner, Sam. When he'd first met her in Namibia she had seemed to him like a feral cat, all hissy and ornery, but in the house in Hippo Rock after a while, she'd been like a lioness in a zoo – restless, pacing, maybe looking for a way out. He ought not to be surprised Sonja had walked out, but it had happened sooner than he'd expected.

He leaned on the railing of the deck. Somewhere over in Kruger a lion called, soft and far away. The wood owl kept asking.

Hudson wondered who *he* was and why Sonja might even want to hang out with him. Fun? No, life wasn't just meant to be about fun, but Hudson had seen enough killing to know that while having a good time might not be the secret to happiness, neither was getting shot or shooting people. Sonja Kurtz might not have got that memo yet.

He finished his beer. He felt blue enough to have another, but he had an early start the next morning, driving a party of American birders around the park. He didn't want to drive with a hangover, so he went back inside, closed the doors and climbed into bed.

Hudson replayed the evening's brief conversation with Sonja over and over in his head, seeking some meaning, wondering what he could have done differently. She had seemed so intent on walking out, without giving him the chance to defend himself – not that he had done anything wrong. Why?

Their lovemaking had been in turns wild and passionate, and slow and tender. He loved her body and she'd said she dug his, but that wasn't enough. The only time he'd seen her eyes soften and her lips curl into a real smile was when she talked about her daughter, Emma, who had graduated from her archaeology degree and was living and working in Australia. Sonja had said more than once that she was pleased Emma had ended up in such a safe country.

Sonja, however, couldn't seem to function in a place without danger. He'd talked last week about them getting away for a while, to the beach in Mozambique, or spending a few nights in Kruger together, but she had always changed the subject back to her work. She didn't seem to want to make plans with him. He didn't know exactly what it was that they'd had, but now she was gone he knew he wanted her to stay.

He felt hurt, hard done by, and a little angry. He hadn't intended on setting up house with anyone, but he had enjoyed it. And now she had walked out on him over nothing.

Sleep didn't come easy, but when it did he dreamed of Sonja.

Chapter 3

Captain Sannie van Rensburg wanted to retch. She was no stranger to death, but the body of the woman in the camouflage fatigues lying at her feet had been partially devoured by vultures. It wasn't the first time she'd seen a human in this state, but it still shook her.

Sannie had investigated several murders in the course of her work as a detective in Nelspruit, but she had hoped she would see few dead bodies – except for those of poachers – when she transferred to the SAPS, South African Police Service, rhino poaching investigation unit, based at the Kruger Park's main camp, Skukuza.

'We might never have found her out here in the middle of nowhere if it wasn't for those vultures,' said her partner, Warrant Officer Vanessa Sunday.

Vanessa was from the Cape and had transferred to Skukuza with her husband, who was an ecologist with South African National Parks. She was young, smart and keen.

'You're right. Lucky the morning game drive from Lion Plains found her when they did.'

Sannie straightened, put her hands on her hips and looked around her. The bush was quiet, save for a grey go-away bird who gave his eponymous call from somewhere nearby. A handful of vultures had taken up position in a leadwood tree and watched her enviously.

'Where exactly are we again in relation to the contact between the female anti-poaching unit and the rhino poachers?' Vanessa asked.

Sannie pointed to the south. 'We're on the Lion Plains property now. The shootout happened over there, to the north. The lodge at Lion Sands, the neighbours on the Sabie River, is actually closer than the one on this property, so the women headed there for safety.'

Vanessa shook her head. 'I was used to seeing bodies on the Cape Flats with all the gang wars, but I didn't expect my first case up here to be a multiple shooting.'

Sannie knelt again, trying to ignore the horribly mutilated face and the empty eye sockets, and checked the woman's pockets. 'As we suspected, the ID book is that of Goodness Mdluli. Her sister was wounded in the contact with the poachers and died in a chopper on the way to Nelspruit.'

'Shame.' Vanessa circled the body, looking for tracks. Sannie noted how she moved to keep any tracks between her and the sun, to use the shadows to help her read the signs on the ground. 'We've got boot prints all around.'

'Those poor tourists on the morning drive, having to see this.' Sannie took a deep breath and rolled the body onto its side. Two entry wounds in the back. 'She was shot down while she was running.'

'You'd think the poachers would have run back to Mozambique after the contact. Instead they took the time to hunt down this girl.'

Sannie nodded. 'Yes, and it meant them moving further away

from where they came from to get her, assuming they did walk through the park from Mozambique.'

They both looked around at the sound of an approaching vehicle. Its engine stopped but Sannie and Vanessa were out of sight of the nearest game-viewing road.

'Coming in,' said a woman's voice.

Sannie stood and peeled off her rubber gloves. Two women, one white and one black, wearing fatigues that matched the dead woman's, appeared through the bush. The older woman looked to be in her forties, with auburn hair tied back in a ponytail, blue eyes and a fit figure.

'Miss Kurtz.'

'It would have been Sonja if we'd met last night. You're Captain van Rensburg.'

'Sannie. It's odd that we meet this way.'

'Not in my world, probably not in yours. Hudson Brand told me you once investigated him for murder.'

'Yes, I did.'

Sonja looked to the woman next to her. 'This is Tema Matsebula. She was with me last night.'

'Good morning, madam,' Tema said. 'How are you?'

'Fine and you?'

'I am also fine.'

Sannie introduced Warrant Officer Sunday to the women.

Sonja looked at the body on the ground. 'Goodness Mdluli.'

Sannie held up the identification card. 'So it says here. She was shot from behind. When last did you see her alive?'

'When she ran away from our patrol, leaving her sister, Patience, bleeding and screaming in the bush.'

Sannie raised her eyebrows. 'So you think Goodness got what she deserved?'

Sonja looked at the ruined face, the bloodied uniform. 'No one deserves to be shot in the back.'

'Front's OK, though?'

'Her sister wasn't a great trainee, neither of them was, but she was caught in an ambush. Looks like someone hunted Goodness down and executed her.'

'Why?' Sannie asked. Two more detectives from the SAPS rhino poaching investigation unit and the South African National Parks environmental crime investigation unit were busy working the crime scene where the poachers had been killed and Patience initially wounded. Sannie hoped they'd be able to provide some answers.

'I don't know.'

'I'm in overall charge of the investigations,' Sannie said. 'I've spoken to two other members of your anti-poaching patrol this morning. One of them told me you and the Mdluli sisters had argued, more than once, that they resented you giving them certain orders and that you criticised them in front of the others.'

Tema cursed in xiTsonga under her breath.

Sonja held up a hand. 'It's fine, Tema. The truth is, neither of them would have passed the course. Their lack of commitment wasn't reason enough for me to shoot Goodness in the back, Captain, and neither was her running out on her sister and her comrades. That would have earned her a *klap* from me.'

'*Klapping* staff, even para-military recruits, isn't allowed in the new South Africa,' Sannie said. 'I may need to interview you.'

'I've given a witness statement to the other detectives just now,' Sonja said. 'If you want more from me you'll have to arrest me. They're not charging me over the deaths of the two poachers I killed, and I've got to go see someone about a job.'

'No, we're not charging you or any of your people. Not yet, anyway. We'll open an inquest docket into the killings of the poachers. All your statements, from what I know of them, indicate that the poachers fired first. They'll most likely have illegal firearms, which also counts in your favour. Unless we turn up any discrepancies there probably won't even be a coronial inquest. We'll open murder dockets into the deaths of Patience and Goodness.' Sannie didn't think Sonja Kurtz had gunned down her own recruit in cold blood, and the location of the body and the timeline didn't support such a theory, but it was her job to cover all eventualities. 'If I need to question you more can I find you at Hudson Brand's house?'

'No.' Sonja's phone rang. She answered it and moved a few paces away.

Sannie shook her head at Sonja's abruptness. She looked at the girl dressed in camouflage who had been standing next to Sonja, and realised she was familiar. 'I know you.'

'Yes, madam.'

'You don't have to call me that. You worked at Hippo Rock?'

'Yes. I was a maid. I cleaned your house once.'

'That's right, when we first moved in. You came with Shadrack, the labourer.'

'Yes. Shadrack Mnisi, he is my next-door neighbour.'

'My husband and I still get Shadrack to come and sweep and trim back the bush around our house. He's a machine, that guy, and cheery, too. There's a waiting list of owners who want to have him work at their places.'

Tema nodded. 'Yes, he is a lovely guy. People think that because he is a little slow that he can't work, but he would do anything for a friend. We grew up together.'

Sannie felt a little bad that she hadn't recognised Tema at first. 'How do you like this work, anti-poaching?'

'It is good. It was scary, last night, but also . . .'

'Exciting?' They nodded in unison.

Sonja was still talking into her phone as she came back to them. '*Ja*, come along Ivory Drive from little Serengeti, you'll see my *bakkie*, a cop car and the vultures.'

'Who's that?' Sannie asked when Sonja ended the call. 'I hope you're not inviting sightseers; this is a closed crime scene.'

'It's our master tracker, Ezekial Lekganyane, from the Leopards Anti-Poaching Unit. He teaches the women how to track. I'm getting him to follow the man who did this.'

'Man?'

Sonja jerked a thumb over her shoulder. 'There's spoor on the road back there. It's been brushed with a branch to make it look like a leopard's drag mark, but even I could tell it was done in a rush, by a man. I can see a partial print in the bush, but Ezekial will be able to follow it.'

Sannie was annoyed with the way the other woman was taking over her investigation before it had begun, but she knew it would take time to bring in a police tracker. The dog unit based at Paul Kruger Gate had been called out an hour earlier to track another poaching gang inside the national park. 'All right.'

Sonja had squared up to her as if she was expecting an argument, but simply nodded. 'Well, I'll go and meet Ezekial on the road.'

'Sonja?'

She looked back. 'Yes?'

'I'm sorry for the loss of your trainees. Please remember this is a police investigation – don't do anything rash.' She took a business card out of her jeans pocket and gave it to Sonja. 'Call me if you come up with something.'

Sonja nodded, took the card, and turned and walked away.

*

Sonja fumed as she followed Ezekial through the bush. Tema was behind her.

The van Rensburg woman was prettier than she had imagined. She was blonde and blue-eyed with a nice smile. Sonja wondered if she'd been wearing the tight jeans and long brown flat-heeled boots last night. Brand was a ladies' man and she could picture him flirting with the cop whose husband was away. A sundowner had turned into a bottle of wine and dinner, maybe more.

Ezekial was another man women found attractive. Sonja had reprimanded Goodness and Patience for tittering like schoolgirls and whispering between themselves during their first lesson with the master tracker. He had played up to the Mdlulis but Sonja, standing back during the class, had noticed how Ezekial's attention kept wandering to the graceful Tema. He had made a show of comforting her when he arrived at the road by the murder scene and Sonja had chivvied him along to get to work.

Sonja was glad he was here. She was reasonably proficient at reading spoor but there was no way she could have picked up the small signs that Ezekial was finding as easily as if they were flashing blue lights in the veld.

Ezekial held up his hand and Sonja and Tema froze. Sonja raised her LM5 slowly. Ezekial looked back, his right hand touching his nose and sticking upwards. Sonja heard a huff of exhaled breath and the large grey bulk of a white rhinoceros trotted across the game trail fifty metres ahead of them. Ezekial grinned, then returned his gaze to the ground ahead and led off.

Sonja thought about the deaths of Patience and Goodness. Patience had been stupid, running from the leopard; she'd been lucky the cat hadn't chased and caught her, and, eventually, unlucky that she had stumbled into the poaching gang.

Goodness had been cowardly, though running from gunfire wasn't particular to any race or gender in Sonja's experience. To run was human; to stand and fight took training and courage. Tema had absorbed the theory and gone with her gut and her heart and advanced on the enemy in the face of danger.

Tema was talking to Ezekial now as they walked.

'Let him do his job, Tema.'

Tema looked back. 'Yes, madam, sorry.'

'Call me Sonja, and do your job. Keep your eyes open.' She was a good kid, Sonja thought. There was no surliness in her reply. Goodness and Patience, however, *had* resented taking orders from her and Sonja didn't know if it was because she was white, foreign or a woman, or perhaps all of the above. But Goodness had not deserved to die, as van Rensburg had taunted.

'Yes, Sonja.'

Ezekial was leading them further to the west, deeper into the Lion Plains property, closer to the perimeter fence of the Sabi Sand Game Reserve. Lion Plains was on the edge of the reserve and it was no secret locally that the lodge was in trouble.

A few years earlier Lion Plains had nearly been turned into an open cut coalmine. It had been the subject of a successful land claim by the local people, the traditional owners who had been granted ownership of the land by the government. The community had been seduced by the lure of jobs and money to sell the mineral rights to an Australian-owned coalmining company. Tema, who had been working as a maid and studying to be a field guide prior to applying for a position with the Leopards, had told Sonja that the discovery of a breeding pair of rare Pel's fishing owls on the property had been enough to put an end to the miners' plans.

However, the lodge had taken a hit through lost bookings while the mine saga played out, and had never fully recovered. Sonja had seen, and avoided, a reporter and photographer from *The Lowvelder* newspaper at the scene where she had shot the poachers, and she knew the lodge's name would once again attract publicity for the wrong reasons. Shootings of poachers were not uncommon in the Kruger and its surrounding reserves, but losses among military, police and anti-poaching operatives were mercifully rare, so the deaths of the Mdluli sisters would be worldwide news.

'What will happen to us now, Sonja, to the Leopards?' Tema asked her.

'I don't know, in the long term, but training's been suspended,' Sonja said as they walked.

Tema clenched her fists. 'I have a child. I will have to go back to working as a maid, but I may not be able to get my old job back at Hippo Rock. There are too many people looking for work and not enough positions.'

'You worked there? I didn't know. I know a man who lives there, Hudson Brand. I'll see if he can talk to management for you.'

'Thank you.'

'I didn't know you had a child.'

'A girl,' Tema said. 'Her name is Shine.'

'I have a daughter as well, Emma.'

'Sure?'

'Don't sound so surprised, Tema. I am human, you know.'

'I'm sorry, madam, Sonja. I didn't think you were married.'

'I'm not. Long story.'

'Nor me,' Tema said, sadly. 'Long story.'

Ezekial stopped and studied the ground. Sonja moved past Tema. 'What is it?'

Ezekial took a few steps to his left, then back to his right, casting about. 'This man is good. He is employing active counter-tracking. See, here, where he has trodden on some long grass, but then straightened it again. Also, where he has crossed game trails he has tried to do so without leaving a track. Where he has had to, he has brushed out the track.'

'But you're still following him.'

'It is not easy and, as I say, he is good.' Ezekial looked up and grinned at her. 'But I am better.'

Sonja saw Tema smile and Ezekial winked back at her. She hoped it wasn't because of her trouble with Hudson, but she really did not have time for these two to be flirting on the job. 'Is he armed?'

'Yes, with an AK-47.' Ezekial pointed back the way they had come. 'He set the rifle down on the ground at one point and I could see the imprint of the AK's butt plate in the dust.'

Sonja processed the information she had. The two men she had killed were Mozambicans, both armed with the same rifles as this man. That meant the machine gunner had gone in a different direction, possibly across the Sabie River and back into the Kruger Park and Mozambique to the east. This man, possibly the one who had shot Goodness, given the location of her body, was heading deeper into South Africa.

Ezekial led off again. 'He was moving faster here,' Ezekial called over his shoulder. 'He was getting nervous; perhaps he heard the helicopters again and was running, taking less time to cover his tracks.'

They had increased their pace as well. Sonja and Tema were alternating between a fast walk and a jog through the bush. Sonja kept watch for game, though she knew Ezekial was not just looking at the ground ahead of them. His skills were phenomenal, particularly given he was only in his late twenties.

'The fence.' Ezekial stopped and pointed to the ground. 'Check.'

Sonja stopped behind him. Ezekial had led them to a dry watercourse that passed under the Sabi Sand reserve's perimeter. The fence was a substantial affair of barbed wire, several electrified strands and two rows of coiled razor wire at the bottom. However, the ground at the base of the streambed was irregular. Large rocks had been placed there to fill gaps, but their quarry had pulled them aside and wriggled under the fence.

Ezekial circled a crisp, clear boot print with his finger in the dust. 'His right boot has a split in the sole. This will be easy to identify.'

Sonja carefully stepped over the track on the road and down into the streambed. She knelt and inspected the razor wire.

'Threads from a green shirt here, and quite a bit of blood. He'll have a nasty gash on his back.'

Sonja took out her phone and called Sannie van Rensburg. She gave the location and the information about the fugitive being slashed on the fence and his boots with the distinctive split in the sole. Van Rensburg told her the police dog unit was still busy in the Kruger Park, but would be at her location, on the outer side of the fence, as soon as possible.

'I'll leave a pile of stones near the spot where the guy went under the fence.'

'No, wait there,' Sannie said. 'I want to see you again as well, ask you some more questions.'

Sonja ended the call without replying. She had another appointment.

Chapter 4

Julianne Clyde-Smith's lodge, Khaya Ngala, which meant the house of the lion, had raised the bar in an already crowded luxury safari accommodation market in the Sabi Sand Game Reserve.

Sonja was greeted by a man in dark trousers and a pressed white shirt who handed her a cold towel, followed by a glass of champagne once she had wiped her hands and face. Ezekial hefted her backpack out of the rear of the Hilux and a porter whisked it away.

'I'll call you tomorrow,' Sonja said to Tema.

'Yes, Sonja, goodbye,' she said, moving to the front passenger seat so she could be next to Ezekial.

As Ezekial passed her Sonja touched him on the arm. She spoke softly. 'Tema's been through a lot in the last twenty-four hours. Keep an eye on her, like a brother – at least for now OK?'

He nodded, then got in the truck.

Ezekial, Tema and Sonja had back-tracked to the scene of Goodness's murder after tracking her supposed killer to the fence line. The South African Police Service dog team would take over tracking the fugitive from the other side of the fence, which was outside the jurisdiction of the Leopards, who were employed only to work within the Sabi Sand Game Reserve.

Before they had left the fence line, Ezekial, whose father was a bishop in the ZCC or Zion Christian Church, asked Sonja if he could say a prayer for the deceased members of the Leopards.

Sonja, feeling slightly self-conscious, had held hands with Tema and Ezekial.

'Lord, we pray for the souls of our sisters Goodness and Patience. Their lives were too short but we know they are in your arms now.'

Tema had wiped tears from her eyes. Sonja envied her ability to grieve now, on the spot, for her comrades. She knew, from bitter experience, that the Mdlulis would visit her in her nightmares in the days, weeks, months and maybe years to come, along with too many others.

Tema had given her hand a tight squeeze and Sonja had felt her own heart lurch, just a little.

She spared them a final glance outside Julianne's lodge as they drove off. Ezekial was handsome, professional and devout. Tema could do worse than him, but she had also seen the way women fawned over the tracker. She had meant what she had said to Ezekial; she didn't want him working his charms on her while she was vulnerable.

Sonja gave the towel back to the man and followed him through the lofty thatch-roofed entrance to Khaya Ngala, sipping her champagne as she walked, taking in her surroundings. She was off duty indefinitely now that training and operations for the Leopards had been suspended.

Although she had been born on a cattle farm in Namibia, Sonja had spent part of her teens living in the staff quarters of a private game lodge in Botswana where her father had worked as the maintenance manager – when he wasn't too drunk to stand up.

Whether tented, or a mix of traditional and modern architecture, like Khaya Ngala, these lodges all set high standards and tried to outdo each other in their quest for luxury, wildlife sightings and dollars.

'Miss Clyde-Smith is waiting for you on the deck, madam. Lunch will be served whenever you're ready.'

Sonja had barely slept at the hotel and she was wearing the same camouflage fatigues she'd had on during the contact. She'd put them back on because she'd expected to be walking in the bush again that morning. Her shirt was stained with dirt, blood and sweat, but she cared as little about how she presented to Clyde-Smith as she did about the ostentatiousness of the woman's lodge.

The location, however, was something else. Khaya Ngala was set atop a granite koppie and the elevation afforded an uninterrupted view out over the best Africa had to offer. A bull elephant guzzled water up into his trunk from a waterhole at centre stage. A trio of elegant giraffe waited nervously for their turn, scanning their surrounds for the predators that would wait to take them when they were at their most vulnerable, drinking. The wildlife was nice, but she was intrigued by Julianne's offer.

'Sonja, so glad you could make it. Can Charles bring you some wine?'

'Not for now,' she said. She took Clyde-Smith's hand. She was a good-looking woman; handsome rather than beautiful was the word that sprang to mind. She had dark hair, pinned up not too neatly, and wore a simple white loose-fitting blouse untucked over jeans and sandals decorated with African beadwork. From the pictures Sonja had seen in newspapers and online Julianne also affected a casual personal style, a bit like Richard Branson. She was anything but casual, however, when it came to the business of making money.

'Have a seat, enjoy the view. Water, please, Charles.' The man who had escorted Sonja in gave a slight bow and went to the bar. 'I hope the police didn't give you any grief.'

Sonja shook her head. A family of warthog, a mother and three piglets, trotted disdainfully in front of the elephant. In reply he shook his big head at them and the babies scattered.

'I fired in self-defence, following our rules of engagement.'

Julianne handed her a menu and she scanned it. When Charles returned with the water he asked for their order.

'I'll have the springbok carpaccio and the eye fillet medallion, rare, please.'

Julianne smiled. 'A fellow carnivore. Excellent. I'll have the same, Charles, and tell the sommelier to select a nice red.'

'Very good, miss.' Charles departed.

'I'm not staying long enough to drink a bottle.'

Julianne held up her hands. 'I wouldn't dare presume, but being in Africa is the closest I get to having a holiday, so I'll work my way through a red eventually. You mentioned rules of engagement. From what little I know of it, your background suggests you're open to bending them.'

Sonja leaned back in her chair. A market umbrella gave them shade. 'I follow the rules, unless they don't suit me.'

Julianne raised an eyebrow, but didn't reply. The silence stretched between them.

'I told you yesterday, I'm not looking for a job.' Sonja was interested in what Julianne had to say, but there were too many do-gooders with too many harebrained schemes about how to save wildlife and how to stop poaching.

'Yet here you are.'

'I heard your menu was worth checking out.'

'Ha!'

Charles returned with the wine.

'Would you like to taste?' Julianne asked her.

'Sure.' Sonja swirled the wine in the glass, sniffed it and tasted it. 'Shiraz, my favourite.' It was superb, and when she checked the bottle the label confirmed it. 'Saxenburg Select. One of the country's best.'

'Life, as they say, is too short for cheap wine.'

Charles poured for both of them. 'Life's too short, full stop.' Sonja looked out at the elephant and the piglets, which had snuck back to the waterhole for a drink.

When the waiter left, Julianne proposed a toast. 'To life.'

Sonja clinked glasses with Julianne and they sipped.

'You assassinated one of the top rhino horn speculators in Vietnam, Tran Van Ngo.'

Sonja set her glass down. 'You can't believe everything you read in the newspapers and online.'

'And fomented a civil war in Namibia and blew up a dam in order to save a fragile ecosystem.'

'You really have to cancel your subscription to *Soldier of Fortune* magazine.'

'If they had a centrefold, you would have been it. We can joke all we like, but what my intelligence tells me is you're a mercenary who chooses to fight for a cause.'

A cause? It was true she'd blown up a dam to save the Okavango Delta, but she'd taken the job for money. She had travelled to Vietnam to assassinate Tran on a mission of revenge and it had cost a good man, a journalist who had helped her, his life. She wasn't sure it had been worth it, and it hadn't slowed the trade in rhino horn.

'Taking out the man in Vietnam didn't stop rhino poaching,' Clyde-Smith said, as if reading her mind, 'but it had an impact. If we hit the man behind the gang that killed your two women last night then you will neutralise a syndicate that takes maybe sixty rhinos a year. That could be the difference between an increase in this year's poaching figures and a decrease over last year's.

You could help turn the tide, buy the security and conservation forces – and the species – some much-needed breathing time.'

They paused while their starters were served. Sonja savoured her glass of wine, but took water in between each sip. The sun was rising fast and despite the shade she knew the dangers of dehydration in the dry, dusty bush. She needed to keep a clear head. They had gone over some of this already, in the Lion Sands bar last night, and while she had told Clyde-Smith she wasn't interested, the other woman was right; she had come here to try to make some sense of Sam's death, to prove to herself it hadn't been in vain. Maybe this was a way to honour his sacrifice.

With the Leopards' training suspended indefinitely there was nothing to keep her in Africa, but she wasn't ready to go back to her home in Los Angeles yet. The truth was the first world bored her. Her military and mercenary service had hurt her – she had an ongoing battle with post-traumatic stress disorder – yet paradoxically she never felt more together, saner, or more alive, than when she was out in the bush with a gun in her hand.

Sonja was smart enough to realise that she needed to break the nexus between violence and her peace of mind and that someone, probably her, would get seriously hurt in her pursuit of adrenaline and fulfilment. She was like an addict, never able to give up completely, never able to get a good enough high.

'If I get caught in Mozambique on an assassination mission I'll spend the rest of my life in some hellhole.'

'That didn't stop you in Vietnam, and anyway, I am most certainly not talking about assassinating anybody.'

'I have nothing to say about that.' Vietnam had been personal, but Sonja wasn't about to go into that with Julianne.

'What if I told you that the man running this poaching syndicate in Mozambique – his name is Antonio Cuna – was one of the biggest rhino horn suppliers to Tran Van Ngo, the man you *allegedly* killed?'

Sonja set down her knife and fork and pushed back her chair. 'I'd say you're playing me and it's time for me to go.' She started to stand.

'Wait, please,' Julianne said. 'There's someone I'd like you to meet – and it would be criminal for you to miss out on the fillet.'

As if on cue a man walked out of the indoor dining area and bar. In contrast to Julianne the man was dressed about as formally as someone could in this part of Africa. He wore a crisply ironed Oxford shirt, striped tie, chinos and polished brogues. He carried a laptop computer under one arm.

'Sonja, this is Lieutenant Colonel, retired, James Paterson.'

'How do you do?' he asked, smiling, as she took his hand. She wasn't surprised by the rank. Paterson's bearing and clothes had ex-officer written all over them, but unlike most of the senior ranks she had met he seemed genuinely pleased to meet someone who might soon fall under his command, if that was what the arrangement was to be. He was a good-looking specimen, physi- cally, and his eyes mirrored his smile. Many officers, in Sonja's experience, looked at a point in the middle of your forehead when addressing you, so as not to make eye contact like a normal civilian would.

'James Paterson?'

'Yes.' He gave a short laugh. 'Same as the author but only one "t". Don't worry, I get it a lot.'

Sonja's eyes dropped to his tie. 'Those are the British Army Intelligence Corps colours – green, white and red.'

He had red hair and he fixed her with his green eyes. 'Well, you should know. Just like me you're an African who served with the British Army, in the same corps as me.'

'You two seem to know all about me,' she said. It was not a pleasant feeling.

'You served with The Det in Northern Ireland, 14 Intelligence Company.'

Sonja shrugged. 'So?'

Julianne leaned forward. 'I hadn't heard of your unit until James told me about it,' she said. 'James – he's global head of security for all my companies, by the way – explained to me that The Det, as you call it, was unusual in that it was made up of men *and* women from the British Army who underwent a tough SAS-style selection course and then carried out undercover surveillance operations in Northern Ireland against the IRA during the Troubles.'

Sonja nodded. 'The higher-ups figured, correctly, that a male squaddie watching terrorists wouldn't stick out quite as much if he had a woman on his arm, and that solo female operatives would arouse less suspicion than lone men.'

'And you,' Julianne said, 'with your Namibian accent, would have been less likely to have been fingered as a British soldier. Your mother was English as I understand.'

'*You understand?* I suppose you even know that she passed away recently. What's my shoe size?' Sonja was feeling like an animal being backed into a trap. Her instincts were aroused. 'You two can stop playing games and cut to the chase, or I'm out of here, with or without the fillet, the smoked trout, peri-peri langoustines, the homemade malva pudding, the lemon meringue pie or the chocolate fondant.'

'You don't miss anything, do you?' Julianne said. 'Did you memorise my menu?'

'Surveillance training. The detail counts.' Sonja took a long look at Paterson. 'Part of my training was to remember faces and I've seen yours – not in the army, but around here. At the Paul Kruger Gate, maybe, waiting to get into the park?'

He flashed her his nice smile. 'Very probably. Also, although I spend most of my time here at the lodge I own a house at Hippo Rock, where you've been staying lately.'

Sonja sat back in her chair. 'OK, now that is just creepy. Am I under surveillance, or have you been stalking me?'

He laughed. 'Neither. I'm on the Sabi Sand's security committee. We vet applications for new staff, contractors, firearms permits, the decision to arm your all-female anti-poaching unit, that sort of thing. Your name and temporary address in South Africa have come across the committee's desk a couple of times.'

'Hmm.'

James opened his laptop. 'The women you were training – that experiment is over. They'll go back to being domestics, mothers, unemployed.'

'You sound like you're happy about that.'

'Oh, no, you misread me completely,' Paterson said. 'I don't want them to go back to what they were doing, at least not the good ones.'

'Really?'

Julianne interrupted. 'I'm not the first person to think it's worth setting up a special unit to take down the poaching kingpins, to tackle the problem at its source.'

Sonja shook her head. 'No, nor even the richest. Prince Bernhard of the Netherlands tried it with Operation Lock back in the nineties, recruiting a secret force of ex–special forces soldiers to hit poaching gangs across international borders.'

'Yes, and it cost him his country. He had to abdicate,' Julianne said. 'I'm not looking for Rambos. I could find scores of white Afrikaans-speaking former recce-commandos who'd like to take on a mission like this, ditto high-minded former Green Berets from the States or Bear Grylls wannabes from the UK.'

'So why pick me?'

'Partly,' Paterson stepped in, 'because you're a woman.'

'I'll try not to find that condescending or sexist,' Sonja said.

'Good, don't. Just as it made sense for the British Army to send you to Northern Ireland because the IRA wouldn't expect us to use women, a female tourist, perhaps part of a couple, will stick out less in Mozambique than a couple of burly white men would.'

'I get it,' Sonja said. She wanted to make sure they weren't just playing at soldiers. 'Still not interested.'

Julianne leaned closer to her, elbows on the table. 'We're not just talking about Mozambique. I have lodges elsewhere in southern and east Africa and poaching's a problem wherever there's wildlife. We've got intelligence that the poachers are becoming increasingly organised and sophisticated, across borders, and we need a force that's agile, smart and resourced enough to fight on several fronts. You could pick anyone you want, whatever salary they demand. Think how a unit comprised of excellent operators from a variety of backgrounds would work. You could select a couple of your Leopards, black xiTsonga-speaking local women, local men, perhaps people fluent in Portuguese and other languages if you know any.'

'It sounds like your everyday run-of-the-mill undercover police operation,' Sonja said.

'Yes.' Julianne slapped a hand down on the table. 'But the police aren't up to it, especially across borders and in different parts of the continent. In some cases the known criminals are wanted by the police, but the cops are so crooked they never act on that information. We'd force them to act, by gathering irrefutable evidence of where the fugitives are, and exposing them publicly. The honest cops, and there's no shortage of them, are hamstrung because they don't have the resources or the jurisdictional authority to carry out the sort of operations we're proposing.'

'So it's a surveillance operation you're talking about, not a hit squad.'

Julianne held her hands up, palms to Sonja. 'I'm not recruiting assassins.'

'At Julianne's instruction,' Paterson said, 'I now spend most of my time as her head of security sourcing intelligence on rhino, elephant and bushmeat poaching in and around where her game reserves and lodges are located. I have a network of informers and I regularly supply information to the South African and other police forces, but we lack our own expert reconnaissance and surveillance team on the ground, here and in the other countries where we operate.'

'I had you pegged for wanting to cull a few poaching kingpins,' Sonja said.

Julianne shook her head. 'I'm mad, maybe, for spending so much time and money on this, but not crazy. Nor am I a murderer. What you'd be doing *would* be questionable in the eyes of the law, but I'm not telling you to kill poaching kingpins. Get me, get James the intel we need, and we'll shame the various authorities into action.'

Sonja turned the proposal over in her mind. 'If we could track poaching gangs in Mozambique from their jumping-off points we could not only work back to who the ringleaders are, but also tip off the South African army and national parks so they could ambush the gangs once they cross the border.'

Julianne leaned back in her chair and smiled. 'You said it, not me. It would be dangerous, but I'd offer handsome remuneration and insurance policies to all involved, medical aid, and the promise of the best legal representation in the world if there's trouble.'

Sonja raised her eyebrows. 'Medical aid? Wow.'

Julianne laughed. 'You're not in this for the money, are you?'

Sonja folded her hands across her lap. 'I haven't said yes, yet.'

Paterson turned his laptop around so she could see the screen. There was a photo of an African man in a suit, shaking hands with another man, who Sonja recognised as the President of Mozambique.

'You want me to assassinate the President?'

'Very funny,' Julianne said. 'No, the man we're after is on the right. That's the man I mentioned before, Antonio Cuna, a prominent local politician in the town of Massingir and the head of the biggest rhino poaching syndicate in that part of Mozambique.'

'So?'

'So it was one of Cuna's men who killed your partner, Sam Chapman.'

Sonja remained outwardly calm, but she gripped the underside of the table to steady herself in her chair. Just the mention of Sam brought back a rush of emotions.

'You're sure?' she asked, and was annoyed that the croakiness in her voice might betray a little of how she was feeling.

Paterson looked her in the eyes and she saw a kindness there, sympathy without condescension from one soldier to another. 'Cuna's gang had a monopoly over the area where Sam was killed. It was one of his people, for sure.'

'Catch Cuna,' Julianne added, 'and you potentially find the man who killed Sam. The man in the photo you are looking at, a friend of the Mozambican President, was the number one supplier of rhino horn to Tran, and no doubt in charge of the man who pulled the trigger.'

'I see.' They were trying to hook her, but perhaps she was ready to take the bait.

'What makes you think we could bring someone like Cuna down if the police in his own country won't touch him?'

'He's a politician,' Julianne said. 'Like all of them he's got his eye on the next election. He can afford to keep paying off the local cops, but if we throw enough mud at him some of it will stick. He might lose favour with the President or, better yet, the government might decide to cut its losses and act. By helping the South Africans interdict and ambush his gangs once they cross the border we'll starve him of rhino horn and revenue. It won't happen overnight, but we'll get him, and the others behind the horrible trade.'

James and Julianne weren't nutters, Sonja saw, and they were working to some sort of strategy. Clyde-Smith was the wide-eyed idealist, but one with a business brain, and Paterson had the look of a man who could get things done on the field of battle and off it – a soldier with a diplomat's touch.

She had more questions, plenty of them, but her phone vibrated in her pocket. She took it out and looked at the screen. It was Tema. She hadn't had the woman's number in her phone until today, as she'd told her to call if she wanted to talk about the killings. Sonja knew that for some people talking things through helped. But not for her.

*

Tema felt the adrenaline coursing through her veins. This was the second most exciting and terrifying thing that had happened to her in her life. The first had been the previous evening when she had been involved in the gun battle with the poachers.

Ten minutes earlier, Shadrack Mnisi, her next-door neighbour for her entire life, had staggered past her house, one arm reaching awkwardly behind him to touch the wound that had soaked the back of his green shirt with blood.

Tema had rushed inside and handed Shine back to her mother.

'What is it now?' her mother asked.

'Shadrack has been cut. His back is bleeding.'

Her mother had clucked at her. 'Men. They are always fighting.'

'Shadrack doesn't fight, or drink, you know that,' Tema had replied in xiTsonga. She had only been talking about Shadrack this morning, to the policewoman, van Rensburg. What she hadn't told the detective, because she didn't think it was relevant, was that Shadrack's father had been a poacher, who snared impala and other antelope for bushmeat. He would often be selling a haunch of impala illegally in the neighbourhood. But that didn't mean Shadrack was a criminal, far from it. Shadrack loved the bush and had learned to track from his father. He'd confided to her that he wanted to be a field guide, but he could barely read so the thought of sitting exams for his FGASA – Field

Guides Association of South Africa – qualification had stymied a career working with wildlife on the right side of the law.

'Mother, take care of Shine, please, I must go see.'

'See what?'

'I'm not sure.'

Tema walked out of the house and followed Shadrack, who was walking through the gate of his mother's modest home. Tema stopped, looked around to make sure no one was looking, then cast her eyes down at the ground.

She saw the tracks Shadrack had left in the dust of their unpaved road. There was a split across the sole of the right boot, exactly the same as the one Ezekial had showed her in the bush. Tema froze in the middle of the road.

She took out her phone, a cheap Nokia held together with tape that had been given to her by one of the Hippo Rock home owners. She called Sonja Kurtz.

'Tema?'

'Sonja. I have found the man we were tracking before, with Ezekial.'

'You're sure?'

'Yes, he lives next door to me. His father was a poacher. He's cut on the back, from the razor wire, and he's wearing a green shirt and the same boots we saw the tracks from, in the bush.'

'Tema, be careful. Call the police. Tell them where he is. Where are you?'

'I'm at my mother's house, where I live. The man, Shadrack, is my neighbour. There were police here earlier, questioning people, going door to door. I think they're still somewhere here.'

'All right, but call the emergency number as well.'

Tema glanced at the house next door to her own. Shadrack had gone inside now. She looked up the street and saw a police *bakkie* turn onto her road. 'We're in luck, I can see the police now. I'm going straight to them.'

'Be careful, keep me on the line. That man will have a gun. Where is he now?'

'In his house.'

'Don't go in there, Tema.'

Tema ran up the street, past Shadrack's place. She couldn't believe it. She knew him well, and they were friends – she even thought he might have a crush on her. She recalled showing off her new Leopards uniform to him, when she had started her training, two months earlier. All that time he must have known that one day they could come face to face in the bush. His crime angered her now. She had to get to the police. She waved the police vehicle to a halt and as she passed his house she imagined him stepping out with his AK-47 and taking aim at her. Shadrack didn't step out with a rifle, but someone else did. A man emerged from between two houses, Mrs Mabunda's and Mr Nyathi's. Tema felt as if she was in a dream when she saw him raise an AK-47 to his shoulder.

'He's got a gun!' she called to the two policemen, who were getting out of the *bakkie*.

One reached for his pistol, but the rifleman opened fire and sprayed him with bullets. The policeman fell back. The second managed to draw his weapon, but the man with the AK was moving now, advancing, firing as he walked. A head shot put the officer down, killing him instantly.

Tema screamed, adding her voice to a dozen others. Women ran into their houses, babies in their arms, and men scattered. Tema's training kicked in; she ran across the road and found cover behind a parked car.

The gunman jogged to Shadrack's house. There was yelling from inside and the pair of them emerged, then ran to a battered red Isuzu *bakkie* and got in.

'Sonja, are you there?' Tema gasped into her phone.

'Yes, was that gunfire?'

Tema related what had happened.

'Stay where you are. I'll be there as soon as I can. I'm calling the police.'

'All right.'

Tema ended the call. As the Isuzu disappeared, dust in its wake, Tema took a deep breath, got up and ran to the fallen policemen. People were peeking from their doorways, but no one else was out on the street.

The first man she reached was dead, but the second officer was alive. He'd been wearing body armour and had taken two rounds there that had winded him, but he had another bullet hole in his leg and the side of his head had been creased by a bullet.

'First aid kit, in the *bakkie*,' he wheezed.

Tema found the kit and took out a pressure bandage which she wrapped around the man's leg.

'Get me to the radio, please.'

Tema helped the man up, with difficulty as he was overweight, and he leaned on her as they limped to the truck. He called in the shooting, but began slurring his words.

Tema checked his wound again. The bandage was already soaked.

'You're bleeding out. I've got to get you to a doctor. Get in.'

She settled him in the passenger seat of the police truck, got in the driver's seat and started the engine. She'd never owned a car, but had learned to drive in preparation for her anti-poaching course.

The Toyota lurched and stalled as she took her foot off the clutch too quickly. Tema forced herself to calm down, remembered her instruction and started again. This time she moved forward smoothly then ground through the gears as she accelerated.

Her phone rang.

'Tema, it's Sonja. The national parks' helicopter is grounded at Skukuza after being hit last night. I'm at Khaya Ngala and

Julianne Clyde-Smith is readying her chopper. I'm coming to you. Where are the men now?'

'Driving south, on the gravel road from Huntington back towards the R536. I'm going the same way, trying to get a wounded policeman to the doctor.'

'Sheesh,' Sonja said. 'Don't do anything silly.'

'This man is a murderer. Shadrack is with him. We're nearly at the tar road. He's heading right, towards Mkhuhlu. They're in a red Isuzu *bakkie*, gangster's paradise plates,' Tema said, using the common nickname for a vehicle registered in Johannesburg, Gauteng Province.

'Get your policeman to hospital. We'll keep track of the Isuzu until the cops arrive. I'll call van Rensburg and tell her our man's on the run, not far from the Kruger Park.'

Tema closed on the speeding vehicle, the needle on the speedometer climbing to a hundred. She looked at the officer next to her. 'We'll be at the doctor's soon, hang in there.'

'That man killed my partner.'

'He killed two of my friends in the anti-poaching unit I was training to be a part of, as well.'

'You've got guts, sisi. How bad do you want these guys?'

'Very bad.'

'Get me close enough to them and I'll shoot the driver.'

Tema nodded. 'All right.'

Chapter 5

Doug Pearse, Julianne's personal pilot, flew the Gazelle helicopter, and James Paterson was sitting in the front passenger seat.

Sonja sat in the rear, the side door removed, her LM5 assault rifle across her lap. Julianne, who was barely able to contain her excitement, was next to her. Sonja had tried to tell Julianne that it might be safer for her to stay at the lodge, but it seemed that despite her talk of wanting to employ professional surveillance and anti-poaching teams to implement her strategy, she still wanted to see some action herself. Paterson's quiet professionalism, however, was a nice counterbalance to his employer's over enthusiasm.

'I see the Isuzu now,' Paterson said, his voice monotone. 'Eleven o'clock. There's a police *bakkie* in pursuit.'

Sonja shook her head. 'Tema. The cops from Skukuza are only just getting out of the Kruger Park.'

'I'm circling to the right, outflanking them,' Doug said. 'If I overfly them they'll see us or our shadow.' They swooped over the township below and Doug brought the chopper around.

Julianne spoke into the intercom: 'If they turn off into Mkhuhlu we might lose them. They'll ditch the car and do a runner.'

Sonja leaned out, the slipstream catching her ponytail. 'Up ahead, the road narrows with steep banks on each side, just past a bend. Put down there.'

'You want to use my helicopter as a roadblock?' Julianne turned to look at her, eyes wide.

'*Ja.*'

Paterson looked to his employer. Clyde-Smith nodded. 'Do it,' James said.

'Well, this should be fun,' Doug said.

He brought the helicopter around until he was hovering just above the surface of the road, at the end of the mini canyon Sonja had spotted.

'Turn side-on to give me a clear shot. Be ready to lift off if he doesn't stop.'

They couldn't see the Isuzu now, but the driver would be in range soon, with enough time to brake, Sonja hoped. She brought the butt of the LM5 up to her shoulder.

As the truck closed on them she saw two faces through the windscreen. She aimed at the driver but held her fire.

'They're not slowing,' Clyde-Smith said.

'Steady,' Sonja told Doug through the headset microphone.

The driver of the car reached out of the window and pointed a handgun at her. She saw the pistol buck his hand. That was her 'go' signal. She was officially defending herself and the others in the helicopter now. She squeezed the trigger repeatedly, wishing she had the fully-automatic military version of the rifle. Empty shells spat from the rifle's ejection port as she stitched a line of holes across the windscreen.

Still the driver kept coming. Sonja fired another burst. 'Up,' she commanded.

Doug brought the chopper up, just in time for them to see the

Isuzu flash under the skids, with not a metre to spare. 'After him.'

As Doug banked, Sonja saw a police *bakkie* scream up the hill in pursuit. Sonja knew she must have hit the driver of the fleeing truck, as the Isuzu now started to swerve on the road.

Another vehicle was coming towards the Isuzu from the other direction, and the driver swung back into his own lane, hit the brakes and then overcorrected. He lost control and the truck left the road, went into a ditch and rolled.

'Bloody hell, did you see that?' Julianne said.

The other woman was almost gleeful, Sonja thought, but she herself was working. 'Put us down, close.'

As Doug set up for landing in an improvised roadside soccer pitch, locals started converging on the crash scene. Sonja watched as the police truck pulled up. She saw a woman in camouflage get out. Tema strode towards the Isuzu, which had come to a stop, right side up. She had a pistol held up in two hands, the way Sonja had taught her to shoot.

The driver's side door opened. A man crawled out, raised his right hand and pointed a pistol at Tema.

'Shoot,' Sonja urged her.

The man fired first.

Tema stopped and seemed to falter and for a moment Sonja feared she had been hit, but instead she dropped to one knee, to make herself a smaller target. As the helicopter touched down Tema fired twice. Through her fear for the younger woman Sonja felt a surge of pride; those long weeks of hard training had paid off. The gunman was down.

Sonja jumped from the chopper and, rifle still up, ran to the Isuzu. She circled around it, ready to fire. Inside, however, she saw that the passenger was immobile, an AK-47 lying across his lap and a bullet hole in his forehead. Sonja reached in and put her fingers to his neck.

'One dead here,' she called.

'Same here,' replied Tema.

Sonja went to her. 'Nice shooting.'

'Thank . . . thank you.' Tema held the pistol loosely in her right hand.

'Next time, don't wait so long. Him pointing a gun at you is all the provocation you need.'

Tema stared at her and Sonja saw the tears well in her eyes and her shoulders start to shrug as the spasms overtook her. Slinging her rifle over her shoulder, Sonja went to her, wrapped her arms around Tema and hugged the young woman to her body.

'You did well, my girl.'

*

Hudson Brand left his party of six American birdwatchers at the reception desk of the Protea Hotel, Kruger Gate. The thought of going back to the empty house in Hippo Rock was mildly depressing.

He'd lived alone, more or less, for years, and it had been surprising to him how quickly he'd become used to Sonja being around.

Hudson had lost his first true love in terrifyingly violent circumstances when he'd served in Angola during the border war in the 1980s, and he knew that had made him wary of settling down with a woman. Also, in truth, he liked being single.

Yet after little more than a week he'd found himself looking forward to sharing his life with Sonja. The house had felt, well, homey, for the first time, and they had settled into a nice mini routine. She would leave early, conduct her training for the Leopards during the day and get home around four thirty. They'd have a drink on the deck overlooking the river then kiss, make love, and he would cook.

He remembered the smell of her hair, the feel of her toned

body against his, the warmth of her when he woke in the middle of the night. A couple of nights she'd had nightmares, and he'd held her, damp with sweat, in his arms until she had stilled. In the mornings afterwards she had been unwilling to discuss her dreams. He hadn't pushed it.

Hudson needed a drink.

The Protea had a nice safari feel to it. The reception area was open plan under a high thatched roof. He walked along the dark-timbered deck past the main bar and restaurant then followed the elevated walkway towards the Sabie River. Spread out along the bank, overlooking the Kruger National Park, was a terrace bar with a few thatched cabanas on stilts.

Hudson saw that the regular barman, Mishack, was on duty.

'Howzit, Mishack?'

'Fine and you,' he said, but missing was the young man's trade-mark smile. He was good at his job and normally had an easy, welcoming manner.

'Fine. Castle Lite, draught, please.'

'Sure.'

Mishack pulled the beer but kept his eyes downcast. 'Bad day?' Hudson asked.

Mishack looked up and blinked. 'My brother, Shadrack, was killed today. A friend of mine walked past the scene of a shooting and recognised Shadrack's body, and that of our cousin. My friend called me with the news, I still can't believe it.'

'Hell.' Hudson knew Shadrack, who had worked around his house at Hippo Rock. 'What happened?'

'Some anti-poaching people shot him. They say he was hunting rhino in the park and killed one of those women, those Leopards, and that both Shadrack and our cousin had guns.'

Hudson whistled. He was tempted to say he couldn't believe it, but the cash on offer for rhino horn was enough to turn even dedicated national parks rangers and police. A poor young man such as Shadrack could have earned more than a year's worth of wages from taking a single rhino. 'I'm sorry.'

'I can't believe it,' Mishack said.

Hudson reached over the bar and put a hand on his shoulder. 'I'm sorry for your loss, man.'

A party of tourists sitting in the nearest cabana was waving to Mishack, trying to get his attention. 'Thank you, I have to go.'

Hudson took his beer to a table by the deck railing and sat down.

The Sabie was wider here than in front of the house where he lived, though at this time of year the water was restricted to a narrow channel. A breeding herd of a dozen or more elephants was browsing contentedly in the reeds in the middle of the mostly dry riverbed. Hudson sat for a while, enjoying his beer and the tranquillity.

He heard a chair scraping on the wooden deck beside him and turned to see a red-haired woman taking her seat. She wore cut-off denim shorts and a lime tank top. She was carrying a paperback.

'Sorry for the noise,' she said.

'No problem.'

'I hope I didn't disturb the elephants,' she said.

'Oh, don't worry about them. They're feeding, which means they're nice and relaxed.'

'Cool.' She watched the herd for a few moments then opened her book. 'I've just been reading about elephants in the Kruger Park as it happens.'

He made a show of peering around at the cover of her book. '*Ivory*. I've read it.'

'I'm enjoying it,' she said.

'That's the one about modern-day pirates, right? Kind of far-fetched, but I liked it.'

She smiled as Mishack brought her a cocktail, set it down and carried on with a tray of drinks for the other tourists. 'What girl doesn't love a pirate?'

He raised his beer to her and she picked up her drink and took a sip.

She set her glass down and closed her book on her lap. 'You don't sound South African, originally.'

He shook his head. 'I'm a mongrel. Half American, half Portuguese-Angolan.'

'That's more an exotic pedigree, I'd say, than mongrel. Are you a guide?'

'Yes. Just been out on a birding tour today.'

'Sounds exciting.'

'For some folks. This group came from the States; for some it's their ninth or tenth visit. Where are you from?'

'Cape Town. I'm a journalist. I'm here on holiday.'

'No game drive this afternoon? It's great wildlife viewing this time of year.'

'Oh, I like all kinds of wildlife. Actually, I'm happier just sitting here, watching the elephants and reading, than chasing about the park trying to spot the Big Five.'

'I hear you.' He sipped his beer.

She was pretty, flirty, maybe mid-thirties. So much his type it wasn't funny. She finished her drink.

Hudson hesitated. He thought of Sonja and how unfair it was that she had lashed out at him, thought the worst of him. He hadn't deserved that. 'Can I buy you another?'

She licked her lips. 'Sure.'

Hudson called Mishack over and ordered refills for both of them. He introduced himself to the woman.

She held out her hand. 'Rosie Appleton.'

'Pleased to meet you, Rosie.'

'How lucky am I? I get to avoid the crowd and still end up with my own private safari guide.'

*

Sonja finished with Captain Sannie van Rensburg for the second time that day, and accepted a lift with Tema's uncle, who had come to the scene of the car wreck and shooting in his tiny, rusting Ford Bantam *bakkie*.

While the local police from Hazyview had taken over the investigation of the killing of the two men, Sonja had first called van Rensburg letting her know that she and Tema were sure there was a connection to the shootings in the Sabi Sand Game Reserve. An ambulance had taken away the injured police officer, and it looked like he would be fine, unlike his partner.

Tema's uncle tried to insist that Sonja ride in the front, in relative comfort, but Sonja chose instead to sit in the open back with Tema. She wanted time with the girl, to make sure she was OK.

'I am,' Tema said, when Sonja enquired.

The initial shock after the shooting was wearing off, although Sonja knew the trauma would manifest itself again, in other ways – nightmares, flashbacks. But for now, Tema seemed composed.

'I'm just sad,' she said, 'about Shadrack. I thought he was such a good boy – man – so harmless.'

'It never ceases to amaze me,' Sonja said, 'what men are capable of.'

Tema looked into her eyes. 'Oh, I know what men are capable of, I just thought Shadrack was different.'

Sonja had thought Hudson Brand was different. Maybe he was. Maybe nothing at all had happened between him and the van Rensburg woman. She didn't feel anything for the men they had killed just now – from her cursory inspection of the bodies it looked like both she and Tema had hit each of the two men. Tema's second shot had been meant for the driver, but when he fell the bullet had gone into Shadrack, inside the vehicle, and that's what concerned the younger woman the most, that she might have killed the neighbour she had known since childhood.

'I need to see Shine, my daughter, to hold her,' Tema said.

'I know how you feel.' Sonja was just pleased that Emma was somewhere safe, without guns, doing what she loved.

Tema's uncle sped down the R536, through the settling gloom. They passed the entrance to Elephant Point and then Hippo Rock Private Nature Reserve. Sonja thought of Hudson Brand and wondered if she should ask to be let out there. However, she had left her pack and dive bag at the Protea Hotel's concierge after checking out that morning, still unsure of where she would spend the night.

'Julianne Clyde-Smith has offered me a job, starting right away,' Sonja said to Tema.

'I am pleased for you. I have to get used to calling white women Madam again, that is if I can find another job as a domestic.'

'I wanted to talk to you about that.'

Tema smiled. 'If you are staying in South Africa I would be so happy to be your maid.'

Sonja had to laugh. 'No, I don't want or need a maid. The job I've been offered, I can recruit my own team.'

'Anti-poaching, like the Leopards? Serious?'

'Don't get too excited. It will be a different job, more dangerous. You have to think about your daughter.'

'Last night we learned how dangerous this job can be. I don't think the others – Lungile, Lucy, Mavis, poor Patience and Goodness – truly realised.'

'Being part of this new unit would mean you would be away from your daughter, sometimes for weeks on end.'

'If I got a job in the Sabi Sand Game Reserve even, or in the park, I would be away for weeks, living in staff quarters. My mother would take care of Shine, just as she did when I was a maid at a lodge. We are used to hardship.'

'This work, it would involve surveillance, following people, living in the bush, watching where the poachers are based, who their leaders are, who is dealing in rhino horn and ivory. We might be working outside of South Africa, undercover.'

Tema nodded. 'I understand. My father was a Shangaan from Maputo, in Mozambique. I speak Portuguese, as well as English and xiTsonga.'

Yes, Sonja thought, *and you're bright, courageous and dedicated.* 'If you come with me, I will make sure they pay you a good wage, that you have medical aid, and that Shine will be looked after.'

'Looked after when?'

'In case . . .'

'Oh,' said Tema. 'That is good. It is fine. If I hadn't had my baby I was going to join the army. I wanted to try and become an officer, but there were not enough vacancies for women. I thought the Leopards would be the next best thing. I want to help my country, Sonja, help the animals and make sure they are still around for my daughter's generation to appreciate them.'

Sonja swallowed hard and looked away. Tema's uncle turned into the hotel's driveway, near the ladies who were packing up their roadside curio stalls for the night. The entry gate to the Kruger Park was closed.

The uncle pulled up under the covered parking area at reception. Sonja looked Tema in the eye. 'As far as I'm concerned, you're on the team.'

'Oh, thank you, Sonja.' Tema put two hands on her heart. 'You have made me so happy.'

Sonja waved them goodbye and Tema climbed down and got into the cab with her uncle.

It had been a shitty couple of days, but Sonja was pleased that she'd at least been able to give Tema something to smile about after the terrible time she'd had. The girl might still live to regret it, but Sonja sensed she had the strength of mind, body and heart to make a good operator.

She needed a drink, so instead of going straight to the concierge or trying to sort out a room for the night she followed the dark planking of the walkway towards the bar down on the river.

It was a pretty spot, set amid massive old jackalberry trees that lined the banks of the Sabie River. Off to her right was the circular open-air boma, where staff were setting tables for the nightly buffet. A fire was already burning in the central pit and lanterns cast golden light on the proceedings.

Sonja broke into a smile when she saw, still some way ahead of her, Hudson Brand emerge from the men's bathroom near the upstairs bar and head towards the river. Sonja felt affection for him flood through her. Perhaps she had been too quick to judge him; she had let her emotions after the firefight cloud her judgement. She quickened her step to catch up with him, but she didn't call out to him, planning instead to surprise him.

Hudson walked up the steps to the deck overlooking the river and signalled to the barman, at the bar on the left, with two fingers.

Sonja slowed as she approached the steps and watched as he took a seat next to a red-headed woman, who threw back her head and laughed loudly at something he said as he sat down.

Sonja saw how the woman played with her hair with the fingers of her right hand. She leaned closer to Hudson and touched him on the arm to punctuate some flirtatious point. He laughed. The barman came and Hudson took a beer and a cocktail from a tray. The man cleared half a dozen empty glasses from the table between them.

It was too much for her to take in, and she was in no mood for a confrontation or more excuses. Sonja turned on her heel and retraced her steps. As she walked she took her phone out of the breast pocket of her fatigues and dialled.

'Excuse me, madam.'

Sonja looked up from the phone. A young woman in the hotel's uniform was ushering a party of guests in safari clothes into the main bar, near reception. She put up a hand to stop Sonja.

'What is it?' Sonja asked, not even trying to hide her annoyance.

'Ma'am, sorry, but a leopard has been spotted in the hotel grounds, over there beneath the walkway.' The woman gestured to the lushly vegetated central area, surrounded by the bar and upstairs restaurant on one side and walkways leading to the guest rooms on the other.

'So?'

'So, ma'am, we're asking everyone to please move inside, into the bar, until the leopard has gone.'

'No.' The big cat had obviously crossed the Sabie River, which this late in the winter dry season was very low. It was probably in search of one of the bushbuck that lived around the hotel.

'No, ma'am?'

'No.' Sonja lifted her camouflage shirt to show the woman the nine-millimetre Glock pistol on her hip. 'I spend my nights in the bush on anti-poaching patrols surrounded by leopards and lions.'

'Well, I'm asking nicely, ma'am, and safety is our priority here.'

'Noted, now leave me alone.'

The young woman looked for a moment like she might stand up to Sonja, but two more guests, speaking French, had just wandered up from the viewing deck bar so the woman turned her attention to softer targets.

Sonja walked on, dialling again, and stopped by the hotel's curio shop, whose nervous staff were peering out the window. She waited for the call to go through.

'Sonja?' Julianne Clyde-Smith said on the other end.

'I didn't know you had my number,' Sonja said, somewhat taken aback.

'Yes, and I took the liberty of saving it to my phone. We're very thorough, you know.'

'I do know.' Sonja shrugged off her irritation. They'd done their background checks on her for good reason, and the level of information they'd gathered on her told her they were serious about taking the fight to the poaching syndicates and gaining usable intelligence on them. That was good; this was no game for amateurs.

'Have you made a decision about my offer?'

Sonja paused, wavering. She was not a woman given to indecision. In the heat of battle one had to make split-second decisions. A bad decision was sometimes better than taking no action at all. She thought again about Hudson Brand, about giving herself a holiday and turning her back on long cold nights in the bush, mosquitos, wild animals, and, inevitably, more blood.

Then she saw him. Them.

Sonja dropped back behind a giant decorative clay pot, which was almost as tall as she was. Hudson Brand was coming along the walkway, from the deck bar, holding the hand of the red-haired woman he'd been talking to.

The young female manager stopped them, but she had a chat with Brand and he was allowed to move on, without even showing her his gun. Brand led the woman towards Sonja, but she stayed out of sight. They turned right and headed off towards the guest rooms.

Sonja made a fist with her free hand. 'Yes, I've made a decision.'

Chapter 6

Tema packed her camouflage uniforms and her civilian clothes in the green kitbag she had been issued with when she joined the Leopards.

Her mother walked into her bedroom, carrying Shine. 'Are you sure you want to do this?'

Tema felt something squeeze her heart as she looked at her daughter's curls, her plump cheeks. For a moment she wavered, but then told herself the best chance Shine had was for her to work hard and make enough money to guarantee both their futures. 'I'm lucky to have a job. The Leopards are being put on hold. The other girls are all out of work for now.'

'It's so dangerous. It's not our fight.'

Tema pursed her lips. Her mother had never been into the Kruger National Park, nor the adjoining Sabi Sand Game Reserve. She'd told Tema many times that she thought people were mad going into animal country. Her people had been banned from even entering the park through most of the apartheid era in South Africa, unless they worked in menial jobs in the reserve.

'I don't like it,' her mother said.

Tema came to her and took Shine from her arms. She loved her little girl's smell and the warmth of her tiny body. 'The money will be good, according to Sonja. I'll be able to send you some, and put some away for Shine.' The baby gurgled and she held her to her breast and kissed her head.

Her mother took the child from her and it was like losing a limb. Tema drew a breath and told herself to harden up, an expression Sonja often used.

'You should go and see Shadrack's mother, before you leave.'

'Mother . . .'

'You need to see the result of your actions.'

Tema sighed. Shadrack's family and their small community were once more seeing the result of the actions of poachers. As long as young men kept accepting money from the middlemen and poaching kingpins for horn, then the toll of dead rhinos and dead people would continue.

Her mother had told her that Mrs Mabunda's son had been picked up by the police last week. He was just fifteen years old, but a man had offered the boy and three of his friends ten thousand rand each to take a rifle into the Kruger Park and try to shoot a rhino. The inexperienced teenagers had been caught almost immediately by an army patrol on anti-poaching duty. They had been watching the drift where the boys crossed the river.

'I will go see his mother,' Tema said. Whatever he had done, Shadrack had been her friend, and she had been up half the night replaying the terrible, yet adrenaline-charged moment when she had fired her weapon.

Tema left her bag by the door, went outside into the bright morning sunshine and trudged through the dust to the house next door. A dozen *bakkie*s and cars in varying stages of disrepair were parked outside the house, other mourners come to pay their respects. A crow wheeled overhead, squawking down at her.

71

Tema walked up to the open front door. A man stepped into the doorway, blocking her way. He wore a black vinyl jacket and folded his arms across his chest. She recognised him, but not by name – he was one of Shadrack's uncles.

'How dare you come here?'

Tema looked down. 'I'm sorry, I've come to pay my respects.'

'Get away from here, you traitorous bitch.'

She looked up. 'You have no need to call me that.'

'You sell out your own people, you shoot a poor simple boy you have known since childhood; what else am I to call you?'

Tema swallowed. He had the look of a bully. Shadrack's mother had gone to work more than once with bruises on her face when her husband had still been alive and his brother, this man, looked like the kind who would hurt women. Too many men, Tema knew, were like that.

'Yes, Shadrack was my friend, but I don't know what happened to him, why or how these people convinced him to work for them.'

He pointed a finger at her. '*These people* are your people. You are the murderer, you are a disgrace.'

Tema felt small. She thought she was working in anti-poaching *for* South Africa, because the wildlife belonged to everyone – that was what Sonja had said. But she knew that some people in her community thought they had a right to take animals, birds, fish – whatever they wanted – from the game reserve and the Kruger Park. It was true what the man said; to some she was the enemy.

There was movement behind the man and Anna, Shadrack's mother, brushed the man aside. She was wearing her best Sunday clothes and her eyes were red from crying. 'Tema.'

Tema felt her bottom lip start to tremble. She looked down, and clasped her hands in front of her. 'I'm so sorry.'

Anna came to her, down the two steps and wrapped her big soft arms around her and pulled her to her bosom. 'So am I,

Tema. I've known you since you were a baby, carried you, cared for you.'

Tema looked up again, the plump smooth cheeks as familiar to her as her own mother's face. 'They had guns.'

'So the police told me. But I don't know how that happened. You knew Shadrack, you knew how gentle he was, what kind of boy he was.'

Tema nodded. None of it made sense. 'They were shooting at us, at me and the policeman, at the helicopter.'

'My Shadrack was shooting at you?'

Tema looked down at her feet.

'Answer me, girl.'

'The other man . . .'

Anna put a finger under Tema's chin and lifted her face. '"The other man"? Tell me, was my Shadrack pointing a gun at you and shooting?'

Tema blinked. It was suddenly hard for her to breathe. 'He had an AK-47, a rifle, like the poachers use, and his boot was cut.'

'Boot?'

'We tracked the man who killed Patience Mdluli; maybe he also killed Goodness. He was wearing a pair of boots and the sole of the right boot was sliced. He also cut his back on razor wire, leaving the Sabi Sand reserve, and I saw that Shadrack had a cut on his back and his shirt.'

Anna looked away and wiped the tears that had sprung again.

'I'm so sorry,' Tema said. 'It wasn't just me who was shooting.'

The older woman nodded. 'I saw my son. My little boy. He was riddled with bullet holes.'

Tema felt her own tears welling. 'I was just doing my job.'

'You did a very good job.'

Anna turned her back to Tema. The uncle stepped up to the doorway again and pointed his finger at her.

'We will not forget you,' he said.

Tema wiped her eyes and glared back at him. He slammed the door in her face.

She walked back to her house. Tema would have given anything for Shadrack to still be alive. However, the man with him had been doing his best to kill her, the policeman, and the people in the helicopter. Tema and Sonja had done what they needed to do to protect themselves and the others with them.

Shadrack had become mixed up in this terrible business somehow, and he had at the very least been an accomplice to a serious crime.

Tema's mother met her at the door, her arms folded across her chest. 'You are leaving now?'

She nodded. 'Miss Kurtz, Sonja, is coming to pick me up.'

Tema walked past her mother to her room and picked up Shine from her cot. It was second-hand, a gift from one of the white women whose houses she'd once cleaned. The baby's jumpsuit she had bought from a stall selling second-hand clothes donated by people overseas to help poor Africans. One day, she told herself, my daughter will have new clothes, a good education, and a fine house. She kissed Shine, held her tight to her chest, then set her down.

The baby smiled and gurgled up at her. Tema blew her a kiss and went back to her mother.

'I'm going to walk for a bit,' Tema said. She hefted her kitbag onto her shoulder.

Her mother held her at arm's length, her bony hands on her shoulders. 'Be careful.'

'I will.'

'You believe in what you are doing.'

Tema nodded, then swallowed as she felt tears rising again. 'I do, but it's hard sometimes.'

'The right thing often is.'

Tema hugged her mother and walked out of the house.

Chapter 7

Hudson Brand woke up in the master bedroom of the house at Hippo Rock, alone.

He had no safari clients today and had slept in. He opened the curtains and the glass sliding door. The morning air was still crisp as he walked out onto the wooden deck overlooking the Sabie River. A fish eagle circled, looking for breakfast, and then dived.

Hudson shaded his eyes with a hand and saw the bird skim the water and take off with a wriggling barbel in its talons.

He went back inside, pleased with the way the day had begun, and went to the bathroom and dressed. When he got to the refrigerator he surveyed its meagre contents and was reminded of Sonja; he detested tomato sauce but hers was in the door.

He thought about Rosie Appleton as he took out an egg and the remains of a packet of bacon, along with two slices of bread.

Hudson knew the duty manager at the Protea Hotel, Simone, and she had told him it was no problem for him to escort Rosie to her room while the hotel staff looked for the leopard that had invaded the hotel grounds. Hudson was an experienced safari guide so would know what to do if he encountered a big cat on the walkway – stand still, stop Rosie from running, and pray it wasn't an old cat with bad teeth who was going to make its last meal the easiest one of its life.

When he got to the room Rosie had asked him in for a drink.

'No, thanks,' he'd said, replaying the conversation in his head.

'I'm scared,' she said.

He didn't believe her; the half-smile betrayed her.

He'd been tempted.

Even now, he didn't quite know why he hadn't gone in for that drink, why he'd begged off, saying he had an early start this morning, when he didn't.

He supposed, now, as he scooped the bacon and egg onto the bread and took his breakfast, and a Coke, out onto the deck, that things were over between him and Sonja, if they had ever really been on at all.

A herd of elephants was making its way down the well-trodden game trail on the dusty red earth bank on the Kruger Park side of the river. In the lead was the matriarch, head and shoulders above her eldest daughter, and with a new tiny calf in tow.

The elephants had it simple. The women were in charge and the males followed them around, waiting for a chance to have sex. When they were done the guys drifted off, sometimes forming small bachelor groups where an old bull would be accompanied by a couple of young males, known as askaris, or guards. Eventually, when the females returned and the askaris went into musth, they would challenge their mentor and they'd all duke it out. The winner would get the girl. Simple.

Hudson enjoyed being a lone bull. He'd never been much of a boyfriend and would have made someone a lousy husband. He did his best to stay away from other men's wives and as a safari guide he never had to wait too long before some tourist suffered a bout of khaki fever – a common malaise in Africa where tourists succumbed to the rough-and-tumble charms of the person showing them around. He'd had female clients who cried at their first sight of an elephant in the wild and Hudson Brand was always there to hold a hand. Africa, Hudson had often said, made one hell of a wingman.

So what the heck was wrong with him now? He finished his breakfast, left the elephants to theirs, and went inside and put his empty plate in the sink.

There was a knock at the door, which was surprising as he hadn't heard a car pull up outside. Hippo Rock was the kind of secluded bolthole where people valued their privacy, so it was very rare for a neighbour to show up without prior warning. When he opened the door he saw it was Anna, Shadrack and Mishack's mother, the matronly woman who was in charge of the estate's laundry.

'Anna, how are you? I'm sorry for your loss. I didn't expect you to be working today.' And nor did he expect her to have walked here, a kilometre or more from her laundry.

She wiped her eyes. 'I wanted to see you.'

'Well, come on in.'

Staff never visited the homes of owners on the estate, unless it was to clean or do some other chores. Anna looked around, as if uncomfortable to be seen infringing on a resident's privacy, then drew a breath and walked across the threshold.

'Would you like tea? Coffee?'

'Coffee, please.'

'Three sugars and milk?'

'Yes, please.'

Most of Africa hadn't got the sugar memo yet, though Hudson had managed to cut down to two. He put on the kettle.

'Take a seat here in the kitchen. What can I do for you?'

'They say, the other owners who know you, that you are a detective, like a policeman, as well as being a guide.'

Hudson poured and passed Anna her cup. 'Yes, I'm a private investigator, part-time.'

He had served in the US Army as a young man. His American oil-man father had taken his Angolan wife back to the States after meeting her in Africa and getting her pregnant. His father had left his mother for another woman when Hudson was very young and his mother had died when he was a teenager. He fully believed he might have ended up in prison if the army hadn't got him first. A secondment to the CIA had brought him to Africa – America was covertly funding anti-communist rebels in Angola and Hudson spoke the local language, Portuguese, and had some family still in the country. Things had turned sour for Hudson and he had almost been killed in South West Africa, now Namibia, when he had uncovered American involvement in the South African Defence Force's illegal slaughter of rhino and elephant in the areas where they were fighting. Corrupt military people and spies were involved in shipping rhino horn and ivory out of Africa.

Hudson had left America's employ and, ironically, ended up fighting for the South Africans in the largely Angolan 32 Battalion, known either as the Buffalo Soldiers, thanks to their cap badge or, due to their reputation, the Terrible Ones.

After the war in Angola he had stayed in Africa, following his passion for the mother continent's wildlife by becoming a safari guide. To supplement his meagre income he had started working as a private investigator. He had stumbled upon a niche business, investigating fraudulent insurance claims lodged by people who had faked their own deaths.

'You can help me?' Anna said.

'Is it about your son?'

She nodded and pressed the handkerchief in her fingers to her eyes. 'He did not do the things they claimed.'

'This is really a matter for the police.'

'They already told me, the woman, the one who also lives here, van Rensburg, that they will not be treating his death as murder.'

Hudson sipped his coffee. 'That sounds right. Based on police procedure they've probably taken out what's called an inquest docket, rather than a murder docket. His death would only be investigated further if you have grounds to make them think he was innocent.'

'He was innocent. He was a good man, Mr Brand.'

Hudson sighed. 'This rhino horn business, it corrupts very good men, Anna. I had a friend who worked as a guide, inside Kruger, for national parks. He loved wildlife, rhino in particular, but the gangs got to him, offered him more money than he could have possibly imagined.'

Anna looked up and fixed him with her eyes. 'My son was not like that. He did not care about money. He could barely count, Mr Brand, and he loved his life, working here and living with me.'

'Captain van Rensburg's a good woman, Anna, a fair person. If you take your concerns to her, she will listen.'

'I tried. She told me the same thing as you just did, that it is just about the money, that even good people do bad things. My Shadrack had never picked up a gun in his life, even though his cousin, who was with him, had been in trouble with the police.'

'Then what was he doing in that car, with the other man? I spoke to Mishack at the hotel yesterday and he told me both Shadrack and his cousin were carrying firearms.'

Anna seemed to hesitate, but nodded. 'His cousin *was* a bad man. Somehow he convinced Shadrack to get in the car with him, and gave him a gun.'

'But why would your son do such a thing?'

Anna set her cup down, hard enough to spill some. 'Sorry.'

Hudson put up a hand. 'No need to be. I understand how you're feeling.'

'The policewoman asked the same questions. I don't know how Shadrack ended up in that car, but I need someone to find out. My son did not kill anyone, and he did not kill a rhino – he loved all animals. Come to our house and I will show you his dogs. He took them in and cared for them, better than most people in our community.'

He was sympathetic to her, but it looked to him, as it no doubt did to Sannie van Rensburg, like an open and shut case. 'I'm not sure I can help, Anna.'

'I can pay you, but I do not have very much money. I can do your washing and ironing for free, for a very long time.'

Hudson could imagine how little Anna had. Mishack, her other son, was a good guy, and from what he knew of Shadrack, he had been as well. Shadrack was a hard worker, and Hudson was unaware of anyone at Hippo Rock ever having anything other than a good word for him. He thought about the big bag of washing in the back of his Land Rover and how he might otherwise spend the day rather than sitting by the washing machine and hanging his clothes out to dry.

He sighed. 'OK. How about I talk to Captain van Rensburg and see what she has to say?'

'How much will it cost me?'

'One load of washing and ironing,' he said.

She raised her eyes and he saw the hope there, shining through the tears. 'Serious?'

'It's a *big* load of washing.'

She forced a smile. 'You need a good woman.'

He stood up. He thought about Sonja and, try as he might, he couldn't picture her in a pinafore pegging up clothes on a line. Well, maybe . . .

'Let me take you back to the laundry.'

*

Sonja picked up Tema from her home but didn't drive straight to Khaya Ngala. Instead she headed in the opposite direction, through Hazyview and along the R40, a winding road through scenic hills covered with banana and pine tree plantations.

Just before the town of White River she turned off at a roundabout to access the Casterbridge Centre.

'I'm going to try and recruit someone else,' Sonja had answered when Tema asked her where they were going.

The centre was a popular stop-off for tourists and locals alike. It had a hotel, a small cinema, a couple of restaurants and cafes and a range of boutique shops and galleries that sold arts and crafts, up-market clothing and handmade furniture.

Sonja parked and Tema opened her door. 'Just a minute.'

Tema looked to her. 'Yes?'

Sonja reached for her rucksack and fished inside it. She pulled out a black metal pocket-sized torch. 'You were the best recruit in the Leopards training program, Tema. When you all officially graduated, I was going to give you this as a gift.'

'Thank you,' Tema said. 'It looks very nice.'

'It's not just a torch.' Sonja turned it around in her hand so Tema could see a small switch on the base, where the battery cap screwed in. Sonja flicked the switch then pointed the lens towards Tema. 'Now, watch what happens when I press the on switch at the top, which normally turns on the light.'

Sonja pressed the button and instead of the bulb lighting up the blue light of a taser cackled and screeched loudly in the confines of the car.

Tema jumped in her seat, then laughed as Sonja handed it to her. She pressed the button and grinned again.

'That's 100,000 volts, enough to put someone down,' Sonja said. 'Come on, let's go.'

They got out of the vehicle and walked along a covered walkway past a line of shops selling gifts, furniture and crafts.

Sonja continued on until they came to a jewellery store. 'This must be it.'

A grey-haired man behind a counter looked up when she rang the bell on the security door, and buzzed her and Tema in.

'Can I help?' he asked.

'I'm looking for Mario Machado,' Sonja said.

'Mario?' the man called.

Tema bent to admire some bronze castings, one of an elephant and another of a warthog. 'These are beautiful.'

'Mario made them,' the jeweller said. 'He's got quite a talent as a sculptor.'

Among other things, Sonja thought to herself. Sonja had met Mario when they were both working as military contractors in Afghanistan. He had served in the old South African Defence Force's 32 Battalion in Angola, as had Hudson, so he knew how to fight. He had been born in Mozambique when it was still a Portuguese colony, and spoke the language fluently. She'd had a fling with him, but that wasn't why she was recruiting him; he knew the first country they were going to operate in, could pass as a local, and would be handy if the bullets started flying. Hudson Brand would have ticked all the same boxes, but she had less of a personal connection to Mario and she wasn't mad as hell at him.

Mario came through the door that led to the studio behind the showroom. He wore a workman's apron and his tanned, muscled forearms showed beneath rolled-up sleeves. Sonja remembered those hands of his, which he now wiped on a cloth; they were big, but the fingers were surprisingly soft.

He looked at her and his dark eyes widened with surprise. 'Sonja!'

'Mario.'

He came around the counter and put his arms around her. Sonja was not good with public displays of affection and was acutely aware of Tema watching her and smiling as Mario kissed her on each cheek and then held her at arm's length.

'It's so good to see you again, but how did you find me? What are you doing here in South Africa? Where have you been?'

She stepped back from him, breaking contact but embarrassed by the fact that her cheeks were starting to burn. 'One question at a time, Mario. Can we talk somewhere?'

Mario looked to the jeweller. 'Roy?'

'Of course.'

Mario untied and shrugged off his apron and tossed it behind the counter. 'We can go to Zannas Cafe across the road. The coffee is good.'

'Fine.'

Sonja introduced Mario to Tema and Mario led them back out of the Casterbridge Centre, through the car park and across the busy R40 to another cluster of eateries and shops. They took a table outside under an umbrella and ordered coffees from a waiter.

He was sitting opposite her, but leaned forward, elbows on the table. His hair was still thick, wavy and dark, though salted with a little more grey since the last time she had seen him. She remembered running her fingers through it.

'Fewer people know me on this side of the road. So, to what do I owe the honour?'

Mario had sensed the need for discretion, which was good, Sonja thought.

'I'm putting together a specialist anti-poaching team, Mario.'

He sat silently for a moment, as if digesting this news, then said, 'I've had offers to do security work in the past, but I prefer my sculpting to endless patrols in the bush or long nights sitting in an observation post.'

'This is something different.'

He smiled, showing perfect, even white teeth. 'As it's you, I had a feeling it would be. Tell me. And your charming young friend here?'

Tema looked down, embarrassed, but Sonja spoke for her. 'Tema's already proved herself, in combat, as a very good operator. She killed a man the other day.'

He raised his thick, dark eyebrows. 'Was that you I read about, the all-female patrol that was ambushed?'

'Yes,' Sonja said.

'You want me to join an all-female unit?'

She heard the mockery, but ignored it. 'No. Men and women, undercover, behind the lines, initially in Mozambique, elsewhere after that, wherever the poaching kingpins are based.'

Mario leaned back now as the waiter delivered their coffees. He said nothing.

'How exactly do you two know each other?' Tema asked, breaking the silence.

'We worked together in Afghanistan.'

'I wondered if you would end up here,' Mario said, 'looking for revenge.'

'I came here to do voluntary work, to train the Leopards, the all-woman anti-poaching unit.'

'And that's all? Just to train.'

'My role's changed; I'm working for Julianne Clyde-Smith now.'

He nodded. 'Billionaire businesswoman, philanthropist, ardent environmentalist, and now she's setting up a hit squad, hey? I wouldn't put it past her. She talks tough about poaching all the time.'

'I didn't say anything about a hit squad, Mario. We'll be gathering intelligence, helping the national parks and security forces catch the heads of poaching syndicates, the people who bribe their way out of arrests and convictions.'

'Yes, yes, yes, I am sure. So why are you coming to me? I am no intelligence officer.'

'You speak Portuguese, you grew up in Mozambique, so you know the country, the people.'

'And?'

Sonja looked across the courtyard to the jewellery shop. 'You're good at your art, your sculpting, but you're not an artist, Mario. You're a soldier.'

He regarded her, not saying anything for a while. 'You are preparing to mount cross-border surveillance operations, but your first member of your new team is a young girl – no offence, Tema – whose sole qualification so far is that she has killed in battle. And now you want me, an ageing warrior. Why? You could find a hundred, a thousand, men – and women – to volunteer for anti-poaching work.'

Sonja nodded. 'This isn't glorified security work, Mario. We're going to war, or we at least need to be able to fight if we're exposed. The pay will be good, better than you get here.'

His gaze shifted from Sonja across the R40 to the serenity of the jewellery shop and studio. 'Roy has been mentoring me. I work on commission. I can always come back.'

Sonja looked into his eyes and saw herself. 'You and I know this isn't just about the money, never was, not even in Afghanistan.'

He showed his even white teeth. 'I'm in.'

Chapter 8

Captain Sannie van Rensburg sat at her desk in the detectives' office in the Skukuza Police Station, at Number 1 Leopard Street, located on the staff-only side of the camp, behind the public post office.

Vanessa Sunday came in, bringing two cups of rooibos tea. She set one down on Sannie's desk. 'There's a guy out front, asking to see you.'

Sannie looked up from the pile of dockets she was reviewing. 'Who?'

'Damned fine looking. Tall, dark, handsome. Sounds American. A Hudson . . .'

'Brand.'

'You know him?'

'We're neighbours, of sorts. I'll go see him.'

Sannie walked out to the charge counter. 'Howzit, Hudson. What can I do for you?'

'I'd like a few minutes of your time, if you can spare it.'

'Let's go to the interview room.'

Hudson gave a small laugh. 'Last time I was there you were

accusing me of murder.'

'Well, you killed the *boerewors* the other night,' Sannie said.

'I like my steak still mooing, but not my sausage.'

'You're forgiven, though you'll never be a proper South African if you keep cooking *wors* like that. Come through. Would you like tea? Coffee?'

'No thanks, Sannie, I had a cup just a while back, with Anna Mnisi.'

'Anna? Our Anna, from Hippo Rock?' Sannie had joined the police force in the dying days of the apartheid regime, but she had done so because she wanted to see justice offered to all South Africans and to help make her country a better, safer place. Her parents had thought her too liberal, but she had worked with people of every background all through her career and did not consider herself racist. However, she was curious as to why Hudson would be socialising with their laundry lady. Immediately, she felt bad for thinking that way.

'Yes. It was her son, Shadrack, who was shot in the *bakkie*; one of the two guys who were allegedly firing on Julianne Clyde-Smith's helicopter.'

'Allegedly? I saw the bullet holes in the chopper.'

'Well, we both know that until someone checks the damage to Julianne's chopper it could have just been one man firing.'

Sannie sipped her tea, then put it down. 'Good point. I'm not handling this case, by the way; it was out of the park and game reserves so the guys from Hazyview caught it. However, your friend Sonja called me as soon as it happened as it seems to be connected to the spate of shootings in the Sabi Sand the other night.'

'How so?'

'What's your interest in this, Hudson? Is Anna paying you to investigate her son's death?'

'A load of free washing.'

'*Eish*, maybe I should become a private investigator. Let the police do their job, Hudson.'

He put his hands up in self-defence. 'I'm not saying they won't, but I'd feel a whole lot better, and I'm sure Anna would too, if you could maybe take a look at this. You know Anna, you know her son.'

'That's not quite true, Hudson.' Shadrack was a good worker around Hippo Rock.

Hudson leaned forward. 'Can you give me something, anything, to maybe let Anna down gently? If this is a slam dunk I don't want to waste your time or mine, even if it means I get my jockey shorts starched.'

Sannie smiled. Hudson was a friend, but she had to keep their relationship professional when it came to investigations. On the other hand, she felt for Anna. She was a lovely woman, now in mourning and grappling for answers as to why her son had taken up arms and gone on the run with his cousin. She could see the bind that Hudson was in.

'All right,' Sannie said. 'Here's what I can tell you, but it will be no comfort to Anna. I spoke to the detectives investigating the shooting of Shadrack and the other guy – his cousin as it happens. The cousin shot and killed a police officer in Huntington and wounded his partner. He and Shadrack then gapped it. Shadrack had been fingered by an anti-poaching patrol member.'

Hudson pulled out a notebook. 'Mind if I take notes?'

'No problem,' Sannie said. 'The patrol member was sharp, she noticed Shadrack had a cut on his back and his shirt was ripped and when she followed him up the street to his house – she was his next-door neighbour – she noticed a slit on the sole of one of his boots in the tracks he left on the ground. The wound on his back and the distinctive boot prints matched those of a suspect the patrol tracked out of the Sabi Sand. We took casts of the prints from the game reserve and they'll be compared to Shadrack's today.'

Hudson looked up from his notebook. 'The anti-poaching unit operator – you said "she"?'

Sannie nodded. 'Tema Matsebula, a member of the Leopards, the all-female unit. The one your friend Sonja was heading up. She's one tough cookie. Used to be a maid in Hippo Rock, but now she's handy with a gun as well as a mop.'

'You said it's not good news for Anna,' Hudson said, 'and I agree it looks bad for Shadrack, but so far all you've got is some evidence indicating he was inside the Sabi Sand. Anna told me her husband was a bushmeat poacher. Shadrack could have been inside the game reserve setting snares to catch impala.'

Sannie paused. She had already given Hudson more information than she should have, but the truth would come out eventually. 'Hudson, the crossover between the shooting of Shadrack and his cousin and my cases leads back to the Sabi Sand reserve, where Sonja's tracker picked up Shadrack's spoor. If Shadrack wasn't dead I'd be charging him with the murder of Goodness Mdluli. She ran away from the contact with the Leopards and it looks like Shadrack tracked her down and killed her.'

Hudson gave a low whistle and closed his notebook. 'Why?'

'I don't know,' Sannie said. 'Poachers who stumble into contacts with the security forces sometimes stand and fight, but usually they try to run from us. These guys opened fire first on the Leopards and after the contact was over at least one of them went looking for, or found, Goodness, and shot her in the back.'

'Murder?'

'Could be,' Sannie said. 'They were both local, the girl and Shadrack. Maybe there was more to this than a chance gunfight in the bush.'

'Anna's convinced Shadrack had nothing to do with poaching. I just think we should do a little more digging.'

Sannie shrugged. 'Of course, we'll have to see if the boot print is a definite match, and the postmortem being done on Shadrack will tell us more, but I'm afraid it looks like Anna's son was just another poorly paid young man who was corrupted by the poaching syndicates. When you look at the money even a foot-soldier stands to make from killing a rhino you can understand why they take the risks.'

Hudson put his book and pen in the pocket of his khaki safari shirt. 'How's Tom doing?'

Sannie and her husband Skyped most days, unless either of them was busy with work, but she missed the physical presence of him; if anything it was his touch, just holding him, that was hardest to do without. 'He's fine. I think he's enjoying being back at work as a protection officer. He liked being on the farm, but I think he was always a bit envious of me going back to police work.'

'It's like an itch, isn't it,' Hudson said.

'Yes, I suppose so. And something more. When I was having the kids, and before I went back into the service, I always felt like I should be doing something, that there were people I should be helping.'

Hudson pushed back his chair and stood. 'I know exactly how you feel.'

She looked him in the eyes. He was a good-looking man and she enjoyed his company, but she had no desire to cheat on Tom. 'Hudson, please, leave this investigation to the police.'

He nodded. 'I will, I promise.'

Sannie led him out past the charge desk and into the sunshine. She wanted to make sure he was not going to interfere with the investigation. 'I think I'll finish my tea out here, it's such a beautiful day, and it's too cold inside. Stay for a cup?'

'I might.' Hudson's phone beeped and he looked at the screen. 'Sorry, I'll have to take a raincheck on that cup of tea. Tracey Mahoney's got an urgent job she needs doing.'

'I understand.' Tracey and her husband Greg ran a safari company from their home in Hazyview. Sannie had interviewed her in the past in relation to a case, checking on Hudson Brand's movements as it happened. She was a feisty Englishwoman and Sannie knew most of Hudson's work came from her.

'Got to pick up some rich dude from Mozambique from the airport. He's asked for me by name.'

Sannie smiled. 'Price of fame. You will leave the investigation to me, right?'

'Yep. Especially as my day job just intervened. I can't say no to cold hard cash.'

Hudson walked towards his Land Rover. Sannie sighed. She knew Hudson had the itch, and as soon as he'd transferred the client to wherever he was going Brand would be sniffing around like a bloodhound. 'Hudson?'

He turned to her. 'Yup?'

'I'll talk to the investigating detectives at Hazyview.'

'Thanks.' He smiled and touched the peak of his baseball cap. 'Appreciate it.'

*

'I'm in heaven,' Mario Machado said, as he walked slowly around the private dining room in the wine cellar at Khaya Ngala Lodge and reverently slid a bottle of Rust en Vrede from a rack.

'Keep your mind on the job, Mario,' Sonja said. 'Take a seat.'

Mario reluctantly, gently, replaced the bottle and sat at the table next to Ezekial Lekganyane, who he had just met. On the other side of Mario was Tema – Sonja didn't want Tema and Ezekial distracting each other during the briefing.

Not that Tema and Ezekial were gazing lovingly into each other's eyes right now. Instead, Ezekial was holding a set of state-of-the-art night vision goggles up to his eyes and Tema was fiddling with a laser-guided directional microphone. There was a host of other brand-new surveillance tools laid out on the heavy leadwood-topped dining room table.

'Tema, Ezekial, put down the toys for now.' Sonja pressed a switch on the wall and a white screen was lowered from the ceiling at one end of the room. She used the remote in her hand to turn on a hidden data projector. The same image of the men she had seen on James's laptop appeared on the screen.

'The man on the right, if you don't know, is the President of Mozambique. The other is our target, Antonio Cuna, the commander of what is probably the largest rhino and elephant poaching syndicate in Mozambique. I use the word commander rather than kingpin or crime tsar or any other name that might somehow glorify what he does. What we are about to embark on is a military operation. He is the commander of the enemy forces we're facing.' She looked around the table, making eye contact with each of them. 'We are taking the war on poaching to the enemy, across the border, and even though we are just gathering intelligence, some of what we are doing could be construed as illegal. There is no doubt it will be dangerous. If any of you wants to leave, now is the time to do so.'

Tema and Ezekial exchanged glances. Mario's dark eyes were solely, intently fixed on the face of the man they were after. Tema and Ezekial shook their heads.

'Then it begins. I'll take questions at the end of my briefing.'

Sonja used a series of slides, some she had taken from James Paterson, others she had found herself, to illustrate, firstly, the situation they faced. Cuna was, she explained to her team, a prominent businessman and provincial-level politician in Mozambique. He enjoyed high-level patronage in the government and the local police were on his payroll. He used intimidation, violence, bribery, and, on occasion, murder, to grow and protect his poaching empire. He had been identified as the operator of the largest force of poachers in Mozambique.

South African military and police intelligence estimated that he personally bankrolled fifteen separate poaching teams, each made up of a skilled tracker, a shooter armed with a heavy-bore hunting rifle, and one or two bearers who doubled as a protection party, usually armed with AK-47s.

'As Tema and I found out recently,' Sonja went on, 'the poaching teams have access to increasingly more sophisticated weaponry, including machine guns, hand grenades and night vision devices. These men are motivated and they're trained. We have reports of former, possibly serving, members of China's People's Liberation Army being paid to offer specialist military training and advice to these men.'

She looked at their faces again. Mario had raised his eyebrows at the mention of heavy weapons, but it was nothing he hadn't faced in the past.

Sonja's next slide was of a dead rhino, its horn hacked off, down to the white bone. A group of rangers in green and crime scene officers in white forensics suits worked on and around the carcass. 'This is what we're fighting for. As you know, around one thousand rhinos are killed each year in South Africa. Their horn is not used as an aphrodisiac as some people still believe, but rather as a hangover preventative, or simply as a status symbol to show that the owner has money and power. The primary market for horn is not China, but Vietnam.'

'You've been there, I believe,' Mario said.

She frowned at him. 'Our mission: conduct a close target reconnaissance of the villa where Antonio Cuna lives and the rural property where his poaching teams rest up and train.' As per military doctrine she repeated the mission so that they all understood it.

'That's it?' Ezekial asked.

'I said I'd take questions at the end, Ezekial. That's the way we conduct briefings from now on. But, yes, for your benefit, that is it for the moment. We are not an assassination squad and we are not the police. We're going to get up close and personal with this man and the people he works for and we're going to work out exactly when his teams leave, and where they cross the border into South Africa. We'll feed that information back to the security forces here, and they will hopefully act. We're going to see who he meets, where and why, and get enough dirt on him to bring him down. From the little I know of him so far,' Sonja paused as she flicked through two more slides to one that showed an older photo, a scan of a black-and-white image from a book, 'Cuna was also a soldier in Frelimo's army during the Mozambican civil war. As a commander he had a reputation for fearlessness, and unlike many other senior officers, Colonel Cuna liked to put himself in the front line, alongside his men. He had a taste for battle and risk and his men respected him for it.'

'You think he might make a mistake,' Mario said.

'Yes. The execution of this mission will take place in three phases, the first –'

The door of the private dining room opened and James Paterson entered. 'Sorry to interrupt.'

'I'm in the middle of a briefing,' Sonja said. There was nothing in her tone that masked her displeasure.

'Normally I'd never interrupt, Sonja, but I've got breaking news about our target.'

'What?' She was over her annoyance in an instant.

'Cuna is in South Africa, right now. He flew into Kruger Mpumalanga International Airport near Nelspruit, from Vilanculos, today.'

'How do you know that?' Sonja asked.

'I have a source at the airport. I pay, he tells me when certain people fly into or out of Mozambique.'

'Where will Cuna go?'

'He's a golfer. He likes the course at the Sabie River Club, near Hazyview. He stays there sometimes. He has some legitimate business interests in the area, but the police suspect he also controls some local crime and poaching gangs made up of expatriate Mozambicans, mostly illegal immigrants, living in Hazyview.'

'Will the cops be tailing him?' Sonja asked.

James shook his head. 'Not enough resources; plus he's a foreign national and he's not wanted for any specific crime here in South Africa. Otherwise they would have stopped him or picked him up at the airport.'

Sonja knew that one of the keys to success in battle was to be flexible and adaptable. All the same, as her briefing would have outlined, she wanted to give her new team some training in close target reconnaissance and surveillance. Mario would have some of these skills and Tema had sat through a lecture on the subjects, but Ezekial, as far as she knew, was more used to following animals in the bush than people on a golf course.

There was another knock on the door of the dining room and Julianne let herself in.

'I hope I'm not interrupting. I was on a Skype call to the UK, but I just got James's SMS. It's terribly exciting, isn't it?'

Sonja frowned. Julianne's face was lit with almost childish glee, just as it had been when they'd chased down the two poachers in her helicopter. 'It's dangerous, that's what it is.'

'Can I borrow your laptop, please, Sonja?' Ezekial asked.

She didn't know what the tracker would want it for, but she slid it across the desk to him.

Paterson looked to Sonja. 'I agree with you, it's a less than ideal situation, and if you'd rather not send the team in then I'll respect your decision. However, we do have an opportunity to tail Cuna while he's here, in our country, not forty kilometres from us, instead of mounting a cross-border operation.'

Sonja had the feeling he meant what he said, that he would not railroad her. But Paterson was right – the chance was too good to pass up. The fact was, a surveillance operation on home ground, in a public place, would be a better way to put her team through its paces, and for them to learn something, than in a different country where they would have a hard time explaining themselves if something went wrong. In South Africa, for better or worse, they were all licensed to carry firearms and there was no law against playing golf. 'All right, James, but we do this on my terms.'

'Of course,' he said. 'Cuna's going to a golf course, but he's not likely to have flown to South Africa just to play eighteen holes. This gives us an opportunity to see who he meets and, if we can get close enough to him, find out why he's really here.'

'Julianne,' Sonja said, 'do you have a set of golf clubs?'

The billionaire grinned. 'Yes. Can I come too?'

'No,' Sonja said. 'You'll attract too much attention.'

'Of course, I understand. But take the chopper, you'll be there in no time. I'll get my assistant Audrey to call the Club and tell them we've got some VIP guests flying in to play a round.'

Ezekial looked up from the laptop. 'Sonja?'

'Yes?'

He swung the computer so she could see the screen. 'Here's a satellite image of the course. I've just sent it, and a golfer's guide to playing it, to the printer. We can study the layout in the helicopter.'

Sonja was impressed. 'Good work.'

He laughed. 'It's just Google Earth.'

Sonja pushed back her chair and stood. 'All right. Saddle up. Dress is smart casual, everyone carries a sidearm and spare magazines, concealed radios from the stack on the dining table here, and I'll bring an LM5. I'll give my revised orders on the helicopter. We leave in ten minutes.'

They all looked at her.

'Move!'

They filed out of the briefing room and Sonja walked briskly back to her accommodation, a tastefully fitted-out detached chalet that was normally reserved for visiting pilots who had to stay overnight after dropping off guests. Sometimes pilots escorted well-heeled guests on flying safaris around Africa.

Sonja unbuttoned her camouflage shirt and shrugged it off. She replaced it with a khaki bush shirt, which would not look out of place with her green and brown trousers. She traded her combat boots for trainers. She took her LM5 from the locked cupboard and stuffed two spare magazines into the side pockets of her trousers.

Her phone buzzed and she answered it as she closed the door and strode out to the helipad. She was pleased to see the others emerging from their rooms.

'Kurtz.'

'Sonja, howzit, it's me, Hudson.'

'Sorry, can't talk right now, Brand.'

'*Brand*? I'm not one of your soldiers, you know.'

'I know. I've got to be somewhere, in a hurry.'

'Sonja, we need to talk.'

She had a mental image of them sitting on the deck of his house at Hippo Rock, holding hands under a full moon, a bottle of wine in the ice bucket between them, elephants splashing across the river. It had been the first time she'd been happy in a long time, and then things had changed. People had been killed; he'd cheated on her.

'No.'

'Later?' he said.

'I have to go.'

'Where?'

'Hazyview. I'll be back at Khaya Ngala later today.'

'When?'

'I don't know.'

'Sonja, I want to talk about us, but I also need to ask you some questions, important ones, about the two guys you and your operator, Tema I think her name is, killed on the road to Mkhuhlu.'

'I really don't have time for this.' Sonja wondered, however, what Brand's interest was in the shooting. He was a private investigator. She immediately felt protective of Tema. 'It was a righteous shooting. Leave it.'

'I'm sure it was. I'd appreciate your take on some stuff that's come up, though.'

The blades of Julianne Clyde-Smith's helicopter were turning and the others had overtaken her and were climbing in. Mario had a set of expensive golf clubs over his shoulder, which he stowed in the rear of the helicopter then boarded.

Brand persisted. 'I'm in Hazyview now. Maybe we can meet somewhere. Tell me where you're going to be. We can get a coffee, or a drink.'

Paterson waved to her and gave her a beseeching thumbs-up. She returned the gesture. It was time to go, but the image of Hudson laughing and flirting with the woman at the hotel wouldn't disappear. 'What happened to your other drinking buddy?'

'Who?'

'Red hair, short skirt.'

'What? Oh, I can explain . . .'

'Save it.' She ended the call, boarded and strapped herself in as they lifted off. Below them the thorny bushveld of the Sabi Sand Game Reserve soon gave way to the barren earth and well-grazed fields of the populated area outside of the protected wildlife zone. Ahead of them, in the distance, was the more densely populated area of Mkhuhlu, where the men had been killed.

Things were moving fast, maybe too fast, but Sonja felt a calm descend over her. What Hudson had or hadn't done with other women was the least of her concerns now – they had a target and they were going to war.

Chapter 9

Hudson Brand watched the helicopter come in low, from the east, and settle somewhere behind where he was having coffee in the outdoor dining area of the golf club. Out on the course was his client for the day, Antonio Cuna.

'They tell me you are the best safari guide in the lowveld and that you speak Portuguese,' Cuna had said to him after shaking his hand in the cool, thatch-roofed arrivals hall of Kruger Mpumalanga International Airport in the hills behind White River.

'Well, you got the second part right,' a bemused Hudson had replied.

Cuna was, like himself, part African and part Portuguese. Tracey Mahoney occasionally paired him with visitors from across the border seeking a day or two in the Kruger Park, or foreign tourists who wanted a daytrip to the Mozambican capital, Maputo, as an add-on to their South African safari holiday.

'You asked for me?' Hudson had asked him in Portuguese.

'*Sim*. A colleague of mine was on one of your tours once,' the man had continued, also in Portuguese. 'He spoke highly of you, and my English is not good. I thought that after my game of golf you might drive me back to the airport through the Kruger Park and show me some wildlife.'

'Of course.'

Hudson could see the man had money, by the fit and labels of his clothes and the expensive clubs he'd brought with him – and now he knew it was all for a daytrip to play golf, and maybe do some business.

He was right about the business, but he now doubted it was legit.

Hudson took the compact Zeiss binoculars he always carried with him from the breast pocket of his khaki shirt and trained them on Antonio Cuna and his golfing partner, who were about to tee off from the third hole. With the Mozambican was James 'King Jim' Ndlovu, an ex-colonel in the South African Police Service, who had been stood down on suspicion of corruption. The King had once been in charge of the station at Hazyview, and the word was he was a major player in rhino horn trafficking and poaching. He'd been stopped at a tollbooth on the N4, after a tip-off, and was found to be carrying a couple of million rand in a suitcase in the trunk of his SUV. The Hawks, South Africa's elite crime squad, hadn't had enough to send King Jim away, and he was politically connected, but he wasn't going to get his old job back any time soon.

On the hole behind Antonio and King Jim was an interesting couple. He wore dark glasses and a cap, his thick salt and pepper hair, mostly pepper, protruding from underneath. His arms were muscled and he walked with the upright bearing of a man who'd spent time in uniform, perhaps also police or military. On his arm, when she wasn't hacking the fairway or the green, was an attractive African girl in high-waisted shorts and a pink tank top.

The pair had come from the direction in which the helicopter had landed and Hudson wondered whether the man, like Cuna, might also be from Mozambique. There was no racial segregation, officially, in the new South Africa, but in reality mixed race couples were not an everyday sight yet. In Mozambique and other ex-Portuguese colonies it was much more common; he was living proof of that. Hudson swung his binoculars to the caddy who stood a few paces behind the couple. He was being anything but frivolous, scanning the grounds around them, and continually moving his eyes to the two men playing ahead of them.

As well as the golfers on the course there were three families enjoying an outing, their kids playing near the restaurant, and a handful of people were lounging by the resort's pool.

Hudson lifted his binoculars again and scanned the golf course. On the far side he picked up movement and re-focused. There was someone walking. It was a woman. She wore a green cap, khaki bush shirt and camouflage trousers. It was fairly typical safari gear these days, but Hudson's job required him to be an observer.

Sonja.

He shifted his gaze to the two men. Cuna had just teed off, and while King Jim was setting his ball the Mozambican was talking. Hudson noticed that Antonio had his hand up to his mouth, but he was definitely speaking because James was nodding his head.

'Why don't you want anyone lip-reading?' Hudson asked himself aloud.

He drained his coffee, got up and walked through the restaurant back to the car park where he'd left Tracey's Fortuner with its *African Safari Adventures* magnetic sign on the side. He unlocked it, opened the boot and took out his camera bag. He brought it with him, habitually, whenever he did a transfer, in case he came across a spectacular wildlife sighting in the Kruger Park or the Sabi Sand. If his clients at the time didn't mind him snapping a few frames, then Hudson liked to indulge his passion for photography.

He returned to his seat. He hefted his Canon digital SLR camera and took aim. He used a Sigma 50–500 millimetre zoom lens. He couldn't afford a long-range Canon lens, but this one was versatile and useful for wildlife photography – and surveillance. He scanned the tree line on the edge of the course and saw Sonja again, still walking. He extended the lens to its full reach and the shutter release whirred.

Hudson lifted the camera again and zeroed in on the trio playing golf. The caddy now mimicked Sonja, lifting his fingers to his ear. They were talking, in radio contact. The caddy said something and the black and white couple stopped pretending to have fun and looked back, talking to the younger man.

When Hudson panned, using the magnification of his zoom lens in lieu of his binoculars, he couldn't find Sonja. The walking path around the course was empty of people. She had gone to ground.

From the car park behind him Hudson heard a vehicle engine revved hard and the squeal of brakes that needed new linings. There was shouting and the slap of boots on a polished concrete floor.

Hudson left his camera and made for a stone pillar supporting the terrace roof and ducked behind it.

Three men, each wearing a balaclava and armed with an AK-47, burst out onto the restaurant terrace. 'Everybody down.'

People screamed.

The man who had given the order pointed his rifle at a family. 'Quiet, no noise or I'll shoot you all.'

The terrified patrons dropped to the ground.

'No one look up, no one say a word. Everything will be fine.'

Hudson had dropped to his belly, and as he leopard-crawled along the grass, using his knees and one elbow to propel himself into a bed of flowers, he reached under his shirt to the pancake holster on his hip with his right hand and drew out his Colt .45 pistol.

'Heads down everyone, that's the way,' said one of the gunmen.

Hudson peered through the petals as he buried himself deeper in the garden. The man who was talking was moving slowly around the guests, some of whom were whimpering. He paused beside one woman, bent, opened her handbag and took out her purse.

Hudson slowly reached into the breast pocket of his shirt and pulled out his phone. He looked at the screen and selected the Messages icon, then scrolled through the list until he found the last time he had tried to contact Sonja.

*

Sonja felt her phone vibrate in her pocket.

Two men, AKs, coming your way.

The message was from Hudson Brand. That surprised her. Slowly, she raised her head. Antonio Cuna and a man Ezekial had informed her was a former local police commander, King Jim someone, were not more than four metres from where she lay in the thick riverine bush, at the edge of the putting green on the fourth hole. At last the men had come close enough for her to hear what they were saying to each other.

Sonja had no idea how Hudson Brand knew where she was or what he could see, but she slowly looked around. A low rise obscured her view of the lodge and its restaurant-cum-clubhouse.

Their targets were so close Sonja couldn't risk speaking into her radio. Instead, she forwarded Hudson's message to Tema's mobile phone.

'Antonio, my heart is heavy,' King Jim was saying.

The Mozambican was hunched over his putter, taking a practice swing, the club's head a few centimetres from his ball. He didn't look up. 'Why?'

'You have betrayed me.'

Cuna stopped his club, mid-swing. Sonja watched as he slowly turned to the bigger man. King Jim's build and belly spoke of a life of profit and excess, but Sonja also saw the power in the ex-cop's big hands, his broad shoulders.

'I hear you have been talking to the South African police about me,' continued King Jim, 'how you planned to plant some horn in my house. Added to that, if that were not bad enough, you bring more police, more soldiers to my backyard by trying to shoot down a fucking helicopter. Man, are you crazy?'

Cuna straightened. 'What are you talking about?' he asked in his accented English.

'And you bring assassins with you, to try and ambush me on a golf course?'

'Who?'

'The man in the sunglasses and cap with the cute girlfriend and the muscle-bound caddy on the hole behind us.' King Jim turned and gestured to Mario, Tema and Ezekial with his left hand. His right went under the Polo windcheater he wore, to a shoulder holster under his arm.

Sonja cursed to herself. Either King Jim had been expecting an ambush, or to be tailed, or Sonja's team had been too obvious. To make matters worse Sonja saw, over the mound, two men moving, rifles coming up to their shoulders.

'Tema, get down, two tangos to your right, AKs. Take cover,' Sonja said into her radio; despite the risk she had to give her people warning.

As King Jim raised his pistol Antonio swung his golf club faster than a cobra striking, and the bigger man screamed and staggered as the club connected with the side of his head and he dropped his gun. Then the gunfire started.

The men with the AK-47s stopped and turned outwards, away from each other. One fired at Cuna, who just had time to drop and grab King Jim's pistol and roll off the grassy mound, towards Sonja. King Jim came to, crawled away, then stood and looked around, dazed.

Cuna opened up and King Jim's body danced before he hit the ground again.

This wasn't Sonja's fight, but her people were under fire. She could see Ezekial lying on the ground, frantically pulling clubs from Julianne Clyde-Smith's golf bag. The young man's pride had been hurt when Sonja told him he would be undercover as Mario and Tema's caddy, but a smile had returned to his face when Sonja told him he would be packing her LM5 assault rifle among the clubs. Tema and Mario had drawn their pistols, but the man with the AK targeting them was forcing them to lie low as he advanced from tree to tree.

Sonja had a clear shot at the gunman's back. She stood, wrapped her left hand around her right and fired twice. It was a long-range shot, but at least one round found its mark and the hit man pitched forward. She saw Mario get up and move forward.

By standing, however, Sonja had exposed herself to the other rifleman, and Antonio Cuna. The man with the AK-47 shifted his aim to her, but Sonja was quicker, pivoting and pumping four rounds at him. He dropped to the grass, but Sonja couldn't tell if she had hit him. Cuna crawled towards the stand of trees in which she was taking cover, once more crouching behind a tree.

Sonja held up her pistol and pointed it at the Mozambican. He raised his gun as well.

'Who are you? Police?' he asked.

'Security.' They were in a stand-off, pistols pointed at each other, but it didn't last. The surviving man with the AK-47 stood and ran at them, firing on the run.

Sonja and Antonio turned their guns on the running man in unison and their combined firepower was too much for him. His bullets went high and wide as their shots brought him down.

Her phone rang and Sonja fished it out of her pocket, one-handed. 'Hudson? Kind of got my hands full here.'

'There's one more coming your way.' He was puffing as if he was running while talking. 'The third guy was holding up people in the clubhouse, but he's outflanking you now, coming in from the south end of the course, any minute. I'm on my way.'

Sonja looked in the direction Hudson had indicated and Antonio raised his head at the same time. A rifle fired and Cuna fell backwards. Sonja crawled to him. Blood was frothing out of a hole in his chest. She placed a hand against the wound.

'Lie still, your lung's been punctured. You've got a sucking chest wound.'

He looked up at her, eyes wide. 'Help . . .' he croaked.

'You ordered the killing of Sam Chapman, the American wild-life documentary maker?'

The man stared at her.

Sonja moved her red-soaked hand and the blood started bubbling again. He groped for the wound, but she knelt on his arm.

'Help me . . .'

'Tell me what happened. I'll save you if you give me the truth. You'll be arrested, but you can probably buy your way out.'

'You . . . you're Chapman's woman. You killed Tran, the Vietnamese.'

'What of it?' Sonja looked up, scanning the tree line. The man who had shot Cuna would be getting close.

'He . . . he . . . was not . . .'

'Wasn't what?'

Sonja glanced up and saw a face and the business end of an AK-47. She ducked as the man fired. Sonja raised her hand and fired twice, then her pistol was empty.

'Shit.' Sonja reloaded, and while the action was as instinc-tive to her as brushing her teeth, in the less than two seconds it took, the gunman had stood and charged towards her. He fired first and she dived and rolled behind a tree. Bullets tore into the foliage above her head. She readied herself to meet him, but then heard the sound of a different weapon firing, a double tap.

Sonja popped up and saw that the man was face down on the ground. Someone had shot him.

Breathing hard, she walked to the man, kicked him, and saw he was dead. She went back to Cuna and dropped so that her right knee was on his chest. He screamed in pain.

'Shut up, you fucking wimp.' She rested the barrel of her pistol between his eyes. 'What were you trying to say to me before, about Tran.'

His mouth curled up at the edges. 'Tran wasn't the man who ordered the death of Sam Chapman, your man, he wasn't even a boss. You and that journalist who went after him got your facts wrong.'

He was taunting her. The young investigative reporter who was helping her had been caught by Tran's people and tortured and killed. She had taken out Tran, but the journalist's death had taken any satisfaction she might have otherwise gained from her revenge mission. 'Who was in charge, who gave the order to kill my man?'

Cuna coughed and blood ran over his lips. 'It wasn't me.'

'Then tell me who it was.'

He gave a weak shrug. 'If I tell you, I will be a dead man.'

'All right.' She tightened her finger around the trigger. 'I'll save them the time.'

'Sonja!'

She didn't take her eyes off Cuna. She recognised Hudson's voice behind her but didn't turn to look at him. 'Go away, Brand.'

'What's with the "Brand" again? Don't kill that man, Sonja.'

'Get lost, Hudson, this is none of your business.'

Cuna stared back at her. She willed him to make a move, to try and overpower her, so she would have an excuse to shoot him.

Hudson's shadow fell over them. 'This man needs a doctor, Sonja.'

'He needs to talk sense to me right now or I'm going to kill him.'

Cuna's eyes went to Hudson.

'I'd do as the lady suggests and tell her what she wants to know,' Hudson said to him.

There was the sound of sirens, getting closer. Cuna looked back to Sonja. She knelt harder on his chest and he screamed in agony.

'For crying in a bucket,' Hudson said. 'He's bleeding out.'

'There . . . there is an organisation . . . they call themselves the Scorpions . . .'

'Who's the head?' Sonja asked. She put her palm over the bullet hole to still his ragged wheezy breathing.

'I . . . I don't . . .'

'Sonja.'

'Shut up, Brand.' She slapped her captive's face with her free hand. 'Stay with me. Give me a name or I swear I'll kill you right now.'

'They . . . they will kill me.'

'No, I will.'

'Hey, drop the gun,' a woman called.

Sonja looked over her shoulder. Captain Sannie van Rensburg was striding across the fairway holding a pistol up in two hands. Her female partner was a step behind her, also with her weapon drawn.

'Shit.' Sonja stood and holstered her pistol. 'Thanks for nothing, Brand.'

Hudson dropped to his knees beside her. He ripped open Cuna's shirt and held a balled hand towel, taken from the poacher's golf bag, to his wound to staunch the bleeding.

He looked up at her. 'Dammit, Sonja, I just saved you from a murder charge. What were you thinking?'

She glared at him. 'I was thinking I was finally going to find the man who ordered Sam's killing.'

'Well, this guy would be no use to you dead. His pulse is weak and he's just passed out.'

'Paramedics are coming now,' Sonja said.

'I can try talking to him in hospital,' Hudson said.

'What makes you think he'll talk to you?'

Hudson gave a small smile. 'Well, I did just save his life.'

'Ha!'

Sannie van Rensburg and her partner reached them. 'All right, everyone stay put. Vanessa, check those men.'

'They're all dead,' Hudson said to her, 'but this guy needs help.'

The paramedics caught up, pushing their gurney. They took over from Hudson, who wiped his bloodied hands on the manicured grass of the golf course.

'You're not on your regular beat in the national park,' Hudson said to Sannie.

'Vanessa and I had a meeting with the Hazyview detectives; we were on our way back to Kruger when the call came over the radio. Instead of a garden-variety robbery, we find two rhino-poaching kingpins and a team of hired guns. I'm going to see if I can get anything out of Cuna.'

Ezekial, Tema and Mario jogged over to the group. 'Are you OK?' Mario asked.

Hudson turned at the sound of the voice. 'Mario Machado?'

Mario looked from Hudson to Sonja. 'What's he doing here?'

'I was about to ask the same question,' Hudson said.

Sonja looked from man to man. Neither was smiling, and while they clearly knew each other, there were no hands extended in friendship. It dawned on Sonja that they had both served in the apartheid-era South African Defence Force's Portuguese-speaking 32 Battalion.

The two men looked each other in the eye. Sonja saw Hudson's hands slowly clench into fists. Mario jutted his chin out.

Sonja was intrigued, but before she could ask either of them what this was about James Paterson showed up.

Paterson was wide-eyed at the carnage. 'Sonja, are you all right? How's the team?'

'We're fine.'

'I was out by the chopper at the landing pad, on a conference call with Julianne and some of her people in the UK when I heard the gunshots.'

'Well you missed the party. Are you armed?'

He shook his head.

'Then just as well you stayed out of the way.'

'I did call the police. Can I have a word, please, Sonja?'

Van Rensburg was walking alongside the paramedics, who were wheeling Cuna across the fairway. Sonja walked away from the group with Paterson.

'We need to go,' James said in a quiet voice.

'The policewoman told us to stay here.'

'Do you want to do that, or would you rather have a shot at catching some criminals who have just killed some of Julianne's anti-poaching unit operators?'

'In the Sabi Sand?' She hadn't heard of an attack.

'No. I'll explain in the chopper. Or you can stay here and talk to the cops.'

Sonja cast her eyes over the bodies that lay strewn on the golf course. 'No, I don't particularly want to stay here. Tell me, what do you know about an organisation called the Scorpions?'

He raised his eyebrows. 'Where did you hear about them?'

Sonja nodded towards the departing medical team. 'Cuna.'

'Interesting. I can brief you more on the Scorpions – if they exist at all – on the chopper. Bring your people and let's get out of here while the policewoman is busy.'

'Where are we going?' she asked.

'Zimbabwe.'

Chapter 10

Sannie van Rensburg sat at a table in the golf club, a cooling cup of coffee in front of her, and took notes as Hudson Brand recounted his version of the day's events.

She was furious that Sonja Kurtz and the others had run to the Khaya Ngala helicopter and taken off while she was trying to question the injured man, who had drifted in and out of consciousness as the paramedics wheeled him to the ambulance.

Sannie flipped back a page in her notebook. 'You say Cuna asked Tracey Mahoney to assign you to him especially.'

'Yes.'

'Why?'

Hudson shrugged. 'It happens sometimes, though usually with people I've guided before. I speak Portuguese, so Tracey often gives me Mozambican clients. As you know, most people that side of the border don't speak English.'

'Yes, but this one does. We know about Antonio Cuna. He's university educated – three degrees in fact – and speaks Portuguese, Russian – from his time abroad during the civil war being trained as a Frelimo cadre – and English, which he learned in Moscow.'

'I could tell by his clothes he was well off,' Hudson said. 'And since you're in the anti-poaching squad and seem to know all about him I take it he's a rhino poaching kingpin.'

Sannie nodded. 'Alleged, of course. In Mozambique that means he has enough money to buy his way out of any prosecution. He hasn't committed any crimes, per se, here in South Africa, which is why I can't hold him. The only break we caught today was that Cuna's wound looks serious enough to keep him in the Nelspruit Mediclinic for a few days at least. That, and the fact that King Jim got his comeuppance at last. I'll need to question Cuna about their meeting.'

Hudson sipped his coffee. 'Everyone in town knew King Jim was dirty, the local Don of Hazyview. What was this, a hit that failed?'

Sannie took some cold coffee. 'Looks like it. The dead gunmen, including the one you got, were Jim's guys. I recognised one and the Hazyview officers confirmed the others were local. Jim invites Cuna to come and play some golf, talk some business, and has his guys make it look like they were robbing the club and the Mozambican gets killed in the crossfire.'

'Yeah,' Brand said, 'but that doesn't make sense if it's clearly obvious to the police that the hit men are . . .'

'. . . working for King Jim.' Sannie nodded. 'That's what bothers me about this, as well. OK, Jim wouldn't have been expecting you and your girlfriend Sonja and her people to be here, following Jim and Antonio and carrying guns, but all the same, it's amateurish. Jim didn't stay out of prison this long by being dumb – he was actually a pretty smart cop in his day, before he went bad.'

'Word on the street was that he was still controlling poaching on this side of the border.'

Sannie knew Hudson was right, and while King Jim had been the subject of ongoing investigations he was dead now, so it didn't matter what she said about him. 'He was. We were sure of it but, like I said, he was clever, so we hadn't been able to catch him out. Everyone from Hazyview to Kruger who's worked for him is too scared to help us out. He was ruthless.'

'So maybe,' Hudson ventured, 'he was arrogant enough to think he could rub out his rival from across the border in public, in broad daylight, and get away with it.'

'Maybe.' But there was something else at play here, some*one* else. 'What was Sonja Kurtz doing here? And why did she get into Julianne Clyde-Smith's helicopter? Is she working for her?'

'I guess she is.'

'She's your girlfriend.'

'Stop saying that, please, Sannie. She's not.'

'She was staying with you at Hippo Rock. Did you have a falling-out? Is that why she didn't come to dinner the night that I came over?'

Hudson looked away, out over the course, where players had already returned to the greens.

This was South Africa, Sannie thought to herself, even in the wake of a shootout the golfers wouldn't be put off.

'We were friends,' Hudson said. 'We had a thing; I don't know what else to call it.'

'A thing? English is my second language; do you mean a fling?'

'Your English is just great, Sannie. No, it wasn't a fling; it was more of a thing. We met in Namibia. I was there on an investigation, she was trying to find her daughter, who had been kidnapped. It was messy. We kind of connected and I guess we thought it was worth giving it a shot, seeing each other again. But . . .'

'But?'

'She's got issues, and that's an understatement. She thought I was cheating on her and she walked out.'

'When?'

'Day after the gunfight she and her female anti-poaching unit, the Leopards, got into.'

Sannie was taken aback. 'What? The day after you and I had dinner? Don't tell me she thought you were sleeping with me?'

Hudson held up a hand. 'Hold your horses. I told her there was nothing between you and me. She's still hurting, Sannie. I think she finds it hard to trust men – people. She saw me with a female reporter at the Protea Hotel.'

Sannie raised her eyebrows. Hudson was a handsome guy and she'd heard talk around the park that he was a ladies' man, but she thought him a fundamentally decent person.

'No, no. Nothing like that,' he said. 'There was a leopard in the hotel grounds and I escorted Rosie, the reporter, back to her room.'

'Rosie? Not Rosie Appleton?'

Hudson took a moment to recall. 'Yes, that was her surname. Do you know her?'

'She's from that travel magazine, *Escape*. But she's a hard hitter, very pushy, and her stories often get picked up by the national newspapers and television. She's been trying to get permission from the Joint Operations Command to interview undercover operatives who infiltrate poaching gangs. She's said she won't reveal anyone's identity, but the powers that be don't think it's worth the risk. She's a snooper.'

'She told me she was here on vacation.'

'She was talking rubbish,' Sannie said. 'I knocked back two requests from her to ride along on our sensitive operations.'

'She also asked me if I had any contacts in the security forces, police or anti-poaching teams.'

'What did you tell her?'

'I've been around enough reporters to know to stick to my name, rank and serial number.'

'Anyway,' Sannie said, 'forget her. Tell me, why was Sonja here? Why was she threatening Antonio Cuna?'

He shrugged. 'Like I said, we're not together. We're not really talking much at the moment. She was offered a job with Julianne Clyde-Smith at Khaya Ngala, that much I do know.'

'Anti-poaching?'

Hudson nodded and finished his coffee.

Sannie couldn't help but feel annoyed. 'Clyde-Smith's like all foreigners – she thinks she knows better ways to fight poachers than we do. She's always in the news media talking up the problem and how she spends more than anyone else on anti-poaching.'

'And does she?'

Sannie had to concede. 'She does. She's proof of the fact that if one reserve, one national park, one farm spends more on anti-poaching or comes up with a new initiative, then the problem moves on somewhere else.'

Hudson signalled the waitress. 'So Julianne Clyde-Smith enlists Sonja Kurtz to further protect her estate from poaching? I'm thinking aloud here.'

Sannie considered what she knew of Sonja Kurtz, from what Hudson had told her, briefly, and what the Joint Operations Command knew of her, gleaned as a result of the killing of Sam Chapman by poachers a few years ago and her recent engagement to train and mentor the all-female Leopards Anti-Poaching Unit. 'Sonja's a mercenary, with experience in Northern Ireland with the British Army, and in Sierra Leone, Angola, Iraq, Afghanistan and the flare-up in Namibia a few years ago, all via the private military company Corporate Solutions, which went out of business after one too many scandals. She's between jobs, but she doesn't come cheap.'

'Because she's good at what she does,' Hudson continued.

'And in the space of the last few days,' Sannie ordered a Coke Light in response to Hudson's second cappuccino, 'she and her girls have killed a couple of poachers, taken out two more who probably killed two of their own operators, and very nearly assassinated Mozambique's top rhino poaching boss, Antonio Cuna.'

'I never said she was about to assassinate Cuna,' Hudson said.

Sannie shook her head. 'Of course not, Hudson. I was late arriving, but I saw her with her pistol pointed at his head.'

He puffed his cheeks out.

Sannie continued. 'This was a military operation, Hudson. Sonja and her team of hired guns arrive, flown in with James Paterson, Clyde-Smith's ex-military intelligence officer head of security, and twenty minutes later Hazyview's number one organised crime figure is dead and Mozambique's top poaching kingpin is in hospital. Am I the only one who sees a link here?'

Hudson didn't answer so she asked another question. 'Who was the guy in Sonja's team? Older, dark-haired, good-looking?'

'Mario Machado.'

'I saw you two sizing each other up. Who is he?'

'He's a sculptor, a pretty good one.' Hudson looked away from her again. She could tell he was clenching his jaw because of the movement of the muscles beneath his tanned skin.

'A sculptor and . . .'

Hudson took a breath. 'An asshole. Back in the day he served in 32 Battalion, in Angola.'

'Your old unit.'

Hudson sipped his coffee then put it down. He wasn't looking at her, still gazing out over the greens, but Sannie felt like instead of manicured golfing greens, he was seeing a killing field on the other side of Africa. 'You know what they called us, our Portuguese nickname?'

Most people Sannie's age or older knew of the battalion's fearsome reputation and kill ratio. '*Os Terriveis*, the Terrible Ones.'

'Yup. It was people like Mario Machado who gave us that name.' He looked back to her, into her eyes. 'None of us were saints, but that guy was a demon.'

'So what's Sonja doing with another trained killer, a pretty girl who's handy with a gun, and a master tracker? Has she put together her own "A-Team"?'

Hudson seemed to mull over her words. 'I don't know. Let me ask you a question.'

'OK.'

'Do you think Shadrack, the labourer from Hippo Rock, was really up to being part of a highly organised rhino poaching team, and shooting a female operative in the back?'

'That's called changing the subject,' Sannie said.

'What's your gut feeling?'

'This isn't an American cop show, Hudson. I work on evidence and fact, not on hunches.'

'Come on, you know what I mean – every investigator also has to trust their instincts from time to time.'

She shrugged. 'I was surprised, but the evidence so far points squarely at him.'

'And the guy he was with, his cousin?'

'Oh, now him I have no doubts about. He was known to us. He had a string of fines dating back to when he was a juvenile and he'd done prison time for car theft and firearms offences. You know, plenty of the car hijackers from Joburg have become involved in rhino poaching. They're violent men who know guns and they're not afraid of anything. The return for taking a rhino far outweighs the gain and even the risk of taking a car these days. Shadrack's cousin's career path was always leading towards rhino poaching.'

'Yup.'

'So what's your point?' Sannie asked.

'I'm not sure, and that's the truth. Do you have the postmortem results on Shadrack yet?'

'No. Given the circumstances it's not a priority.'

'Tell that to his mom, Anna. If your forensic evidence – blood types, the wound on his back, gunshot residue on his hands – all matches the circumstantial evidence, then I think we owe it to her to explain as soon as possible that her son was a criminal.'

'I feel sorry for Anna, but it's not up to "us", it's up to me. Hudson, we're friends, and I respect that you make your living as an investigator, but this sounds more like a grieving mother clutching at straws. Don't lead her on, please, or get in my way.'

'Understood.'

Sannie sighed. 'The fact is I did talk to the Hazyview detectives today about Shadrack.'

Hudson raised his eyebrows. 'And?'

'And it's not great news. His late father was a bushmeat poacher who snared antelope to sell for food.'

'That doesn't make Shadrack a criminal,' Hudson said.

'No, but you and I both know someone has been setting snares inside Hippo Rock to catch our buck.'

Hudson nodded. Illegally trapping and killing buck for bushmeat was a big problem in most of Africa's national parks, but one which was often overlooked because of the coverage given to rhino and elephant poaching. Curious predators, such as lion, wild dog and leopard also fell victim to wire snares set to catch herbivores. The State Veterinarian based in the Kruger Park had recently been called to Hippo Rock to dart and treat a hyena that was being slowly strangled by just such a trap. 'You think Shadrack could be the culprit?'

Sannie shrugged. 'The Hazyview guys were going to come out to Hippo Rock to talk to Shadrack's colleagues and check up on his last known movements. I told them that as I lived there I'd ask around.'

Sannie hadn't forgotten her original question. 'And your friend Sonja? Where does she fit into all of this, and why did she take a job with Julianne Clyde-Smith after the Leopards' operations were suspended?'

Hudson looked out over the fairway, and Sannie thought he was mulling over the same questions as she was, and possibly coming to the same conclusion.

'I'll answer the question for you,' Sannie said at last.

He looked at her and raised his eyebrows.

'She got a better offer.'

'How so?'

Sannie watched a couple of uniformed officers combing the bush around where Sonja's team had been when the gunfire started. They were looking for bullet casings. 'Hear me out. What if Julianne Clyde-Smith has put together some sort of elite team, maybe to take the fight to the enemy in the way that we – police, national parks and the army – can't?'

'Sounds a little far-fetched.'

'What else were they doing here? I bet they got wind that Cuna and King Jim were going to be here, perhaps even a heads-up that something was going to go down. An assassination attempt's a good cover for one more extrajudicial killing.'

Hudson rubbed his chin. 'You said yourself, King Jim's people were too scared to share information with outsiders.'

Sannie knew that was the weakness of her argument. Also, her professional pride didn't want to acknowledge that someone in the private sector might have access to better intelligence than she and her colleagues did. 'Yes, I agree with that, but someone, somewhere, knew something about this meeting.'

'What do you know about the Scorpions?' Hudson asked.

The question took Sannie by surprise. 'I take it you're not talking about the old name for the Hawks, the serious and violent crimes unit?'

'No,' Hudson replied. 'I thought the name was slightly ironic as well – a crime gang with the same name as South Africa's former elite police unit. Cuna said something to Sonja about them when she had a gun pointed at his head, just as you were arriving.'

'Your friend can be most persuasive.'

'The Scorpions?' he tried again.

'Between us?' she said.

He nodded.

She decided she could trust him as, like it or not, he was a party to the current round of investigations into the bloodshed in her patch of South Africa. 'We're not sure about the Scorpions. There has been talk of them in the past; depending on who you speak to they're run by the Chinese, the Vietnamese, South Africans, Mozambicans, or Russians. Our best guess is they're international, controlled by one man whose identity we don't know, and they're bigger than just rhino horn.'

'Ivory?' Hudson asked.

'Yes, and drugs, guns, abalone, pangolins – anything of high value. If even half of the myths about the Scorpions are true then we're dealing with a serious organised crime syndicate. Their interests are said to stretch from here across to Namibia and north and east as far as Tanzania and Kenya.'

'How do you fight an organisation like that?'

Just talking about the scale of the problem threatened to leave Sannie disheartened. 'The best we can do is gather intelligence and work to keep our wildlife in South Africa safe. We can share information with our neighbouring countries and try to encourage them, but in the end, as with most things in this country, we're hamstrung by politics and money.'

Hudson drained his cup. 'Two things that probably don't concern Julianne Clyde-Smith too much at all.'

*

Julianne never tired of the view from her house at Khaya Ngala. Like the lodge's suites it was set up high and built among the smooth red granite boulders that made up the koppie, although her African home was out of sight and earshot of the guests.

Through the full-length glass wall of her office she looked out over the same waterhole that could be seen from the deck and dining room. A herd of perhaps two or three hundred buffalo were milling around, and through the open balcony door she could hear their low bovine grunts and moos, and their musty odours were carried in on a warm gentle breeze.

Julianne heard the squeak of rubber-soled boots on the polished screed concrete floor. She looked over her shoulder and saw James walking down the hallway.

'They're on their way to Zimbabwe,' he said.

Julianne turned away from the view. The buffalo were moving on and she wondered if the predators were out there resting up before going on the hunt later, just like Sonja would, presumably, once the sun went down. James stood in front of her desk. 'What happened today?' she asked.

'Cuna killed King Jim. His men were eliminated. Kurtz almost terminated Cuna.'

'Almost?'

'She had a pistol in his mouth, literally, and was questioning him when the police arrived,' James said.

A herd of eight zebra was slowly approaching the waterhole, in single file. The lead animal stopped short, head raised, alert for danger.

'I'm scared, James. I'd never admit that to anyone else. It's high risk, bringing in Sonja and her people. We've upped the ante.'

James walked around the desk until he was behind her. 'It's like this, in combat, sending soldiers into battle. It's exciting, heady, but there's always the risk some of them won't come back. Take solace in the fact that people like Sonja, her man Machado, they live for this sort of thing. The younger ones want to prove themselves. It's age old, timeless.'

Julianne shivered involuntarily as she felt James's fingers on her shoulders. She swivelled her head as he began to knead the muscles. The next sound she uttered was a low *mmm* as his fingers moved higher, along her neck, to the base of her skull.

'You're tense.'

'I am. There's a lot at stake – the acquisition of Lion Plains, the other properties in Zambia and Tanzania; not to mention the team's first surveillance mission turning into a pitched battle.'

'You need to blow off some steam, Jules,' he said.

'Yes.'

The fingers of his left hand moved higher still, digging harder and harder into her scalp, just how she liked it. He reached around her with his right and started deftly undoing the little buttons of her crisp white shirt. Fingertips brushed over her nipples, making them strain against the lace of her bra.

Abruptly, his hands left her and she felt her nerve endings yearning for his touch. 'Keep touching me.'

'No.'

She turned and looked him in the eye. 'Do as I tell you.'

'I'm sorry, no, it's not right,' he said, casting his eyes down.

Her eyes followed his and she could see where he was looking, his arousal in plain view. 'If you want to keep your job, you'll do as I tell you.'

He looked up at her now, and she saw how the left side of his upper lip curled to an insolent sneer. He began unbuttoning his own shirt.

'What do you think you're doing? Stop that.'

He ignored her and shrugged off his shirt and dropped it on the floor. His hand moved to his belt buckle.

'You're being highly inappropriate, Colonel Paterson. As a military man you should know how to follow orders.'

He came to her, put a hand behind her neck and kissed her hard. Her whole body responded, even more so when she put a palm on his chest and shoved him away.

James took a step back and glared at her. He lowered his hand inside his pants.

'Stop. Now,' she commanded.

He shook his head and continued, his eyes feasting on her cleavage, her expensive French lingerie. She knew, exactly, how the contrast of the pastel tones, the pale skin of her belly and the blue of her jeans aroused him.

Julianne's right hand struck fast and hard, delivering a hard, satisfyingly loud slap to James's cheek.

He folded his six-foot-three frame to his knees and Julianne wrapped her hands in his hair and gripped him, hard.

*

The Cessna bucked as it hit an air pocket and Sonja was shaken awake. She lifted her head from the warm Perspex window, blinked and was greeted by the stunning sight of the Zambezi River below and the bitter smell of vomit.

She looked over her shoulder and saw Ezekial holding a paper bag up to his mouth. Tema was rubbing his back, comforting him. Sonja glanced at Mario, beside her, who grinned.

Sonja had little to smile about, but at least she'd been able to snatch twenty minutes' sleep. The sun was turning red as it entered the band of dust. The river glowed like lava. The pilot, a young woman who looked barely out of school, banked and lined up on the dirt strip.

On Sonja's lap were some printouts James Paterson had handed her when they'd boarded Julianne Clyde-Smith's private jet at Kruger Mpumalanga International Airport, after their passports were stamped by South African Home Affairs immigration officers. They had then flown to Harare, Zimbabwe, where they had cleared customs and boarded the smaller aircraft for the ninety-minute hop to the Zambezi Valley.

James had been almost apologetic when he had briefed her on

board the helicopter from Hazyview. At Julianne's behest he had asked Sonja and her team to act as a fire force, an old military term in this part of Africa that referred to a quick reaction unit, deployed to put out the insurgency equivalent of bushfires. This was a world away from running an undercover surveillance operation and gathering evidence for law enforcement agencies. In any war there was a phenomenon known as 'mission creep', which was to be avoided – it meant setting out to do one job and then being dragged into doing something completely different. Sonja hadn't agreed to work for Julianne to be a hired gun, and while she would have liked more time to plan and discuss the mission with her team the fact was that there were people like them in trouble in Zimbabwe, and they needed reinforcements. It wasn't what she signed up for, but the soldier in her couldn't say no.

Sonja raised her voice over the noise of the engine as she orientated her team. 'Below us is Zimbabwe, on the south side of the Zambezi River; Zambia is over there, to the north, where you can see the mountains rising. That camp you can see in the distance is Nyamepi, the main public campsite for Mana Pools National Park on the Zimbabwean side.'

Ezekial wiped his mouth and tried to focus. Mario laughed and Sonja elbowed him hard.

'Julianne Clyde-Smith has set up a new camp, in a hunting area on the border of Mana Pools, but her concession is devoted solely to photographic safaris. Paterson thinks that the absence of hunters from her area made poachers think her concession would be a soft target. Two weeks ago one of the major pools away from the river was laced with cyanide and thirty elephants were poisoned and their tusks taken.'

'My gosh,' Tema said.

'Yes, terrible,' Sonja said. 'As well as the elephants a number of lions, hyena, a leopard and about a hundred vultures were also found dead from feasting on the poisoned carcasses.'

The aircraft lurched again and Ezekial grabbed on to Sonja's seat back to steady himself. 'Last night, another pool was poisoned. Julianne's manager here, Ian Barton, sent his anti-poaching squad out as soon as a game viewer came across another ten dead elephants, half of them with their tusks removed.

'The patrol picked up spoor of the poachers and started tracking them, but the bastards stopped moving and set up an ambush, perhaps because they were burdened with ivory and knew they couldn't outrun the anti-poaching guys. They killed two of the five-man stick. Another, the patrol's leader, an ex-professional hunter originally from Germany, was shot dead by a national parks ranger when the survivors stumbled into a parks patrol that had been called on to provide support.'

'What a disaster,' Mario said.

'Exactly,' Sonja agreed, 'which is why we've been called in.'

The Cessna's wheels touched the ground, bounced once, then settled and they juddered their way down the dirt strip. The pilot turned at the end and then taxied up to a thatch-roofed open-sided lapa.

'Here, at last,' said the pilot.

Sonja opened her door, and while the air outside was hot and heavy it was a relief from the stench inside. A tall man with grey hair and arms and legs tanned mahogany came to greet her. He didn't smile as he extended a hand. 'Ian Barton.'

'Sonja Kurtz.'

He introduced himself to Tema and Mario and waited for Ezekial, who was retching on the ground at the rear of the aircraft.

'Are you going to be all right?' Barton asked Ezekial.

'He'll be fine,' Sonja answered. 'Sorry to hear about your men.'

Barton cast an eye over all of them. 'You're my reinforcements? The men I lost were hardened professionals, all with experience hunting and killing poachers.'

'We know what we're doing, Mr Barton,' Sonja said.

'Ian.'

He had the look of a man in shock, Sonja thought, though he was still arrogant and misogynistic enough to give a small shake of his head when his eyes moved from her to Tema.

'You'll want to freshen up,' he said to her as he led them to an open-topped Land Rover.

'Hurry, get your gear on board,' Sonja said to the others. She looked at Barton as she climbed into the passenger seat next to him. 'No, we don't need to powder our noses, we need to get to the scene of the poisoning.'

'You think the poachers would be brazen enough to come back for the remaining ivory?'

'Wouldn't you?' she asked.

'Parks and wildlife have told us to stay away from the water-hole. They're watching it.'

'Will they stay out overnight?'

'Maybe not. They rarely get their basic pay, let alone overtime.'

'Just get us there, please, Ian. But first we need weapons and gear, whatever you have. We couldn't bring our own guns into Zimbabwe.'

He drove fast to the lodge, an impressive new construction on a sandy bank of the Zambezi, looking across the wide river towards Zambia. Sonja noticed that Ezekial was looking better now he was back on terra firma as they followed Ian across a wide teak-timbered deck, through a deserted bar and dining area, to the staff accommodation and back-of-house section of the lodge.

'Our guests flew out today,' Ian said as he unlocked the door of a brick building. 'They cut short their visit, rattled by the news of the contact. The first poisoning attracted worldwide attention and condemnation, and it also brought a slump in our bookings. Julianne's worried the shootings, so close to where our guests were at the time, will bring down our business before it even gets off the ground.'

'I guess that's why we're here,' Mario said.

Ian switched on a light, illuminating a gun rack that ran the length of the storeroom. Military kit was piled on three trestle tables.

'Find yourselves uniforms and weapons,' Sonja ordered. Not wanting to advertise the real purpose of their trip to the customs officers at Harare Airport, they had all travelled in civilian clothes. She picked up an AK-47, and when she placed her hand on the grip it felt sticky. When she inspected her fingers she saw the flakes of dried blood.

'We were able to retrieve the weapons from our dead operators,' Ian said.

Sonja wiped her palm on her pants. 'Tema, if you can't find trousers to fit you, just put on a camouflage shirt.'

'I could have handled these local poachers on my own, you know,' Barton said.

'Not with two men down you couldn't. If I was in your situation I would have asked for reinforcements.'

He put his hands on his hips. 'Well, I didn't ask for you. When I sent my sitrep to Julianne she called and told me you were on your way, whether I liked it or not.'

'We're here to help, nothing more.' Sonja selected a camouflage shirt and buttoned it on. The Zimbabwean police and customs officers, under the instructions of their despotic regime, were paranoid about foreign military incursions into the country, so Sonja had not even been able to bring her load-bearing webbing gear to carry ammunition, food and water. She selected a belt, adjusted it to fit, and clipped on two canteens. A simple green canvas satchel would do as a makeshift carrier for the six full banana-shaped magazines she found for her AK-47.

When they were all changed and ready they went back to Ian's game-viewing Land Rover and climbed in.

'What are our orders, Sonja?' Tema asked, raising her voice

over the rush of wind as Ian raced along a dirt road over the dry, dusty floodplain that ran parallel to the river. A baboon barked an ominous warning call from the high branches of a Natal mahogany tree.

Sonja saw the anxious look in the young woman's eyes. 'When we get to the ambush site Ezekial will cast about for spoor and lead off. Mario, you'll be behind him, then me, then you, Tema. Make sure you keep checking our six – our rear.'

'Yes, Sonja.'

'I'm coming as well,' Ian said, from the driver's seat beside her.

She looked at him. Her initial reaction was to challenge him, but she thought better of it. His pride had been hurt and she knew how childish men could be when it came to their fragile egos. Also, he knew the local area and they didn't.

'My men were killed,' he continued. 'You know what that's like, to lose someone you were responsible for?'

Sonja nodded.

'Rules of engagement?' Mario asked.

Ian grunted and looked around. 'Simple. One thing our fucked-up government does not worry about is human rights. Up here they operate a shoot-to-kill policy. You see a poacher in a national park, you kill him, dead, one-time.'

Sonja felt the familiar pre-battle cocktail of dread and excitement intoxicate her. She looked into the faces of each member of her team. 'This wasn't what any of you signed up for. Anyone who wants out, speak up now. There will be no blame and no shame.'

None of them said a word. Sonja cocked her rifle.

Chapter 11

Hudson stood as Rosie Appleton walked up the steps and was greeted by a waiter at Kuka, a restaurant in the Perry's Bridge centre, a collection of eateries and boutique shops on the outskirts of Hazyview, on the R40.

Rosie pointed Hudson out to the maître d' and joined him at his table. She came to him, took his proffered hand and kissed him on the cheek. The sun was taking the heat of the day with it, behind the hills that rose to the escarpment and South Africa's highveld.

'This *is* a pleasant surprise,' she said as she took a seat opposite him at the outside table under an umbrella. 'I'm glad you called, I didn't expect it.'

'My pleasure, and thanks for coming out here to meet me.'

'Like I said on the phone, no problem, as I had to meet some friends here in Hazyview in any case.'

The waiter came to them. Hudson ordered a Castle Lite, Rosie a glass of sauvignon blanc.

'Friends or contacts? You're not here on vacation, like you told me.'

'Is that a question or an accusation?' she asked.

'Observation.' The beer was cold, good. Rosie was even prettier than he remembered.

'Has my reputation preceded me?' She crossed her legs.

He returned her smile. 'Maybe. I hear you're looking to interview undercover anti-poaching operatives.'

Rosie shrugged, sipped her wine. 'OK, working holiday. I never stop working, really, that's my problem.'

'I was wondering . . .'

She leaned a little closer to him and twirled a lock of hair in the fingers of her left hand. 'Yes?'

'Have you heard of an organised crime syndicate called the Scorpions?'

Rosie sat back. 'Maybe.'

'What kind of an answer is that?'

'The kind that indicates we may have some bargaining to do, you and me, Mr Hudson Brand, safari guide slash private investigator.'

'You've been googling, I see. I don't do much investigating these days.'

She raised her eyebrows. 'Really?'

'Really.'

'Then how come when I tracked down the families of the two poachers killed on the road to Mkhuhlu the other day the mother of one of them, who works as a laundry lady on your estate, told me that you were investigating the death of her son, Shadrack?'

'That's a favour to a friend.'

She sat back in her seat. 'Level with me, Hudson. We're both on the same trail. We can help each other.'

'Why do you say we're on the same trail?'

She smiled. 'OK, I'll go first. At least one of the two poachers who was killed was part of the gang that crossed the border from

Mozambique and tried to shoot down the national parks heli-copter, as well as killing the two girls from the Leopards.'

'Not Shadrack?' Hudson asked.

'No, his cousin. I'm sure you know a lot of the families in this area are originally from Mozambique and their members cross back and forth across the border, legally and illegally.'

Hudson nodded.

'The cousin had form and my source tells me he was a Scorpion.'

'And Shadrack?'

'Seems he was a new recruit,' Rosie said. 'His first mission didn't end well.'

'He'd joined the Scorpions?' he probed.

'Your turn, what do you know about Shadrack? His mom wasn't keen on telling me much.'

'Well, I know there's no "type" when it comes to criminals, and the money on offer in the rhino poaching business could corrupt a saint, but Shadrack was a nice kid, you know?'

She sipped her wine.

'He was kind, friendly, maybe a little slow.'

'Good cannon fodder,' Rosie ventured.

The thought had crossed Hudson's mind, but he wasn't convinced. The crew that Sonja's girls had come up against in the Sabi Sand Game Reserve sounded like well-trained profes-sionals; why would they recruit a guy with learning difficulties? 'I want to try and get hold of the autopsy report on his body, when the medical examiner gets around to it. It won't be a priority.'

'You can get that?' she asked.

He grinned back at her. 'You're not the only one with sources. So tell me, what do you know about the Scorpions?'

'For a start, they exist. The authorities here in South Africa are still clinging to the hope that the Scorpions are some kind of rural myth, but they're for real. My person tells me the police and army here are worried, as are the law enforcement people in half a dozen other African countries.'

'How do they work?'

Rosie ran the thumb and index finger of her right hand up and down the sides of her glass, leaving a trail in the condensation. She gave an exaggerated pout. 'And here I was thinking you called because you wanted to spend time with me. You saved my life at the hotel and I was hoping to repay the favour.'

Hudson laughed. 'You weren't in any danger.'

'No, but does this have to be all business? I *am* sort of here on a break. As well as researching an article on the links between organised crime and poaching I'm also staying a couple of nights in some lodges to do some travel pieces for *Escape* magazine. I could do a feature on you.' She winked at him.

Hudson knew he had to be careful. She was coming on to him and he had to admit that part of him, a certain part of him, was enjoying the attention. His mind, however, told him he needed to make things right with Sonja. Also, he knew that however she might act, Rosie was a journalist, and for her, the story was everything. 'Well, maybe I can take you on a game drive or two,' he said cautiously.

'Maybe you could drive me to the first lodge I'm doing a story on, Khaya Ngala, and you could stay over. In the guide's room, of course.'

She was a pistol, Brand thought. 'We'll see. Where do they get their money from? Who's the leader of this gang?'

'Oh, they're more than a gang. Basically, the Scorpions are all about cornering the market on high-value illegal wildlife products – rhino horn, elephant ivory, abalone, pangolins, and vultures.'

'Even vultures?'

Rosie nodded. 'There's a market for vulture meat in west Africa and some local people here in South Africa, particularly

Zululand, believe that because vultures can see so far that using their heads for *muti*, traditional medicine, will help them see into the future – next week's lottery numbers, the next big business deal, that sort of thing.'

'I've heard of those uses, but I wouldn't have thought there was enough money in vultures to interest organised crime.'

'Well, the Scorpions get their partners in the field to poison the carcasses of rhinos and elephants they've killed because vultures give away the locations of the kills and alert rangers, police and the army. Taking vultures out of the ecosystem helps the poachers and makes a few bucks at the same time.'

'Bastards,' Brand said. 'You said "partners".'

Rosie sipped some more wine. She seemed to be enjoying holding court now and showing off her knowledge. 'The Scorpions enlist existing poaching gangs to partner with them. They offer modern weapons, silencers, night vision gear, and training in modern military tactics.'

'So the Scorpions are well funded, organised and probably use ex-military people.'

'Yes. Ex–special forces according to my source.'

'And if some local poaching big shot doesn't want to join Scorpions Inc?' Hudson asked.

Rosie ran her right hand across her neck. 'The Scorpions wipe him out, and his family, and any of his foot-soldiers who don't come on board. They're ruthless, Hudson.'

He saw how focused she was, how the flirting had dropped away. 'You're not just here to interview undercover anti-poaching operatives, are you?'

'I want to break the story on the Scorpions – hell, I want to help put them out of business. Do you think you can help me?'

'I think you need to be careful, if these people are as organised and as dangerous as you say they are,' Hudson said.

'Don't patronise me, mister. I've covered South Africa's military involvement in the Central African Republic, been a stringer in Afghanistan; this is just another war zone for me. The only difference is that it's closer to home.'

He didn't underestimate her. 'You heard about the shootout at the Sabie River Lodge golf course here in Hazyview this morning?'

'Yes,' Rosie said.

'Is Antonio Cuna a member of the Scorpions syndicate?'

Rosie rocked her head from side to side, pondering the question. 'I had him down as a maybe, but after the gunfight on the green I'd now say he's a yes, for sure.'

'Why?' Hudson asked.

'Cuna's a big-time operator in Mozambique, probably the largest of the independents, or so I thought. He's got direct links to very senior people in Vietnam; he allegedly had a hotline to Tran Van Ngo, the kingpin who was assassinated in Ho Chi Minh City two years ago. You know anything about that?'

'Nope,' Hudson lied. Sonja Kurtz had killed Ngo, on a mission to avenge the death of her partner. She had as much as admitted it to him. He wanted to find out how much Rosie knew about that, or if she was just fishing. This was like a game of chess, with drinks. Hudson called the waiter over and ordered another round. 'Was it Cuna, acting on Tran's orders, who had that American wildlife documentary maker killed?'

'So, you do know about Tran's assassination.'

Hudson shrugged. 'I read the papers, check the internet every now and then.'

'OK, I'll level with you, even if you're playing it cool with me. I like you, Hudson.'

He sighed, internally. That's what Sonja said to him, sometimes.

Rosie continued: 'Sonja Kurtz, retired mercenary, killed Tran Van Ngo. She was also at the golf course when Cuna was

135

wounded by King Jim's men. Had a gun shoved down Antonio's mouth from what I hear.'

Her sources *were* good, and everywhere apparently. 'Go on. What makes you sure Cuna's joined the Scorpions?'

'King Jim. One thing about the Scorpions, from what I hear they don't have a toehold in South Africa and our country's own *tsotsis* want to keep it that way. We're proudly South African here in the Rainbow Nation, and local is *lekker*, even when it comes to crime. King Jim's been running rhino poaching this side of the border since he was the Hazyview police chief, and Cuna's brazen raid into the Sabi Sand Game Reserve, not to mention his attempt to shoot down a helicopter, will draw even more heat onto the reserves in this part of the country. Jim and Cuna had a truce, of sorts, but as of their last friendly golf match today – usually a peaceful way to discuss business – Jim signalled he was finished with Cuna. I believe he was trying to send a message to the Scorpions.'

'But Jim's ambush was in turn hijacked by Julianne Clyde-Smith's flying squad.'

'Led by your girlfriend, Sonja Kurtz.'

'She's not my girlfriend.' Hudson was getting tired of those words.

Rosie gave him a wink. 'Cool. Does this mean this is a real date, then? Dinner?'

Hudson checked his watch. The waiter returned to check on their drinks and lit a candle on the table between them.

'Come on, where else do you have to be? It's on me. I have an expense account.'

'OK,' he said, relenting. It wasn't difficult. 'How did Clyde-Smith's people know about the meeting between King Jim and Antonio Cuna?'

'Their intelligence is as good as – maybe better than – that of the South African authorities. She's got a guy called James

Paterson, ex-army, who makes it his business to keep tabs on all sorts of people and groups, including the Scorpions. I had an off-the-record interview with him once. He's impressive, committed, and straight up and down.'

'And Julianne?'

'She's putting a hell of a lot of money into anti-poaching. I think she gets off on it, but that doesn't belittle her commitment. She probably spends more on security than the rest of the lodges in the Sabi Sand put together, which is why she hasn't lost a rhino on her property. Same thing goes for her lodges in other African countries, although there was news of a mass elephant poisoning at her property in Zimbabwe, near Mana Pools, yesterday.'

Hudson was aware of Julianne's reputation. Her glossy tourism brochures always talked up her commitment to protecting animals, not to mention her many philanthropic projects in the communities living near her lodges and reserves.

'So what do you think went down at the golf course?' Rosie asked. She was making good headway with her second glass of wine and seemed to be enjoying herself.

Hudson replayed the day's events in his mind. 'Cuna had no bodyguard, no weapon. He sure wasn't expecting anything.'

'No, but King Jim was, and so were Julianne's hit squad.'

'Hit squad? That's a bit rich, isn't it?'

She was stroking her glass again, the candle's reflection dancing in her mischievous eyes. 'They were loaded for bear, as you Americans might say, and tailing King Jim and Cuna. Paterson knew something was up, though he hasn't been returning my calls lately.'

Hudson let himself ride along on Rosie's conspiracy express. 'Someone tipped King Jim off that Cuna was joining or had joined the Scorpions; King Jim was angry at Cuna for crapping in his backyard; Julianne Clyde-Smith saw an opportunity to join in an ambush and do some collateral damage when the bullets start flying?'

'Yes!'

'That's a stretch.'

'This is Africa, Hudson. Nothing's a stretch.'

Hudson thought back to how Sonja had acted on the golf course. She had been working apart from the rest of her team, close to where Antonio and Jim were playing. Maybe the whole thing was personal for her, more payback for the death of Sam. Like most firefights it had been a confusing affair, but when the bullets had started flying Sonja's team was well positioned to take on King Jim's hit squad. Would a successful businesswoman whose reputation for philanthropy equalled her ability to make money really bankroll a vigilante-style hit squad? As Rosie said, and as he himself had learned through some of his cases, people were capable of anything. He took a drink.

'Sonja had a chance to take out Antonio Cuna, but she didn't,' Hudson said, playing devil's advocate. 'She wasn't on an assassination mission.'

'Were you in the army?' Rosie asked.

Hudson set his beer down. 'Angola, 32 Battalion.'

'OK, so you're officially a bad-ass. Did you ever kill anyone in cold blood, execution-style, shoot prisoners, that sort of stuff?'

'No.'

'So maybe there's a difference for Sonja and her team, subtle though it may be. It's OK to start firing when there's a gunfight going down, or at some guys with AK-47s posing as armed robbers, but a different thing to put a gun to someone's head and pull the trigger.'

'Hmm.' He rubbed his chin. 'Maybe.' He didn't want to tell Rosie, but in his opinion if Sonja had been on a mission to kill Antonio Cuna as well as King Jim, she wouldn't have had a second thought about despatching the rhino poaching kingpin, quickly and cleanly.

'Do you believe in coincidences?'

'No.' Not when it came to investigations, he didn't. 'Although it does seem odd that Sonja and her operatives appeared to be tailing two gangsters on the day that one of them was about rub out the other one.'

'My point exactly,' Rosie said. 'I'm starving, let's eat.'

'Shouldn't you be getting back to the Protea Hotel?'

She shook her head. 'I'm staying in Hazyview tonight, a place called the Rissington Inn.'

'I know it.'

'What's the food like there?' she asked.

'The crocodile tail curry and bobotie samosas are excellent.'

'Great, then let's eat there and I won't have to worry about driving back to the hotel drunk,' Rosie said. 'I've got a nice buzz on already.'

Hudson realised he had been snookered. 'I should get home.'

'To what?'

It was a good question. He would be alone, with not much food in the refrigerator, and the supermarkets would be closed soon. The thirty-five-kilometre drive from Hazyview to Hippo Rock could be quite perilous at night, with drunk drivers, cars without headlights, and pedestrians and cows meandering along the unlit road.

Hudson weighed up his options. He could stop drinking now and drive home, or he could go back to Rosie's hotel with her, get pleasantly drunk over dinner and then stay the night at the Rissington Inn. She twirled a finger in her hair and smiled at him as she waited for him to decide.

'OK, I'll come for dinner. If I need a room the owner usually does me a good rate.'

'I like you, Brand. You're tough, but you're also a boy scout. Maybe you can show me how to tie a few knots after dinner.'

Chapter 12

Nervous energy, the thrill of the hunt, excitement laced with a dash of fear – call it what you want, but the possibility of impending contact with the enemy had charged Sonja's mind and body.

She moved carefully, watching where she put her feet and then sweeping her eyes and the barrel of her AK-47 in a 180-degree arc to her right. Mario, in front of her, covered the left, and Ezekial, their forward scout and tracker, focused on the ground and the bush in front of them.

As she finished her sweep she saw that Ian, behind her, had picked up their rhythm and was also covering the right. Tema, who continued to impress Sonja with her skills and concentration, took a few steps then turned and swept the 180 degrees to their rear. Her job was to make sure no one was following them.

Sonja's gaze moved slowly to her front again and she allowed herself a couple of seconds to look at Mario from behind. He was still in pretty much the same shape as he'd been in Afghanistan. She remembered the smoothness of his skin, save for the two puckered scars where a bullet had entered and exited, by his right shoulder. She had touched the wounds the one time they'd had sex.

The years had flown and in the intervening time she'd met Sam, fallen in love with him, and then lost him. It might have been love with Hudson Brand, if she had given it time, but their relationship, if she allowed herself to call it that, had rekindled the memories, good and bad, of devoting herself to another. Mario had been a fling, the result of one too many brandies, but they had gone their separate ways as friends. He was gentlemanly enough not to have raised it or joked about it since she had found him at the silversmith's gallery.

He turned, covering his side of their route, and their eyes locked, briefly. He gave a half-smile and she looked to the opposite side, in case he could guess what she had been thinking.

Sonja heard the click of fingers and stopped. She looked forward. Ezekial had his right arm up, his hand now clenched in a fist. She looked back to Ian and motioned with a downward gesture for him to drop to one knee. Tema had done so already, and was facing rearward. *Good girl.*

Sonja moved slowly forward. Mario had his rifle up into his shoulder, covering Ezekial. Low and slow, she went to the tracker's side.

Ezekial tilted his face up and touched the side of his nose. Sonja sniffed the air.

'Smoke,' she whispered into his ear.

He nodded. Sonja concentrated and caught a whiff of cooking meat. It had to be their quarry. The tracks Ezekial had picked up spoke of a large group of men, about twenty. Most of them were bearers, carrying the ivory from the poisoned elephants. It had been like following a highway, their tracks impossible to disguise. They were operating with impunity, which, in itself, made Sonja doubly cautious.

'Pull back,' she said.

They reformed twenty metres to their rear and Sonja gave her orders.

When they set off again adrenaline was filing their nerve endings and senses to needlepoints. Each step was slow and deliberate, all weapons were raised, all eyes straining to read and interpret the ghostly glowing green landscape in their night vision goggles.

Mario and Ian had moved wide and to the right in a flanking manoeuvre, while Sonja took point and led Ezekial and Tema directly in the direction the smoke was coming from. The poachers had followed a well-worn hippo path, the big animal's rounded feet leaving a raised *middelmannetjie* hump between its right and left legs, but Sonja's group weaved among the trees and bushes on either side, in case a sentry was covering the track.

As the smell of smoke and *braai*ing meat became stronger, so too did the murmur of voices. These men were either stupid or they were supremely confident of not being followed.

They were close enough now to see embers flying skywards and orange light reflected on the trees. A man laughed, too loud, and someone was cautious enough to shush him.

Sonja dropped to her belly and Ezekial and Tema did the same. They leopard-crawled closer. Sonja motioned for each of them to take up position behind a tree – Tema a leadwood and Ezekial a Natal mahogany.

The campfire glowed bright in her goggles, which intensified any ambient light. Casting her eyes over the group, it became immediately apparent to Sonja why the men were so confident. Seated at the centre of the feast that was now getting underway was a man in the uniform of the Zimbabwe Parks and Wildlife Service, his green beret hanging from the tip of the barrel of his AK-47, which was propped against the fallen tree most of the men were sitting on. The four men either side of the senior ranger, who wore officers' insignia on his epaulettes, were dressed in khaki bush gear with good boots on their feet, and an assortment of packs and military-style webbing gear and rifles was piled next to them on the ground or resting against the trunk. Another ten men squatted or sat in the dirt around the fire, but these wore older, more ragged clothes; they would be the ivory bearers, Sonja thought. A cook was carving a leg of antelope, probably kudu.

Sonja had told her people, and Ian had seemed content to let her give the orders, that after they had established the location and number of the party they were tracking they would take up position and keep them under observation until the early hours of the morning, once all or most of them were asleep. They would then, following Sonja's lead, move into the enemy position, disarm any sentry who might be awake, and separate men from weapons and tie all of them up. They would then radio for national parks rangers to come and take the poachers into custody.

Sonja knew that no plan, according to Rommel, himself paraphrasing an earlier German general, Helmuth von Moltke, survived contact with the enemy, and the presence of a senior ranger in this group was about to prove the old adage correct again.

Sonja was mulling over her chosen course of action and settling down to at least watch what transpired between the ranger and the rest of the gang when a shot rang out. The ranger she had been watching toppled backwards off the log. Men yelled to each other and scrambled to pick up their weapons.

From the right flank, where Mario and Ian were, muzzle flashes lit up the darkness. A man screamed. Others crawled behind the fallen tree or stood, not knowing which way to run.

'Shit.' Sonja stood. 'On me.'

Tema and Ezekial got up and moved to her, following as she moved closer.

Some of the poachers were firing wildly towards Mario and Ian, who were returning with one or two aimed shots at a time.

'Fire at the men with guns, not the bearers,' Sonja said. 'Make every shot count.'

Their only advantage, now that surprise was lost, was the fact that they had night vision devices and so, as long as they stayed away from the fire, they were invisible – at least until they fired.

Sonja ran forward through the darkness, Tema close behind her. Ezekial opened up, prematurely, with an overeager burst of automatic fire. Consequently, he drew fire from a man armed with an AK-47.

Sonja dropped to one knee, raised her rifle and took aim at the man who was firing at Ian. She let off two shots and the man dropped. Tema leap-frogged past her, getting closer to the poachers, and Sonja covered her.

Mario was up and moving, charging towards the enemy from the right flank. He dropped a man in his path with a double tap and Ian paused to fire at another man, who also fell to the ground. Men were scattering everywhere.

A man with a hunting rifle stopped and took cover behind a tree. He took aim at Mario and Ian, but Sonja was quicker and put two rounds into his back. His body slammed into the trunk and he slid to the ground.

Sonja scanned the bush for more armed targets, but there were none. She was at the campfire. 'Re-org!'

At her shouted command the others swept through the position the poachers had been occupying, checking for dead and wounded. Sonja heard screaming, then a single shot.

'Report,' she ordered, dropping to one knee beside the last man she had shot. She tossed his rifle a metre away and put two fingers to his neck. He was definitely dead. 'One dead.'

'Two dead here,' Mario called from the other side of the fire.

'One here,' Tema said.

'On me,' Sonja called to them. They came to her and Tema and

Ezekial, with a whispered reminder from Tema, took up positions around Sonja, facing outwards in different directions.

Sonja looked to Mario and Ian. 'What was that last shot?'

'Wounded guy went for his gun,' Mario said, 'so I finished him.'

Sonja's eyes went to Ian's. He looked away for a split second, then back at her and nodded.

'Who fired first?'

Ian squared his shoulders. 'I did. That senior ranger – his name is Obert Mvuu – heard something. I saw him look our way.'

Sonja hadn't seen any such movement from where she was looking, but now was not the time for a fight, out here in the middle of the bush. 'We'll talk about this later, in the debrief. Let's collect up the weapons and call for an uplift.'

'I'll organise a vehicle,' Ian said.

'You do that.'

Tema was staring down at the body of a man. Her lower lip began to tremble.

Sonja went to her, but did not touch her. 'Are you going to be OK?'

She nodded. 'I just need a moment to compose myself.'

'We will talk, later, I promise. Ezekial?'

He came to her. 'Yes, Sonja?'

She gestured to the man at Tema's feet. 'Check his pockets. See if he's carrying ID, a phone, anything that will tell us something about him.'

Tema stepped closer to the body, preventing Ezekial from getting to it. 'I will do it.'

Ezekial looked to Sonja, who nodded. 'Check the others.'

Sonja walked to the mound of tusks, the whiteness of which almost glowed by the light of the moon. She shook her head. It was madness, what people killed and died for. Ivory, rhino horn, gold, diamonds – the cost of all of them was horrendous.

Mario came to her. 'How are you doing?'

'I'm fine, you?'

'OK. Pretty good, in fact. I haven't done this shit for a while. It never gets old, does it?'

She looked at him. He had the eyes of a nineteen-year-old, clear, sparkling and excited. 'It is what it is.'

'Come on,' Mario nudged her arm with his, 'don't tell me it's not a rush for you. It's why we do this, or at least why I used to.'

'It's not meant to be fun, Mario.'

His eyes became older and the fingers on her forearm gripped in a way that was not painful, not intimate, just sincere. 'We won. We did good.'

Sonja looked at the bodies around the campfire. She had fought in several conflicts and was hard pressed to justify the causes of any of them. This one, however, was a battle to protect innocent animals. They may not have been worth more than humans, but they never did anything stupid or greedy or killed for fun.

She cast her gaze over to Ian, who was on his radio. Mario released his grip on her arm. 'Any news?' she called to Ian.

'Uplift in twenty minutes.'

Ian pulled a pack of Zimbabwean Newbury cigarettes from his uniform shirt pocket. He offered one to Sonja. She shook her head; she had quit a couple of years ago, but the sound of the tobacco catching and the smell of the smoke still triggered a craving.

She gestured to the body of the park ranger. 'You say you know him?'

Ian nodded. 'Obert Mvuu; he's as guilty as sin. It was an open secret around here that Obert was running an ivory and bushmeat syndicate. He was the local big man and everyone was afraid of him; too scared to report him to the higher-ups. His brother's a provincial governor, very high up in the party, and Obert gets shuffled from national park to national park so he can line his and his family's pockets, but he never stays long enough for the good people in parks to catch him in the act.'

'Why did you execute him?'

'I told you, he heard us, went for his gun.'

Sonja could tell a lie when she heard one and Ian's body language gave him away. 'Was he responsible for the deaths of your men?'

'Yes. The poachers were often a step ahead of us; it would seem that they would strike wherever we weren't patrolling. I had to supply national parks with briefings on our patrols so they could de-conflict – make sure none of their guys bumped into ours and started shooting. Obert was telling the poachers where we'd be patrolling and that was helping them, and that was frustrating, but no one was getting killed. This last time he used the information I supplied to set up an ambush.'

Sonja rubbed her chin. 'Why? If he was taking a cut, or running things as you say, and it was working to his advantage, why would he risk his men in a gunfight or run the risk of being involved in a murder rap?'

'I don't know. I just know he deserved to die.'

She felt her anger rise. 'And you took it on yourself to be his executioner and, more importantly, put my people at risk by triggering a gunfight that we could have avoided.'

'I told you, Sonja, Zimbabwe operates a shoot-to-kill policy. This is my country and we play by our rules.'

'You said this man was well connected, politically. The police could make trouble.'

Ian shrugged. 'Well, that's my problem, isn't it? Your job here is done and I thank you and your people for your assistance, but the best thing for you all would be to get on a plane at dawn and fly out of here.'

'We'll do that,' Sonja said.

'This is a war and our enemies are becoming increasingly aggressive and better resourced. Obert Mvuu wasn't alone; he had backing in the form of weapons, training and ready-made markets for the ivory his gang took.'

'Organised crime?'

'About the only thing here that is organised, yes. We believe the ivory taken here in the valley is transported across the river to Zambia and bought and shipped from there.'

'Who are the buyers? Chinese?'

Ian dragged on his cigarette, exhaled and coughed. 'Maybe. It's easy to think they're behind it. There are so many Chinese here and in Zambia building roads, logging forests, developing new mines, so there's a ready conduit out of Africa to Asia for anything you want, legal or illegal.'

'You don't sound totally convinced.'

'My guys caught a poacher, a bearer actually, a couple of months ago, and I interrogated him. His job was to ferry ivory across the Zambezi from our side to Zambia. He'd then carry it through the park on the Zambian side to waiting vehicles. He mentioned seeing a white man. The bearer overheard this guy talking on a satellite phone in a foreign language, not English. He thought it might be Russian.'

Sonja wasn't surprised. She'd had dealings with the Russian mafia in Africa in the past. Like the Chinese, the Russians had existing networks and alliances in Africa thanks to both countries' support for Cold War independence movements and military uprisings. 'You ever hear of an organisation called the Scorpions?'

Ian stubbed out his cigarette and, as Sonja once had, followed the old soldiers' habit of putting the butt in an old-fashioned plastic camera film container he took from his pocket, so as not to leave a sign for an enemy. 'What did Paterson tell you about them?'

The briefing had been just that – brief – because of the rush to get them to Zimbabwe. 'It's a nickname for a criminal organisation that's trying to corner the market on poaching in South Africa and Mozambique.'

'And here,' Ian said.

'So Obert Mvuu was part of the Scorpions?'

Ian turned away, tilting his head. 'Listen. Vehicle coming?'

'Answer me, Ian,' Sonja persisted. 'Did you know Obert Mvuu would be with these men tonight? It's a big haul of ivory. Was Obert here to make sure it got across the river without interference from any national parks patrols?'

He looked back at her. 'All I can tell you is that when I reported to Julianne about the loss of my men, I told her that I had checked in at Nyamepi Camp and was told Obert was on leave for two days. His car was still at the staff compound. I told Julianne I thought Obert was going to link up with the poachers.'

Sonja didn't need him to explain the rest. 'And you didn't have enough shooters to go after him.'

'That's correct,' Ian said. 'I asked for help and Julianne sent you and your team.'

'And you told Julianne that if you could track and catch the gang then you would have an opportunity to take out Obert Mvuu.'

'No, I told Julianne that we had an opportunity to catch Obert in the act.'

'*Catch* him or kill him?'

Ian shrugged his shoulders again. 'Does it matter?'

'It does to me and to my people. I'm not running a hit squad here, Ian, and I'm nobody's hired assassin.'

'Well, thanks to you my people will be safer, and so will the wildlife here now that Obert's tickets. I've heard plenty of politicians and landowners talk tough about poaching, but Julianne's prepared to put her money where her mouth is. She knows how to deal with the poachers' bosses.' Ian drew a finger across his neck.

Chapter 13

Hudson Brand was pleasantly drunk. He and Rosie Appleton sat on the verandah of the Rissington Inn bar. They were the last two guests still up.

'So, do you want that room?' Chris, the owner, asked Hudson.

'He will,' Rosie said. 'He's too drunk to drive home.'

'Very sensible,' Chris said. He gave Hudson a key. 'Now I'm going to bed.'

''Night,' Hudson said. 'I won't be far behind.'

'One more drink,' Rosie insisted.

Hudson checked his watch. 'Sheesh, midnight already.'

'You have somewhere to be at the crack of dawn?'

'Nope, business is slow.' Chris departed and the waitress came over.

Hudson ordered a wine for Rosie and, 'I'll have an ABF.'

'ABF?' Rosie asked.

'Absolute Bloody Final.'

She laughed at his joke and twirled her hair again. When the waitress had turned her back to them, Rosie leaned over from her wicker chair to his and put a hand on his knee. 'I'm pissed.'

'I'll take you to bed.'

'Now you're talking.'

'Alone.'

Rosie leaned back and the drinks came, quickly – the waitress was obviously as keen to get to sleep as her boss had been. Rosie took a couple of sips. 'Sorry, that's me, out.'

It was odd, Hudson thought, as Rosie had been quite lucid until a few minutes earlier. He'd thought she'd been handling her drink very well and they had both eaten heartily at dinner – she the crocodile and he the delicious mother-in-law's chicken and prawn curry. 'OK, I'll see you to your room.'

'I'm getting a sense of . . . what's that thing called?' Rosie said.

'What thing?'

He held her arm as they crunched and lurched along a gravel path towards Rosie's garden suite. Hudson would come back to the main building, where they'd had dinner, to his smaller room after he saw Rosie safely to her room. At least there was no risk of them bumping into a leopard here in Hazyview, unlike the last time he'd escorted her to a hotel room.

'That thing where you think you've been here before.'

'Déjà vu,' Hudson said.

'Yep. That thing.'

Hudson led her to her suite. 'Key.'

'Oh.' She rummaged in her handbag and giggled. 'Here it is.'

Hudson took the key from her after she'd had three attempts at getting it in the keyhole. He opened the door and she walked in. 'Well, I'll say –'

Rosie grabbed him by the shirtfront and pulled him to her, raising herself up on her toes and planting her lips on his. Her mouth was soft and warm and her touch sent an instant charge through his body, to one region in particular.

Hudson put his hands on her shoulders and managed to ease himself away. 'You're drunk, Rosie.'

'No, I'm not.' She'd stopped slurring and giggling. 'I know how people in small towns talk, I just wanted to get you away from the bar without it looking like you were about to cheat on your absentee girlfriend.'

'Sonja's not my —'

'Save it. I don't care either way. I'm not used to being refused, Hudson. Come inside, let's have some fun.'

She kissed him again and ran a hand down his spine, dropped her handbag on the hotel room floor and grabbed his butt. She broke the kiss and whispered into his ear, 'Do me.'

What the hell, he thought, *why not?* He hadn't slept with Sannie or Rosie, but Sonja thought he had, and had broken off contact with him. If she was so hell-bent on believing he'd cheated, then he may as well have some fun.

He wrapped his arms around Rosie, put his hands under her bum and she jumped up onto him, wrapping her legs around him. He savoured the feel of her petite body in his bear-like grip. He moved to one of the whitewashed walls, pressed her against it and kissed her hard. She ground her body against his and Hudson felt the desire flood through him like a drug.

'Yes,' Rosie said. 'Bed,' she mumbled through their kisses.

Hudson carried her across the room and lay her down on the starched white duvet cover. She reached up and found his belt buckle and undid it. Hudson kicked off his shoes. She unbuttoned her shirt and Hudson drew a short, sharp breath at the sight of her lacy pale blue bra and the swell of her breasts.

'You like?'

'Oh, yeah,' he groaned.

While Rosie clearly wasn't as drunk as she'd seemed, Hudson hesitated. Rosie had no such qualms and sat up, reached out and undid his zip. She lowered his shorts and traced the outline of his erection through the fabric of his underpants. Rosie leaned forward and placed her mouth on him, biting

152

him softly through the fabric. He half closed his eyes.

Hudson ran his fingers through her hair, massaging her scalp, and increased his pressure when she, too, let out a low moan of pleasure.

Rosie moved her mouth from him and looked up into his eyes as she began to free his penis. The crooked grin appeared again and made him smile and sigh.

'Give in to it,' she whispered.

Hudson closed his eyes.

Rosie stopped touching him long enough to unzip and pull down her denim skirt. Her pants, which matched her bra, were sheer enough for him to see the tight curls beneath the lace.

Hudson took a breath. 'Rosie, I shouldn't.'

She laughed. 'Relax, I don't want to marry you, just have sex with you. What's wrong with that?'

Indeed, he could almost hear a part of his body saying, *what's wrong with that and what's wrong with you? For crying in a bucket, man-up.*

'Touch me, please.'

He moved a hand to her bare thigh, stroking the skin on the inside. It was so soft, so smooth. Hudson wanted to taste it. His fingers trailed over the sheer fabric of her pants. She had a hand on him again. The desire was agonising.

Rosie took his hand, pressed it to her and he closed his fingers, cupping her, kissing her mouth again, hard, as he felt her heat radiating against his palm.

'I want you. Now,' she said into his ear as he kissed her neck. 'Condom?'

But try as he might, he could not force Sonja's face from his mind, no matter how tightly he screwed his eyes shut. It wasn't guilt that he felt, more like sorrow; a sense of loss for something that probably hadn't existed, but which he thought both of them had longed for.

His body stiffened. 'Rosie, I'm sorry, I can't.'

She opened her eyes wide. 'You're kidding, right? It doesn't *matter*, Hudson. I won't tell anyone, not Sonja, not anyone here. You're a single man, for goodness sake.'

He eased himself away from her. He saw the longing in her eyes and felt bad he'd let things get this far.

'She doesn't *love* you. Don't be a fool. She left you.'

It was true. Sonja had walked out on him, but he felt like there was something more he could have done to help her, to show her how he felt. Rosie reached up and took his hand.

She looked so inviting, so desirable. He thought of all the women he'd been with. Rosie was smart, funny, beautiful and sexy. *Would it really matter?*

His phone rang. He stooped and picked up his shirt and fumbled for it. He looked at the screen.

Sonja.

*

Sonja held the phone up, hoping the one bar of signal would stay steady this time. She'd tried calling Hudson three times.

There was, Ian had told her, little or no signal in Mana Pools National Park, but on the drive from the ambush site back to the lodge her phone had beeped. It was a text message from her daughter, Emma, telling her all was good with her and there was no need for her to reply, just say hi when she could.

Sonja had told Ian's driver to stop the open-top Land Rover. She was standing in the back of the vehicle. Thinking about the contact, and the dead bodies in the *bakkie* that was trailing them, and what Ian had told her about expecting to find the corrupt ranger he had killed, Sonja had an urge to talk to Hudson, to get his take on the gunfight that had gone down at the golf course.

And she had wanted to hear his voice. She felt guilty at how abrupt she had been with him after he had helped her, and for leaving so suddenly with no explanation.

Sonja looked at the screen, saw that the number was dialling. She willed him to answer, even though it was late at night. Abruptly, the call ended. At first, Sonja thought her line had dropped out, but when she checked the signal strength it had stayed steady on one bar.

'Shit.'

She tried again, but this time her call went straight through to voicemail.

'Hudson, it's Sonja. I . . . I'm in Zimbabwe. Some stuff has happened here. I just want to talk to you, to ask you some questions. And, well, I don't know. Hope you're OK. Call me, if you can, though I may not be in signal, so leave me a message.'

'Shall we go?' Ian asked.

Sonja looked at the still-glowing screen of her phone. It faded to black. Hudson had cut off her call. 'Yes.'

It took them half an hour to drive back to the lodge on the edge of the Zambezi. When they arrived Ian supervised two of his maintenance staff to unload the bodies of the dead poachers. Sonja stayed with him, dismissing Tema and Ezekial, but Mario stayed to help move the corpses to the lodge's spare portable cold room, which thankfully was empty of food.

When they were done, Ian had one of his staff, Taffy, short for Tafudzwa, unlock the bar fridge and drinks cabinet.

The three of them sat at the bar, with Taffy pouring. Sonja nursed a Klipdrift Brandy and Coke Zero.

'You need to get out of Zimbabwe tomorrow, Sonja,' Ian said.

'No argument from me, but will you be OK?'

Ian drained a Bollinger's Lager and signalled Taffy to open another. 'No one's ever OK here, but we manage. The police will come, there will be shit, but we'll carry on. It's the way of this country.'

Mario sipped his Scotch, neat, no ice. 'How will we get out?'

'There's an aircraft coming into the Mana Pools airstrip tomorrow morning. It's bringing in one guest. You'll fly out on that plane. But we need to get you out of here early, before the national parks guys and the police arrive. If you don't mind, I'll take the credit for all the shootings.'

'We're not looking for medals,' Mario said.

Sonja was uneasy about everything to do with this mission. There had been too little time to plan and she had not been told that Julianne had had her sights on a particular target, Obert Mvuu. However, like Mario, the last thing on her wish list was glory for what had happened this night.

'I'm tired,' Ian said. 'I'm taking this beer to bed.'

Sonja looked to Mario. 'Last one for us as well?'

Mario nodded.

'Good night, Taffy, you can leave us if you like,' Sonja said to the barman. He nodded his thanks.

Ian extended his hand to Sonja. 'Thank you. I know you have concerns about tonight, but I was impressed by you and your team. Trust me when I say that this lodge, this national park and this country are better off as a result.'

Sonja was tired as well, and too exhausted and confused to argue. She had no choice but to accept Ian's story about why he had opened fire first. The fact was that he had avenged the death of his men, a poaching gang had been all but eliminated, and all her people were going home safe. She wasn't precious enough to question things further. Sonja's concern was not with Ian Barton, but the people who employed him – and her.

If Julianne wasn't running a hit squad, she at least seemed to be manoeuvring Sonja and her team into situations where battle was inevitable and the presence of high-profile targets, such as Cuna, King Jim and now local strongman Obert Mvuu, seemed to be a given. She had her doubts about Ian Barton; she felt sure that he knew, and had probably passed on to their superiors, that they were likely to find Obert with the gang and that his killing had been preordained.

'Night, Ian.'

He waved and walked out of the bar.

Sonja stretched on her stool, raising her hands above her head, and winced.

'You OK?' Mario asked.

'My neck and shoulders are killing me.'

He got up and moved behind her. 'Allow me.'

She almost told him no, but as soon as she felt his fingers on her she gave in.

'I remember doing this to you in Kandahar,' he said softly, reading her mind.

'Me too, but this is not the time for that kind of thing.'

'What kind of thing?'

She swivelled her head and saw his boyish grin. 'Ow. Not so hard.'

'Hard is good. Your shoulders are a mess of knots. Look down, let me loosen you up.'

The feeling was, she had to admit, hypnotic, as he kneaded and pinched her tired muscles. She'd had precious little sleep these past few days and had been keyed up, ready for action, most of the time she had been awake. She surrendered, temporarily at least, to his touch.

'Who were you calling, from the Land Rover?'

'Hudson Brand.'

Mario snorted.

'You two don't like each other. Why not?'

'It was over a girl; a long time ago, in Angola.'

'Care to tell me more?' Sonja asked.

Mario's fingers paused. 'He took her away from me, but she came back to me, and then she died. He blames me for her death,

157

saying I put her in danger, but it was Angola. I don't have to tell you what war zones are like, but for Hudson it was easier for him to channel his anger against me.'

'He took your girlfriend?' Sonja was surprised.

'Ha! You clearly don't know too much about our Mr Brand. He is quite the ladies' man. You know of this syndrome, khaki fever?'

She nodded. 'I grew up in a game lodge in Botswana, remember. I know very well how female clients fall for their handsome khaki-wearing guides when on safari.'

'Well, in the guide's textbook, under khaki fever, the entry reads, "See Brand, H."'

She wondered. Hudson was good-looking, he wasn't too old, he was heterosexual, and he was single. Why wouldn't he be playing around with all the women he wanted? Did she have a right to judge him? Sonja told herself she hadn't wanted to settle down with him in any case. And tonight it seemed as though he had deliberately ended her call. She gave her imagination free rein and pictured him bedding some bimbo tourist.

'You're tensing up even more. Relax, Sonja.'

'Tell me about this girlfriend of yours.'

Mario paused for a second, as if recalling. 'I loved her. We – 32 Battalion, the South Africans – were fighting on the side of UNITA in Angola, you know, the anti-communists?'

'Yes,' Sonja said.

'The girl, Ines, was part of UNITA, but I found out she was a spy for the communists, for the MPLA, the Angolan army. Brand and I were friends, for a while, but Ines liked him too much. She left me for him, or rather he seduced her away from me. She came back to me, but in the end it was tragic. I tried to cover for her and she told me she had stopped spying, but UNITA found out about her, from an informer and . . . took her away. I never saw her again.'

'I'm sorry about your friend.'

'It was war.' His fingers moved up the nape of her neck, into her hair. He pressed against her scalp.

'Too hard?'

'You can go as hard as you like there.'

She hadn't meant it as a double entendre, but she felt Mario move closer to her, the warmth of his body against her shoulders as his fingers pressed deliciously firmly into her temples. It felt like exquisite torture.

Sonja reached for the countertop and found her drink. She took a long draught and felt the brandy warm her insides while her skin began to sizzle. She needed to think about tonight, about the events of the last few days, and about what, if anything, James Paterson and Julianne Clyde-Smith had been setting her up for. Right now, though, the mix of sensations on and in her body was overriding her brain.

'We should go to bed,' she said.

'That's the best offer I've had in years.' He laughed to counter the sultriness of his deep voice.

She gulped more brandy and Coke and wiped her lips. 'Ain't going to happen.'

'Just joking. But I feel wired, don't you? I wouldn't be able to sleep now, not after tonight.'

'You sound like you enjoyed getting shot at,' she said.

Mario stopped massaging and peered around, into her eyes. 'You, the great Sonja Kurtz, mercenary? You are telling me combat doesn't turn you on?'

'Not in that sense, no. You have a one-track mind, always did, Mario.'

'Oh, do not get me wrong,' he said, putting his talented fingers back to work, 'killing does not give me a hard-on. I am not a madman. But you have to admit, it's the best drug around. I love my sculpting, and the peace and quiet of my life in White River, but it is in moments like tonight, and only then, that I feel truly alive. You know this feeling, right?'

She nodded into his hands.

He moved back to her shoulders, and they felt less tense. His touch was pleasurable rather than painful now. His thumbs were on her shoulder blades, circling, and his fingers – she only now noticed how long they were, something she hadn't remembered from Afghanistan – were resting above her breasts, the tips of each middle finger almost reaching her nipples.

Sonja looked down and saw the two little peaks swelling against her uniform shirt. She felt a surge of adrenaline burst through her veins and her cheeks turned red and hot. Mario was bending over her, his stubble almost scratching her burning skin. She held her breath.

Sonja set her drink down on the bar, slowly, and brought her hands up to cover Mario's, to stop him moving any further. She tilted her head to look up at him, to tell him to stop, and then he kissed her.

He did it softly. She kept her mouth closed, and shut her eyes, but the contact electrified her. She parted her lips a little and he pressed home his attack, still without urgency or force. She wrapped her fingers around his hands and squeezed, holding on to him, her body needing the contact.

Damn you, Hudson Brand.

Mario moved around her, so that he was between Sonja and the bar. He put his arms around her and drew her to him. She clutched him and he kissed behind her ear. He leaned into her and she opened her legs and felt the swell of his erection against her body.

'I missed you, after Afghanistan,' he murmured.

They had both discussed it at the time, rationalising it as a bit of fun, a fling, with neither of them wanting anything ongoing. Had she misread him? she wondered. Was he looking to see more of her? Sonja hadn't contacted him and when Mario had messaged her a couple of times on Facebook she had ignored him, just as she ignored most people who contacted her out of the blue. She used social media primarily to stay in touch with her daughter, Emma, and monitor her movements.

He kissed her mouth again and she responded, opening hers and revelling in the feeling of his tongue, of hers in his mouth, their lips crushing together now, desire taking over.

He ran his hands along her arms and the feel of him sent a shiver through her.

Mario put his hands on her waist and lifted her from her bar stool. Sonja let him guide her as he swung her around. She felt him start to raise her and gave a small jump so she ended up sitting on the polished wooden bar. Mario reached up, while maintaining eye contact, and started to undo the buttons on her camouflage shirt.

Sonja leaned back, her palms on the counter as he went about his work. To his credit, he didn't go straight for her, instead he kissed a line from the underside of her chin, down her neck to her cleavage.

'You're wearing lace,' he said.

'You were expecting Mr Price?' she laughed.

'I can't even picture you in a discount clothing store, let alone buying lingerie there . . .'

'I didn't expect to be going to the golf club on a mission, let alone Zimbabwe.'

It was the nicest bra she owned; she'd bought it and the matching briefs in Nelspruit, in a lingerie shop, when she'd decided to visit Hudson. *Foolish.*

Mario traced the first of her nipples with his fingertip through the sheer fabric then lowered his mouth to it. The cocktail of the warmth of his mouth, the flicking of his tongue and the roughness of the material was enough to elicit a low moan from her.

Yes, she thought, *this is what I need*.

Mario continued what he was doing, which was very good, and freed her other breast with his left hand. When he moved his mouth there he sucked, too greedily.

'Ouch.'

He glanced up at her. 'Sorry.'

'It's OK. Be gentle.'

'Yes, ma'am.'

'Don't call me that.'

'OK,' Mario said.

'I didn't mean to sound so harsh.'

'It's fine.' He went back to sucking her nipple, more gently this time.

Sonja focused on getting back into the groove. She closed her eyes and enjoyed the sensation. There was still a risk someone could walk in on them, perhaps Taffy because he'd forgotten something, or a security guard. That made it hotter for her.

Mario was working her belt buckle and the top button of her jeans.

'Help me take your pants off,' he whispered.

'No. I'll leave them on.' It was one thing to get a thrill out of the *thought* of someone walking in on them, but she didn't want to be caught half-naked.

She unzipped and lay back, then shrugged her pants down so the waistband was midway down her thighs. As she did so Mario unzipped his cargo pants. She saw how hard he was, how ready for her.

Mario bent over and kissed her there. She shivered again. Sonja's first thought, when Mario had started massaging her shoulders, was that there was no way she would have sex or indulge in inappropriate physical contact of any kind with someone under her command. At that moment, though, she had decided that as soon as they got back to South Africa she would tell Julianne

Clyde-Smith and Paterson that she was quitting. She didn't like the way things were playing out; either they were dropping her into dangerous situations without proper planning and forethought, or the opposite: they were setting her and her people up to be on-the-spot executioners. Either situation was unacceptable. Too much was not right. *This*, what Mario was doing, was wrong.

'Stop, Mario.'

'Fuck,' he said. 'Relax.'

'Do *not* tell me to "relax". Back off.' Sonja heard footsteps. 'Someone's coming. Stop it. Pull your bloody pants up.'

Sonja slid off the bar, raised and zipped her pants, hastily buttoned her shirt and grabbed her half-drunk brandy and Coke. She took a long sip, needing it, and slumped back on the stool as Ian Barton walked across the timber decking. Mario sat on the sofa, trying to control his breathing. Ian's eyes flitted between them.

'Couldn't sleep?' Sonja asked. She could feel her cheeks burning.

Ian looked to her. 'I had a call from a contact of mine, a policeman based at the national parks headquarters at Marongora, about eighty kilometres from here on the main road. We've got trouble; more precisely, *you've* got trouble.'

'What kind?'

'Charlie 10. The Central . . .'

'. . . Intelligence Organisation. I've had dealings with the CIO in the past.'

'Apparently they've found out you're here and someone is coming to interview you. Why?'

Sonja drained the drink. The ice had long melted. 'I tried to assassinate the President of Zimbabwe a few years ago. They never really forgave me for that.'

'That could explain why the cops are coming out now, in the middle of the night. Investigating the deaths of several poachers could easily have waited until tomorrow,' Ian said.

'I was wondering if they might have been waiting for me at Harare Airport, but I figured that since we arrived on a private jet and went straight to a chartered aircraft they wouldn't notice me.'

'Yes, well, the local cops knew you were here, thanks to the park's rangers. Obert Mvuu probably reported your presence to someone higher up. Your aircraft arrives at eleven tomorrow, in time for you to connect to the Comair Flight back to Joburg from Harare at fourteen-hundred. I called Julianne's office to try and get her jet again, but Doug Pearse has taken it to Pretoria for maintenance. I checked with Comair, and there are plenty of seats on tomorrow's flight so you can buy a ticket for cash at the airport; hopefully that will keep you a step ahead of the CIO. For now, though, you can't stay here.'

'Any ideas?'

Ian nodded. 'There's a place called Chitake Springs, have you heard of it?'

'Yes,' Sonja said.

'Legendary game-viewing location about forty kilometres away from the river,' Mario weighed in.

'Correct,' Ian said. 'We've got a tented camp there. I'll get one of the guys to drive you there now. We've got permission to drive at night on anti-poaching patrols. The rangers don't need to know who's on board the Land Rover. I'll wait here and deal with the police and CIO. You can hide out at the bush camp until your flight arrives.'

'Will you be OK?' Sonja asked.

'I'll be fine. Hopefully you'll make it through the airport at Harare. The CIO are evil, but not terribly efficient. I'll tell the local guys you're out on patrol, looking for the bearers who escaped the gunfight.'

Sonja looked to Mario. 'We'd better get Tema and Ezekial up and ready.'

They started to walk to the tents they had been allocated. Ian put a hand on Sonja's arm. Her instinct was to shrug him off.

'I just wanted to say thank you, again, for your help,' he said.

'I feel like I was set up, used.'

His face betrayed nothing. 'Obert Mvuu was a criminal and a traitor to his country and the parks and wildlife service. He had the blood of humans as well as animals on his hands.'

'Yes,' Sonja replied, not feeling gracious, 'and now you have me, a wanted political criminal to pin the blame on for his killing. You'll stay out of prison, but your patch of Africa will be safer. Let me tell you something . . .'

He squared up to her. 'What?'

'If I get caught at Harare Airport, when I get out of prison I'll come looking for you.'

Ian nodded. 'I'd expect nothing less from you.'

Chapter 14

Chitake Springs was one of Africa's best-kept game-viewing secrets. Sonja had heard of it, but had never been there.

She, Mario, Tema and Ezekial sat on folding green canvas safari chairs on the edge of a bank that dropped almost vertically past their toes about ten metres down to a mostly dry riverbed.

The morning was cool and crisp, the sun, not long up, bathing the dry bush behind them in mellow red-gold. From the opposite bank came the lowing and the bovine smell of a herd of buffalo whose lead element had stopped at the precipice and was now staring malevolently at the sitting humans.

'Are they going to come down to drink?' Tema asked.

'They will,' said Ezekial, 'but they are cautious. This place is a natural ambush site for lions. They could be anywhere, hiding under a bush or tree on the bank on our side or the other side and we'd be lucky to see them if they charged. They can launch themselves from the higher ground, down onto the buffalo when they are drinking.'

Ezekial handed Tema a pair of binoculars and pointed out a big buffalo bull with spectacular horns. When Tema had trouble finding the bull, Ezekial was quick to stand and move behind her and place his hands over hers, guiding her line of sight. The length of time Ezekial spent touching her was too long for mere friends.

This was, Sonja thought, like sitting in the seats of a natural amphitheatre with a ringside view of an imminent gladiatorial fight. There was an air of anticipation among the group, which was better than them brooding about the events of the previous days and nights.

Sonja had deliberately set up her chair so that Tema and Ezekial were between her and Mario. She regretted her decision to momentarily give in to his advances, even though they hadn't gone all the way. Perhaps there had been more chemistry between them in Afghanistan. It hadn't helped that Ian had almost walked in on them, but she had decided that would be it for her and Mario. It had been a mistake and it was time for her to move on.

Mario had looked at her, hopefully, when they were shown to their respective safari tents at the camp at Chitake, but Sonja had dashed his hopes of a second try with a curt shake of her head. She had been tired, but it was the sort of exhaustion that made sleep impossible. She had tossed and turned on her stretcher, thinking about her near miss with Mario, her elevated and unfulfilled desire, and how Hudson Brand had cut off her call.

Men.

'Look.' Mario pointed to the opposite bank. 'They're coming down.'

Here and there on the sandy riverbank the water from the natural springs seeped to the surface, and it was to these small pools that the buffalo were making a beeline. They would take a few steps, pause and sniff the air, but as the lead animals moved further down the bank their thirst and the steepness of the sandy game trail forced them to increase their speed. Dust clouds began to swirl as a mini stampede began.

Sonja felt her phone vibrate in her pocket. Out of habit she had it turned to silent. She was surprised to get a signal here in the middle of nowhere, and even more so when she checked the screen and saw she had three bars of signal on her international roaming SIM card.

Hudson's name was flashing on the screen. She stood, ignored Mario's question about who was calling, and walked away from the others and the bank. She answered the call.

'Brand.'

'Howzit, Sonja?'

'What do you want?' She kept walking.

'I saw you called me last night. My battery went flat before I could answer and I only just borrowed a charger this morning. I called straight away; I haven't even listened to your message.'

'Where are you?'

'At a hotel, Rissington, in Hazyview.'

'Why?'

There was a pause. 'Why? What's with the third degree?'

'It's not the third degree, unless you're guilty of something. Anyway, I don't care where you spent the night, or with whom.'

'Sonja, I didn't spend the night with anyone. Where are you?'

'Zimbabwe.'

'You called. What did you want?'

'I wanted . . . I wanted to talk to you about some stuff, about poaching, and that guy, Cuna. I need more information on a group called the Scorpions, an organised crime syndicate.'

'I might be able to help you there,' Hudson said. 'I've picked up some information on them from a contact.'

'That woman journalist?'

He paused again and she thought she could picture his embarrassment. 'We can talk about where I got the information later. Are you coming back to South Africa?'

'I am.'

'Sannie van Rensburg wants to see you. She's pissed off that you left the country.'

'Where were you last night?' Sonja asked, changing the subject. She didn't care about the police officer or how she felt.

'I told you, at the Rissington Inn, having dinner.'

'With who?'

'Sonja, please . . .'

'Was it with her?'

Hudson sighed. 'Rosie Appleton, yes. And yes, she has information about the Scorpions. I can tell you what I know, happy to. You know, nothing happened between us.'

'I wasn't inferring that anything had,' Sonja said.

She had wanted so much to hear his voice and she was still not convinced he hadn't ended her call deliberately and then slept with that woman, who clearly wanted him. And to top it all off she felt guilty about what had nearly happened between her and Mario.

'How's Mario?'

How can he read my mind? Sonja thought. 'OK. Why?'

'Watch him. He's dangerous.'

'How so?'

'He's a psycho, Sonja. I tried to warn you about him. He comes across all sensitive and kind, what with his sculptures and all, but he's a stone-cold killer. He's one of those guys who really enjoys it. I'm sure you know the type. They don't last in military units – usually don't even make the grade – and in mercenary outfits they're the ones who cause all the trouble.'

She did, indeed, know the type, but she hadn't pegged Mario as a psychopath.

'I knew him in Afghanistan. He wasn't like that.'

'You ever work with him, get into a gunfight with him alongside you?'

'No.' They had worked as personal protection officers, bodyguards, in Afghanistan, and while Sonja had seen action, Mario hadn't been around at those times. 'Except for last night, and he did just fine.'

'He had a nasty habit of shooting unarmed prisoners of war in Angola.'

Sonja remembered the wounded man crying out for help last night, the single shot in the darkness, and Mario's explanation that the man had been going for his gun. She didn't say anything to Hudson, though. 'Whatever.'

'Well, *whatever* you do, keep an eye on him.'

'He told me about Ines,' Sonja said. There was a pause on the other end of the line. She filled the void. 'He said you took her away from him.'

Another pause. 'Yes. I did. I don't want to talk about that. When are you due back?'

Sonja sighed and checked her watch. 'We should get picked up in twenty minutes for a flight out of where we are now back to Harare Airport. Plan is that we catch the Comair flight to Joburg this afternoon and then an Airlink connection to Skukuza tomorrow morning.'

'Can I pick you up from the airport?'

'No date planned for tomorrow?'

'Sonja . . .'

'I've got business with Clyde-Smith and someone else. Have you got hard intel on this group, the Scorpions?'

'I don't know how hard my info is, but we need to talk.'

'About work.'

'OK, about work,' he said.

'Come to Khaya Ngala tomorrow; I'll square it with Julianne. She can put you in a room in the staff quarters. Shoot for seventeen-hundred.'

'All right, I'll be there.'

Sonja ended the call. She thought about what Hudson had said about Mario and how he had all but agreed with Mario's take on what had happened with the girl, Ines, when they were younger. She would need to grill Mario about what had happened during the contact last night.

She put her phone in her pocket and had started to turn back to where the others were when she caught sight of something moving, through trees on the opposite side of the dirt road from where she was standing. Sonja froze.

As safari guides and soldiers were taught, she looked *through* the leaves and branches, not at them. There it was again. Sonja stayed still, all senses alert. She thought of what Ezekial had said, about how lions followed herds of buffalo and set up ambushes. They had passed a pile of bones on the way to the viewing spot, proof that lions had feasted very close to where they were all sitting, enjoying the sight below.

Sonja had no weapon on her; the AK-47 Ian had lent her was in a bag beside the chair where she had been sitting while watching the buffalo. There were public campsites at Chitake Springs, not just the one Ian operated, and if she or the others had been seen carrying rifles the tourists might have panicked and called national parks.

Sonja saw a stout leadwood tree off to her right. She dropped to a crouch and made her way to it. She took cover and watched the bush where she had seen the movement. If it was a lion she knew she would have to stay still, as her movement would attract it, but she would also need to alert the others.

Holding her breath, she peered through the foliage until she saw it again. This time, however, she saw bluish gunmetal. It wasn't an animal, it was a rifle, and holding it was a man, whose form slowly emerged.

He moved with exaggerated caution, scanning the bush to his front and each side and glancing down before taking a step, to make sure he wasn't going to stand on a dry twig that might snap, or stumble on a rock.

The man held up a hand, telling her there must be others behind him. He had come to the roadway where Sonja had been standing and he scanned left and right. When he was satisfied there was no one in sight and no traffic approaching he darted across and, as Sonja had done, found himself cover and conceal-ment behind a tree. He looked over his shoulder and waved for his comrades to move.

Sonja counted them. There were three more, all with AK-47s. They were well dressed, in bush clothes, but not the uniforms of the Zimbabwe Parks and Wildlife Service. The first man who had crossed covered the others as they moved past him. These men were well trained.

When the man began to stand and turn to follow the others, Sonja made her move. She crept silently through the bush, doing as he had done, watching her footfall, but moving faster, more confidently than he had.

Sonja remembered that Tema, like her, had been checking her phone while they watched the buffalo. Sonja took her phone out of her pocket and, as she walked, tapped out an SMS. *Contact rear. Hold fire.* She had no time for more, and hoped Tema would receive it. At this stage Sonja didn't know for sure who the men were, other than that they were not dressed as rangers. For all she knew they could be some Zimbabwean special police unit or even operatives from Charlie 10, the Central Intelligence Organisation. While they might be coming to arrest her, that did not give her the right to open fire on them indiscriminately. With a bit of luck Julianne Clyde-Smith could find a lawyer or pay a big enough bribe to keep her out of prison in Zimbabwe, but not if she murdered some intelligence officers in cold blood.

The man paused, perhaps because those ahead of him had also stopped. Sonja reckoned their lead element must at least be in sight of her people on the edge of the riverbank, over-looking where the buffalo were drinking. She could hear the buffalo grunting and lowing and the splash of hooves in the shallow water.

The man was alert and she pondered the best way to disarm him, quietly, without killing him. It wouldn't be easy, she thought, but then she caught a break.

The man took his right hand from the pistol grip of his AK-47 and unbuttoned the flap of the left breast pocket of his shirt and took out a mobile phone. Sonja took the Leatherman tool from her belt and opened the knife blade. She moved fast and silent through the grass and came up behind him. As the man studied the screen she reached around him and put her hand over his mouth and pushed the point of the knife into his neck until blood began to flow.

'Drop your rifle or I'll open your throat.'

He writhed in her grip and tried to reach for the trigger. Sonja pushed the blade a little deeper to still him and he groaned into her palm. 'I said drop it. Get on your knees.'

This time he complied. Sonja snatched up his rifle and put the barrel to the back of his head.

'Who are you?'

'National parks rangers. Anti-poaching.'

'You're not in uniform.'

'We are poor, the government has no money.'

'Bullshit,' Sonja said. 'Your clothes are new, as are your boots. Are you Charlie 10?'

The man started to turn his head and she caught the flash of confusion in his eyes.

'Give me your phone.'

He picked it up from the grass where he had dropped it, and Sonja saw his thumb start to tap the keys. She swung the AK-47 around and smashed the butt into the side of his head. The man dropped the phone and toppled sideways, unconscious or at least severely stunned.

Sonja checked the screen. The last message read, *Kill them.*

She scrolled up and saw the brief exchange. The owner of the phone had reported that he had the 'targets' in sight. Then the order to kill had been given. Whoever was after them, their intent was not to arrest them or take them alive. Sonja took out her phone and saw that Tema had replied to her earlier message, saying they were standing by.

Sonja tapped out a reply. *Targets hostile. Shoot to kill.*

The man groaned, pulled himself to his hands and knees and tried to stand. Sonja delivered a swift, vicious kick to his ribs. The man cried out and clutched his side. Sonja brought the rifle up to her shoulder and took aim between the man's eyes.

'In about thirty seconds your men are going to come in range of my people. I've given the order to take them out. As soon as the first shot's fired I'm going to kill you, unless you start talking now. Who sent you the message?'

The man blinked up at her. 'You're a woman.'

Sonja laughed. 'So, you think I won't kill you?'

The man shook his head. 'We were warned, you are a warrior. We were told not to underestimate you. But if you think you can stop the people who give me my orders – you, one woman – you are mistaken.'

Sonja took up the slack on the trigger. 'I don't need your shit. I need to know who they are. Zimbabwean? Chinese? Vietnamese?'

'Obert was my boss, the national parks warden you killed.'

'Is this a revenge attack, for Obert?'

The man shook his head. 'None of us liked him. He was our boss, but he was just a middleman. He took too big a share of the profits. We would have killed him eventually, or the higher-ups would have taken him out if they'd learned how he was robbing them.'

'OK, but who are these "higher-ups"? I need names.'

'I don't have their names. Obert met with them, not us.'

Sonja was frustrated. She wanted to get to Tema, Mario and Ezekial, to join them in the fight. However, there was much more to what was happening here than Ian Barton knew or had let on. Barton had thought Obert Mvuu was the local poaching kingpin, but now it seemed he was just another pawn.

'You're not helping me . . .'

'Alfred . . . I have a name. I have a wife, two children, please.'

'Yes, Alfred, and I have a daughter, and you would have happily left her without a mother, you piece of shit. I'm going to kill you now.'

He put up a hand, a stop gesture. 'Please. Obert mentioned something once, about "the Russian".'

'Male or female?'

'He did not say. I assumed it was a man. He said . . .' Alfred closed his eyes, concentrating on remembering a conversation, 'He said, "The Russian is flying back to Johannesburg to be with his other insects", or something like that.'

'Insects?'

'Some sort of insect. He actually said *rize.*'

'What language is that, Shona? What does it mean?'

'Yes, my language. It is the insect with the claws,' Alfred pronounced it as *craws*, 'and the sting in the tail.'

'Scorpion. That's an arachnid, Alfred, not an insect. I can see why you're a poacher, not a guide. How did Obert know the man was Russian?'

'Obert spoke that language; he was Ndebele and was trained in Russia with Joshua Nkomo's men as a fighter for the Chimurenga, the liberation war. He said it was good to talk Russian again.'

Russia's organised crime gangs had a foothold in Africa, so it wasn't beyond the bounds of possibility that the Scorpions were backed from there. Sonja pushed the tip of the barrel into the skin and bone between Alfred's eyes, forcing his head back. 'Give me more. A name.'

'I don't . . .'

'Goodbye, Alfred.'

'Wait, wait. I heard one name only. Obert called the man Nicholas, or something like that. The man corrected him – they spoke English for a little bit – his name was not Nicholas, but something similar. I could not hear the rest.'

'Who sent you the SMS just now, telling you to kill my team and me?'

Before the man could answer or stall they heard a burst of gunfire from the direction of Chitake Springs, the curtain-raiser on a chorus of shooting that followed. Sonja glanced towards where the noise came from, but all the while she kept her eye on Alfred, using her peripheral vision.

Alfred lunged, as she expected he would when he thought she wasn't watching him, and tried to grab his rifle back from her. Sonja pulled the trigger. He fell back, dead, his blood mixing with the red soil of Africa.

Sonja ran through the bush, rifle up, scanning the trees ahead for targets. The shooting had died down, but every now and then there was still a short burst or a single aimed shot.

She heard Mario calling out a target indication, saying there was a lone gunman behind a fallen tree. 'Seventy metres, one o'clock.'

She pictured the spot, based on where his voice had come from. She would be getting almost that close to the riverbank. Of the buffalo there remained only a cloud of bovine-scented dust rising in the wake of their panicked stampede.

Sonja had spent much of her lifetime, from her childhood in the Namibian bush on her parents' cattle farm through to her time in Botswana's Okavango Delta in her teens and then as an adult in war zones around the world, training her eyes to pick up movement and targets. She saw the rifle's barrel poke above a fallen tree. When the head popped up Sonja fired from behind.

'One dead enemy!' she called.

'Cease fire,' Mario said in reply.

Sonja ran to the man she had just shot, confirmed he was dead and kicked the rifle away from his body. The sound of a vehicle engine made her pause. It could have been one of the tourist trucks leaving but, when she concentrated, she could hear that it was getting louder. It sounded like the rattle of an old Land Rover.

She moved through the bush, weapon still up.

'Over here,' Mario said.

She passed a second, then a third dead man.

'Report,' Sonja said.

'Tema's hit.'

Sonja fought down fear that rose in her chest and constricted her heart and lungs. She found them. Ezekial had taken off his shirt and was tying it, tight, around Tema's left leg.

'I'm sorry, Sonja,' Tema said.

Sonja shook her head. 'Don't be. How bad is it?'

'Not serious,' Mario said, 'but she needs a doctor.'

Sonja spun and pointed her AK at the Land Rover that crashed over several saplings as it charged towards them. She relaxed, a little, when she saw that Ian Barton was at the wheel. He climbed out.

'I was on my way, to take you to the Mana Pools airstrip, when I heard the gunfire. I just got a call on the radio. The CIO are here and they're heading to the airstrip.'

'How do they know we're heading there?' Sonja asked.

He shrugged. 'One of my staff, maybe, or someone in national parks. We have to go, *now*.'

They lifted Tema into the back of the Land Rover and climbed in around her in the open cargo area. As Ian drove they passed two dead men. The toll was mounting, but Sonja felt no sense of achievement, even though the immediate threat to Julianne Clyde-Smith's Zambezi River lodge had been neutralised.

Mario interrupted her thoughts. 'What will you do if the CIO get to the airstrip first?'

'I'm not coming with you.'

'What?'

'You heard me,' she said.

Tema raised herself up on an elbow. 'You can't stay here, Sonja. We have to get back to South Africa.'

'*You* do. And get yourself looked after. Mario, make sure Paterson and Julianne send Tema to the best surgeon in Nelspruit. Ask for Dr Bongi.'

Mario nodded. 'Please, Sonja, if you stay here the CIO will get you.'

She shook her head. 'No. If they don't catch me here they'll have people waiting in Harare.'

Mario looked her in the eyes. 'What about us?'

Sonja knew he was thinking about what had happened last night. Nothing like that was going to happen again. She'd had too much to drink, but the fact was she would not have slept with him if she had any intention of them continuing to work together. 'We're through.'

'What do you mean, Sonja?' Ezekial asked.

'This business is finished. I'm quitting, and this anti-poaching unit no longer exists. Mario, you can tell Julianne, if I can't reach her by phone first.'

Tema winced, but Sonja was sure it wasn't just because of the bullet wound. 'Sonja, please.'

'No,' Sonja said. 'We've been set up from the beginning. If Julianne wants a black ops hit squad then I'm not going to command it. We were told we'd be used for surveillance and reconnaissance, and instead we've been dropped into one fire-fight after another.'

Mario put a hand on her forearm. 'Sonja . . .'

She shrugged off his touch. 'I told you, it's *over*. All of it.' Sonja looked to Tema and Ezekial. 'I'll give you both good references, and if I get back to South Africa I'll do my best to see that you both find good jobs, assuming you want to stay in anti-poaching.'

Sonja banged on the roof of the Land Rover's cab.

Ian Barton stopped the vehicle and craned his head out of the driver's side window. 'What is it?'

Before the others could begin to explain to Ian what had happened, Sonja had disappeared, into the African bush.

PART 2

The Day

I ngwe stretched and yawned, stood and shifted her position on the wide branch high in her favourite sycamore fig tree. From her vantage point she surveyed her domain, a large swathe of the Sabi Sand Game Reserve.

It was daylight, the sun high and hot, and the leaves of the tree bathed her in dappled shadows. The breeze ruffled her whiskers.

She settled on her belly, full from another impala, and rested her chin on a paw. But sleep did not come.

Instinctively, as soon as she heard the unfamiliar noise she lowered her ears and squeezed her body into the bark to minimise her profile. Through golden eyes she watched the human.

He moved slowly, cautiously, swinging his long arm from side to side, hunting. As careful as he was, the twig he had stepped on had been enough to alert Ingwe, for she was a far better hunter, a more efficient killer than this man could ever be.

Ahead of the man was Mkhumbi, the rhino, a dim-witted creature if ever there was one. He could barely see and while his hearing was good he was too engrossed in chomping the grass with his big wide mouth to hear the human sneaking up on him.

Mkhumbi relied on his sheer size to protect him from Ngala, the hated lions who roamed the veld in big prides or in coalitions of males. But Mkhumbi, like all of them, had to be wary of humans. Trouble was, for all his size and brute strength the rhino was generally as docile as the Nguni cows that grazed outside of the reserve, where Ingwe, if she was feeling hungry or mischievous, would sometimes wander in search of a tasty goat or calf.

The man stopped, within visual distance of Mkhumbi. He raised and steadied his long arm. It bucked in his hands, but the sound was not loud, as it often was, more a cough that carried on the soft breeze and made Ingwe settle yet lower onto the branch. The rhino took a few paces, staggered and fell onto its chest, raising a cloud of dust as it hit the ground.

Mostly, these things happened at night, occasionally interfering with Ingwe's nocturnal forays.

And now, something even stranger happened. The machine arrived overhead, its blades clattering and whirring, blowing dust and leaves and twigs and rocking the boughs around Ingwe. The machine settled in a small grassy clearing and the man with the long arm, clutching Mkhumbi's freshly sawn horn, ran to it, climbed in, and then disappeared into the sky.

Odd, very odd.

Ingwe settled again, chin on paw, and slept, as the flies settled on Mkhumbi's lifeless body.

Chapter 15

Hudson Brand had been driving for four days and had crossed into Malawi from Chipata, Zambia, at dawn. His left leg was cramping again so he pulled over. The distance he could drive without a break was getting shorter by the year.

He was a long way from South Africa and, as good as it was to be out on the road in Africa again, this was no holiday. He hoped his journey wouldn't be a waste of time; already the cost of fuel had eaten a crocodile-sized chunk out of his meagre bank account.

From his home near the Kruger Park he had driven north to Musina and crossed the notoriously chaotic border at Beitbridge into Zimbabwe. The country was still on its knees, economically, thanks to its ill-thought-out land redistribution program. Between two and three million Zimbabweans were living legally and illegally in South Africa, having fled their home for the promise of work across the border. Those who didn't queue for hours at Beitbridge waded through the Limpopo River, dodging military and police patrols.

By contrast, when he crossed the Kariba Dam wall from Zimbabwe into Zambia it became evident how quickly a country's fortunes could change with the benefit of just a few years of stable, relatively democratic government. Many of the commercial farmers who had been kicked off their farms in Zimbabwe had migrated north, and Zambia's agricultural sector had been brought back to booming life in a few short years, creating prosperity and jobs.

Hudson climbed down from his old Land Rover, stretched and walked around the vehicle to take a piss, something that was almost impossible to do without company in Malawi. In this poverty-stricken country the roads weren't congested with traffic, but rather with people walking or cycling everywhere. It wasn't more than thirty seconds before he heard the ding of a bicycle bell. As he zipped up he waved to the cyclist, a man in a threadbare suit and a natty purple tie who trundled slowly by.

He got back into the Land Rover and continued driving. The air was warm, the sun bright, and occasionally he glimpsed Lake Malawi on his right. Eventually he came to the turnoff he'd been looking for to Makuzi Beach. He took it and followed three kilometres of winding sand road.

Hudson had no idea if she would be there. Sonja's team had returned to the Sabi Sand Game Reserve. He'd been to see Tema at the Mediclinic hospital in Nelspruit, where she had spent a night following relatively minor surgery before being allowed to leave. She was already up and walking. Neither she nor Ezekial knew where Sonja had gone and nor had they heard from her. Hudson avoided contacting Mario.

Village huts and straggly crops gave way to lawn and palm trees as Hudson approached the beachside lodge and camping ground which, fortunately, contained only one vehicle, a rented four-by-four with South African registration.

Hudson stopped outside the reception building and got out. There was no one around. He checked his watch: lunchtime.

He walked past an office and through an open-walled bar to a bleached timber deck.

In front of him was a white sandy beach dotted with rocks and a few grass-thatched umbrellas. A banda, a simple structure of four poles supporting a bed-sized raised platform topped with a grass roof, held the only evidence of habitation – a brightly printed kanga, a woman's wrap, a T-shirt and pair of shorts hanging over the railing around the platform.

Hudson walked down the stairs to the beach and kicked off his sandals. The white sand was warm and squeaky underfoot. He raised a hand to shield his eyes and saw a figure swimming, out near a small rocky outcrop in the lake.

As he walked towards the water's edge the person turned towards shore. Fifty metres out, where the water obviously became too shallow to accommodate her powerful stroke, she stopped and stood, and Hudson felt like her hand was around his heart, giving it a little squeeze.

She mirrored his stance, shielding her eyes, and stood there, silhouetted against the water that shone a shimmery blue-grey under the sun's glare. She was wearing a simple black bikini, her hair tied back in her trademark ponytail; sporty, sexy. Hudson kept walking until he was in the water up to his knees, where he stopped.

Sonja started walking again but also stopped, two metres from him, hands on her hips. 'What the fuck are you doing here, Brand?'

He smiled. 'That's one of the many things I like about you, Kurtz.'

'What?'

'Your manners.'

'Am I supposed to just fall into your arms?'

He rubbed the stubble on his chin with two fingers. 'Hmm, nice thought. A simple howzit would probably suffice.'

'How did you find me?'

'I have my sources.'

'Emma's the only person who knew where I was. And I told her not to tell anyone.'

Hudson had got on well with Sonja's daughter in the short time he'd known her. 'Don't blame her, I told her that you were in danger.'

'Am I?'

'Maybe. You're hiding.'

'I don't hide from anyone.'

'Licking your wounds then, like a lioness.'

'I trusted Julianne Clyde-Smith but she dropped me and my people into one firefight too many. I like being in control.' Her mouth turned up, just a little, at one corner. He remembered that half-smile. He liked it. Also, while she maintained her pose, it seemed to him as though she had relaxed, just a little.

'There's stuff I want to talk to you about; the Scorpions, Julianne, but all that can wait.'

'Are you here to apologise?'

'I didn't do anything wrong, Sonja.'

She stared him in the eye. 'Did you sleep with Sannie van Rensburg, or that journalist woman, Appleton?'

'No.'

'OK.'

He didn't know what he had expected, maybe for her to be madder at him, or not believe him, or turn him away. Maybe she'd had a change of heart.

'So?'

'So what?' he asked.

'What's the other stuff you wanted to talk to me about?'

It was as close as he'd get to an apology from her for misunderstanding him, for walking out. He took the two steps needed to close the gap between them, took hold of her wrists and drew her arms around him until she relented, and held him properly.

She felt cool and wet against him as her body moulded into his, but her mouth was warm and inviting. It felt like coming home, a concept fairly unfamiliar to Hudson Brand. The long drive, the tedious border crossings, their fights mattered not at all.

Sonja wrinkled her nose. 'You stink.'

He held her tighter then tried to pull her down, into the water. As he'd expected she threw him, like an unarmed combat instructor had done to him at Ranger School in the US Army, and he fell, laughing, into the clear fresh water of Lake Malawi.

He came up spluttering and reached for her again. Sonja took his hand and allowed herself to be dragged down into the water with him, where they embraced again and moved, in unison, kissing all the while, to where it was deep enough for them to float together, as one.

When they took a break from their kissing, he couldn't tell how long it had been, she nuzzled into his neck as he looked down. The sunlight caught countless tiny grains of mica that glittered the colour of gold in pale sand sculpted into flawless tiny dune lines. They called it the Lake of Stars, but right now, with this strong-willed, slightly bruised woman in his arms, he was as close to paradise as he reckoned he'd ever get.

Sonja broke their embrace, eventually, and stood and led him out of the water, across the sand to the bungalow where she had been staying.

He walked in and saw her clothes and things scattered about the room. He missed that feminine clutter in the house where he lived.

They kissed again, moving in lock step to the bed. Hudson lay her down and looked at her, savouring the sight and the memory of her as he got out of his wet clothes. She undid her bikini top and he dropped to one knee. Those nipples.

He kissed one, gently sucking, revelling in the feel of it swelling under the touch of his tongue. Sonja wrapped her fingers in his hair and he moved to her other breast. Slowly, he kissed his way down her belly and she lifted her hips so he could slide her pants down. He climbed up onto the bed.

Hudson kissed the inside of her thighs, where the skin was so soft, and felt her fingers again urging him on. He'd missed her, missed this, and his body was yearning for hers.

Sonja positioned herself and guided him so that he was on his side next to her, she on her back, legs drawn up. They lay like that, staring into each other's eyes, and she smiled.

'I've missed you,' he said.

'I'm sorry.'

'It's fine.'

He reached out and teased her nipple with his fingers as he moved, rhythmically in and out of her. She moved a hand between her legs and began stroking herself as he kept going. Hudson loved this feeling, so close to the edge but deliberately not tipping over, and felt, wished, it could go on like this for the rest of the day, the rest of the night, the rest of his life.

In time, though, her breathing changed, now coming in short gasps. He felt her body start to stiffen.

She closed her eyes, but her nods told him to keep going. He bucked his hips, faster now, and moved his fingers from her nipple so that he could wrap an arm around her as she shuddered to her climax with him inside her.

After catching her breath she opened her eyes, and looked to him again and nodded.

Hudson needed no urging. He closed his eyes, surrendering to the pure, primal need deep inside him. When he was done and his breathing had returned to something approaching normal he spooned her. He kissed the back of her neck.

'I love you,' he said, for the first time, not even thinking before saying the words.

'Ja,' she said. 'Same.'

*

Sonja lay propped up on one elbow on the bed, the sheet half covering her. Hudson was on his back, lightly snoring. The afternoon sun was behind them, shining out onto the lake, turning it a silvery grey. The horizon blurred with the sky so that she could hardly tell where it was.

She didn't know where this would go, with Hudson, but right now she had the very rare feeling of truly being in the moment, and not caring what was over the horizon, let alone where it was.

He stirred and blinked. 'What time is it?'

'Three.'

'I'm sorry I fell asleep.'

She reached out a hand and stroked his cheek with the back of her fingers. 'It's OK, you must have been tired from all the driving.'

'A little . . . and the workout.'

'Oh, yes, that was quite exhausting.'

He turned his head and kissed her fingers. The touch of his lips electrified her, all over again.

'How did you get here?' he asked.

'I crossed illegally from Zimbabwe to Zambia, over the Zambezi River in a canoe I "borrowed". I caught minibus taxis through Zambia to Luangwa Bridge and then hitched a lift with an English couple in a rented four-by-four. They left here yesterday. At the Zambian border, at Chipata, I told the immigration and customs people I'd lost my passport, but had another one – they let me go through and then I entered Malawi legally.'

'You're incredible.'

She waved her hand in dismissal. It wasn't the first time she'd crossed a border illegally. 'So tell me, what brought you all the way here, apart from what we just did – not that I'm complaining, mind you.'

'You're enough. But I'm also working an investigation and a lot of the questions I'm asking are leading me towards Julianne Clyde-Smith. I'm hoping you can help me.'

'Go on.'

Hudson propped himself up on one elbow. 'The poaching and the war against it is escalating in the Sabi Sand, Sonja. Since you've been away there have been four rhino killed on three different properties.'

She shrugged. 'The battle's a long way from being won. The poachers move from reserve to reserve, park to park.'

'This is more than just cyclical. I'm convinced of it. The latest attacks all happened in properties bordering Khaya Ngala. Julianne Clyde-Smith has been talking tough in the media, locally and internationally, telling the world that she's got a zero tolerance for poaching and how she's staked her professional reputation on not losing another rhino.'

'Big call, and a stupid one,' Sonja said.

'She's using her tough stance on poaching as a marketing tool. In her interviews she's talked about bringing in ex-military people to train locals and help them take the war to poachers, wherever she has lodges. The news of the shootout in Zimbabwe broke on Facebook and went viral. She hasn't mentioned you by name, but she's out there boasting about the body count. Julianne's a public hero.'

Sonja thought about Hudson's news; she'd deliberately stayed away from internet news sites and only used Facebook briefly to message Emma, to let her know she was alive and well. 'Julianne's waging an information war as well as using boots on the ground.'

'Yes. She's also announced she's buying Lion Plains.'

'They had a bad run of poaching incidents prior to my arrival in South Africa.'

'Yep,' Hudson said. 'I went back through the stats on rhino poaching for the last couple of years. Lion Plains lost only two rhinos in that period until March this year. Their anti-poaching efforts seemed to be no better or worse than anyone else's, but in the last six months they lost seven.'

Sonja nodded. 'The Leopards were formed because of the spike in rhino killings in that area. We were having some success with aggressive patrolling.'

'Yes.' Hudson reached to the side table for a water bottle, which he offered to Sonja. She took it and had a sip and passed it back to him. 'And then you came up against a full-scale incursion by poachers armed with an RPD light machine gun – unheard of up until now – and a gang that seemed intent on taking out your patrol and a national parks helicopter.'

Sonja had realised the attack on her all-female unit was unusual, weaponry included, but she hadn't made the connection with the recent history of rhino losses in that part of the Sabi Sand reserve. 'You think the Scorpions were targeting that lodge, and us, deliberately?'

'I can't say for sure,' Hudson said, 'but the numbers don't stack up. They don't have any more rhino in that part of the reserve than any other section, though now they have a heck of a lot fewer, and they were still being targeted.'

'Were?'

'I checked,' Hudson took a swig from the water bottle, 'not a single report of a rhino lost or contact with poachers since that night when your girls were killed. Contrast that to the last few months.'

Sonja thought about the situation she'd walked into when she'd taken on the role of training the Leopards. The owners of the Lion Plains lodge had made no secret of the fact that they were losing the battle against poaching and that the negative publicity they were receiving was affecting bookings. 'No contacts with poachers since Julianne Clyde-Smith's offer to buy the lodge was accepted.'

'Bingo.'

Sonja slotted the pieces together in her mind. 'So Julianne, what, protects her property like Fort Knox and to hell with her neighbours? She hasn't lost any rhino in the last couple of years, has she?'

'No. The word behind the scenes in the Sabi Sand is that Julianne is rubbing a lot of people up the wrong way. She doesn't exactly have a reputation as a team player, and it's not only Lion Plains that's been losing rhinos. Remember, these animals are free ranging throughout the Sabi Sand, so if a neighbouring property loses a rhino then that's an animal that won't be wandering onto Julianne's patch again.'

'Even without Julianne's help, the work the Leopards were doing and other security measures Lion Plains put in place were having an impact,' Sonja said. 'They told me that the publicity they were receiving, worldwide, by having an all-female unit in the field had actually boosted their bookings for a while, but they didn't have the training to take the fight to the enemy. That's why I was called in.'

'How did Lion Plains find you?'

Sonja propped herself up against the bedhead with a pillow. 'There's an NGO in the UK that lines up ex-military people from overseas to mentor and train anti-poaching units. Friend of mine runs it.'

'You and your Leopards could have driven up the purchase price of Lion Plains,' Hudson said. 'It was a basket case, poaching-wise, until you came along.'

'So the best way to take me out of the picture was to give me a job. That way I couldn't convince Lion Plains to carry on with the Leopards. Damn.'

'I'm guessing, of course, but maybe she thought it was better to have you inside her tent pissing out, than outside pissing in.'

'Crude, but accurate,' Sonja said. 'I feel used.'

Sonja thought about the chain of events since the night she and Tema and the others had been ambushed, the string of gunfights, and how they might be related, if they weren't a series of one-off encounters. She'd been in actual war zones where she'd seen less action than she had since returning to Africa. 'What do you know about the Scorpions?'

'A little more than I did since the last time I saw you. Rosie gave me some info.'

Sonja felt herself bridle instantly at mention of the other woman's name, though she realised she had no right to think badly of Hudson after what had happened between her and Mario. She regretted few things in her life, but that was one of them. While Hudson had been sleeping Sonja had toyed with the idea of telling him about Mario, but she didn't want to hurt him. It had been her mistake and she would have to live with it. She chose to believe Hudson when he said that he had not, in fact, slept with Rosie or Sannie.

'Ian Barton, Julianne's lodge manager in Zimbabwe, filled me in some more.'

'So,' Hudson said after they had swapped notes on the shadowy poaching organisation, 'Julianne Clyde-Smith is at war with the Scorpions and using you to spearhead her attack, but she may also be working a strategy that leaves some lodges or properties vulnerable to increased poaching, which she then uses to her advantage.'

Sonja had already come to the same hypothesis. 'This is crazy. If it's true, we have an internationally renowned businesswoman with more money than she knows what do with acting like a gangster, standing over people to break their family business when it doesn't suit her. And at the very least, she put the lives of my people at risk, not to mention mine,' Sonja said. 'I want to look her in the eye and find out why, exactly.'

'There's more news from home. Tema's in Tanzania, along with Ezekial and Mario.'

'What the hell are they doing there?' Sonja had declared the unit disbanded and while she didn't control the other members of the team she was surprised they seemed to have stayed together.

'Your guess is as good as mine, but from what I can work out Julianne Clyde-Smith and her head of security James Paterson are up there as well.'

'She's got three lodges in Tanzania, I saw it in her glossy self-published coffee table book at Khaya Ngala.'

'Yup, and guess what?' Hudson said.

Sonja gritted her teeth, then said, 'She's shopping for more property.'

'Yup.'

'She's called me half a dozen times this week, and emailed me, wanting to know where I am. I haven't replied,' Sonja said. 'I was finished with her.'

'Was?'

'I don't mind going into battle, but if someone's putting me and my people in danger without telling me why I'm fighting, I get annoyed.'

Hudson half smiled. 'I've seen you annoyed.'

She ignored his flippancy. 'I was told we were being used to gather intelligence, by conducting close target reconnaissance missions and working undercover.'

'And instead,' Hudson said, completing her thought, 'you and your people have been used in some anti-poaching version of Operation Phoenix. You know about that, right?'

Sonja nodded. 'Your CIA used assassins during the Vietnam War to target Vietnamese civilians suspected of being high-level Viet Cong cadres and sympathisers. People were wrongly accused by informers who were looking to get even with them for whatever reason, and innocent people were killed.'

'Yep,' Hudson said. 'Julianne's playing with fire.'

What burned Sonja was that she had been used and that was unacceptable.

'They're working a strategy,' Hudson said, also thinking aloud. 'I've been talking to the security people in the Sabi Sand and some of the lodges. Julianne offers the services of Paterson and her anti-poaching people and helicopter to some lodges, but not to others. They're funnelling the poaching gangs into corridors through the reserve –'

'Leading them straight to Lion Plains, which is behind on its security levies because it's going out of business.'

Sonja got up and walked across the bungalow's floor to the window. She stood there, naked, looking out over the lake. 'That looks like smoke, across the lake. Fire.'

Hudson got out of bed and came up behind her, wrapping his arm around her body, drawing her to him. 'It's not smoke. Believe it or not, those black clouds are actually flies.'

She turned her head to look up at him. 'Serious?'

'Yep. Lake flies. Millions of them. Fishermen on the lake have been known to be suffocated by those swarms, which fill their mouths and noses.'

'I've never heard of them.' Sonja was tempted to add that choking on a swarm of flies was a terrible way to die, but there were few good ones. She knew. Even in this staggeringly beautiful corner of Africa, death and darkness were never far away.

'I need to talk to Tema, and I want to learn more about exactly what Julianne and Paterson are up to. Tema and Ezekial don't know what they've got themselves into and I don't want them selling their souls for Julianne Clyde-Smith's cash without understanding what that job will do to them.'

'If Julianne is running a hit squad then Mario Machado's the right man for the job,' Hudson said. 'What was it like working with him?'

Sonja hoped her embarrassment didn't show, but just in case she looked back out at the clouds of flies that were coalescing and moving along the lake like a mini storm front. 'Professional, though I did notice he had a tendency to shoot first and ask questions later.' She needed to change this conversation, or rather get back to the salient point. 'I want to find Tema, and Clyde-Smith.'

'Like I said, they're in Tanzania.'

Sonja gave him a half-grin. 'Just across the border from Malawi. There's a crossing near the northern tip of the lake. Fancy a road trip?'

'With you? You bet.'

Hudson kissed the back of her neck and she reached around behind him and pulled him even closer. She dug her fingers into his skin, which was still warm from being in bed.

'It won't be all play, Hudson.'

'Well, we don't have to leave right away, do we?'

Chapter 16

The rush of air into the back of the helicopter snatched at Tema's green uniform shirt and adrenaline surged through her body as the Tanzania National Parks – TANAPA – ranger with them pointed to the four men running across the grassy plain below.

Mario was up front in the co-pilot's seat and he directed the pilot to sweep around the targets. Mario looked back at Tema, Ezekial and the ranger. They had been searching the Grumeti Game Reserve since the call for assistance had come to Julianne Clyde-Smith from the Fort Ikoma gate and ranger post southwest of Julianne's camp in the Kuria Hills.

Tema pictured the map Mario had shown her before they took off. The Serengeti National Park resembled, she thought, a musleman holding up his left arm, bent at ninety degrees, viewed from the front. The Grumeti reserve, where private safari operators leased concessions from the Tanzanian government, was a narrow strip of land that ran across the bodybuilder's bicep. The annual wildebeest migration was busy crossing this area and would re-enter the park at the imaginary man's forearm.

Julianne and her people had been scouting the reserve, looking for locations for a proposed new tented camp. At the same time, she, Mario and Ezekial had been working with the TANAPA people on anti-poaching patrols, searching for a gang of elephant ivory poachers who had been working in the area. Tema had thought that when Sonja left them in Zimbabwe that she would once more be out of a job, but Julianne had offered command of the team to Mario. Tema wasn't happy Sonja had gone, but she needed the money that was still on offer.

'We've got them. We'll give them a chance to surrender,' Mario yelled to them.

Tema leaned out of the door hatch. She was surprised how much she had learned to love flying in such a short period of time. She followed Mario's lead and cocked the AK-47 she had been issued. The TANAPA ranger in the middle, and Ezekial on the other side, did the same. Ezekial, she noticed with a glance, was still terrified of being airborne.

She gave Ezekial a reassuring smile. She had gone home to her mother and Shine after being released from hospital. Ezekial had come to visit her every day. They had been out on a few dates and while they had kissed, many times, they had not had sex. Ezekial had made no secret of his desires, but Tema wanted to take things slower than she had with the first man she had slept with. He respected her wishes and told her he would wait as long as it took.

The pilot came abreast of the fugitives, flaring the nose of the chopper to slow it to their running pace. The men had already ditched the four tusks they were carrying. At least two of them were armed, one with what looked like a hunting rifle, the other with an AK.

Two of the men, the bearers, stopped and put their hands up.

'They're surrendering,' Tema said.

But then the man with the AK raised his rifle and fired a long burst at them.

Tema's training kicked in and she took aim and squeezed off three rounds. The pilot pulled up on the collective, causing her to miss. All the men started running again, though.

'Go back, go back,' Mario screamed into the intercom, but this pilot, a Tanzanian local, clearly had less stomach for the fight than Julianne's regular pilot, Doug Pearse had when flying. 'Turn around or I'll have you fired!'

Reluctantly the pilot wheeled around. Tema had heard that another flier had been killed by poachers recently so the man's trepidation was understandable. She, too, felt the fear, but her desire to get the man who had just shot at them – at her – was stronger. She also wanted to get back into the fray.

By the time they had circled around, the poachers had made it to a granite koppie a cluster of boulders studded with trees that stood out like an island in the sea of grass.

'Shit,' Mario said, 'they could be hiding anywhere in there.'

They circled a few times, all of them straining to see any sign of movement. Mario fired a few random shots into crevices, hoping to draw fire from the poachers or panic them into surrendering or running. It didn't work.

Mario looked over his shoulder again. 'The only way to get these bastards is on foot. Are you game?'

'I think we must return to Fort Ikoma, to get more men,' the ranger said, over the noise of the engine.

Ezekial looked to Tema. She spoke, loud and clear. 'We go!'

'Yes,' said Mario. He looked to the pilot. 'Put us down. Orbit above us. You,' he said to the ranger, 'be ready to give us covering fire if these guys show themselves.'

The ranger nodded and Ezekial swallowed bile and bravely winked at Tema. He was as ready for the fight as she was. She could see it in his eyes, and right then she saw the warrior in him and knew she wanted him to be her man, the father of her daughter, if he wanted them.

Tema had been talking to Sonja by phone and instant message and she had been quietly watching Mario and their superiors, gathering intelligence for her former mentor. Sonja had ordered Tema to tell no one that she and Hudson were investigating Julianne Clyde-Smith's dealings, but Tema thought it was now time to let Ezekial in on the secret. On the other hand, Sonja had drilled into her the need to follow orders.

The pilot brought the chopper down, and when the skids were just a metre off the ground Tema, Mario and Ezekial jumped out. As Sonja had taught them, Tema and Ezekial took a couple of paces and dived into the grass, rifles out. The helicopter lifted off above them and peeled away.

'Up,' Mario yelled.

They moved in bounds, one running while the other two covered him or her. Tema was moving slower than the men because of her healing bullet wound, but her heart was still pounding as the granite boulders loomed larger in her vision. At any moment she expected to hear the *pop-pop* of an AK-47 or the deeper *crack-thump* of a heavy-calibre slug. She tried not to think of what they would do to her body, though she had already experienced firsthand what bullets could do.

Tema had her rifle up, safety off and her finger outside the trigger guard. When they were twenty metres from the koppie Mario used hand signals to tell her to prop, to get down on one knee and cover him and Ezekial.

She knew Mario was telling her to stay and keep watch because of her leg; nevertheless, she felt mildly cheated. Ezekial looked to her and grinned. This was scary, terrifying in fact, but they were so pumped up they were both enjoying themselves. Tema told herself that covering the men and watching for movement was just as important as the work they were doing.

Tema scanned the shiny pinkish rocks. She caught sight of a flash of movement near the crest of the outcrop and trained her rifle left. She had taken up half the pressure on the trigger and almost squeezed all the way, until she saw the dainty little grey antelope that had leapt from one rock to another. It was a klipspringer – she knew from her studies that these little bucks had circular hooves that acted like suction cups to help them gain purchase on the rocks they liked to inhabit. The klipspringer looked down at her, apparently at ease, but as it rotated its head something else startled it and it took off, bounding from boulder to boulder.

To the right of where the animal had been and in the direction where it had last looked, Tema saw another movement, the bobbing of a head. She moved slowly, at a crouch, through grass, until she had a better view of the far side of the boulder where she had seen the man.

Tema took aim at the spot and waited. From the other side of the koppie Mario called out something to Ezekial. The head appeared again and Tema confirmed it was one of the armed men, the one with the hunting rifle. He would be the member of the gang who was responsible for actually killing the elephants. He was taking aim, at Mario or at Ezekial. Tema took a breath, steadied herself and exhaled partially. The back right rear of the man's skull was in her sights. She squeezed the trigger.

'Contact front,' she yelled as she fired, the words rushing from her like a machine venting air. The man's head was no longer visible. She heard a clatter and saw the rifle slide down over the smooth surface of a boulder and bounce down to the rock below.

Tema was up now, racing to the foot of the little hill and scrabbling up the first rocks.

'Talk to me,' Mario called.

'One tango down.' Tema wanted to tell Mario that she was on the move, but she didn't want to alert the poachers, as well. In xiTsonga she called out: 'Ezekial, I'm climbing the rocks, cover me, but don't advance.'

'Affirmative,' Ezekial called back.

Tema was on her own now, climbing, and the adrenaline was charging her with what seemed like superhuman strength. Sonja had put the Leopards through a military-style obstacle course that she had ordered constructed, and one of the challenges was to walk along a set of high bars with cross rungs spread a metre or so apart. Sonja had told them that getting over this obstacle was all about confidence. Tema moved the way she had then, keeping her head and eyes up, looking ahead for targets, not down at her feet and ignoring the odd twinge of pain from her healing wound. She trusted her mind and body to work together and she stepped purposefully from rock to rock just as the klipspringer had, by instinct.

She saw a man's back flit past the gap between two boulders. Tema raised her rifle, but wasn't quick enough. Also, she didn't know if the man was the remaining one with the gun or one of the unarmed bearers. She forced herself forward. Now that she'd seen another of the poachers her feet started to feel heavy. Something inside her was telling her to duck down, to take cover, but Sonja had told her that at times like this she had to fall back on her training and her heart.

'My heart?' she had asked.

'You have the heart of a hunter, of a leopard,' Sonja had told her. 'Listen to it, give in to it.'

Tema felt, heard the beat, like a war drum that pushed her onwards. She jumped to the top of the next rock and looked down. A man scurried beneath her. He was unarmed, but she saw the fallen man's rifle, on a granite ledge beneath her. The man scrambled over the slippery rocks.

'Stop!'

He froze and glanced over his shoulder.

'I said stop.'

Even though she was pointing a gun at him the man just sneered at her and kept crawling. Tema trained the barrel of her AK-47 on his back. When his hand touched the wooden stock of the hunting rifle she squeezed the trigger. The weapon bucked twice and the man sprawled forward. He slid down the face of the rock, taking the rifle with him and leaving a long smear of blood.

Tema didn't feel anything, other than the need to move on, to finish the job. She hopped to the next rock, searching for a new target. Gunfire echoed around her and she dropped into a slide, down the long sloping face of a granite boulder.

When her boots met firm ground again she looked left and right, searching for another target. She saw a movement and a man, startled by the noise behind him, turned and started to raise his arm as if bringing a weapon to bear.

Tema brought the AK-47 to her shoulder and pulled the trigger. Instead of the first of the two shots, the double tap, that she'd intended to fire, she heard a sickening click. She was sure she was not out of ammunition so her rifle had jammed.

Sonja had drilled the procedure for this into all of the Leopards countless times, on the rifle range and before their first patrol. Tema ducked behind the nearest rock, grasped the rifle's cocking handle and pulled it back to find the source of the problem, either a double feed of two rounds into the chamber, or a dud round.

Tema fully expected the man she had aimed at to run, or, worse, to open fire in her general direction. Instead, she heard an animalistic wail. When she peeked around the rock she was confronted with the sight of the looming bulk of one of the bearers. In his hand, held aloft, was a panga, a wicked-looking machete, and not the gun she had mistakenly thought he was carrying.

Before Tema could shake free the misfed or damaged rounds, the man was on her. She held her AK up in two hands and the force of the downward blow of the machete clanging on the steel of her rifle jarred up her arms. She smelled the man's body odour, saw the wild killer look in his jaundiced eyes.

The man barrelled into her, pushing her against a rock. As he raised his hand to deliver another slashing stroke she sidestepped, reversed the AK-47 and rammed the steel butt plate up at the man's jaw.

She had only landed a glancing blow, but it was enough to snap his head back and stop his arm. Tema shook the rifle and frantically tried to chamber another round, but he came at her again, slashing wildly. The blade dinged on her barrel again and slid down the metal, digging into a finger on her left hand. She yelled with pain and let go of her weapon. The man seized his momentary advantage and pushed his bulk into her. He used his fist, clasped around the hilt of the panga, to punch her in the face.

The father of Tema's daughter had hit her, when she was pregnant, which was why she had left him and she felt the rage inside her rise and erupt out of her as her attacker's foul breath washed over her. As Sonja had taught her, she let the adrenaline take care of the pain and allowed her suppressed hatred to guide her. Controlled violence, that was what it was all about, Sonja had said.

Tema brought her right knee up as hard and as fast as she could into the man's groin, and when he started to double up she stabbed him with two fingers in his eyes. As he screamed she pushed harder and harder.

As the man staggered and tried to back away from her, Tema grabbed her rifle with two hands again, this time with both at the barrel end, and swung the AK-47 around like a club in a wide arc. When she connected with the side of the groaning man's head he dropped his panga and toppled over. He didn't move.

Tema stood there, over him, panting. She cleared her rifle, let the working parts fly forward and, for a second, aimed it at his head, her finger around the trigger.

A burst of gunfire nearby made her look away from the unconscious poacher. She swung the gun around when she saw movement at the top of a rock, but lowered it a fraction of a second later.

'Don't shoot, it's me,' Ezekial said.

'This one is out cold,' she said.

'So I see.' Ezekial climbed over the rock and came to her. 'You're bleeding. Are you OK?'

Tema looked at her hand. The cut was deep, but she felt no pain, not yet anyway. 'I'll be fine.'

'All the same, let me bandage it.'

Tema stood there, physically shaking.

Ezekial put his rifle down, pulled the field dressing from his chest pouch and wrapped the pad and bandage around her finger and hand. 'I got one, as well.'

'Good for you.'

'Yes. He went down like a sack of mealie meal. It was the one with the AK-47. He got off a few shots at me, but I drilled him, one-time.'

Mario appeared through a cleft, a handheld radio pressed to his ear. 'Bring the chopper now. You don't need to worry for your safety or your precious aircraft. We've got them all. I say again, the poachers are all dead. Out.'

Tema heard the helicopter's engine and looked up. It was circling around, coming towards them. The pilot hadn't even been game to orbit above, offering them support from the ranger on board as Mario had directed. She was disgusted with his cowardice.

Ezekial knelt by the unconscious bearer. 'This one's still alive, Mario, but he needs medical help.'

'Move away from him,' Mario said.

'I need to check that head wound first, and we have to carry him down the koppie to the chopper.'

'I said get away.'

Ezekial looked up at Mario, who was bringing his AK-47 to bear. 'Hey, what are you doing?'

'I'm not going to tell you again.'

'No!'

Mario pulled the trigger. One shot.

Ezekial yelped, then stood unsteadily and wiped droplets of blood from his face. 'What . . .' He stared down at the dead man, then to Mario and, finally, Tema. 'What have you done? You murdered him, in cold blood.'

Ezekial looked skywards, put his hands in his hair, doubled over and vomited. Tema looked away.

Mario flicked his safety catch to safe and looked at Ezekial. 'He tried to kill your girlfriend with a panga. In any case, he was unconscious. He didn't feel a thing.'

Ezekial wiped his eyes and mouth with the back of his hand. 'Tema?'

Tema tried to steady her nerves. Right now she was terrified of what Mario might do if she showed what he perceived to be weakness. She bit her tongue.

Ezekial stared at her.

'Enough of this,' Mario said. 'We have more work to do.'

Ezekial bent down, retrieved his rifle and started to climb down from the rocks.

'Ezekial?' Tema called.

Mario walked over and stood next to her. He put his hand on her shoulder and although it creeped her out a bit she didn't flinch. 'Don't worry about Ezekial. He'll get over it.'

'I'm not so sure,' she said. 'He's very religious. His father's a bishop.'

'You did well today, very well.'

'I was well trained,' Tema said. 'No offence, Mario, but I miss Sonja.'

He removed his hand and knelt and picked up the panga next to the dead man. When he straightened he said: 'I miss her too.'

'What would you do if she came back?'

Mario seemed to ponder the question. 'I don't need to be the commander of this team. I'm happy to take orders from Sonja, but I'm not sure she has the stomach for this fight any more. I heard she killed the man who was responsible for the death of her partner, but that was a personal vendetta. I don't think her heart's in this war, like it is for you and me.'

He was reaching out to her, which was good. If she could gain and keep his confidence she might glean more information from him for Sonja about what Julianne Clyde-Smith was up to. 'Make no mistake, I'm here for the money, as well as my love of wildlife. I have a daughter to raise and I want the best for her.'

'In that respect, in many others, you are very like Sonja. She should be proud of you.'

'Thank you.'

'Will you talk to Ezekial for me, tonight, see how he is feeling?'

'Why? Do you care?'

'I wouldn't want him to do anything foolish, like talk to the wrong people about what he saw here today.'

Tema looked Mario in the eye. 'You want me to make sure he doesn't do that? He knows what he saw.'

'Yes, and I know what I saw – you shooting that other guy in the back.'

'He was going for the hunting rifle and he ignored my order for him to stop.'

'I know that and you know that, but if the Tanzanian police were of a mind to do a thorough investigation they'd find the man had no gunpowder residue on his hands because he was a bearer, and they'd see your bullet in his back.'

'Are you threatening me, Mario?'

He shook his head. 'No. We're at war. You're a soldier, a natural. You're learning that in the fog of battle things are sometimes not what they seem. What I will tell you now is that today you may be hailed as a hero, but tomorrow you could be persecuted as a criminal for what you just did. We must all be careful, we must all look after each other.'

'And if one of us splits from the group, reports something he thinks he saw?' she asked.

'Then he – or she – is no longer one of us. They become the enemy, and you know how we deal with them.'

Chapter 17

James Paterson heard the helicopter then saw it coming in across the golden grassy plains to the west of Kuria Hills.

He left the air-conditioned comfort of his suite and trudged up the hill to the helipad, past the back-of-house functions of Julianne's camp. It never ceased to surprise him how ramshackle and grubby were the workshops, staff accommodation, vehicle parks and other essential elements behind the facade of a luxury safari lodge. The tourists were served up a Hollywood view of Africa, but the builders there to work on the septic tank squatting over a charcoal brazier and a pot of mealie meal were the real deal. So, too, was the grimy, sweat-stained man he now shook hands with.

'Howzit, Mario,' he said, returning Machado's crushing grip.

'Good day's work.'

Paterson watched the others. The TANAPA ranger, a young man, looked shaken. Ezekial, the preacher's son, deliberately avoided eye contact with him and strode away. Tema walked with the fluid gait and cold stare of a leopard slinking through the long grass. She slowed as she came abreast of him and Mario.

211

'You know the drill,' Mario said. 'Clean your weapon, get a feed, Tema. Remember what I told you.'

'Yes,' she said, then carried on.

'How did she do today?' Paterson asked once she was out of earshot.

'Sonja trained her well,' Mario said.

'News of the contact has spread fast. The ranger radioed his own sitrep.'

'I know, I couldn't stop him,' Mario said. 'He was a pussy. Tema is more of a man than he is.'

'The news of the shootings has already reached the ears of a senior government minister, who has complained to the head of the National Parks Department and the chief warden of the Serengeti. We've fielded calls from both and the minister is not happy.'

'So? Just another politician complaining.'

'Actually, it's good news. The minister in question is, I'm told, in the pay of the Scorpions. Him complaining so soon of "foreign mercenaries" killing Tanzanian citizens in cold blood means we've landed a blow in the right place, straight to their solar plexus, as it were.'

Mario grunted. 'You deal with the politicians. To my mind they're worse than the poacher vermin Julianne is paying us to exterminate.'

'We don't use words like "exterminate", Mario. You're misinterpreting your job.'

The Portuguese man took a step closer to him. He didn't flinch. 'You and I know exactly what is going on here. I have no problem with it, but I expect you to be man enough to use plain language, to not veil your words like some lying coward politician.'

James put his hands on his hips. The man was a blunt instrument, but he was good at his work.

'You did well today, Mario, you and your people. You'll be rewarded accordingly. Talk to me about Ezekial. What was wrong with him just now?'

Mario ran his fingers over his grime-encrusted stubble. 'He's weak. He's a good tracker, one of the best I've seen, but his heart's not in the dirty business.'

'Will he talk?'

'Not if we have anything to say about it.'

'We meaning you and the girl, Tema?'

Mario nodded. 'She's got the look, you know.'

Paterson nodded. He'd seen her eyes in the faces of men he'd served with in Iraq and Afghanistan. Killing became a job for these people, nothing more, and they were generally very good at it.

'She'll keep him in line,' Mario went on.

'I thought you suspected there was something going on between them, that they were sweet on each other.'

Mario shrugged. 'Maybe they were, but that will be in the past after today. You should have seen the way she turned her back on him just now when the job had to be finished. You told me you wanted a message sent to the Scorpions, no?'

'Yes. And as I said, it's been received loud and clear. We're going to rattle them.'

Mario held his AK-47 in the crook of his left arm. With his right hand he opened the breast pocket of his camouflage shirt and took out a short stubby cigar. He lit it and dragged deeply.

Paterson turned, slightly, as Mario blew the smoke his way.

'Tell me,' Mario said, then inhaled again, 'have we really been Julianne's hit squad all along? Was the whole spiel about surveillance and reconnaissance just a lie to get Kurtz on board? If it was, you can drop it now.'

'You, like me, are employed by Julianne to protect her reserves and assets and fight poachers. You seem more at home with a more fluid battle space than Sonja did.'

Mario exhaled and spat. 'You're talking like a politician again, *James*. I'm pulling the trigger. I at least deserve to know who is ultimately giving the orders here. If you're running some sort of rogue operation at arm's length from Julianne then that means that if it all falls apart she'll be able to deny she knew anything about it and you'll hang me out to dry. Enough of my enemies know enough about me to make sure I'll take the fall for you.'

'You want me to spell it out?' James asked.

'Yes.'

James drew a breath. 'Julianne plans to do whatever it takes to put the Scorpions out of business. She's got more balls than any man, certainly any politician I've ever met. She knows half of these bastards would never do a day in prison even if we served up enough evidence to send them to the gallows. That's why I'm on board with her. Are you?'

Mario showed his perfect, even teeth. He took another puff of his cigar. 'I am. I won't say anything to her, or anyone else, as long as you back me up.'

'That was my job as an intelligence officer and it's still my role today. I'll do the targeting . . .'

'Yes, and I'll do the shooting, and the commanding officer will get all the glory.'

James nodded. 'That's exactly how it should be.'

'All right. One more thing.'

'What's that?' James asked.

'Tema gets a pay rise. I don't want to lose her and I want her to know that you – and your silent commander – appreciate her.'

'Done. Fifty per cent OK?'

Mario nodded. 'It's more money than she could ever hope to make in South Africa as a maid.'

'Are you going soft in your old age, trying to uplift the previously disadvantaged people of South Africa?'

'No, and you can lose that tone in your voice, Paterson.'

James bridled silently. He needed this thug, so he bit back the retort that was forming in his mind.

Mario used his cigar to point at James. 'I served with scores of good African men in Angola. They bled and died for your apartheid regime and when the war ended people like you tossed them on the scrap heap.'

Paterson said nothing. He knew the story of 32 Battalion's fearless soldiers and how the new South Africa had no need for them and no compassion for them. Many ended up working as mercenaries, others in high-risk security jobs such as ferreting out heavily armed illegal goldminers from deep underground where no police officer would dare go. It seemed this cold-hearted killer had a soft spot somewhere beneath his leathery, tattooed skin.

'Are you finished, Mario?'

He put his cigar back in his mouth and nodded.

'Good. Now I have some news for you. Sonja Kurtz is coming back to us. Julianne wants to welcome her back with open arms.'

Mario narrowed his eyes and exhaled. 'Sonja's not the sort of woman given to changing her mind once she's made a decision.'

Paterson shrugged. 'Julianne wants her to head up your team again, just as you started out. How do feel about being under Sonja?'

Mario grinned and winked. 'Under her, on top of her, behind her, it's all good as far as I'm concerned.'

The man was a boor, but Paterson made a mental note that Mario seemed to think he had a chance of bedding Kurtz, or perhaps already had. It was the sort of information that Julianne paid him to collect and interpret. He allowed himself a brief fantasy of what Sonja might do to Mario, preferably with a riding crop, if she knew he'd been talking about her in that way. 'Good. Keep me informed about Ezekial.'

Mario gave a theatrical bow and tugged his forelock. 'Yes, my liege.'

*

As he drove through Tanzania, Hudson Brand was feeling happier than he had in as long a time as he could remember.

He would have pinched himself, to make sure he wasn't dreaming, but he was too busy hanging on to the steering wheel of the Defender as he navigated a rough, corrugated stretch of gravel road, a deviation around resurfacing work on the main road. It seemed to him that much of Tanzania was one giant road-building project in progress.

Sonja was next to him in the Defender, dressed in a green tank top and matching short shorts, her feet propped up on the dashboard. She looked over at him and smiled. In the short time he'd known her he reckoned he could have counted on the fingers of both hands the number of times she had smiled – really smiled. However, what buoyed him was that most of those times had been in the last few days. It lifted his spirits and moved his heart to see her like that.

She had her phone out and was sending Emma a message on Facebook, updating her with their progress through Tanzania. Sonja had told him that Emma was thrilled when she'd learned she was back with Hudson.

'What was the name of the place where we stayed at the northern end of Lake Malawi?' she asked him.

'The Blue Canoe, Matema Beach.'

'Ah, yes. But it's called Lake Nyasa on the Tanzanian side of the border.' She glanced up from tapping the phone and winked when she caught his eye. 'In fact, how could I forget that place?'

They had made love on the sand there, in the middle of the day. The few staff were having a siesta and she had spread out a towel to sunbathe. Hudson had lain down next to her and before they knew it they were naked. Afterwards they'd swum in the lake, locked in each other's arms.

From Matema they had travelled north, stopping on a farm outside the town of Iringa, where it had been cold enough for them to wear long-sleeved T-shirts to bed and spoon each other in the roof-top tent on Hudson's Land Rover. From there they had dropped down to the warmer, drier bushveld of Ruaha National Park.

It was there, in Tembo Camp on the Great Ruaha River, that the real nature of their trip through Tanzania had once more intruded. Tema had called Sonja on her phone and, as Sonja and Hudson had watched a bull elephant walking silently past their vehicle not more than three metres away, ambling down to the river to drink, Tema had told them how Mario had executed a poacher in cold blood during a gunfight in Tanzania in the Grumeti reserve.

Just hearing Mario's name had again annoyed Hudson, but he knew he had to stay professional. Tema had also told them that Julianne had been inspecting sites for a future camp in the area where she, Mario and Ezekial had tangled with the elephant poachers.

Glancing now at Sonja, who was messaging her daughter as he drove, he could almost pretend, for a moment, they were like any other couple fortunate enough to be overlanding through a beautiful expanse of Africa, but it was an illusion. They were travelling as hard and as fast as they could through Tanzania, sharing the driving and only stopping to feed or relieve them-selves. They had spent the last night in the capital, Dodoma, in a B&B on a winery on the outskirts of town. He told himself that he would at least take the time to show Sonja the natural majesty of the Ngorongoro Crater and the Serengeti before their impending date with Julianne Clyde-Smith.

At Dodoma, Hudson had used the wireless internet to do some research and found out that the Grumeti area had been hit hard by poachers recently. A game-viewing vehicle full of tourists had also been held up by armed gunmen which was as serious for local tourism as it was unusual. He had tracked down and called a woman he knew who ran a safari operation in the reserve and had told Sonja he had arranged to meet the woman on the road during their travels, at a lodge called Maramboi, located in a conservation area between Lake Manyara and Tarangire national parks.

It was getting dark as they approached the turnoff to Maramboi and Sonja had to brake hard to avoid hitting a giraffe that ran across the main road that separated the two parks. They went left and passed through a pretty floodplain land-scape studded with palm trees. A herd of zebra trotted parallel to them for a moment, their hooves raising a cloud of dust that burned red-gold in their wake.

After a few kilometres of winding road they came to the lodge. Its car park was busy at this time of day, with stretched Land Cruiser game-viewing vehicles disgorging tourists clad in khaki and green and floppy bush hats. Hudson saw a brace of vehicles with the Maasai Journeys logo emblazoned on the sign.

'Those vehicles belong to Helen Mills, the woman I told you about.'

'How do you know her?' Sonja asked as she negotiated the Defender into an empty parking spot.

'She used to work in the Sabi Sand managing a lodge there.'

Hudson and Sonja got out, glad to stretch their legs, and went to reception. They were in luck; despite the crowds there was a safari tent free for the night. The duty manager showed them to an open-sided lounge area where they sat on a couch and filled in registration and indemnity forms. The manager left them and said he would send a porter to carry their luggage and show them to their tent. While they waited, Hudson scanned the room. He saw a flash of blonde hair and a trim figure, from behind, in khaki.

'That's Helen,' he said.

He caught her eye and waved to her. Helen excused herself from a party of tourists and came over to them, smiling broadly.

Hudson didn't tell Sonja, but he'd had a fling with Helen when she'd worked in the Sabi Sand a dozen years earlier. She'd then travelled to East Africa and fallen for her driver guide, a young Maasai guy. Helen had married the guide and now ran a mobile safari operation with him in Tanzania.

'Well, hello, Hudson Brand, nice to hear from you and even better to see you.'

She came to him and kissed him on the cheek. Hudson introduced Helen to Sonja.

'First time in Africa, Sonja?' Helen asked, mistaking her for a client and Hudson for a guide.

'I was born in Namibia, grew up in Botswana,' Sonja said.

'That's a no then,' Helen said, still smiling.

'We're friends,' Hudson said.

'Up here on business or pleasure?' Helen asked. She also knew of his sideline as a private investigator. 'Sorry I didn't have time to answer all your questions when you called; I was busy herding cats, i.e. my lovely clients.'

'Join us for a drink?' Hudson suggested. He signalled for a waiter.

Helen looked back to her tourists. 'The porter's with them, so they should be fine. Sure.' The waiter came and took their orders.

'I'm glad we could meet, but when I called I didn't expect it to be out here on the road,' Hudson said.

Helen sagged into the lounge. 'To tell you the truth we had to let a few of our driver guides go. Our business has taken a hit lately.'

'Sorry to hear that,' Hudson said.

'Nas and I,' she looked to Sonja, 'Nas is my husband, well, we managed to get a concession from the government just outside the Serengeti, not far from Fort Ikoma. It's a beautiful parcel of land and we set up a small tented camp there. It was prime real estate, but we ran into trouble. There were ivory poachers working the area and we did our best to track and catch some of them, but they were a violent crew. They held up one of our game viewers out in the bush and robbed all the tourists at gunpoint.'

'That's serious,' Hudson said, feeling he was stating the obvious. It was the incident he had read about online.

Helen nodded. 'Yup. And bad for business once they all started talking on TripAdvisor. Our bookings nosedived and then, to make it worse, the poachers shot down a helicopter we had contracted to help us in our anti-poaching efforts. The cost of the chopper nearly broke us, and when it crashed the publicity that followed was the last nail in the coffin for us.'

'I'm so sorry, Helen,' Hudson said.

'It could have been worse,' Helen said.

'How so?' Sonja asked.

'Well, we managed to sell the lease on the concession to another operator. We didn't want to – the person who bought it had been pressuring us for some time to sell – but in the end we had to and she made us a pretty good deal. Not quite as much as she was first offering, but it allowed us to keep the mobile safari business going.'

'She?' Sonja said, sipping her Klipdrift and Coke Zero.

'Um,' Helen said, 'I might have said too much. Under the terms of the deal I'm not supposed to say who it was until the buyer goes public with the news.'

'This mystery person wouldn't have been a very rich British businesswoman, would she?' Hudson asked.

Helen looked to him. 'Well, like I said, I can't say, but, what the hell, if you ask around Arusha you'll probably find out a certain chick with a double-barrelled name has been shopping for property in our part of Tanzania.'

The duty manager came over to them, with a porter in tow.

'Mr Brand, Miss Kurtz, Gregory here will show you to your room. Helen, sorry to interrupt, but one of your American tourists has a problem with her hair dryer.'

Helen sighed. 'Sorry, duty calls, guys. Maybe see you later?'

'Sure,' Hudson said as he and Sonja stood. Hudson looked to Sonja and saw she was thinking the same thing as him.

*

Julianne Clyde-Smith got up from the desk in the office of her camp in the Kuria Hills, in the north of the Serengeti, when she heard the game-viewer vehicle pull up outside.

She walked out and felt the sun's sting. She swatted away a tsetse fly before it could bite her; the loathsome insects followed the vehicles into camp but thankfully didn't hang around too long. Rosie Appleton, the reporter, got down from the vehicle, and after she'd accepted a cold towel from one of the camp's employees, Julianne approached her.

'Hi, Rosie, I'm Julianne, nice to meet you.'

Rosie gave a small laugh. 'You're probably one of the most recognisable businesswomen on the planet!'

'Well, I'm just trying not to get under the feet of the people who actually do all the work around here.' Julianne introduced Rosie to Amelia, the camp manager, who had followed her out. 'Amelia can have someone show you to your room and we can chat later if you like.'

'Well, you're the reason I'm here,' Rosie said, 'so is now good for you?'

'Sure,' Julianne said. 'That way you can go out on an afternoon drive if you wish.'

'Perfect.'

Julianne led Rosie through the reception area. 'You'll see that all of the accommodation and common areas here are canvas; it gives the feel of being in safari tents, but the framework is actually all made from recycled steel. If we had to dismantle this camp there'd be no footprint left.'

'Very environmentally friendly.'

'There's a private dining room off the main area; I thought we could chat there.'

'Sure.'

They went past the well-stocked bar and Julianne pointed out a herd of zebra grazing just below the deck in front of the dining room. 'They're part of the migration, just passing through, but the grass is good up here in the hills, so they're in no rush.'

'Looks like just the right place to chill,' Rosie said.

'I love it here.'

'I bet you do.'

They went into the dining room, followed by a waiter.

'I'll have coffee, please, Samuel,' Julianne said. 'Rosie?'

'Sure, same, thanks.'

They sat in green canvas director's chairs across from each other at a heavy, polished teak dining table.

'I hear you don't grant too many interviews,' Rosie said.

'I'm selective,' Julianne said. 'And mostly people want to talk to me about business matters, but as your magazine focuses on wildlife issues I was happy to agree to meet you. I'd rather talk about conservation than corporate takeovers any day.'

Rosie set a digital voice recorder down on the table, checked that the red light was on, then took a notebook out of her leather satchel. Julianne regarded her. She was pretty, but those blue eyes had a hard edge to them. She was dressed for the bush, but in a practical rather than tourist style, in a denim skirt, leather sandals and a nicely fitting short-sleeved khaki shirt. Julianne knew from the file Paterson had prepared on the young journalist that Rosie was smart, probably straight – she had been seen having drinks with Sonja Kurtz's sometime lover Hudson Brand – and tenacious as an investigative reporter.

Her magazine's exposé on abalone poaching and its links to Chinese triads had been picked up by national newspapers, television programs and online news services abroad. Rosie opened her notebook – she was also thorough, taking notes as a back-up in case her recorder failed.

'So, Julianne, where did your love of Africa and interest in conservation begin?'

Julianne knew media interviews could go one of two ways. Either the reporter began with a hard-hitting question to put the interviewee off balance, or, as in this case, the journalist started with an easy question to try and put the subject at ease and get them talking. Julianne was mildly disappointed; she'd prepared herself for a tougher approach.

'I came to Africa twenty years ago on what was supposed to be a once in a lifetime safari holiday. It turned out to be anything but.' Julianne had told the story so many times at wildlife fundraising events, interviews like this one, and at other public speaking engagements that she felt like she could retell it in her sleep. She carried on, honestly saying that it was hard to pinpoint what had hooked her about the continent and its wildlife. 'I don't know whether I was bitten by something, breathed something in or drank something, but this place, this Africa, got under my skin, like those wicked barbs on a buffalo thorn tree, and wrapped its tendrils around my heart and took hold.'

Rosie nodded as she wrote, in Pitman shorthand, Julianne noted. The way she laid the notebook down told Julianne that Rosie assumed she could not decipher the strokes and dots on the page. If Rosie had done her homework she would have known that Julianne started work at eighteen as a personal assistant to a middle manager in a clothing factory after graduating from a secretarial college in the East End of London.

'How far would you go to save an endangered species, such as the rhino, or to stop the illegal trade in elephant ivory?'

That's better, Julianne thought to herself, seeing Rosie's interview strategy for what it was – starting off with the easy question and then switching tack fast, to keep the interviewee off balance. 'I'd do, within the limits of the law, anything.'

Rosie jotted down the answer then leaned back in her chair. 'Good answer.'

'What do you mean?' Julianne asked. She was on guard, had been since the beginning of the interview, but she was here for the same reason that Rosie Appleton was – to find out how much the other woman knew and how best to use that information to her advantage.

'You put the words "within the limits of the law" in the middle of your response so that I couldn't simply cut your quote to read "I'd do anything".'

Julianne crossed her leg and placed her hands together in her lap. Rosie was right. 'Well, I meant what I said.'

Rosie took up her notebook again. 'The laws regarding poaching differ greatly from country to country. In Zimbabwe and Botswana, for example, where you also operate lodges and run anti-poaching operations, there's a shoot-to-kill policy. Anyone seen trespassing in a protected game reserve or national park and carrying a weapon can be shot on sight. Should this law be introduced in other African countries, such as South Africa and here in Tanzania?'

'It's not up to me to dictate to the various governments in whose countries I operate game lodges how they should make or enforce their laws. As I said before, I am prepared, within the limits of the law of the land, to do anything, and fund any program or initiative, that will protect Africa's wildlife.'

The waiter arrived with the coffee on a silver serving tray and offered to pour.

'It's fine, Samuel, I'll take care of it.' Julianne depressed the plunger and poured Rosie a cup. The simple ritual was, Julianne thought, like the bell in a prize fight. They each retreated to their corners. Round one was done. Time for round two. 'I hear you've been asking around in South Africa about an organisation called the Scorpions?'

'Hey,' Rosie forced a little laugh. 'I'm the one who's supposed to be asking the questions.'

Julianne took up her cup and sipped some coffee. She knew, from countless business meetings and negotiations, that when one party was silent the other often felt the need to fill the void. Rosie might have been thinking the same thing because she also took some coffee and sat back, looking at her. If it was to be a battle of wills, Julianne had nothing to lose. After all, Rosie couldn't very well go back to her editor, having landed an interview with Julianne Clyde-Smith, with only forty words' worth of copy.

After what seemed like a very long time, though perhaps was no more than a minute, Rosie set down her cup. 'That was going to be my next question to you – what do you know about the Scorpions?'

'I asked first,' Julianne said.

'You're not going to give me anything until I tell you what I know, are you?'

'You're a very smart young woman, Rosie.'

'All right, I'll play along. There's a tendency, based on history, to think of wildlife poaching as opportunistic, localised crime. Corrupt national parks rangers or politicians rape the lands they're supposed to be protecting, evil Chinese and Vietnamese businessmen get poor Africans to put their lives on the line to smuggle out a few rhino horns or elephant tusks or pangolin or whatever. But it's all a bit ad hoc.'

Julianne sipped some more coffee, remaining silent.

'But,' Rosie continued, 'up until now no one's thought of illegal wildlife products in the same way as, say, drugs or human trafficking; that is, that it might be organised crime. I did a story on abalone smuggling in the Eastern Cape and found out that triads in Hong Kong and Shanghai were involved, but that they, too, were at war with another organised crime outfit fighting for control of the abalone market. That's when I first heard the name "the Scorpions".'

'I read your article, and the follow-up stories in the rest of the media, though there was no mention of the Scorpions.'

Rosie shook her head. 'No, I left out the name of the rival organisation for two reasons. One, I only had it from a single source – he wasn't the most reliable sea captain around and a bit of a drunk – and I couldn't corroborate the name; and two, I didn't want to let them know I was on their trail, at least not then.'

Julianne smiled. She liked this smart, tenacious, pretty young thing. 'And now?'

'Now I'm getting ready to break the story. The Scorpions aren't something out of a novel; they're real. They operate like the mafia, with a sophisticated ranking system, and a series of what I describe as franchises. The local operators, in most cases poachers and kingpins who've been hunting in their own patches for years, now form part of a much bigger organisation. They're benefitting from bigger markets and better support. The average foot-soldier in a Scorpions franchise has gone from being some desperately poor guy in ragged clothes carrying a rusty old bolt-action rifle to a well-trained, well-equipped, well-armed warrior. The Scorpions' hierarchy provides support and expertise; I'm guessing there are ex-military people involved.'

Julianne decided it was time to weigh in. 'One more question from me.'

Rosie pursed those pretty lips. 'One more.'

'Do you have any indication of where the top people in the Scorpions hail from?'

'No. The temptation would be to think it's someone or some

organisation from the Far East. Asia is a big consumer of rhino horn, ivory, pangolin and other endangered species. But I don't want to fall into racial stereotypes. The Chinese triads were at war with the Scorpions, and from what I could gather a couple of those groups, the Hong Kong guys and the ones from Shanghai, had joined forces to try and fight off the Scorpions. They lost. Seemed the Scorpions' poachers were better armed, better organised and better led.'

'Russia,' Julianne said, then leaned back in her chair.

Rosie made a note. 'That's it. One word? Is that all I get?'

Julianne gave the younger woman her most charming smile. 'No, you'll get more. You strike me as the type of person who could get just about anything you want.'

It was Rosie's turn to be silent now, though she was looking back at Julianne in a slightly different way. She set her notebook down and twisted a lock of her hair in her finger while she waited.

'Some of my anti-poaching operatives had a contact with a gang in Zimbabwe. You may have heard about it?'

Rosie nodded, but didn't say a word. She took up her pen and notebook again.

'My people questioned one of the survivors of the . . . engagement . . . and found out they supplied ivory to a white man in Zambia who spoke Russian.'

'You think the Scorpions are Russian mafia?'

Julianne shrugged. 'The weapon of choice of many poachers in Africa is the AK-47; there are hundreds of thousands of these rifles left over from the various liberation struggles, and armies that allow their guns to filter out into the black market. However, my teams are increasingly coming across state-of-the-art Russian-made hardware – latest generation night vision goggles, brand-new heavy-calibre sniper rifles; body armour. This is the sort of stuff the militaries in countries such as Mozambique, Zimbabwe and Tanzania have on their Christmas wish lists. It's expensive.'

Rosie was scribbling furiously. She looked up. 'The white Russian is a first for me.'

Julianne entwined the fingers of her hands. 'I can see the head-line now.'

Rosie looked her in the eye. 'Give me a better headline.'

'Ask me the right question and I will.'

'The armies and national parks services of the countries in which you operate your safari camps are all aware of the Scorpions, even if they won't go on the record. They can fight them, if they're not in bed with them, but coordinating their efforts is a bureaucratic and political nightmare. You're the one unifying force in the fight against poaching in these countries.'

'Go on,' Julianne said.

'"Within the limits of the law", are you, Julianne Clyde-Smith, at war with the Scorpions?'

'Yes. I'm going to, within the limits of the law, destroy them.'

Chapter 18

Sonja Kurtz had never seen so many animals in one place. The Ngorongoro Crater was such a visual feast of wildlife she wasn't sure whether the Serengeti, where they were heading next to meet up with Julianne Clyde-Smith and James Paterson, could better it.

She and Hudson had stayed at the Lemala tented camp just inside the rim of the crater. The string of luxurious safari tents and a communal bar and dining area were located in a lush forest atop the high walls of the caldera, which Hudson said was the correct term for an inactive volcano.

A prime benefit of the camp's location was that it was close to the Lemala entry gate into the park below. This meant that when they entered the crater that morning, just after six as the sun was struggling up, they were one of the first three vehicles to make it to the floor. Hudson told her that further around the rim, where the main gate and most of the lodges were located, dozens of vehicles full of impatient tourists would be queuing to enter.

As it was, for the first few hours of the day they had several game sightings to themselves on their side of the arena.

Hudson was leaning out the driver's side window of his Land Rover and had picked up fresh pugmarks in the dust of the road heading towards the Lerai Forest. 'Lioness.'

Sonja felt the thrill of the hunt as Hudson followed the spoor and she scanned the golden grass that stretched away to a small lake beyond. 'I see her!'

Hudson accelerated a little, but stopped about a hundred metres short of the lioness. Sonja had picked up the movement of the dark fur on the backs of her ears, above the grass. The animal had moved off the road and had her nose up, sniffing.

Hudson switched off the engine and took up his binoculars. It had cost them a small fortune to pay the fees to drive their own vehicle down to the floor. He had very little money, she had gathered, but it wasn't a problem for her so she had been happy to pay. While they had been driving hard to get to their rendezvous with Julianne, Hudson had been adamant that Sonja could not miss this iconic African destination.

'Look,' Sonja said, proud that she had once again trumped her safari guide boyfriend, 'there's a male, off to the right.'

'Hey, you're good at this. Watch, he's coming towards her.'

Sonja followed the lions' progress as they trotted towards each other, and realised she had just thought of Hudson as her boyfriend. She wondered if that was the right word. The male lion was a handsome fellow with a luxurious mane so pale it was almost blond. The two animals came together and rubbed their heads against each other in greeting.

'They're going to mate,' Hudson said.

He started the engine and crept a little closer, and by the time they reached the lions the friendly house cat–style greeting had been replaced with snarling and the bearing of fangs.

The lioness lashed out at the male, taunting him with the smack of a big paw to his face. He growled, moved behind her and bit down on her neck.

'I've seen this before, but it never gets old,' Sonja said.

'Yep, I know what you mean.'

They were close enough not to need binoculars. As they both watched the intense, somewhat violent spectacle of the big male mating with the female, her snarling and him grunting through the brutal but short coupling, Sonja reached out across the console box between them.

Hudson took her hand and clasped it, hard, as the male lion finished.

The lions parted, got up and walked around each other once, then flopped down into the grass, sated and exhausted.

'You know they'll do that every fifteen to twenty minutes for a whole day,' Hudson said.

'I know. But I prefer quality over quantity, and at least you're not that fast.'

After they exited the crater via the same gate they had entered through, Hudson drove around the rim and then past a smaller caldera where Maasai warriors herded their cattle amid zebra and wildebeest.

As they descended they continued on through the Ngorongoro Conservation Area, where people and wildlife lived side by side. They passed but didn't stop at the Olduvai Gorge heritage site, where Hudson told Sonja that Louis Leakey had discovered evidence of the earliest human species.

'Ironic,' Sonja said, 'that humanity began in Africa, and ended in so many countries over here.'

They had both, Hudson thought as he drove across the dry, dusty Ndutu Plains, seen the best and worst the continent had to offer, but here he was, an American, choosing to live in Africa, and here Sonja was, too. 'Does Africa feel like home to you?'

She looked over at him and he met her eyes for as long as the corrugations in the road would allow. 'It does right now.'

They entered the Serengeti National Park at the busy Nabi Hill Gate and Hudson queued with a score of driver guides waiting to pay entry fees. Hudson and Sonja's was the only self-drive vehicle in the packed car park, and when Hudson finally emerged from the payment office he saw a pair of Japanese tourists, wearing surgical face masks to protect themselves from Tanzania's ubiquitous dust, taking pictures of his battered, ageing Land Rover. Sonja sat in the shade of a tree, her legs crossed, reading a paperback, ignoring the tourists.

'All set,' he said.

They drove through the park, heading for the first of Julianne Clyde-Smith's two operations in the Serengeti, the semi-permanent tented camp in the Makoma Hills, to the west of the park's headquarters at Seronera. He took it slow as they turned off the main road onto the game-viewing track that wound its way along the Seronera River.

With the great wildebeest and zebra migration well on its way north towards Kenya, the plains game wasn't abundant here, but it was crawling with resident predators who lived in the long grass and marshes of the riverbed, along with elephant, buffalo and enough other herbivores to guarantee some action.

A gaggle of half a dozen game viewers told them there was something interesting across the river, so Hudson found a drift, a shallow crossing point, and headed towards them. 'Probably lion.'

He was right. When they came to the cleared area on the other side, now a car park, they saw a pride of twelve lions, some sleeping under a tree, others lying in the grass. One lazed in the shade of a game viewer, whose tourists peered nervously from their roof hatch down at the lolling cat, which regally ignored them.

'I can't help it, I like lions,' Sonja said.

This was idyllic, Hudson thought. Here he was on safari with a beautiful woman, taking in some of the greatest national parks in the world. He wanted to suggest to her that they forget Julianne Clyde-Smith and just turn around and head back to South Africa, or, better still, just keep on travelling through Africa. He knew, however, that Sonja was like the predators around them; as relaxed as they might look now, their driving force was the hunt. He understood that, even felt it himself. It's what drew him into investigation work, that almost addictive feeling he got when he was on someone's trail.

'Look,' Sonja said. 'That one's seen a gazelle.'

Hudson watched where Sonja was pointing. The lioness in the shade of the vehicle had rolled into an upright position and was now on the move, in stealth mode. She was up and on all fours, but her legs were bent, her belly close to the ground and her tail straight out. She stalked around and then under the chassis of the Land Cruiser, her gaze fixed on a dainty Thompson's gazelle, grazing unawares on the other side of the causeway Hudson and Sonja had just crossed.

'She's going for the Tommy all right,' Hudson said, using the East African nickname for the gazelle.

They watched and waited. Periodically the gazelle would look up and around, and then, in the few seconds during which it returned to eating, the lioness moved fast and low, across the river to a bush that gave her cover just twenty metres short of her target. She dropped even lower, tensed, and gave a little shake of her behind, as if psyching herself up or coiling her muscles.

Camera shutters clicked and whirred on the other vehicles around them and the chatter ceased as everyone drew a collective breath and focused on the big cat.

The gazelle looked up and around and then, when it returned to feeding, the lioness sprang from cover. The flash of movement was enough to alert the Tommy, and the little antelope leapt away.

The lioness ran in long strides, her body and legs at full stretch in each bound. As fast as she was, the cat almost looked as though she were lumbering compared to the frantic blur of the gazelle. The Tommy danced left and the lioness twisted to follow. No sooner had she reached out a paw to try and trip up her prey's rear leg than the little fellow had jinked right.

The lioness followed, but one more zig was too fast for her zag and the predator came to a halt in a cloud of dust.

'Wow,' Sonja said. 'Just wow. My heart's beating. I've seen that a few times in my life and I'm always torn.'

'I know what you mean. You want her to catch something, to see the kill, for the cat to get supper, but you also want the prey to live.'

'Yes,' she said. 'Exactly. It got more like that, not wanting to see a kill, after I had Emma.'

'We can turn around, you know, or just keep heading in a different direction,' he said to her.

She looked at him and for a moment he thought she might actually be considering his proposal.

'No.' The lioness was coming back to her pride, and looking decidedly annoyed as she walked across the causeway. 'I don't miss when I'm hunting. I'm going to find out exactly what Julianne's up to and if it's what we think, that she's running her own personal star chamber, then I'm going to get Tema and Ezekial out before they end up dead or rotting in some African prison for murdering an innocent civilian.'

Chapter 19

Hudson and Sonja spent the night in Julianne's Makoma Hills camp and rose early the next morning for a long drive through the Serengeti.

Hudson Brand crested a ridge and saw, in the shallow valley, the Grumeti River snaking its way from west to east. Here it was little more than a creek, but it was an important watering stop for the hundreds of black dots that studded the short grassy lands around them.

'Well, here it is,' he said.

'What?' Sonja asked.

'The great wildebeest migration, well, the tail end of it at least.'

Sonja and Hudson got out of the Land Rover. She looked around them. 'It's amazing.'

'Nah, this is nothing. Wait until we get into the thick of it, then you'll see what a spectacle it is.'

'Ow.' Sonja slapped the back of her thigh. She squealed again then jumped back into the Land Rover, slammed the door and wound up the window.

Hudson went to the back of the truck, opened the rear door, rummaged in his duffel bag, slapped a fly on his arm and got back in.

'My God, they're the worst insects I've ever come across.' Sonja rubbed her leg, where a red welt was rising. 'That hurts *so* much. Are they tsetse flies?'

Hudson laughed. 'Yes. You don't think you're overreacting just a tad, Sonja?'

She looked at him and pulled a face like an angry buffalo. 'That fly seriously bit me. Look at the size of this lump. My leg looks like I've been pumping iron and taking steroids.'

Hudson produced the elegant slim-line aerosol can he'd found under his dirty underwear. 'Try this.'

Sonja took the can and read the label. 'Avon Skin So Soft spray-on moisturiser?'

'Yes.'

'Have you gone metrosexual on me, Hudson?'

He smiled. 'Trust me, this is the only thing in the world that repels tsetse flies, other than Dettol mixed with water, so if you don't want to smell like a hospital ward then try some.'

She looked at him sceptically, but sprayed some moisturiser on her arms and legs and rubbed it in.

'The added benefit,' he said, 'is that when I travel to tsetse-infested countries my skin is positively glowing.'

She laughed.

The repellent worked, and Hudson explained to Sonja that as well as being die-hard safari aficionados the British Special Air Service had also become converts to the Avon spray-on moisturiser, which repelled midges as well.

They drove on through the Serengeti and Hudson continued to savour the experience. He liked being able to tell Sonja things she didn't know. She was such a self-assured, confident woman that he could see how some men might find her intimidating. She had confessed to him that she'd only had two long-term relationships in her life and that both had ended badly.

He wondered, as they drove past more herds of wildebeest making their way inexorably towards the Mara River, what it might be like to settle down with someone like Sonja if, in fact, she was capable of putting down roots again.

They stopped a few times to stretch, have a snack, and reapply their moisturising tsetse fly repellent. Hudson could feel the mood changing between them, the closer they came to Julianne Clyde-Smith's camp. Sonja had lost the free and easy look; her feet were planted firmly in the footwell of the Land Rover as she cleaned her pistol while they drove. She checked and cleaned her ammunition and reloaded the weapon.

'You look like you're preparing for battle.'

She glanced at him. 'I am.'

After a long morning's drive they came, in the early afternoon, to a T-junction intersection with a giant white animal skull on a plinth.

'Kichwa Tembo,' Hudson said. 'Elephant's head. This is the point of no return.'

'Don't be so melodramatic, just turn right,' Sonja said.

About fifteen kilometres down the road they started seeing the distinctive granite koppies of the Kuria Hills. This was a prime spot, he explained to Sonja, for tourists to come and see the great wildebeest migration in Tanzania. Here, the Mara River, which formed part of the border with Kenya, flowed into the Serengeti National Park, and this time of year, in August, was a prime opportunity to view the massed crossings of the river by wildebeest and zebra.

While it had been busy in the Seronera area of the park, where they had watched the lioness chase the gazelle, the drive through the Serengeti had been much quieter; they had seen no more than half a dozen other vehicles on their route. Now, however, they started encountering more and more safari traffic. Eventually they came to a turnoff, to the left, to Julianne Clyde-Smith's Crossing Lodge in the Kuria Hills.

Hudson noticed Sonja clenching and unclenching her fists as they drove along the access road which wound in and out of large pink granite boulders. They were both tired, hot and dusty from the drive in the un-airconditioned vehicle, but Hudson noted how Sonja became instantly alert as they pulled up and Julianne Clyde-Smith herself emerged from the canvas-and-steel reception building to meet them.

'Sonja, so nice to see you again, and welcome back.'

Hudson came up behind Sonja, and she introduced him.

'How nice to meet you. Are you Sonja's driver?'

Sonja looked to him and back to Julianne. 'Hudson's a friend of mine. He's ex–32 Battalion, South African Defence Force.'

'Three-two Battalion, Hudson?'

He nodded. 'Yes, ma'am.'

'Oh, well, then I suppose you know Mario Machado, whom Sonja recruited.'

'We're acquainted, ma'am,' Hudson said. It was Hudson's turn to clench and unclench his fists at the thought of seeing Mario again. This would be interesting, but Hudson sensed that was how Sonja liked it.

'Sonja's briefed you on the work she and Mario have been doing?'

'Yes,' Hudson said. 'I was on my way on a vacation to Tanzania and caught up with Sonja. I'm giving her a lift.'

'Well, you're very welcome at Crossing Lodge and we'll find somewhere for you to stay. Come in,' Julianne said. 'It's good to see you again, Sonja, and to meet you, Mr Brand. Mario and the others have been busy lately. I'm sure you'll all have lots to chat about over dinner. I've reserved our private dining room for all of you.'

'We're not here to socialise, Julianne,' Sonja said. 'I've come back to work, and the sooner we get started the better. Where's Paterson?'

'He'll be along soon. He and Mario have been working on a new mission for the team. I'll send for him. Meantime, come through to the bar. I must say, Sonja, I'm not used to my employees walking out on me without notice, like you did in Zimbabwe.'

'The Zimbabwean secret police were after me. If they'd caught me I'd be in prison and so, most likely, would Ian Barton and the rest of my team. It was best I disappeared for a while.'

'Quite,' said Julianne.

Hudson followed Sonja and Julianne through the reception area, past the office on the left and a curio shop on the right, down a short flight of stairs to the bar. It was open on the side overlooking a gentle slope covered in grass and dotted with trees. Zebra grazed very close to where a couple of tourists took pictures with their phones of cocktails in the foreground and the wildlife beyond. Julianne led them to a corner table, away from the guests, and summoned a waiter and invited them to order.

'Coke Zero for me,' Sonja said.

'I'll take a sparkling water, please,' Hudson said.

'Champagne for me, please, Samuel.' Julianne beamed at them. 'I feel like celebrating.'

'You said your team has been busy?' Hudson asked. 'Do you mean that your people caught some poachers?'

'Disrupted a major syndicate's centre of gravity, as James would put it,' Julianne said. 'It means we beat some bad guys, a notorious ivory poaching gang.'

'Prisoners?' Sonja asked.

Julianne shook her head. 'No, they put up a stiff fight. Mario and the team took them all out.'

'Killed them,' Hudson said.

She looked at him as she took her glass of sparkling wine from the waiter. 'I know how dirty this business is, rest assured, Mr Brand.'

'Hudson.'

'Very well, Hudson. You must have seen your fair share of combat in Angola.'

He nodded.

'I haven't, but I'm aware of the stakes. I don't like it when anyone is hurt or loses their life, but when people shoot back then our anti-poaching operatives must use the appropriate level of force.'

'The shoot-to-kill policy works in Botswana,' Hudson said, 'and you could argue the only reason there are still a few rhinos left in Zimbabwe is because they still operate under those rules.'

'You may be right.' Julianne shifted her gaze to Sonja and narrowed her eyes. 'Sonja, I know you left because you didn't like the way your team was being managed, but I can assure you we're not operating a de facto illegal hit squad here.'

'I disliked being set up for gunfights where the inevitable result every time was for me and my people to shoot our way out. That was *not* what I signed up for.'

Julianne held up a hand in a conciliatory manner. 'I completely understand, and I've had a long, hard discussion with James about that. From now on, if you still wish to re-join us, you will be involved in every level of planning from beginning to end and you will have an equal say.'

'Except Paterson's busy planning a mission now,' Sonja said.

'Well, that was in train before you called me. However, you're more than welcome to thoroughly vet the plan before anything else happens. In fact, I'll insist on it.'

Hudson sat back and regarded the two women. Sonja was pushing a little hard, he thought, but, after all, the aim of their 'operation' was to find out what Julianne Clyde-Smith was really

240

up to. Julianne was either lying very convincingly in claiming that she was not bankrolling a hit squad, or she was telling the truth.

They had discussed it in the Land Rover on the last leg of the drive to Kuria Hills, from Kichwa Tembo. There was a possibility that Sonja and her team had just had a run of bad luck – or good luck, if your desired end state was wiping out every poacher and kingpin in Africa.

As an investigator, though, Hudson didn't believe in coincidences.

Julianne looked up, past Sonja. 'Oh, hello!'

Hudson turned his head and his heart gave an unpleasant lurch as he saw Rosie Appleton, dressed in denim and khaki, walk into the bar.

'Hudson!'

He swallowed and stood. 'Rosie.'

She came to him and kissed him on the cheek. Through his peripheral vision Hudson saw Sonja's face. She did not look happy.

'Rosie, it seems you know Hudson. This is Sonja Kurtz, she's also from South Africa.'

'Namibia.'

'Oh, yes, right.'

'Sonja Kurtz. I've heard of you,' Rosie said.

Sonja, Hudson saw, was fixing her gaze on Rosie the same way a cobra did before it spat its venom into its victim's eyes. 'Ditto.'

'Rosie,' Julianne said, 'we're kind of in the middle of a meeting here, can I help you with something or get someone to look after you?'

Hudson saw how the reporter's professional curiosity was immediately piqued.

'I was just coming for a drink, but I can sit elsewhere.'

'Hudson,' Julianne said, 'since you two know each other perhaps you might like to wait with Rosie and have a drink while Sonja and I talk business.'

'No,' Sonja said.

'We can go to my office, Sonja,' Julianne said.

Hudson looked back to Sonja.

'No. Hudson's in on this as well. He's going to be part of my team.'

I am? thought Hudson. That was news to him.

'What team?' Rosie asked, unable to hold back.

Hudson wondered why Sonja had shown her hand by letting Rosie know that she was going back to work for Julianne.

'Leave us,' Sonja said to Rosie.

The reporter put her hands on her hips. 'Excuse me? I'm a guest here, and I will not be spoken to in that tone.'

'Perhaps we can reconvene later,' Julianne said placatingly. 'For now, why don't we all just have another drink?'

Sonja stood and closed the distance between her and Rosie, until she was just centimetres from her nose.

'I'm not reconvening for anyone. This is a private meeting. Get out of here before I throw you out,' Sonja said.

Rosie opened her mouth, but the reply died on her lips when she locked eyes, briefly, with Sonja again. Rosie turned on her heel and strode out of the bar.

'Well, that's one way to deal with the media,' Julianne said.

Chapter 20

C aptain Sannie van Rensburg let the African bush take over
her senses as she walked through Hippo Rock Private
Nature Reserve.

Sannie had told the Hazyview detectives – and Hudson – that
she would take on the job of investigating Shadrack's movements
before his death. Her first port of call had been the Hippo Rock
administrative office where Avril, the receptionist who booked
maids and labourers to clean and maintain owners' houses, gave
her some surprising news. Shadrack's last day on earth had been
spent cleaning up around the home of James Paterson, Julianne
Clyde-Smith's head of security.

Sannie and Tom enjoyed their life in the Hippo Rock Private
Nature Reserve on the border of the Kruger Park. They had
only been able to buy the house thanks to the money that Tom
was making working as a protection officer – a bodyguard –
in the Middle East, but it annoyed her that he was away so
much. She knew it was no easier for him, and they were both
looking forward to the day when they could spend more time
together. With the kids in boarding school it was only her

work, back in the police service, that stopped her from going stir-crazy.

Today she had an excuse to work from home, and as she walked along the red sandy road through the reserve, her walking stick clicking out a tattoo with every second step, she took a moment to savour the beauty of where they lived. Everyone who walked in Hippo Rock carried a stick; the theory was that if one came across a hyena or a leopard that standing tall and still with the stick in the air would scare the animal off. Sannie wasn't sure if that would work, but it gave her some measure of comfort.

Although it was terribly dry she loved the bush at this time of year, at the end of winter. The sky was perfectly clear and the day was warming nicely. Winter was mild in the South African lowveld; although the nights could be pleasantly chilly enough for a fire and a good night's sleep, the days were carbon-copy perfect for the middle six months of the year.

With the leaves fallen from the trees, and the bush thinned out by the occasional nocturnal raiding party of elephants from the neighbouring Kruger Park, Sannie had a much better view of the houses she passed than she would have in summer, when the bush was lush and green.

Ahead of her was James Paterson's luxurious bushveld retreat. Like the house that Hudson minded it was on the river, over-looking Kruger, and these were the most expensive homes on the reserve. Sannie and Tom's house was located a couple of kilo-metres deeper into the Hippo Rock estate. It was nice, and set on a little *spruit*, or stream that flowed into the Sabie, but their house was far more modest than the mansions that lined the riverfront.

Sannie had no warrant to search Paterson's house or property, but as she came closer she worried less about legal ramifications of what she was about to do and more about the other owners who lived at Hippo Rock.

She looked around her, to make sure there was no one sitting on their *stoep* or, like her, out for a walk to the communal picnic area where those who couldn't afford a river house could watch the game over in Kruger.

Sannie dealt with law-breakers every day, but she was certain she would be more civil towards a thief or a poacher she arrested than one of her elderly neighbours would be to her if they caught her trespassing on someone else's plot. There were no internal fences between the properties in Hippo Rock and the law of the land, agreed to by all owners, was that one did not walk through the bush onto a neighbour's stand without permission. People here guarded their privacy and the tranquillity of their bushveld paradise jealously.

Taking another glance around, Sannie turned off the track and threaded her way through a dense stand of Tamboti trees. These trees with their distinctive black bark scored into little rectangles were a reminder that danger was a neighbour to beauty here in the African bush. Tamboti was never to be used as fuel for a *braai* because the smoke the wood gave off when burned, while sweet smelling, was poisonous. Sannie kept small pieces of Tamboti bark in her chests of drawers to keep bugs out of their clothes.

She could see the house, and while she knew James Paterson was away in Tanzania, she paused to look and listen. He could have perhaps allowed friends to stay.

All looked quiet, however. Sannie moved cautiously through the bush until she came to the rear of the house. It had the look of being recently renovated, with a heavy dark wood double-sized door and clear-view stainless steel security screens to keep out mosquitos and human – and animal – intruders, but allow a breeze through in warm weather. It was expensive security for a bush house on an estate with next to no crime, save for the occasional opportunistic burglary.

Sannie walked around the house, scanning the ground as she went. She wasn't exactly sure what she was looking for.

There was spoor in the cleared ground between the house and the surrounding bush; all the houses had a perimeter like this in case of fire. She picked up the tracks of bushbuck, baboons, a monitor lizard dragging its long tail on the ground, and a hyena.

The last person to visit this house, then, other than James Paterson and any company he may have kept, was Shadrack, who James had employed from the estate's pool of people to clean up his grounds. Sannie had come across James Paterson a few times. The police based in the Kruger Park occasionally met with the security people in the Sabi Sand and other reserves on the border of Kruger, to discuss anti-poaching strategies and when investigating crimes committed on the reserves. Also, she'd seen James around Hippo Rock. They didn't socialise, but were on cordial first-name terms. He had always struck her as professional, polite and proper.

Completing her circuit, Sannie came back to the front door of the house, which was located on the side away from the river, in a similar layout to the home Hudson was house-sitting. She knew the effect of entering a house such as this – as soon as the door was opened the visitor was confronted with the stunning river view and the wilderness beyond. Sannie scanned the ground, keeping the tracks she was picking up between her and the sun as she cast further away from the house.

Here, she saw tyre tracks and a man's shoe print. It was faint, and it was not a workboot, such as the one Ezckial, Sonja's master tracker, had picked up in the Sabi Sand Game Reserve where the two female anti-poaching operators had been killed.

Sannie walked up the short access road that led from the house to Hardekool Street, the road that ran parallel to the river. They'd had a fairly heavy shower of unseasonal rain, Sannie recalled, just before the Leopards Anti-Poaching Unit had been ambushed.

There was a patch of ground that held deeper, clearer tracks of game, including the large hooves of one of Hippo Rock's resident giraffes. Sannie surveyed the road; this spot was in a small depression and it had obviously held the moisture from the rain and been quite muddy. Here, at the intersection of the roads, in the shade of one of the leadwood trees – Hardekool in Afrikaans, giving the road its name – was the clear, dried imprint of a work-boot. Sannie took out her iPhone and focused the camera on the track. She snapped a picture then got down on one knee to study it and another two imprints.

The man who had made these tracks had walked from Paterson's house to the road. Sannie knew the maids and labourers generally waited by the side of the estate's main roads to be collected in the afternoon by Thomas, the *induna*, or manager, who supervised the estate's workers. The ground would have only been muddy for a short time, so it stood to reason that Shadrack, the only male worker at Hippo Rock who should have been at Paterson's house during that period, had left it.

But when Sannie took a closer look at the tracks she saw that both, one left and one right, looked to be from boots with good soles, with no sign of a cut or other damage.

Sannie stood, brushed the knee of her pants and looked back at the house. She retraced her steps down to the house and decided to cast about once more, looking further around the house, though for what she still did not know.

She heard a rustle above and looked up to see a vervet monkey peering down at her. Sannie wagged a finger at it – the monkeys and baboons were a constant source of worry for the home-owners. A window or door left carelessly open was a gilt-edged invitation for an invasion by primates and a guarantee of an appalling mess.

Sannie walked around the house again, in a wider circle this time, and stopped at the side facing the river. Below the house's brick *stoep*, which sat behind her at head height, was a narrow track that ran parallel to the fence that marked the actual boundary of Hippo Rock. The Sabie River gurgled around some smooth granite boulders about twenty metres from where she stood, hands on hips.

The Hippo Rock security personnel patrolled this road, on foot and quad bike in the morning and evening and at irregular times during the day, looking for signs of intrusion by humans, and by elephant, who were easily capable of breaking through the three strands of electric wire that constituted the fence along the river frontage.

Sannie detected movement in her peripheral vision and turned to see a big bull elephant with an impressive pair of tusks, shining clean and white after he'd waded across a stretch of river. The bull raised his trunk and sniffed the air, perhaps having picked up her scent.

Sannie stayed perfectly still, enjoying the sight of this regal fellow. She marvelled, again, at how quiet these giant creatures were. The elephant, having detected no sign of danger, began feeding on some papyrus on an island in the river. It was not the most nutritional form of vegetation, but at the end of the long dry season beggars couldn't be choosers. It was one of the reasons elephant were prone to break into Hippo Rock at this time of the year – because the reserve did not have resident elephant there were more trees here than across the river in the national park.

People who lived on the river were treated to regular sightings of elephant – not to mention lion, leopard, rhino and buffalo. Sannie and Tom hoped they might one day have enough to buy a property along this multi-millionaire's row. Sannie went back to scanning the ground.

As she walked along the perimeter fence, the road dipped into what would have been a rivulet during the rainy season. Here, as at the intersection of the main road, the water had pooled during the recent rain and the soil had turned to mud. Sannie stepped over the patch, which also held a good amount of spoor, and once more positioned herself so that the tracks were between her and the morning sun.

Ignoring the signs of animals, she zeroed in instead on another boot print. This could have been made by one of the security personnel, but if it had, then he had been stationary, staring out at the river.

Sannie took out her phone and, once more, dropped to her knee to get a better look. This boot looked to be about the same size as the one that had left the imprint by Hardekool Street.

Except that this print, quite clearly embedded in the mud, had been made by a boot with a slash across the sole.

*

Sonja turned off the taps of the outdoor shower on the deck of her luxury suite. Wildebeest snorted and brayed on the grassy slope in front of her as she towel-dried her hair under the sun and pulled it back in a ponytail.

She dressed and walked out and up the hill towards the dining area. The sun was low and red.

Hudson emerged from his suite – Sonja had made a point of insisting they had separate rooms – and joined her on the pathway. He said nothing.

'What's wrong?'

'Me joining the anti-poaching team wasn't part of the plan,' he said.

'No plan survives –'

'First contact with the enemy; I know Erwin Rommel and Sonja's Kurtz's "art of war", but you could have given me some warning.'

Sonja was annoyed with herself. Hudson was right; their plan had been that he would continue his own investigations on the periphery, perhaps even back in Arusha, after she re-joined Julianne's strike force, or whatever term they were using for the team now. It irked her that she had made the decision in an instant, and all because of jealousy. She hadn't wanted Hudson slinking off with Rosie Appleton. She saw her emotions now for what they were – foolish and counterproductive – but backing down was not in her nature.

'And now I've got to socialise and work with that prick Mario Machado,' Hudson added.

Sonja sighed. She really had made a mess of this. She regretted bringing Mario onto the team, and what had gone on between them, but she was sure he would be enough of a gentleman not to put her on the spot. She had made this bed and would have to lie in it, with both of these handsome dark-haired men.

She thought about Julianne Clyde-Smith. She was a powerful businesswoman, used to getting her own way, and it had been clear from their meeting earlier in the day that Julianne was pleased Sonja was back on the team, apart from her comment about Sonja leaving without notice in Zimbabwe. A couple of times during their talk, after Rosie had left, Julianne had leaned closer to Sonja and touched her on the arm to reinforce a point she was making.

They walked up the hill to the lodge and Hudson stepped aside so she could walk through into the dining area of the lodge first. 'OK. Let's do this.'

Tema stood up from a long table as soon as Sonja entered and walked around to her. They shook hands and then Tema hugged Sonja.

'I've missed you so much,' Tema whispered.

'Don't make it too obvious.'

Sonja looked around. Mario had been at the bar. He looked to her, then Hudson, his face souring. Sonja saw Hudson return the look. 'Where's Ezekial?' she asked Tema.

'In his room in the staff quarters. He says he's sick. He hasn't spoken to me since the contact we had with the elephant poachers.' Tema lowered her voice. 'He doesn't know that you've been getting me to spy on Mario, and I think that he thinks I'm some sort of cold-blooded killer like Mario. It's killing me not to tell Ezekial.'

'Not just yet,' Sonja said softly. 'Mario.'

He came to her and offered his hand. 'Nice to have you back, *boss*.'

Hudson took up a position behind her, protectively, she felt. She was between the two men, who said nothing to each other.

Mario glared at him. Sonja looked over her shoulder to Hudson.

He cleared his throat. 'Machado.'

'Brand.'

The silence hung between the three of them. Sonja put her hands on her hips. 'For God's sake, will one of you say something other than a surname?'

Mario looked to her. 'Paterson tells me he's joining the team.'

'Yes,' Sonja said. 'You can leave if you want.'

'I'm not running because of you, Brand.'

'No, you like the work too much,' Hudson replied.

'It's men's work.'

Hudson looked around the bar, to Tema and Sonja. 'Looks like you're outnumbered.'

'These women are more manly than you.'

Sonja held up a hand. 'Enough. You two are acting like schoolboys. We have important work to do and a new mission to be briefed on. If anyone wants out, now's the time to leave.'

The men stared at each other.

'I want a glass of wine,' Tema said. 'Anyone else for a drink?'

'Whisky,' Mario said, not breaking eye contact.

'Double,' Hudson said.

'Good.' Sonja beckoned over a waiter. 'Sit down, both of you, before I tell Tema to taser you.'

They took seats across the table from each other. Sonja was under no illusion that the two would make up and play nice, but that didn't concern her. She needed to find out more about what Clyde-Smith was up to. James Paterson walked in, a laptop computer under his arm.

'The other guests are having dinner in the boma this evening, so we have this area to ourselves,' he said without preamble. 'Tema, you can fill Ezekial in on the mission later, assuming he's still with us.'

'All right,' Tema said.

Paterson opened the laptop and positioned it at the far end of the dining table so they could all see it. He used a remote to open his presentation. The face of a white male, mid-fifties, came up on the screen.

'This is Nikola Pesev,' James said. 'Head of logistics for the UNHCR, the United Nations High Commission for Refugees in Tanzania.'

'He's a poacher?' Tema asked, eyes wide.

'I'll take questions at the end of the briefing,' James said. Tema nodded. 'Pesev is a Macedonian, a former officer in the old Yugoslav army, way back in the Cold War days. He was trained by the Russians and retains links to some former Soviet military people who have become successful "entrepreneurs" – read, gangsters.'

James clicked the remote. An image of a female chimpanzee with a baby in its arms, against a background of emerald-green foliage, flashed up. 'This is Pesev's current stock in trade: baby chimps. Julianne has just taken over a tented safari camp on the shores of Lake Tanganyika, Tanzania, on the edge of Mahale National Park. Mahale, along with the better known Gombe Stream, is one of Tanzania's havens for chimpanzees. Poaching is getting out of hand again. There's a market for baby chimps in the United Arab Emirates – it's trendy for wealthy Emiratis to have their own private zoos – and in Russia, where they're still prized as pets.'

Sonja shook her head. She noticed that Hudson had stopped glaring at Mario and was instead focusing on Paterson.

'As a logistician, Nikola organises road and air transport in and out of Tanzania to support a number of refugee camps east of Kigoma. The camps are holding people from Burundi who escaped the recent violence there when old feuds between the Hutus and Tutsis – the same conflict that sparked the Rwandan genocide in 1994 – flared up in Burundi. The UN workers like to stay at Kigoma on the shores of Lake Tanganyika as it's a lot nicer than living up in the hills with the displaced masses. Pesev recently invested in a lodge on the shores of Lake Tanganyika further south of Kigoma, near Kipili. Pesev's place, Paradise Bay Lodge, is much closer to Mahale National Park and there's an airstrip nearby. Much of his business is UN people on R&R, and we believe that when he charters aircraft to bring people from Kigoma to Kipili he backloads baby chimps stolen from Mahale to Kigoma, then arranges for them to be flown out of Africa on UN cargo aircraft. Questions now.'

'Where does your intel come from?' Sonja asked.

'Like any successful crime figure, Pesev has made enemies. One of them contacted a journalist and provided some pretty damning evidence on Pesev and his activities.'

'Who's the journalist?' Hudson asked.

James looked up. 'Ah, Rosie. Welcome. Right on cue.'

Sonja turned and saw the red-haired South African walk in. She seethed, seeing the woman's smug smile.

'Hello, we meet again,' Rosie said, directing her comment to Sonja.

'So what do you have to say for yourself?' Sonja asked.

Rosie wasn't backing down this time. 'If you hadn't sent me away so rudely before, I could have told you earlier.'

'Ladies,' Paterson said. 'Sonja, please let Rosie speak.'

'Of course.'

Rosie nodded to James, who advanced his slide presentation. A scan of a story from the South African *Sunday Times* came up, a full-page feature headed, *Lid lifted on UN child sex trafficking*.

'This is a story I did when I was on assignment in Uganda a year ago. A female UN worker I met in a bar in Kampala told me she was resigning because she'd reported a colleague, a medic, whom she'd seen touching a child inappropriately in a clinic in Entebbe. She claimed that as well as sexual abuse of minors there were rumours that orphaned children were being smuggled out of the country. The woman's complaint against her co-worker had been buried in a mass of bureaucracy and internal investigations, but when my story broke the UN was forced to act decisively. The medic was charged, deported, and ended up doing time in prison in the US. I couldn't conclusively prove anything about UN transport being used to fly or drive kids illegally out of the country, but the man responsible for logistics there was –'

'Let me guess,' Sonja interrupted, 'Nikola Pesev.'

Rosie nodded. 'My source – I won't name her – stayed with the UN after my story forced them to clean up their act, but she kept tabs on Pesev. She believed he was dirty, and still is, though now she's telling me he's using company transport to ship out baby chimps rather than humans.'

Sonja directed her question to James. 'You say Pesev worked with the Russians when he was in the military and still has ties to them.'

'Yes, which brings me to my next slide.' He advanced the presentation. There was a head shot of Pesev in the middle of the screen with arrows radiating out to a number of Russian-sounding names. 'These are companies for which Nikola Pesev is listed as a director.'

'There's a lot of them,' Hudson said.

'Yes,' said Paterson.

'I've investigated some of these businesses,' Rosie said. 'Some seem legit, others not so, but you could say that about every new business in Russia.'

'He speaks Russian?' Sonja asked.

Paterson nodded. 'Fluently.'

Sonja rubbed her chin. 'Where else has he worked in Africa?'

'The question is, where hasn't he worked,' said Paterson. He gave a half-smile.

'Zambia?' said Sonja.

'Tick. Right across the border from Zimbabwe, in the Lower Zambezi Valley, opposite Mana Pools National Park.'

'One of the poachers we came across in Zimbabwe, in Mana Pools, spoke of the local kingpin there, Obert Mvuu, dealing with a Russian-speaking man named Nicholas,' Sonja said.

'When I interviewed Julianne,' Rosie said, 'she mentioned the report of a Russian-speaking white man buying ivory in Zambia. I didn't let on to her at the time, but the first thing I thought was that the man could be Pesev. It's the corroboration I was looking for. Nikola could very easily be misconstrued as Nicholas, and he speaks Russian.'

'Mozambique?' Sonja asked next.

'Yes,' said James, 'he worked in Massingir, hometown of many of the rhino poaching gangs that enter South Africa. Pesev is currently based in Tanzania, at his place on the lake, but he's more of a consultant than a fulltime employee of the UN these days. He has a remit to travel the continent south of the Sahara to advise and audit the UN's logistics operations.'

Rosie cleared her throat. 'I asked my source if she could trace Pesev's recent movements and she was able to do so, via a friend of hers who worked in the travel booking part of the organisation.'

Paterson took centre stage again. 'Rosie kindly handed the

travel documentation over to me. I crosschecked it with the reports we have from my own sources in Zimbabwe, Zambia, Mozambique, and here in Tanzania. There are several reports, most unsubstantiated, of a Russian-speaking white man having meetings with poaching kingpins and middlemen at the same times and in the same general areas as Pesev's travels through Africa on UN business. It would be easy for Pesev to masquerade as a Russian businessman to disguise his real nationality and job.'

He clicked the remote and Sonja leaned closer to the screen. The dates of Pesev's travels matched up with those of the armed contacts they had been in. It would have been easy for Pesev to get to the Zimbabwe–Zambia border from his business meeting in Lusaka, and in Mozambique he had even been visiting Massingir the day before she and the others had been scrambled to intercept King Jim and Antonio Cuna at the golf course near Hazyview. 'Nikola Pesev is one of the Scorpions,' she said.

Paterson shook his head this time. 'Yes, but there's more, I now believe Nikola Pesev is *the* Scorpion, the head man.'

'What makes you so sure?'

He held up his hands. 'I'm not, but Rosie's information is pointing that way.'

Sonja regarded him. She wondered if he was being overly cautious now that she was back, and whether his orders to Mario and the team – if she were not there – would have been simpler, more direct. 'So our mission is to find out for sure, one way or the other?'

'Exactly,' Paterson said. 'We will mount an intensive under-cover surveillance operation on Pesev. He's at his new lodge on the shore of Lake Tanganyika at Kipili now, and is planning to stay there for a week. Julianne's people have made reservations, though not direct, through a travel company. You'll all be issued fake identities and documentation. I want everyone to make sure they have each other's phone numbers, even the boys who don't play nice, to make sure we're all in communication during the infiltration phase.'

'And if we do find proof Pesev is the head of the Scorpions, what then?' Sonja asked.

Paterson glanced over at Rosie, the journalist, and then to Sonja. 'We compile a dossier of evidence for the Tanzanian police and Interpol and let them take it from there.'

'Of course,' Sonja said.

Chapter 21

Hudson and Sonja were ready to leave Kuria Hills early the next morning. Julianne was up before dawn to say goodbye to them as they had breakfast, and Paterson was in the car park as the porters loaded Hudson and Sonja's meagre luggage into the Land Rover for the road trip to Kipili, on Lake Tanganyika.

'I don't envy you, being the road party on this mission,' Paterson said to them as he leaned against the driver's side door.

Hudson started the engine. 'Well, like you said in the briefing, it's less obvious if we all arrive from different directions.' Paterson had explained that he'd be flying in while Mario and Tema, masquerading as a couple on their honeymoon, would arrive by boat from a luxury camp in Mahale National Park. Hudson and Sonja were going overland, via some of the worst roads in Tanzania. 'We've got a long, hard drive ahead of us, so we need to get moving.'

'What will you do about Ezekial?' Sonja asked Paterson. 'He's a loose end.'

Ezekial had disappeared from the camp. No vehicles or fire-arms were missing; he had simply vanished during the night.

For most people, setting off through the Serengeti National Park in the dark, on foot and unarmed, would be akin to committing a lion-assisted suicide, but as a master tracker Ezekial was a consummate bushman, adept at reading the signs of the wild and avoiding dangerous game. He would be able to survive in the bush for weeks.

'I'll find him,' Paterson said, then added, 'I'm worried about the poor lad.'

Hudson touched the peak of his Texas Longhorns cap. 'Gotta go. Enjoy your flight.'

They drove off along the narrow winding access road from the camp towards the main route that led north, to their left, to the Kuria Hills airstrip and the Mara River just beyond, and right, southwards, in the direction they needed to head, past Kichwa Tembo and on to the Fort Ikoma Gate and the road towards the great lakes.

Against the pink morning sky was a line of black wildebeest silhouettes that stretched away as far as they could see. The animals were heading towards the Mara River. Hudson marvelled at them. They were not, judging by appearances and behaviour, the sharpest critters in God's realm, but here they were, on their annual pilgrimage, travelling thousands of kilometres and guided by a mix of memory and instinct, in search of food, water and a future for their offspring. They grunted and brayed as they walked, shaggy heads tossing as if in conversation with each other.

As they reached the junction of the main road, three Toyota Land Cruiser game viewers sped past them, leaving a cloud of red dust hanging in the still, cool morning air.

'They're in a hurry,' Sonja said.

He looked at her. 'It'll be a crossing, the migration swimming the Mara River.'

She smiled. 'You want to see it, don't you?'

'It's quite a spectacle, Sonja. I know it might seem frivolous given what we're setting out to do, but it's one of those things I think everyone should see at least once in their life. I'd like to show you.'

Sonja reached over and put her hand on his. He felt his old heart constrict a little. 'Thank you for thinking of me.'

'My pleasure, ma'am.'

She smiled and Hudson turned left, instead of right.

They drove a few kilometres down the road and came to the Kuria Hills airstrip. A guide driving an empty vehicle approached them and Hudson waved him down. Hudson asked if he knew where the other vehicles had gone, in search of the crossing, and the man gave him directions.

From the airport Hudson crossed the river via a low-level concrete causeway. He pointed to the left, where the bloated body of a wildebeest, perhaps a drowning victim, was snagged in some rocks.

After they crossed Hudson took a left on a rough track that meandered through a dry tributary of the river. They were still well inside Tanzania and stayed parallel to the Mara, following the tracks of the vehicles ahead of them, and countless others that had made the same human migration in the years before.

'On a hill, over there,' Sonja said, pointing.

Hudson saw the three vehicles they'd been following. They had parked on the crest of the small rise, a hundred metres or so from the river's edge. 'They're waiting up there, watching to see where the animals will cross, so they don't spook them.'

Sonja nodded. Hudson wove between trees and bushes and parked not far from the other vehicles. 'Now we wait.'

Across the river the wildebeest, sprinkled with a few zebra, were amassing. Their numbers were building up, putting pressure on those closest to the Mara. Much of the riverbank was a sheer drop-off, though there was a well-worn section that was not quite as steep, where previous columns had gone down to the river to drink and cross. Dust rose like a brewing storm cloud above the growing herds.

Hudson took out his binoculars. 'There are hundreds of them already, just on the edge.' In the distance were four other long lines, single files of scores of animals all being drawn or pushed to the same point.

'One's going down to the water's edge,' Sonja said.

Hudson shifted his view. Sonja was right. A lone wildebeest – it looked like a bull – had either decided to take the loose dusty track down to the river, or perhaps he'd been pushed over the edge by the crush building behind him. Whatever his motivation he found himself at the forefront. He tossed his head and looked up at where he had just come from.

'Even if he wants to turn back, he probably can't; the others are all crowding the edge of the bank,' Sonja said.

Stuck as he was, the lonely bull made the most of his predicament. He lowered his head, his shaggy beard dipping into the cool, fast-flowing waters of the Mara. He drank. Then he looked up, droplets falling as he tossed his head. Something hardwired into his tiny brain made him take a step, then another. He was in up to his knees.

'My God, the tension is incredible,' Sonja said.

Hudson felt it, too. It was palpable, like a building force rolling across the river to where they were. He took Sonja's hand.

'Is he going to?'

Hudson held his breath. Then, for whatever reason, that single wildebeest decided it was time to stop drinking and start swimming. His first strokes were clumsy, his hooves perhaps sticking in the mud or sand of the riverbed, but by the time he had covered a couple of metres he had triggered one of the greatest natural phenomena on earth.

As if a siren had been sounded or switch flicked, the bumbling, disorganised mob focused itself and leapt, literally, into action.

Behind the leader dozens of wildebeests now began running, staggering, slipping and sliding down the well-worn descent to the river. The ground was loose, bare of grass, and a curtain of dust began to rise as hundreds of hooves churned the sand and soil.

'It looks like they're on fire,' Sonja breathed.

The dust did look like smoke, rising up above them. By the time the first animal was halfway across the river there were fifty more in the water behind him, in files two and three abreast, legs flailing, heads held high out of the churning spume.

The current was strong and the leaders were being swept downriver. They redoubled their efforts and began heading back upstream.

Around Sonja and Hudson engines were coming to life. By the time the brave or foolhardy first wildebeest had crossed the river, safe and sound, the safari vehicles had taken up strategic viewing positions either side of the animals' exit point.

Hudson found them a position, on a rise, with just one other vehicle between them and the crossing point. A continuous stream of wildebeests was now galloping between the vehicles, the water flying from their bodies making a slippery black road in the otherwise powdery grey earth.

It was a spectacle that assaulted all the senses. The smell of the tightly packed bodies washed over them and the noise of their braying carried on the warm breeze from the other side of the river. Hooves pounded the ground as the wildebeests ran from their fears once they had scaled the embankment on the humans' side.

Hudson opened the door of the Land Rover and climbed up on the bonnet of the truck. Sonja joined him and they sat on the roof, in the open with front-row grandstand seats to nature's command performance.

'They're splitting,' Sonja said.

The phalanx swimming against the tide was getting too wide for the exit point, and a splinter group had peeled off to the right of Hudson and Sonja.

'They'll never make it up there,' Sonja said.

The bank they were heading for looked like a sheer vertical climb of several metres. Amazingly, a few seconds after they lost sight of the divergent herd, a shaggy head appeared to their right, hooves frantically pawing at the dirt and dry grass. A wildebeest hauled itself up over the edge.

'Incredible,' Hudson said. On the far bank the mass hysteria was having a similar effect in reverse. Rather than slipping and sliding down the washout to the first crossing point, animals were hurling themselves off the high bank and splashing noisily into the river, which was now churned brown from thousands of flailing legs.

A dazzle of zebra, the reasoning behind the collective noun now clearly apparent, broke from the dusty blue-grey mass of the wildebeest and galloped imperiously down to the water's edge. When the zebra took to the waters they swam like thoroughbred horses in training, heads held high and calm as they easily outflanked and overtook the clumsy, struggling masses of wildebeest.

The animals that had been scaling the mini cliff near Hudson and Sonja found another gully, still steep but less sheer, and the first animal emerged not two metres from where Hudson and Sonja were perched on the Land Rover. The wildebeest looked up, clearly surprised to see the humans, and started to turn back.

'Get down.' Hudson took Sonja's hand and eased her back down onto the hood of the Land Rover. They crouched so their silhouettes no longer broke the outline of the vehicle. The startled wildebeest was met by his comrades coming up the washout. He turned again and, not seeing the human heads bobbing around, charged past them. The next thing Hudson and Sonja saw was their own private stream of animals thundering past, almost within touching distance.

Sonja nuzzled into Hudson and he put an arm around her. He could feel her heart beating, as fast as his, as they watched the unending procession. The smell of wet hair and wild fear was thick in the air. Hundreds of hooves drummed the ground.

A third crossing point opened up and the pressure on the narrow inlet by their vehicle began to ease. Hudson checked his watch. Forty-five minutes after the spectacle had begun it ended, just as suddenly. Those animals that had crossed had moved off, though some stragglers were now calling quietly and grazing on grass as if nothing had happened. On the far bank of the river more wildebeest and zebra were arriving, but as none were in the water these newcomers were content to just mill about and feed on their side. The river was quiet again.

Sonja tilted her head and Hudson kissed her.

'That was amazing; awesome in the true sense of the word, not as in how my daughter uses it.'

He laughed, and it was like a release. Scenes of the great migration crossing the Mara were usually accompanied by the river's crocodiles indulging in their annual gluttonous feast. Hudson had been doing some mental arithmetic during the crossing, working out the time it took one animal to cross and the average number of animals in the river at any one time during the spectacle, which had taken forty-five minutes. 'I'd say we just saw three thousand animals swim that river and not a single one of them was taken.'

Sonja beamed. 'I know. I half expected to see a kill happen, but I'm so glad I didn't.'

'I know what you mean. I feel . . . I don't know. I feel like giving them a round of applause.'

Sonja stood upright on the bonnet of the Land Rover, raised her hands in the air, turned to the grazing animals and started clapping. Tourists in the nearby two safari vehicles saw her and, after some puzzled looks, realised what she was doing and joined her in a standing ovation to nature.

Hudson did the same and they hugged. People whistled as they kissed.

The magic of the moment over, they climbed down, got back in the truck, and drove off towards their own private war.

*

The next day, Tema was on a boat, on Lake Tanganyika. There had been many firsts in her life since she had joined the Leopards and then gone to work for Julianne Clyde-Smith that she had lost count of them.

Some of them, like flying for the first time and being in combat, had been frightening yet exciting, while others, like being in a speedboat bouncing across a vast inland body of fresh water, were simply terrifying. She held tight to the gunwale, her face grim.

'Cheer up, this is fun,' Mario yelled over the screaming engine.

'For you, maybe.'

'I miss the water,' he said.

'I've never been on a boat before. I don't like it.'

He laughed, but it was no joking matter as far as Tema was concerned. She couldn't wait to get to dry land.

For the sake of appearances, and in case Nikola Pesev had a reason to check up on them, Mario and Tema had flown to Mahale National Park the day before and spent the night at Julianne's tented camp on the shores of the lake on the opposite side to Kipili, where they were heading now. They had shared a tent, notionally and in respect to their booking, but Mario had slept in the staff quarters, leaving Tema to soak up the luxury.

They didn't go chimp trekking, the park's flagship activity, but instead spent the day rehearsing their cover stories, as a newly married couple, and discussing how they would carry out their surveillance of Pesev.

Tema felt queasy, but her spirits lifted a little when she saw a green fringe come into view on the horizon. Land. She felt an arm around her shoulders.

'Hey!'

'Relax,' said Mario. 'If someone's watching from shore they'll see a honeymoon couple, not two co-workers. We discussed this, remember?'

'Sure.' She knew that some touching would be part of their cover, and they had talked about it, but all the same it felt creepy when Mario snuggled just a little too close to her. He was handsome, she guessed, but he was also easily old enough to be her father. It was Ezekial she wanted. She'd been more acutely aware of her growing feelings for him since he had disappeared, and it pained her that he had run off before Sonja had the chance to tell him what she was really up to. Tema had sent him an SMS message saying where she was heading, to Kipili, on the shore of Lake Tanganyika, although she had no idea where he was or if he had received the message.

The boatman eased off on his throttle and the craft returned to a more sedate pace as it settled on the glassy water. Other than the uncomfortable feeling of Mario's flesh on hers, she started to feel a little better.

As they approached a concrete breakwater and jetty Tema saw a white man walk down from the single-storey, open-fronted building that looked like a lounge or dining area. He wore a panama hat, and as the driver eased the boat into place she could see the man was their target, Nikola Pesev.

Why, she wondered, had the owner of the lodge come to greet them himself? Surely he would have had a manager or other staff member on duty?

Mario stood and stepped lithely off the boat. He held out a hand to Tema. She took it, gratefully this time, as her legs felt rubbery.

'How do you do?' Pesev asked.

'Hi.' Mario introduced them by their assumed names and the two men shook hands. 'This lovely young lady is my wife. Beauty by name and beauty by nature.'

'Charmed,' Pesev said, touching the brim of his hat. 'Welcome, I am Nikola.'

'Have you worked here for long, Nikola?' Mario asked, as a porter fetched their bags from the boat.

'I'm the owner. I only just built this lodge last year. I was lucky to even get the land.'

'Really?' Mario asked.

'Yes, someone else, another tourism operator, was desperate to buy some lake-front property with a decent beach. I was able to get in first.'

'Who was the other operator?' Tema asked.

'Can we get a drink, please, Nikola?' Mario asked, abruptly. Tema was miffed.

'Um, of course, yes.' Nikola called the waiter. 'Moses will take your orders. If you'll excuse me, I just have to go and check my emails. I must warn you that while our internet is free, it is satellite, so it takes a long time to download and send messages. I hope to see you later.'

Nikola left and after they had ordered Cokes Tema motioned Mario to come out to the balcony area. 'Why did you cut me off like that?'

'It's all right,' Mario said, too condescendingly for Tema's liking, 'we don't want him to get too suspicious of us, by asking too many questions when we've only just arrived. We're here for three days, remember, so we'll give him enough time, enough rope, and he'll eventually hang himself up, or the covert team will find the dirt on him.'

Tema huffed, but kept her emotions in check when the waiter arrived. Sonja and Hudson were to be the 'covert team' Mario had mentioned. Both had experience in undercover surveillance and what James Paterson referred to as the 'black arts'. Hudson, it turned out, was an accomplished lock-pick, and Sonja had been trained in covert reconnaissance by the British Army.

If Tema and Mario couldn't coax enough leads out of Nikola by conversing with him and eavesdropping then Sonja and Hudson would break in to his office, perhaps his accommodation, and search his computer and other digital and physical records. Paterson had brought an array of electrical surveillance gear with him from South Africa and he would be their technological quartermaster.

After they finished their drinks, the porter who had taken their bags returned to show them to their room. Tema and Mario followed him. Tema wondered how this would work. At Julianne's Mahale camp Mario had slept in the staff quarters but now – to maintain their cover that they were honeymooners – they would have to stay in the same chalet. The thought made Tema feel anxious.

They walked along a white sandy track flanked with stones.

The village of Kipili was over the hill, beyond a campground, where Tema saw two South African–registered Land Rovers parked in the shade of a giant mango tree. The tourist occupants were having lunch. She saw that the registration plates ended in MP, Mpumalanga Province, her home. She felt a twinge in her heart, thinking of her mother and her daughter, back home, and for a moment she longed for her simpler, if poorer life.

Mario had told her, last night, of the pay rise he had negotiated with James for her. Her monthly wage would be more than she made in a year as a maid at Hippo Rock, and even her pay with the Leopards had been not much better. Mario told her that with the skills and experience she had amassed in her anti-poaching work she could potentially work overseas, as a contractor, just as he and Sonja had. She didn't like the idea of being even further away from Shine, but the wages Mario had alluded to, all in US dollars, seemed like an incredible fortune. How, she wondered, had she ended up as a gun for hire?

The porter led them into a beachfront bungalow. It was beautiful. In the centre of the room was a king-sized bed. As honeymooners it would have been unusual to ask for separate beds. Mario had said he would sleep on the floor, or on a day bed and, luckily, there was one, overlooking the glittering waters of the lake through wide open sliding doors. A gentle breeze stirred the mosquito net hanging from a wooden frame beneath a ceiling fan.

'It's lovely,' Tema said to the porter.

'Yes, very good.' Mario palmed the man a tip in Tanzanian shillings.

Tema looked around the beautiful room. How her life had changed; until recently, the only chance she would have had of entering a place like this would have been to clean it. The man left. Mario sat down in a wicker armchair.

'Nice, yes?' Tema said, filling the silence.

'Yes.'

'What do we do now?'

Mario winked. 'You know what the porter is thinking we're doing.'

'Mario, please.'

He stood and Tema took a step backwards, towards the door.

'Tema, relax. We just need to spend some time here, for the sake of appearances. I'm not going to hurt you.'

Just him saying that made her heart beat faster, and not in a good way. 'All right, I'll read.'

Mario moved a pace closer. 'How about a drink? There's sherry on the sideboard over there.'

'No, thank you.'

'Then get me one.'

She looked at him. She was not his servant, though he was her superior in the team. It was not in her nature, nor her culture, to disobey.

'Please.'

She exhaled. 'Well, all right. I'm closer.'

Tema turned and went across the spacious, airy suite to the cabinet. Next to a small kettle and tea and coffee was a cut-glass decanter and two glasses. She righted one and poured the golden brown liquid into it. She had never tried sherry.

Tema started and spilled the sticky fluid as she felt his hands on her shoulders.

'Stop, please.'

He kept his hands there, squeezing his fingers together, beginning to knead her shoulders. Tema was too scared to turn around. 'Mario, please.'

'Shush.'

She felt his warm breath on her neck; he had moved his head closer. 'Tema, we're friends, right? You don't need to think of me as your commander always.'

She swallowed. 'Sonja is our commander.'

'Yes, but I'm second in charge, clearly. I'm the one who got you that lovely pay rise. Aren't you grateful for that?'

She felt woozy.

Tema reached around, handing Mario the drink. He took one hand off her and she heard him slurp down the sherry. Then she heard a chink as he tossed the little glass onto the floor.

Her whole body tensed as he caressed her neck with the backs of his fingers. She felt a chill as he trailed his nails down over her collarbone, over her T-shirt, tracing the swell of her breast.

'Please. No.'

'Yes.' His hand cupped her.

Tema was wearing high heels, impractical in the sand but part of her costume as the sexy young wife. She brought a foot up and raked her stiletto down Mario's shin. As he cried out she jabbed her elbow back into his stomach.

'Get off me.'

'Ouch.'

She spun around and Mario swung at her. Tema did the opposite of what he expected, coming closer in to him, inside the arc of his slap. She grabbed his shirt front in her two hands and brought her knee up into his balls. Mario doubled over.

Tema pulled back, her body poised.

Mario groaned as he half stood and lunged at her. Tema was ready and, as Sonja had taught her, she stabbed his eyeballs with the first two fingers of her right hand. Mario yelped like a dog.

'Enough.' He raised his hands.

Tema looked around. She picked up a lamp by its slender stand, and hoisted it like a war club. 'Try something else and I'll finish you off.'

Mario coughed. 'No. Enough.'

'Not quite.'

Tema swung the lamp and the shade fell off and the bulb exploded with a pop as the stand connected with Mario's temple. She went to the door of the suite, opened it and ran out.

'Tema!'

She didn't turn back, even when he ordered her to stop and return. Instead, Tema carried on towards the bar and lounge area of the lodge.

'Help me, help me,' she cried.

Nikola Pesev came walking out of the lodge office. 'What's wrong?'

'My husband. I . . . I hate him,' she sobbed.

Nikola opened his arms and Tema pressed herself against his chest. The tears that wet his shirt were real – she had been truly scared – but as the businessman's arms folded around her, Tema smiled.

271

Chapter 22

Sonja knew things were not going well when she saw Mario's cut and bruised face.

'Where's Tema?'

'She's with the target, staying in his house, since just after we arrived yesterday.'

'She's *what?*'

'I tried to get friendly with her – to keep up our appearance as a honeymoon couple.' He rubbed his eye. 'She wasn't in the mood.'

Sonja put her hands on her hips and sized him up. He didn't seem to think he had done anything wrong, sexually harassing a subordinate. 'For fuck's sake, Mario.'

Hudson stood back, by the Land Rover. He was picking his teeth. He and Sonja were both filthy, covered in a layer of dust from the long, bumpy drive. They had stopped in a terrible hotel in a small town called Kibondo, near the UN refugee camps on the Burundian border that Nikola Pesev provided logistic support for.

Mario smiled and shrugged. 'She's tough, that girl. She's wormed her way into Pesev's affections. He's shown me the red card, threatened to hurt me if I touch her again. Tema's saying she doesn't want to see me, so we've got an asset inside, but I'm persona non grata.'

Sonja shook her head. She would have laughed if the situation wasn't so dangerous.

'I'll set up camp,' Hudson said.

'All right,' said Sonja. 'I'll go check in. Mario, don't let yourself be seen with us.'

'It's OK,' he said. 'I've established a daily routine. I go for a walk past the campground – I spoke to some Australians who were here yesterday – and then to the village. Tema's probably telling Pesev I'm trolling for young girls.'

Hudson was unfolding the roof-top tent from the Land Rover, behind them. 'Makes sense to have a cover based on truth.'

'What did you say, Brand?'

Hudson lowered the ladder support of the tent to the ground and wiped his hands on his shorts.

'I said you're a cocksucker, Mario.'

Mario started towards him, but Sonja stepped in front of him and put her hand up on his chest. 'Stop.' She looked over her shoulder. 'And you zip it as well, mister. Sheesh, it's like dealing with two little boys.'

Sonja could see that Mario was seething. He'd been able to brush off his beating from Tema, but the animosity between him and Hudson was palpable. She'd tried to draw Hudson out, on the long drive, but he'd refused to give any details about his history with his one-time fellow officer. 'Go for your walk, Mario. Ask around in the village, see what they think of Pesev, the new lord of the manor here.'

Mario and Hudson glared at each other for a few seconds, then Mario continued on his way.

Sonja walked down to the reception area and found a barman who took her booking for the camping site. She asked if the owner was around and was told he was at his residence, but would be at the lodge later.

'We have a problem with our Land Rover. I'd really like to talk to him now, if I can, to see if he can recommend a mechanic. Can you take me to him, please?'

'OK, madam,' the barman said.

Sonja followed him along a path that led away from the beachfront suites. They walked past a couple of small thatched bandas with sun beds. The clear waters of Lake Tanganyika looked cool and inviting after the long hot drive in Brand's un-airconditioned vehicle, but Sonja's first priorities were Tema, and the mission.

The path meandered through a stand of reeds and emerged at a beach that was smaller, but just as pristine as the one in front of the lodge. Set back from the sand, flanked by watered green lawns, was a lovely, single-storey whitewashed house.

On the beach in front was a thatched banda and under it Tema reclined on a sun bed. A multicoloured cocktail topped by a little umbrella rested in the shade on a carved wooden side table.

Tema, her young body brilliantly framed by a starkly white bikini, lowered her big sunglasses and regarded Sonja. She gave no sign of recognising her, but set down her copy of *Vogue* magazine and started tapping something on her phone.

Sonja bit her lower lip to stop from laughing.

Nikola Pesev came out of his house wearing swimming trunks and a blue T-shirt. Sonja recognised him from the pictures. He raised a hand to shield his eyes against the glare from the lake and the white sand. 'Hello?'

'Howzit,' Sonja said, 'I'm sorry to bother you at your home, but I need some help. We've got a problem with our vehicle.'

'Hello. There are no problems here at the Paradise Bay Lodge. Please, come in.'

'Hi there,' Tema called from her sun bed. 'Is that a South African accent I detect?'

'*Ja*,' Sonja said, laying it on. 'We're from Nelspruit, here on holiday.'

'O. M. G. I'm from Hazyview.'

'No ways,' Sonja said.

Tema got off the sun bed and Sonja noticed the way Nikola's eyes followed every sway of those hips.

'Howzit, I'm Beauty Baloyi,' Tema said, using her cover name.

'Ursula Schmidt.' Sonja had used her favourite aunt's name often when working in similar situations.

'*Lekker* to meet you.'

'Come in, come in,' Nikola said. 'It's not every day I get the company of *two* damsels in distress.'

'You're in trouble?' Sonja asked.

Tema rolled her eyes. 'Long story. Man problems.'

'Can I get you a cold drink?' Nikola asked Sonja. Tema held up her cocktail to show Nikola she was still fine.

'A Coke Zero would be great if you have one.' Sonja took off the grime- and dust-encrusted baseball cab she'd been wearing.

'Nothing stronger?'

'Well, if you happen to have Klipdrift?'

'Ha! Brandy and Coke, the national drink of South Africa.'

Sonja laughed. Pesev seemed charming and convivial. When he turned and went to a heavy wooden sideboard that served as a bar, Sonja raised her eyebrows in a question to Tema.

He's nice, Tema mouthed.

Sonja wasn't so ready to judge Pesev by the way he presented himself to a couple of women. All Paterson had been able to tell them about his sexual preferences was that he was straight. He'd been married in the past and had relationships with two fellow UN co-workers, both of them African. He was believed to be single at the present time.

'So what's the problem with your vehicle, Ursula?'

'We've had a couple of punctures so we need two new tyres, and there's a problem with the steering.'

'Ah,' he said. 'Are you heading down the lake?'

'Yes, back towards Zambia, then Zimbabwe, Botswana and home to South Africa.'

'The next large town is Sumbawanga. There's a good tyre place there and a couple of mechanics. I can have my workshop guys take a look at it for you if you wish?'

'That would be great. Can I ask, what's your accent? You don't sound like you're African.'

He smiled and handed her a drink. 'In my heart and soul I am, but, no, you're right. I'm from Macedonia. I came here with the UN, and after buying this lodge I'm just about to retire.'

'You look very young to retire.'

'Ha, thank you. You're too kind. I've had a good working life and I like to think I've done my bit. But now the rest of my life is for me.'

Sonja looked to Tema. 'You must love living here.'

Tema shook her head. 'Oh, no. I'm not staying here. I'm actually sort of in transit. It's complicated.'

'If you'd like to explain over dinner, perhaps you'd like to join my boyfriend and me. Nikola, do you eat with the guests?'

He sipped a sparkling water he'd poured from a Perrier bottle. 'I am still new enough to the hospitality business that I love meeting new people and dining with my guests. My friends who work in hotels and safari lodges tell me I will tire of this, but for now I am enjoying it.'

'Great, then if you'd like to be our guests, Mike and I would love to buy you dinner.'

'I eat for free every night,' Nikola said, 'but I accept your kind offer. Perhaps I can bring the wine.'

'Lovely,' Sonja said. 'It's a date. Now, if I could take you up on your offer to get your workshop man to . . .'

Nikola's phone rang. He answered it, in Russian, and said a few words.

'Excuse me,' he said to Sonja.

'Sure,' Nikola turned his back on her, walking deeper into the room. Sonja took out her iPhone, found the voice recorder app and hit the red button. She put the phone down on the bar, behind the bottle of brandy, and dropped her baseball cap on top so that it partially covered it. She walked out, motioning with a flick of her head for Tema to come with her. They left Nikola in private.

'Is that Russian?' Tema asked.

'It is.'

'Wow.'

'Why wow?' Sonja asked.

'I mean, we knew from the briefing that he *can* speak Russian, and now he is, just like the leader of the Scorpions.'

'This is all still conjecture,' Sonja said, taking Tema by the elbow and leading her further away from Nikola's bungalow. 'He could be talking about anything.'

'Will you be able to translate what he's saying, from your phone recording?'

Sonja shook her head. She tipped most of her drink onto the sand. She needed to keep a clear head. 'No, but I'll find someone who can. Paterson flies in later today. He's got all the electronic surveillance gear so we can plant a proper bug and if Pesev does some more talking we'll have more material to work with.'

'I sent James a WhatsApp message when you arrived, updating him. He also knows I'm here in the house.'

'Good work,' Sonja said. She liked Tema's initiative and thought she had done a good job getting so close to the target so soon, even if it did increase the risk to her. 'What have you been able to find out so far?'

'Well, like I said, he is actually a very nice man. Not sleazy, like Mario.'

'Did Mario hurt you, Tema?'

'I hurt him.'

Sonja nodded. 'And Pesev?'

Tema shrugged. 'If he wants me he hasn't made a play for me yet.'

Sonja looked her up and down. 'You're not exactly playing the shrinking violet.'

Tema winked at her. 'Well, I think he likes looking at me. I'm not going to have sex with him, not even for the mission, in case that's what you're thinking.'

'Absolutely not,' Sonja assured her. 'And don't. I'll get you out before that happens.' Sonja had been in that situation herself, when she was a young undercover operative for the British Army in Northern Ireland, tracking a dangerous IRA bomber. She wouldn't wish that predicament on anyone.

'He ducks away every now and then to make calls, but never in front of me, nor does he seem to like to take calls in front of his staff.'

'Anyone visited the house?'

'No, just me. From what I've seen he's very hands-on in the management of the lodge, very particular. He was showing the waiters how to measure the distances between knives, forks and spoons and the plates this morning. I got him talking about his time in the UN.'

'And?'

Tema shrugged. 'He was very passionate about the UNHCR and the work they do with refugees. He's also worked for their education arm, UNICEF. He says he's enjoyed travelling all over Africa but wants to settle down now.'

'Signs of wealth?'

'I took a walk around. He does OK, very, in fact. He's got a Range Rover, late model, out in a garage behind the workshop, and a Discovery 4 kitted out like a safari vehicle, so he's got money. He's also got a fishing boat and a luxury motor cruiser, and a couple of jetskis. He offers snorkelling and diving trips and he told me he likes driving the boats himself. He's offered to take me out, but I don't know if I can handle it after the trip over. I almost lost my lunch.'

'Do it,' Sonja ordered. 'If you can keep him out on the water for a few hours, say, tomorrow morning, it will give Hudson and me time to plant the bugs and have a good look through this place.'

'He's coming,' Tema whispered.

'Sorry about that,' he said, putting his phone in his pocket. 'I hate to keep a lady, or ladies, waiting. Shall we go to the work-shop, Ursula? I can introduce you to my mechanic.'

'Sure.' Sonja started to walk ahead, then stopped. 'Oops, sorry, I think I left my hat inside.'

'Let me get it for you,' Nikola said.

'I'm closer,' Tema said quickly. 'Do you remember where you put it?'

'On the bar, I think,' Sonja said. The girl was fast thinking.

'So,' Sonja said, wanting to keep Nikola engaged, 'my boyfriend and I wanted to stop at Katavi National Park on the way down here but I was worried about the vehicle. I've heard it's pretty remote and the tsetse flies are bad, and so is the poaching. What do you think, Nikola? Should we have risked it?'

'Well the tsetses *are* murder there. As for the poaching, yes, it happens. It's something that sickens me, the amount of elephant ivory poaching here in Tanzania. It's dire in the Selous National Park and spreading around the country. It's unspeakable; I don't know how anyone could kill an elephant.'

'Well, in South Africa, in our Kruger Park, the authorities say there are too many elephants and they should be culled. Same in Zimbabwe. We stopped in Hwange National Park on the way up and you should see the damage to the environment that too many elephants have caused.'

Nikola smiled, but shook his head. He wasn't taking the bait. 'Call me romantic, but I think we must find a way to live with nature, to make room for those elephants to move. The peace parks initiatives down your way need more time to work before we even contemplate deliberately killing such beautiful animals.'

'Here you are.' Tema returned and handed Sonja her hat, with the phone wrapped inside.

'Tema, do you want to come with us for a walk?'

'I think I'll just stay here, maybe move inside into the shade and read, if it's OK with you, Nikola?'

'Fine.'

As Nikola led off Tema caught Sonja's eye and winked.

Be careful, Sonja mouthed.

*

The sight of James wincing as he put his shirt on gave Julianne another little tingle of satisfaction. 'I didn't hurt you *too* much, did I?'

Reclining on the bed, Julianne caught sight of herself in the full-length mirror. The corset she'd brought with her to Tanzania, just for this sort of play, enhanced her figure nicely.

'I thought that was the point, Jules?' He pulled up his underpants.

'I love that you indulge the sadist in me, but you get your turn, sometimes.'

He gave a little sneer as he zipped up his chinos. It was how they played. She would dominate him, tie him up, tease him, hurt him, and then there would come a point when the roles were reversed. He would unleash the beast inside him; Julianne would let him know when she was ready, and then it would be done. But there was no time for that now; he had a plane to catch. Julianne enjoyed the thought of him leaving knowing she'd had the last word.

She leaned over the side of the bed to where she'd dropped the riding crop, picked it up, then got up on her knees and flexed it in both hands. 'Whether Nikola Pesev is the head of the Scorpions or not, I want that lakeside real estate of his. I need it if we're going to expand the chimp camp in Mahale.'

'You don't have to tell me again,' James said.

She reached out a hand to him and he came to her, took it, and kissed her fingers. The smell of their sex was on her. She raised the crop with her other hand and touched the leather end of it under his chin, tilting up James's face. 'I know, James. Just make him an offer he can't refuse.'

'You know me.'

Julianne pulled him closer. 'Yes, I do, you're irresistible.'

He leaned over and kissed her. 'I need to go.'

'I know you do, my love.'

'My love?'

She could feel her cheeks turning red. Damn. 'It slipped out.'

'Do you, Jules?'

'Do I what?' She knew very well what he meant.

The ceiling fan above the four-poster bed turned slowly, stirring the mosquito net. Outside, beyond the balcony, Africa stretched away, beautiful, wild, yet dangerous.

'Do you love me?' he asked.

'You know our deal.'

'Yes, I do. We're colleagues first, you are my superior and I am your head of security and, of late, new business development.'

'Yes, and while you have also become my lover . . .'

'We will not fall in love. I remember the rules,' he said. 'I was in the army, I'm good at following orders.'

He pulled away from her and Julianne slumped back against the bedhead. 'And then I go and call you "my love".'

James laced his boots. 'Is it that bad?'

Julianne ran a hand through her hair. 'I kind of like the sound of it. Just don't ask me to marry you, all right?'

'I don't like taking no for an answer so I rarely ask a question I don't already know the answer to,' James said. He stood.

'Thank you. I mean, I'm not saying that one day if someone asked me that question I would automatically say no, but . . . well . . .' The control she'd felt just a few minutes earlier was slipping away. She was freefalling and her stomach lurched.

'I know what you mean, Jules. We didn't set out to become lovers or fall in love, but these things happen. I work for you, and I like my job. I see it as something more, in fact. It's a rush, what you do, what we do.'

Julianne took a deep breath to steady herself. Yes, a rush. She blew him a kiss. 'Travel safe.'

James walked out the door, then paused and looked back at her. 'I'll deliver Nikola Pesev, one way or another. I know what you want.'

She nodded. Julianne got what she wanted in life, every time, no matter what it took.

Chapter 23

Hudson sat at the bar in the lounge area of the lodge, nursing a Kilimanjaro Lager and checking his emails on his phone.

His WhatsApp beeped and a message popped up from Captain Sannie van Rensburg. *I have questions. Are you on?*

He replied. *Yes, and wi-fi works here. Talk?*

Her voice call came through a few seconds later.

'Howzit?'

'*Lekker*, sort of, how's Tanzania?' She pronounced the second half of the country's name to rhyme with 'mania', in the way most South Africans did. Locals, he had learned, pronounced the zania as 'zan-ear'.

'Nice. Roads are rubbish, though.'

'You can show me your slides when you get back to Hippo Rock. Tell me, are you with James Paterson?'

'He's arriving at my location soon, flying in this afternoon from the Serengeti. Why?'

'I checked out Shadrack's movements before his death – the last place he worked was around Paterson's house.'

283

'Did you find tracks?'

'Some, but I've got questions.'

'Anything else?' Hudson asked.

'I checked with the crime scene investigation guys. An autopsy hasn't been carried out, but preliminary testing showed Shadrack had no gunpowder residue on his hands from an AK-47 or any other weapon, yet he clearly hadn't changed his clothes since he'd received the cut on his back when he was leaving the Sabi Sand Game Reserve.'

'*If* he was in the reserve at all,' Hudson said.

'Yes. The wound that Tema Matsebula noticed could have been caused by something else; it could have just been a coincidence, but the AK-47 he was carrying in the car was no coincidence. I've got enough doubts now, however, so I've requested a full autopsy be done on Shadrack, toxicology, everything, before we release his body to Anna.'

'That's good that there's no evidence he fired the AK.'

'Yes, but we don't know why he got into a vehicle with a known criminal.'

'He was simple, Sannie, you know that.'

'*That* simple?'

'Who knows what line or substance the cousin fed him to get him to ride along with him? Tell me about the tracks you found at Paterson's place.'

'I found out from the staff here that Paterson had booked him for an outdoor clean on the morning of the day when the Leopards were ambushed. I checked the gate register and James was at his house at least part of the day when Shadrack was there. I went to his house and looked around. I found Shadrack's distinctive boot prints down by the river, but not around the house where he would have been working, plus another set of prints that could be James's. It's been a while, but there had been rain, you remember, and a couple of areas still showed the tracks. It's confusing. I want to talk to Paterson about it.'

'Well, like I said, he'll be here soon, but we're kind of busy. We've got an operation going.'

'You have?'

He told her as much as he thought she needed to know. Pesev was not a South African citizen so it was out of Sannie's jurisdiction.

'Do you think your target is a member of the Scorpions?'

She was way ahead of him. 'That's what we're trying to find out. Julianne is playing it cool.'

'You should check your internet. Have a look at *Escape* magazine online; Rosie Appleton has a story running that she filed from Tanzania saying Julianne Clyde-Smith has declared war on the organised crime interests behind poaching.'

'Hmm.' Hudson thought about this news, and made a note to check the site when he'd finished speaking to Sannie. 'That's a big call.'

'She's either full of arrogance, supremely confident of winning this fight, or she's sending a message to someone.'

Hudson rubbed his chin. 'Or all of the above. Julianne's anti-poaching team has been racking up the body count here in East Africa.'

'What's your role in all this? And Sonja's?'

Hudson weighed up how much to tell Sannie. He knew from past experience with her – from the time she had investigated him during a murder case – that she was as straight as they came but was not, as they said in America, afraid to go off the reservation in pursuit of a case.

He answered her question with another. 'What if it turns out that Shadrack was in fact an innocent, just a simple guy who got duped into picking up an assault rifle and riding along with his criminal cousin?'

Sannie paused on the other end of the call. 'You know the answer to that. If that happens I have to open a murder docket, and your friend Sonja and the girl who worked for her will be the subjects of a new investigation. Shadrack was shot in the head and the chest by different weapons, a rifle and a pistol. They both hit him, Hudson.'

'What do you want me to do about James Paterson? Do you want to talk to him by phone? I'm not sure when we'll be back in South Africa.'

'This is irregular.' Again, she waited a few seconds. 'I shouldn't be getting you to help with a police investigation . . .'

'But . . .'

'But you're on the ground in Tanzania and I'm here. Hudson, I don't know if it means anything, but the prints near the river, on James Paterson's plot in Hippo Rock, are a match for the boots that Shadrack was wearing, but there are other workman's boot prints around the house. There have been no other labourers at the house since then – I checked. Can you ask Paterson if he was walking around his house in a set of workboots?'

'Sure. I'll try.'

'Something doesn't add up.'

'I'm hearing you,' he said. 'Anything else?'

'Is Julianne Clyde-Smith out of control with her anti-poaching team?'

It was Hudson's turn now to take a breath. Sannie was an intelligent woman. She'd looked at the string of gunfights involving Sonja and her people, and possibly the subsequent contacts when Mario had been in charge, and she had come up with the same theory as he and Sonja – or at least a similar one.

'Hudson?'

'I don't know.'

'Is that what you're trying to find out?'

'If she is, there would be a lot of people, even some of your colleagues in the police, who would say she's doing a good job, doing what the law enforcement agencies and the military aren't capable of.'

'Yes. But that doesn't make it right, does it?'

'No.' He waited on the line a little longer.

'What else, Hudson?'

'It might go further than just running a vigilante anti-poaching unit.'

'How so?' Sannie asked.

'Sonja and I have looked at where the various gunfights with poachers happened and when.'

'And, don't tell me, they coincide with strategic expansions in Julianne Clyde-Smith's portfolio of safari properties. I read online how she bought Lion Plains not long after the last attack. They said on the news site that the lodge was going bankrupt because of the number of poaching incidents they'd suffered, going right back to the death of Sonja's partner, Sam Chapman.'

'Yes,' said Hudson, 'and there have been similar links in Zimbabwe, where she's acquiring a concession in Mana Pools National Park, and up here in Tanzania. They just had a shootout here near the Serengeti National Park. A gang of poachers was wiped out.'

'All of them?'

'Yes. They opened up on a helicopter, so Julianne's team went in and winkled them out. No prisoners.'

'Business interests?'

'The gang had been responsible for a lot of elephant poaching in the area. Now they're out of business and Julianne's looking to set up a new lodge there. And there's more: I spoke to a woman I know up here, Helen Mills, who leased a concession in the area where the poachers were killed. She was forced out of business by a run of poaching incidents, a robbery, and the downing of a helicopter on her land. She pretty much confirmed it was Julianne who paid her out and is about to take over the concession.'

'Her people wiping out a poaching gang fits the tough line she took in Rosie Appleton's story,' Sannie said. 'You should read the comments when you get a chance, on the *Escape* webpage and all over Facebook, Twitter . . . you name it. She's a celebrity. But would she really risk her reputation by using anti-poaching operations to further her business interests?'

Hudson thought about the question. 'Trouble is, it would be very hard to prove. As a safari operator and landowner it's in her interests to fight poaching, on her own properties and on neighbouring properties. The word is she kept her teams out of Lion Plains until it was too late, until the poaching got so bad that people were scared to go there.'

'*Ja*,' Sannie said. 'But that's like what the Catholics call a sin of omission; it's not what she did, it's what she didn't do, and she could just claim Lion Plains wasn't pulling its weight in the anti-poaching effort.'

'They weren't,' Hudson said. 'And the records of the Sabi Sand Executive Council will show they were behind on their payments, and the news media will see that it was Julianne's team that finally delivered a killer blow to the poachers running rampant on Lion Plains.'

'After the Leopards were put out of business.'

'Yes,' Hudson said. 'The Leopards were Lion Plains's last roll of the dice.'

'Bad timing for Lion Plains.'

'Yep,' Hudson said. Outside he heard a vehicle arriving, then doors closing. He got up from the bar and looked outside. 'Our man Paterson's just arrived. I'll see what I can find out and get back to you.'

'One thing,' she said. 'Be careful.'

'Careful is my middle name.'

Sannie laughed and ended the call.

*

Sonja saw the lodge's transfer vehicle drive past the camping ground and caught a glimpse of James in the back seat.

'Thanks, Godwin, you're a star,' she said to the mechanic, who climbed out from underneath the Land Rover.

'Well, I'm sorry there's not much I can do here, but I've checked everything. Your Panhard bushes and tie rod ends need replacing; that's probably what's giving you the steering wobble, but you'll make it back to South Africa. You can go join your boyfriend in the bar now.'

Sonja laughed. 'I will. He thinks I'm worrying about nothing.'

'Not nothing, but it pays to be safe.'

Godwin dusted himself off.

'I see your boss has got a lot of boats. Does he take many trips across to Mahale National Park?'

Godwin nodded. 'Yes, whenever there are tourists who want to see the chimps.'

'Gee, if I lived across from such a wonderful place I'd be travelling over there myself all the time.'

He started packing his toolbox. 'Well, he does go by himself sometimes, or with friends.'

'Friends? Pretty remote place out here, and he's only just bought the lodge, hasn't he?'

'Well, I mean, Mr Pesev has been visiting this area for a few years now. He used to stay at the other lodge, where I used to work.' Godwin closed the toolbox and stood a little straighter. 'He recruited me, offered me more money.'

'Lucky you. Is he a good boss?'

'Yes, very.'

'Godwin, how long does Mr Pesev stay in the park when he goes?'

He looked around, as though checking if someone was listening. 'One night.'

'That seems quick to go looking for chimps. From what I read, people should go for one night, get up early, go trekking, spend the day, then a second night and come back.'

Godwin shifted his weight from foot to foot, as if he was keen to get away. 'I don't know. I have never been.'

He was unnerved. 'Have you ever seen a chimpanzee?'

Again the eyes darted. 'Yes.'

'But you said you've never been to Mahale National Park.'

'No.'

'Have you been to a zoo?'

'I need to get back to the workshop,' he said.

Sonja smiled. 'It's all right, Godwin, I know Mr Pesev sometimes brings chimps here, from Mahale.'

'Oh.'

'Yes. I'm sure it's for a good reason.'

Godwin nodded vigorously. 'Yes, he says they are sick, that they need medicine, and he takes them to the animal doctors in Kigoma. The United Nations, where he once worked, takes care of orphan baby chimpanzees.'

'I'm sure they do.'

'Yes.'

He touched the brim of his baseball cap. 'I need to go. I am sure your vehicle will be fine.'

'Yes, I'm sure it will be. One more question, sorry.'

Godwin seemed reluctant, as if he had already said too much. 'I must go.'

'Sorry. I just wanted to know, does Mr Pesev have any chimpanzees here at the moment?'

'No, madam. I must go.'

He strode away, and Sonja wondered if she had overstepped the mark. It didn't matter, she told herself. If Godwin went to Nikola and told him what he had said, and Nikola was indeed a criminal, Godwin would be fired – or worse. But if Nikola was legit, then he had nothing to hide.

As far as Sonja knew, there was nothing in the UN's remit about looking after orphan baby chimps. In fact, she imagined it would be rare to find an orphan in the wild. She knew of chimpanzee rehabilitation places in Uganda, on an island, and in South Africa and Zambia, but they accommodated chimps that had once been pets, or were kept in zoos or sideshows. These chimps had either been bred in captivity or taken illegally. The word was that Nikola Pesev was in the business of sourcing chimps the latter way. There would be big money in this trade, perhaps enough to build a luxury lodge on the shores of Lake Tanganyika.

Sonja walked from the campground to the lounge and bar area. When she entered, taking off her cap now that she was out of the sun, she saw Hudson and James standing at the bar.

'Hi, honey,' Hudson said, loud enough for the waiter setting a table for lunch to overhear, 'meet John Price. He's just flown in.'

'Hello, I'm Ursula.'

By the time Sonja had come over to them the waiter had disappeared and they were alone.

'Hudson just told me about Mario,' James said quietly. 'What a cock-up.'

Sonja bridled, internally. 'Well, the fact is that Tema made the most of the situation and has ingratiated herself with Pesev.'

'Yes, so I hear,' Paterson said. 'At least she's on the ball.'

'Machado's a liability,' Hudson said.

Paterson set down the welcome mocktail the waiter had given him. 'He has his uses. You all do, which is why you're all here.'

'I managed to get a recording of Pesev speaking in Russian. It's on my phone,' Sonja said.

'Good work,' James said. 'I have a contact who is trustworthy; one of my sources in fact. He's a professional hunter, a German who used to live in the east. He specialises in taking Russian clients on hunts, so he can translate it. Email me the file, please, and I'll send it on to him.'

'Will do,' Sonja said. 'I also just had an interesting chat to Pesev's head mechanic. Pesev regularly brings baby chimps from Mahale to the mainland, supposedly to get them veterinary care.'

'What?'

'I know, amazing, right?' she said to James.

Hudson seemed incredulous. 'He came right out and told you that?'

'Yes. Either the mechanic is an idiot, which he didn't seem to be, or Pesev is doing something legitimate with chimps that he doesn't bother to hide from his staff.'

James rubbed his chin. 'Do we just confront him with it?'

'Not for now,' Sonja said. 'Let's see what else Tema turns up. Pesev wants to take her on a long boat ride. That will give us a chance to look around, to place some bugs, and she might turn up something herself.'

'Will Tema be OK?' Paterson asked.

Sonja smiled. 'When you see Mario you'll have the answer to that question. She's more scared by the prospect of another boat trip than of any man pawing her. I'll get her to ask to go back to Mahale again, give him some line about how much she loves baby chimps and how she always wanted one as a pet.'

'All right,' Paterson said. 'I'll set up my gear in my suite. Let's convene later, around sundowner time. Sonja, as soon as you send me that recording I'll get my guy onto it.'

'Sure,' she said.

'What now?' Hudson asked.

'Let's go back to the campground,' Sonja said. 'We've got an hour or two to kill.'

*

Sonja and Hudson walked back to the camping ground. Theirs was the only vehicle there. Hudson felt on edge, wired.

'What do you want to do until drinks time?' Hudson asked.

'I need a shower. I'm filthy from crawling around under your Land Rover with the mechanic.'

'Did he think it odd that I didn't come see him?'

Sonja shrugged. 'Maybe, but I think it worked, getting him talking, more than it would have if you'd started asking him questions about orphan chimps. I told him my boyfriend is an ignoramus when it comes to vehicles.'

'You're not far wrong there.'

Sonja took out her phone and selected her email program.

'What are you doing?' Hudson asked.

'I'm emailing James the conversation I recorded of Pesev talking in Russian.'

'CC me, please,' he said.

'Sure.' Sonja hit send. 'Done.'

'I need a shower as well,' Hudson said.

'Join me?'

Hudson felt a jolt of excitement. They were on a mission, and if Pesev was who they thought he was, the head of the Scorpions, it would be dangerous for them. The Scorpions were ruthless in their quest to dominate commercial poaching, and they weren't afraid to kill, but right now all he could think about was Sonja's body.

'Bring your towel.'

Hudson touched the brim of his cap. 'Yes, ma'am.'

Sonja led the way and Hudson admired the sway of her hips. He felt himself stir with anticipation. There was no one about, no attendant, no other visitors, but Sonja still checked the shower first, knocking, and the bathroom next door.

She went in and Hudson followed her. Even before he had closed the door she was pulling off her T-shirt, her caution and modesty vanishing. She pressed herself against him, arms around his neck, and drew his face down to hers. They kissed and he breathed in the smell of her. It aroused him.

Sonja moved her hands to undo his belt buckle and zip. He kissed her neck, working his way down to her breasts as he reached around her and undid her bra. He let her pull down his shorts, then kicked them off. Sonja took a step back, just out of reach and slowly, teasingly, undid her own shorts.

She stopped when they were halfway down her hips and reached into her panties with one hand. She put her other one up, on his chest, stopping him from coming closer.

'Watch.'

She half closed her eyes, licking her lips as she caressed her nipples. When she focused on him again she could see that he couldn't help himself, he had his cock in his hand.

'Stop. Don't touch.'

He felt the desire flood him, telling his brain to take her, to ravage her, but he could see she was enjoying this. 'OK.' He let go and stood there, hard and ready as he watched her.

'I want you to get to the point where you can't bear it any more.'

He smiled. 'I'm close.'

'Not close enough.' She lowered her shorts, stepped out of them and kicked them aside.

Sonja reached up and behind her, for the taps, and turned them on. Water started cascading down over her. She tipped her head back and let the flow run into and out of her mouth as she worked her fingers faster. She swallowed some water, quenching her thirst. Her breathing started coming faster.

Sonja pointed to the low stone bench built into the wall, beneath the showerhead. 'We called these bonking steps, at the safari lodge where I grew up, in Botswana. You've probably heard of them.'

'Yes. You can put one foot up . . .'

'Like this.' She stood, turned her back to him, wanton, offering, teasing. She reached between her legs and went back to touching as she looked over her shoulder, her eyes beckoning him.

He came up behind her, kissed her hard, on the back of the neck, like the mating lion had done to the female. She reached back, grabbed a handful of his butt and pulled him to her.

Hudson moved his hand to where hers had been and took up the rhythm.

'Yes,' she moaned, pushing back against him.

Hudson entered her. Sonja gasped, leaned her cheek against the wall and then started moving with him. She put her hands on the tiles and pushed back from the wall, meeting his thrusts.

Water poured from their bodies, amplifying the sound of flesh against flesh. Hudson closed his eyes, revelling in the feeling of being part of her, of her firm muscles under his fingers, of the warmth of her body and the water.

He reached a point where his arousal was finely tuned, where he was just at the brink and he wished he could stay there, with this woman, for the rest of his life.

'This is good,' she said.

'Yes, it is.'

'I wish we could stay like this.'

It had been too long since he'd felt such a connection. He felt his heart swell and the pure bliss of being with her ran through his body like a jolt of electricity. He wanted all of her, to consume her, to own her, to be hers. Hudson gripped Sonja's hips tighter.

Sonja looked back at him, over her shoulder. 'Open your eyes. I want to watch you.'

*

Mario had spied them as he crested the hill that separated the lodge from the village of Kipili. He had done his job, found someone who spoke English, and quizzed the old man about Nikola Pesev, the latest foreigner to buy property on the lake.

He had watched Sonja and Hudson walk to the showers. He had noted the way she paraded herself in front of him, like an animal on heat, and how Brand had slavishly followed her, nearly tripping over his tongue.

Mario wanted her and he was quietly enraged by the way she had discarded him, how she now flaunted herself in front of Brand.

He skirted the camping ground, using the big mango trees as cover, and made his way to the ablutions blocks from the opposite direction to Sonja and Brand. When they entered the shower, together, he crept across to their block, crouching to keep his head below the window level.

Now he was closer he could hear them.

The slut was putting on a show for him. Mario slowly raised his head until he could peek in through the mosquito mesh–covered window. They had their backs to him. Brand was touching her, moving behind her, but he could see the swell of her hip. He remembered the feel of her.

Mario felt himself harden at the thought of what he would do to Sonja, and to Hudson Brand. He reached into his shorts and started to massage himself.

Brand was increasing his pace, his hips thrusting, and Sonja, the whore, was driving back with equal frenzy. The American tilted his head upwards, unable to hold on any longer, and opened his mouth wide. Mario freed himself and imagined wrapping an arm around the American's neck, then drawing his knife across it.

He wondered what it might have been like if he'd been able to sneak in there now, to kill him while he was deep inside her, then take over from him.

He thought of the pleasure she would experience, the pain he would inflict. He felt his own orgasm rushing on. Sonja was crying out, Brand was grunting like the pig he was. Sonja deserved better than a broken-down safari guide.

Brand had never had the stomach for the killing that was required in Angola. The enemy were ruthless and the men of 32 Battalion knew how to take the fight to them. Brand was soft on prisoners and civilians alike. He had broken the soldiers' code and reported on Mario, accusing him of atrocities. Mario had taken the one thing, the woman, that mattered most to Brand. He remembered Ines, the way she had clawed and scratched at him like a wildcat, and how he had silenced her.

Brand had never been able to prove it was him, but the knowledge of the truth gave Mario a power over Hudson Brand, which he relished every time he saw the man or thought of him. Brand might have Sonja, here, now, but Mario would take her in time, and whenever the shooting started again, as it inevitably would, Hudson Brand would end up with a bullet in the back.

A knife would be more satisfying, more climactic, but a bullet would be easier to write off.

Mario watched Sonja slump against the wall and he unloaded against the warm brick exterior of the shower block.

He would not waste it the next time; he would fill her, have her begging for more of him.

'Hello?'

Mario turned his head. There was an African man in blue overalls, a camp attendant perhaps, waving to him, wondering, no doubt, what he was up to. Quickly, he zipped up and moved away, around the block, back into the shade of the mango trees.

'Who's out there?' Hudson Brand called from inside.

Me, Mario said to himself. *And I'm going to kill you.*

Chapter 24

Sannie van Rensburg sat down at her desk in the upstairs open-fronted loft area of her house at Hippo Rock.

This 'office', of sorts, looked over the Amanzini Spruit, a stream, barely more than a trickle now at the end of the dry season, that ran into the Sabie River some three kilometres downstream, near the house where Hudson Brand stayed.

She opened the screen of her MacBook, tethered her phone to connect to the internet, and logged into Skype. While she waited for her husband, Tom, to come online, she scanned the *spruit* for signs of life. A purple-crested turaco gave its distinctive honking call, and when she scanned the big jackalberry tree that shaded the rivulet she caught a brief flash of the bird's red underwings. Down on the ground the rustle of bushes gave away the estate's resident herd of impala. The bush was terribly dry this year – there had not been enough rain last summer – and the impala were braving the thickets of vine-enshrouded trees along the watercourse. They were extra vigilant in this close, almost jungle-like vegetation, as this was perfect leopard country.

Sannie and Tom had seen the big resident male leopard several times, on the opposite bank of the Sabie River, from Hippo Rock's communal picnic area. The last time was while having drinks with Hudson, and Cameron and Kylie who owned Hudson's house and were visiting from Australia. They were a nice couple. Sannie missed being part of a twosome when Tom was away. As much as she told herself it was nice to have time to herself, the truth was that with the kids in boarding school and Tom in the Middle East, she was often lonely.

A baby's cry made her look up and she saw a flock of trumpeter hornbills, their distinctive *wah-wah-wah* preceding them, swoop through the treetops.

The Skype ringtone brought her back to the computer and she felt her heart give a little lurch when she saw it was Tom. It wouldn't be anyone else calling, but even so these little digital triggers were enough to get her excited.

'Hiya!'

Even after living in South Africa for nine years he still hadn't lost his English accent.

'Howzit, my *liefie*.' She adjusted the laptop so she could see his handsome face better and blew him a kiss.

'Hello, my love. How are you?'

She put one hand on her heart and reached out to the inbuilt camera with the other. They did this as often as they could, depending on their work schedules, but it never seemed enough. 'I'm OK.'

'Just OK?'

'*Ja*.' She waved a hand in a dismissive gesture. 'Some work stuff that's bugging me. How about you?'

'Good news.'

She brightened, seeing his smile. Often he looked so very tired. His contract was to protect some UN officials in Iraq. Tom tried to downplay the danger, but every time Sannie watched the news on TV about the situation in Iraq and Syria she felt her anxiety levels rise. 'Yes?'

'I'm coming home early!'

'Wow. That's fantastic. I can't wait.'

'The UN mission is heading home to New York sooner than expected, but as we're on a fixed contract I still get paid the full amount.'

'That's wonderful.'

Tom held up his hands. 'Wait, it gets better.'

That was good enough for her. 'Go on?'

'I told you the company recently got a new CEO, didn't I?'

'*Ja*, a South African, right? Louis?'

'Yes, Louis van der Merwe. He came to visit us and was briefing us on some new developments, here and around the world. They're starting up an anti-poaching division and they want me to work for them, in South Africa, based in the lowveld.'

'It doesn't get much better than that,' she said, 'although at the moment there's probably been more gunfire here in the bush than in Iraq and Syria combined.'

'Tell me?'

She filled him in on the spate of shootings and ambushes in the war against poaching in their little corner of Africa. 'The info we're getting is that organised crime is responsible for more and more of the poaching here in South Africa, and also in neighbouring countries. There's a syndicate that calls themselves the Scorpions, and we're picking up reports of them working as far up as Tanzania.'

'You think it's true? If so, this would be something Louis really needs to hear.'

Sannie wondered if she had shared too much with her husband, but it was becoming more and more apparent to her that if there was such an organisation it was too big for just one police force or even just one country to tackle. It would require a whole new approach to policing wildlife crimes.

'It seems that Julianne Clyde-Smith has decided to take on the war on poaching as her own personal crusade. The word is that she and her head of security, a guy called James Paterson, are funding sophisticated anti-poaching operations. I've had reason to question some of her methods lately.'

'Paterson? Like the author but one "t"?'

Sannie thought for a moment. 'Yes, that's how he spells it.'

'Ex–British Army?'

'Yes, a South African who served with them, in Iraq and Afghanistan, and before that, Northern Ireland.'

'I met him, years ago, when I was seconded from Special Branch to MI5. We were conducting undercover surveillance on the IRA in London and James Paterson, he was a captain back then, was the military liaison man. I haven't seen him in what, twenty years maybe.'

'Small world.'

'Yes.'

'What do you remember about him, Tom?'

Tom looked up and scratched his head, as he did when he was thinking. 'Very bright, and very hands-on. In Northern Ireland he'd been undercover himself. When he was with us it was like he missed being in the field and kept telling us how to do our jobs. Any chance he got he was out on the streets, wanting to be part of the action.'

Sannie flipped open her notebook on the desk and jotted down some of what Tom was saying.

'He finally got his chance to get into the game.'

'How so?' Sannie asked.

'We were tailing some IRA men who were supposed to be organising an arms deal. They were looking to buy RPG-7s, rocket-propelled grenades. MI6 intercepted the arms seller, overseas, and made sure he didn't make it to Heathrow. When they put him in the bag they had to quickly find someone who could pose as the seller. Paterson was the right man at the right place, so he went in as the salesman.'

'What happened?'

'Paterson went undercover, posing as the arms dealer, and set up a meeting with the IRA guys. They were after a light machine gun and Paterson had one, and a thousand rounds of ammo.'

'Serious?' Sannie said.

Tom nodded. 'They wanted it for an ambush, to shoot up an army convoy, in England – soldiers on exercise. The idea was to take the fight to the enemy, on home soil.'

'Sheesh,' Sannie said.

'Exactly. So the buy was set up and the IRA men came to him. The idea was that they would fire off some rounds, to make sure the machine gun was in good order.'

'Where in England could you fire a machine gun without alerting an entire village?'

'Out at sea. Paterson chartered a fishing boat and picked up the IRA guys at a little village in Cornwall. They went out; he had an MI5 guy with him posing as his henchman.'

'And?'

'And something bad happened. It was never made public, Sannie.'

'I have no intention of making it so.'

'OK. So, the IRA men became suspicious and the guy with Paterson, less experienced than him, said something – I don't know what – that gave them away, and guns were pulled. Paterson's sidekick was killed, but James took out the three guys who were there to make the buy. They say that when he got the boat back to port it was awash with blood.'

'Oh my.'

'Yes. The incident was hushed up. While the intelligence

service lost an operator, an IRA quartermaster and two senior commanders were taken out and a major attack was averted.'

'Tell me something, Tom.'

'Yes?'

'Would you trust Paterson?'

'From what I've heard of him, yes. If Julianne Clyde-Smith was looking for someone to take the fight to the poachers then she found the right man in James Paterson.'

'Thanks. I miss you.'

'I miss you too, my love. I can't wait to get home. I'm finished with this overseas stuff. I miss South Africa.'

'I love the thought of you coming home for good,' she said, 'but this war against poaching is getting hectic. Sometimes I wish we still had the farm.'

'Yes,' Tom said, 'I know what you mean, but the money I'll get from this contract will help us, and having the security of a job in South Africa will mean we can stay at Hippo Rock. It's all going to be good, love.'

Sannie heard a knock on the front door downstairs. She looked around. 'Sorry, someone's downstairs.'

'No problem,' Tom said. 'I have to get going anyway, I have a meeting in five minutes. Bye, my love.' He blew her a kiss.

Sannie returned the kiss, closed her laptop and went downstairs. When she opened the door she saw Anna, the estate laundry lady, standing there. Anna carried a pair of men's boots in her hands.

'Anna, howzit,' Sannie said as she opened the door.

'Fine, madam, and you?'

'Fine. *Ka hisa nomuthla*, hey?'

'Yes, madam, it is hot today. I am sorry if I am bothering you. I got your message.'

'Oh, yes, right.' Sannie had called Anna – she had her mobile phone number for when she needed to check if her washing was ready – and told her she had some questions to ask about Shadrack's workboots. 'Come in.'

Anna walked in, looking around the house. 'I brought Shadrack's boots with me, as you asked. I got your message when I was at the doctor's, then went home to get these.'

Sannie looked at the boots that Anna held up. 'I didn't need you to bring them. I just wanted to ask you about the boots that he was wearing on the day that he was killed.'

Anna looked away for a moment and wiped an eye with her free hand. 'These were his boots, the only pair of work shoes that he owned.'

Sannie was confused. 'So what was he wearing . . . that day?'

'I don't know. When I saw . . . when the police came to get me to identify him, he was wearing nice boots, but they were not his. Do you think he stole them?'

Sannie felt her heart melt. Anna seemed to be shocked by the fact that her son could have stolen a pair of workboots; the fact that he was most likely an armed poacher suspected of killing at least one woman didn't seem to register with her at all. 'I don't know, Anna, what do you think?'

The older woman looked bewildered. 'I found these in his room, under his bed, just like this.'

'The laces are tied together. Would he normally do that, like if he wore another pair of shoes or slops to work and maybe hung these around his neck?'

Anna shook her head. 'No. He cleaned his boots every night and wore them to work here at Hippo Rock every day.'

'So where did the boots that he was wearing come from?'

'I don't know. Maybe a gift?'

'What about his cousin?'

Anna's face soured. 'He was always coming around to our house, showing off his new clothes, his new phone, talking about the parties he went to, the women . . . I always wondered where his money came from.'

'How did he compare in size to your son?' Sannie tried to recall the bodies she had seen at the crime scene.

'They were similar. My sister and I would share clothes, sometimes, when the boys were growing up. They did have the same size feet, if that is what you are asking.'

'Yes,' Sannie said, 'that's what I was thinking. Anna, I need you to think, carefully, please. Do you ever remember Shadrack coming home with a new pair of boots, different from the ones he normally wore?'

Anna frowned. 'I can't remember, no, even though I know it is important. You linked my son to a crime he did not commit by the pattern on the sole of the boots he was wearing on the day he was killed. I would love to tell you that he was not wearing those boots until that morning, but the truth is I do not know. I was working late the day he was killed; he came home before me. He could have found or been given some different boots that day, but I don't know where or by whom. He never stole a single thing is his life.'

Sannie nodded. 'Thank you for your honesty. I will have some people, our forensic scientists, take a look at those boots that your son was wearing, and these ones, if you don't mind, to see what they can tell us.'

Anna held out the boots and Sannie took them, but the other woman held tight a moment longer, not wanting to let them go. 'Please do not be offended, but I do not know if I can trust the police. I was hurt, a long time ago, because I protested.'

Sannie put her free hand on Anna's. 'Please, you can trust me. I have two sons. I know the pain you must feel. I will see what the scientists can tell us about these shoes and the ones he was wearing. Perhaps there is an answer there.'

'All right.' Anna relinquished this last link to her son.

'Do you think it's possible Shadrack's cousin could have given him the boots he was wearing on the day he was killed?'

Anna closed her eyes, then slowly nodded. 'I did wonder if that might have happened.'

'You can see why?'

Anna opened her eyes. 'Yes. If his cousin killed that woman, the others, then he could make it look like my son was the one who did it. I don't wish to speak ill of my sister's son, but as well as being a show-off he was . . .'

'You can tell me.'

'He was bad. I knew it. I didn't ask where his money came from, but there were rumours. If he kidnapped Shadrack, and was later going to set him up somehow then the police, you, would think Shadrack was the one.'

'Yes, that is possible. The evidence is just what we call circumstantial. But both men are dead and we don't have a lot more to go on with.'

Anna was silent, and tears began to well in her eyes.

'Let me get a plastic bag for the boots so I don't get my fingerprints all over them,' said Sannie gently. 'We have to protect what's called the chain of evidence.'

Sannie went into the kitchen, to the cloth bag hanging on the back door where she stored all her old plastic shopping bags for future use. Plastic bags, South Africa's 'native flower', were a blight on the landscape, and she couldn't countenance the thought of them going into the ground as landfill.

The boots safely in a bag, she came back to the lounge room where Anna waited patiently. Sannie noticed that Anna's eyes kept going to the family picture of Tom, Sannie, Christo, Ilana and Tommy.

'You have a beautiful family.'

'Thank you. Your daughter, Clarissa, isn't it?'

'Yes.'

'She's at varsity?'

'Yes,' Anna said, her eyes sad.

'You must be very proud of her,' Sannie said.

'I am proud of all my children, all of them.' Anna looked to the clock on the wall. 'It is late. I need to go.'

Sannie put the bag containing the shoes down. 'Let me drive you.'

'Thank you. That way I won't miss the bus back to Huntington.'

Sannie fetched the keys for her Fortuner and escorted Anna outside. She closed the house door and set the alarm; though in this part of South Africa she was more concerned about baboons or monkeys getting into the house than human intruders.

Anna sat quietly in the front passenger seat as Sannie negotiated the estate's narrow, winding gravel roads to the entrance gate. It was four in the afternoon and there was a queue of people, staff and the employees of building and other contractors waiting to leave.

Sannie always felt mildly annoyed at the fact that even Hippo Rock's most loyal and long-serving staff had to subject themselves and their bags to a search by the estate's security guards every day, in case they had stolen something from one of the houses.

'Thank you,' Anna said as she got out of the car. 'If there is anything else I can do to help in your investigation, please let me know.'

Sannie nodded, and as she sat in the Toyota for a minute longer, watching the people patiently wait while their meagre belongings were searched, she had an idea.

Chapter 25

Hudson Brand nursed a beer at the bar of the lodge. The bleeding sun was being devoured by Lake Tanganyika. Tema, in a white shift dress, was sitting at a table for two on the sandy beach talking to Sonja.

James Paterson walked in, wearing chinos and a blue Oxford shirt. Hudson had gone for a swim in the afternoon, after making love to Sonja, and wore shorts, sandals and a Hawaiian print shirt that Sonja said didn't suit him.

'Aloha,' Paterson said.

'This shirt gets all sorts of comments.'

'Gin and tonic,' Paterson said to the barman. Hudson covered his glass.

Hudson took a sip of beer. 'I had a call from Sannie van Rensburg, the cop investigating the shootings in the Sabi Sand and Hazyview.'

Paterson took his drink. 'I've seen her around. She and her husband moved to Hippo Rock a while ago.'

'Yes. She's following a new lead that one of the killings by your people – by Sonja and Tema in fact – might not have been justifiable.'

'Really?'

'She thinks that kid Shadrack, who worked on our estate, might have been framed by his cousin, the one driving the Isuzu *bakkie*.'

'So that it looked like Shadrack killed the member of Sonja's team of Leopards who ran from the contact?'

'Yes. It's one thing to go down for rhino poaching, or rather attempted poaching, as they didn't get anything that night, but it's another thing to go away for murdering a female anti-poaching unit operator. The cops were closing in on him and Sannie thinks that maybe he gave his boots – distinctive ones with a slit across the tread – and his AK to his intellectually challenged cousin so that if they got caught he'd be the lead suspect.'

'Stupid, but feasible, I suppose.' Paterson looked up at the ceiling, as if recalling something. 'Boots with a split, you say?'

'Yes.'

'Hudson, I need to call van Rensburg. I'll do so this evening; please give me her number.'

'Sure, I've got it here. But what do you need to call her for?'

Sonja and Tema were walking their way, across the sand to the bar and dining area.

'I know whose boots Shadrack was wearing.'

'Whose?' Hudson asked.

'Mine.'

Hudson raised his eyebrows.

'I'd noticed that I'd damaged the sole of one of them – a silly accident with a chainsaw while splitting wood; I was lucky I didn't lose my bloody foot. Shadrack was at my house raking and sweeping and I asked him if he wanted them. Compared to his boots they were damn good quality and he couldn't thank me enough; he thought Christmas had come early. It was a day or two before the Leopards Anti-Poaching Unit was ambushed.'

Hudson nodded. 'Yep, you do need to tell Sannie all of that. It doesn't help Shadrack, though.'

'No, I'm afraid not. Rather it puts him more squarely in the picture. Here comes Sonja.'

Hudson turned and watched her enter. He thought of her naked, in the shower, teasing him.

'Hello, we meet again,' James said to Sonja, pretending, for the barman's sake, that they had only met that morning. Tema followed her into the bar.

'Maybe we should adjourn to the lounge area,' Hudson said.

'Sure, fine by me, honey.' Sonja took his arm.

Hudson got a kick out of hearing Sonja address him that way, even if it was an act. They all sat around a carved wooden coffee table and ordered fresh drinks from the barman to get him out of the way.

Paterson addressed Tema. 'How's it going between you and Nikola?'

'He's taking me out on his boat tomorrow. We're going to Mahale National Park. He says he has a surprise planned for me.'

'That sounds encouraging,' James said.

'The surprise will be if I don't get seasick.' Tema rolled her eyes.

Paterson looked to Sonja and Hudson. 'That gives you two a chance to case Nikola's bungalow and plant some bugs. OK?'

They nodded.

'The maid takes lunch from twelve thirty to one,' Tema said. 'There's no one in the house then.'

'Perfect,' Sonja said.

Tema set down her drink on the table. 'If someone does see you and reports it back to Nikola, you can tell them that I said you could come borrow a book I'm reading. I'll leave it on the lounger out the front of the bungalow. Nikola never locks his suite. He says there are no criminals here.'

310

Paterson scoffed. 'Apart from him.'

Hudson thought that was what they were there to try and prove. He saw Sonja look past him, to the entrance to the lodge, and when he turned Mario walked in.

'Is this a private party, or can anyone get a drink?'

Hudson eyed him, then stood. He felt Sonja's hand on his arm, but he shrugged it off. Hudson saw how the other man swayed a little. 'You're drunk.'

'Yes, well, I'm off duty, and I've come here for a refill.'

'Hudson,' Sonja said, 'leave it. Let him get his drink.'

'Listen to your girlfriend,' Mario slurred. 'Remember, she's the boss here. She's the one who wears the pants. You like it like that, don't you, Brand?'

Sonja got up off the lounge and moved around Hudson so that she was between him and Mario. 'Stop this. Mario, get out of here before you cause a scene and compromise this operation.'

'You owe Tema an apology,' Hudson said.

Mario went to the bar. 'Barman? Hey, where the fuck are you?'

Sonja put her hands on her hips. 'Get out, Mario. I'll have room service send you a bottle.'

'No. You don't tell me what to do any more.'

'Apologise to Tema,' Hudson said.

Sonja looked over her shoulder. 'You're goading him, Hudson.'

'Fucking-A.'

'Brand.' Mario leaned back against the bar. 'You fucking cowboy. Go back to America, or Angola, or wherever it is a bastard like you comes from. Tema?'

Tema stood as well. 'Yes, Mario.'

'I'm sorry for wanting to fuck you.' He burped. 'Maybe you prefer girls to guys.'

Sonja took a step closer to him. 'Mario. Enough. You've been warned. Get out of here.'

He waved a finger at her. 'Oh, you . . . Sonja. I know you're not into girls. I know just what you like. I remember just how you like it, from behind, like the bitch in heat that you . . .'

Hudson let the rage overtake him, but before he could get to Mario Sonja had put him down with a hard, fast sucker punch straight to the nose. Mario yelled and started to slide down the bar. Blood ran through the fingers he held to his face. He growled, low and animalistic, then lunged at her.

Sonja weaved, easily out-manoeuvring the drunk, and by the time Mario had raised his closed fist to strike at her Hudson was ramming the barrel of his Colt .45 into the side of Mario's temple. 'Get up, you worthless piece of shit. Move it.'

Mario put his hands up. 'All right, all right, I'm moving.'

Hudson grabbed him by the shirt collar and thrust him through the doors of the lounge, outside. Sonja and Tema followed them out.

'Give me an excuse,' Hudson said to Mario.

'Ha, you'd like that.'

'Go for your gun, if you've got one, if you're man enough.'

'Want a gunfight, eh, cowboy?' Mario spat blood. 'Want me to draw down on you?'

Hudson stood back. 'Yes.'

'No!' Sonja came to him, but Hudson held out his left arm, stopping her from getting between them.

Mario stared at him. Slowly, he undid the lower two buttons of his safari shirt and used his right hand to uncover the holster clipped to his belt.

Hudson gripped his .45 tight.

'You're supposed to put your pistol back in your holster,' Mario said, his voice distorted by his blood-clogged nose. 'That's a fair fight.'

'Fuck fair.'

'Hudson, he's not worth the effort,' Sonja said.

Mario laughed and winced. 'I'm not going to commit suicide. But you can shoot me if you want, Brand, if you have the balls. You know, if the situation were reversed, and you had fucked two of my women, I would have killed you by now.'

'Sheesh, Mario, shut up or I'll shoot you myself,' Sonja weighed in.

Hudson looked down the barrel of his pistol, past the sights. He hated how the weapon was shaking in his hand, how Mario was making him feel.

'Tell me . . .'

Mario kept his right hand just above his pistol. 'About Sonja?'

Hudson gave the slightest nod of his head.

'I was her revenge fuck, I think, in Zimbabwe. She thought you'd been with someone else. She was using me to get you out her system. She tasted great.'

'Mario!' Tema hissed.

Sonja drew her pistol and pointed it at Mario. 'Get inside, Tema. Hudson, I did not sleep with Mario in Zimbabwe.'

Hudson clenched his jaw and put his finger through the trigger guard of the Colt.

'I did her once before, in Afghanistan.' He grinned at Sonja.

Hudson felt his heart lurch.

Mario continued: 'She was like a leopardess, you know? You're a safari guide, you've probably seen it for real, what that's like. Far more brutal than the way lions do it. She was scratching, biting, and expected me to do the same, and when I was done she just wanted more of the same. It was different with Ines.'

Hudson's eyesight started to swim. He felt the rage overtake him and closed the gap between them and pushed the tip of the barrel hard into the skin between Mario's eyes.

'Shut. Up.'

'She cried, Brand. All the way through.'

Hudson took up the slack on the trigger, then started as he felt a hand on his shoulder. He looked around and saw Sonja's face.

'Get your hand off me.'

'Ha!' said Mario.

Hudson drew back his hand and, still holding the gun to give the blow extra weight, smashed his fist into Mario's shattered nose. Mario screamed in pain, staggered and dropped to his knees. He writhed and moaned for a few seconds then collapsed into the sand.

'Hudson,' Sonja said, 'Please . . .'

He stuck the pistol in the waistband of his shorts and looked her in the eyes.

'Was Mario lying, about tasting you?'

'I can explain . . .'

'So that's a no,' he said.

Hudson felt the rage building inside him, like hot lava ready to erupt from a volcano. His vision went blurry and he clenched his teeth to fight back the vitriol that threatened to spew forth from his mouth.

'It was nothing. I regret it. I was stupid; and in any case when we were in Zimbabwe we were interrupted, so nothing really –'

'Interrupted? So you fully intended to have sex with him.' He took a deep breath. There was no point in him saying anything and there was nothing she could say to make this right. Of all the people she had to let touch her, why did it have to be that disgusting creature lying out cold on the sand? He drew his gun again. Sonja didn't flinch, but he had no desire to shoot her. He swung his arm until he was pointing at the prone figure.

'You can't do that,' she said.

His hand wavered. He thought, in his madness, that if he executed Mario he might excise the cancer that had grown between him and Sonja. He looked to her again. 'How could you?'

314

Sonja was defiant. 'I thought you had slept with Rosie. I thought it was over between us.'

'You didn't give me a chance to explain that nothing happened.'

Sonja looked down. 'Well, nothing happened between Mario and me. I said I'm sorry.'

'No, you said you regret it and you were interrupted.'

She looked up at him again. 'Of course I'm sorry. I apologise, Hudson, from the bottom of my heart. Will you please forgive me?'

He breathed deep again. His shrink had told him that deep breathing would help him control his anger, when he was doing it tough, after Angola, after the things he had seen people like Mario do there. He'd thought that was all behind him, but all the evil, all the hatred, all the ugliness reared up again, as did the image of Ines, alive and beautiful, and dead and desecrated.

He put the gun away again. He was better than Mario on that front. As much as he wanted that man dead, he was not cowardly or criminal enough to shoot an unconscious man.

Sonja reached for him, her hand extended. 'Please, my love.'

He wanted to take her hand, to forgive her, to start again and pretend this had never happened. The trouble was, he couldn't.

'*Adios.*'

Chapter 26

Tema felt quite OK on the boat, a little calmer and less queasy than she had on the trip over to Kipili. It was a beautiful morning. At the same time, she found working undercover exciting and it gave her a natural buzz.

Nikola had given her a seasickness pill and it was starting to work, she thought. His boat was bigger than the one she and Mario had come over in, and the lake was calmer, which helped.

He showed her how to steer and she stood on the top deck, aiming at a mountain peak on the horizon. Her hair was wrapped up in a brightly printed turban and she thought she looked quite sexy in her white top and navy shorts. Nikola had complimented her on how she looked this morning, in a non-sleazy way. She was genuinely enjoying his company. He talked about his time in the UN, the places he'd visited, and mentioned more than once how he loved wildlife. He was interested in her part of the world, but she hadn't let on that she had spent time in the bush. Whether he knew it or not, it was very unusual for any of her girlfriends to have ever visited the Kruger National Park – except maybe on a school field trip when they were little – even though the vast reserve was on her doorstep. She told Nikola she had been studying at a secretarial college in Hazyview when Mario had come visiting friends from across the border in Mozambique.

At one point Nikola went downstairs and returned to the bridge a short while later carefully balancing two champagne flutes. 'You are doing a marvellous job, Beauty. You're a natural skipper.'

She smiled. She thought she really ought not be drinking champagne at this time of the morning after taking a pill, but the sun was bright, the breeze warm, and the water still glassy. If this was undercover work, she wanted more of it. She hoped, secretly, that Nikola would turn out to be the person he seemed to be: the former aid worker who loved the environment and owned what would soon be a successful lakeside resort.

'I never asked you about your name. What does it mean?' he asked, as she stepped aside and allowed him to take over the helm.

Tema leaned against the dashboard, or whatever it was called on a boat. She sipped her drink and loved the feel of the cold bubbles on her tongue. 'Um, it just means Beauty, that's all.'

'Of course,' he said.

Tema laughed. She felt pleasantly light-headed. She didn't drink a great deal, but this champagne must be very strong, she thought. She was pleased she hadn't used her real name. Why, she wondered, had Nikola asked what her undercover name meant?

'What happened last night, with your husband and that other *mzungu*?'

Tema had learned very early in her visit to East Africa that the word meant 'white person'; it was similar to the Zulu word, *uMlungu*. 'Ag, I don't know. I do know that Mario is a pig and that he must have picked a fight with the other guy and ended up second best. That's what the barman told me.'

'Yes, he told me the same thing.' Nikola set down his glass. 'Except your husband's name is Mari*us*, I thought?'

Tema felt woozy. She blinked. 'Oh, yes, sorry . . .' She was finding it hard to form her words. She had made a mistake, that much she registered, but they had all practised their cover stories and committed each other's fake names to memory. Why was she having so much trouble remembering them? Sonja was Ursula, Hudson was . . . Hudson was . . .

Nikola reached over and took her glass from her. 'Who are you, Tema?'

'Um, I'm not Tema, I'm Beauty. For real. That's my name.'

'But not Mario? That's not his name.'

'No . . . he's . . .'

'Mario.'

'No, no. He's Marius, like you said. I'm just, I'm just maybe a little tipsy I think, Nikola.'

'He's Mario Machado, a former mercenary. Your South African friend who showed up here like some unwashed smelly back-packer in that old Land Rover is Sonja Kurtz, and her supposed boyfriend is Hudson Brand, a private investigator. Who are you?'

'I'm, I'm Beauty.' She felt properly sick now and very afraid. She blinked, but Nikola was getting blurrier. 'I'm . . .'

Nikola grabbed her left forearm, hard enough for her to register some mild pain through the fog that overtook her. 'I'm . . .'

'I'll tell you exactly what you are, young lady, and make no mistake about it. You're finished, Tema.'

*

Sonja looked around again and, seeing no one, slipped into Nikola's private suite. She remembered the layout from her first visit and went straight to Pesev's home office, where his computer sat on a masculine, dark wood writing desk with a green leather blotter.

A carved African face mask, Congolese she thought, grimaced down at her from the wall behind the swivel chair. Sonja sat at the desk and started going through the drawers methodically. There were chequebooks, receipts, a petty cash tin and a diary. She opened the little leather-bound book and flicked through it. Pesev was old-school, preferring to use a paper diary rather than an electronic one, or perhaps both. She turned back to the time when this whole mess had begun, when she had been training the Leopards in the Sabi Sand Game Reserve. Pesev was in Mozambique, just across the border, at the time, and in Johannesburg a few days earlier.

Sonja remembered the days with Hudson, how the loss of the women on the patrol that night had quietly freaked her out. She had tried to convince herself she could just live in the moment, just enjoy being in Hudson's arms, and not think about Sam or all the other people she had known in her life who had been killed in action.

She shook her head, to clear it. Now was not the time.

Pesev, she saw, had been in Harare, Zimbabwe, at the same time she and Mario and the others had been killing poachers in Mana Pools National Park. The timing correlations were unnerving, but, again, that was why they were here. It seemed like it wouldn't take too much to confirm Paterson's supposition that Pesev, who spoke Russian, was the man in charge of the Scorpions.

Sonja slid the hiking pack off her shoulders and took out the first bug. Pesev would be no fool, though she suspected he felt secure enough in this remote little slice of paradise not to worry about electronically scanning for bugs. She stood, lifted the mask from its hook on the wall, and secured the device with double-sided tape to the back of the carving before replacing it.

The laptop on the desk was in sleep mode so she sat and pressed the power button. As she suspected, the Mac needed a password to wake it up. Sonja was no hacker so she didn't even bother trying.

She stood and walked out of the office, along the polished concrete floor of the hallway to the master bedroom.

The bed, like the desk, was dark and carved, a four-poster with a big mosquito net suspended from a frame. The maid had already made it up. Sonja went into the walk-in open closet. Pesev had a lot of clothes and shoes, for a man. He was single and rich.

Sonja went to the bathroom and looked out the small window. The camping ground was empty. Hudson had packed the Land Rover and driven away. An attendant was raking the dirt where they had parked.

Sonja sighed.

She forced her thoughts back to the job. Pesev would notice the missing vehicle as soon as he and Tema got back. How plausible would it be, she wondered, for a hotelier to have two couples, guests, break up in the course of a few days? They had to get the information they needed on him and get out of here quick.

If Sonja's suspicion about Julianne Clyde-Smith running a hit squad was true, then as soon as they did prove Pesev was the head of the Scorpions Sonja was fairly sure Julianne would order Mario to kill him.

Given what had happened to Sam, part of Sonja didn't care what Julianne was up to. It was illegal, running an ex officio hit squad outside of the law, and as much as some people might applaud Julianne for taking such a stand, Sonja did not want to be a part of that sort of operation. She had killed plenty of people in her life, but had nearly always been able to justify her actions to herself as morally acceptable.

The one exception to this had been the Vietnamese man, Tran Van Ngo.

Sonja had no problem shooting poachers if they were firing at her, and while she did, in fact, want revenge for the deaths of the two women in her team, she would not kill a man in cold blood again to achieve that.

Quite what she would do with Julianne if she found out she was running a murder squad, she didn't know. One thing was for sure: she would get Tema away from this toxic environment and do her best to find her employment somewhere else.

Her mission would be harder without Hudson, and her life would be emptier.

Try as she might she could not focus solely on placing the bugs in Nikola's house. Her thoughts kept going back to Hudson. She remembered when she was a young soldier in the British Army, undergoing a gruelling selection course to join 14 Intelligence Company, for service in Northern Ireland. Almost as tough as overcoming the physical obstacles on the course was the battle against the mindset of some of the male soldiers and officers she dealt with. 14 Company was at that time as close as female soldiers could get to being in harm's way in a front line, albeit undercover, unit.

The opponents of the concept of women being placed in situations where they might be compromised and face the prospect of having to shoot their way out fell back on an age-old excuse for keeping women off the battlefield: that their male counterparts might become too attached to their female comrades and take foolish risks to protect the weaker sex.

It was nonsense, Sonja thought.

The fact was that most of the acts of heroism she'd seen in her years on the world's battlefields were not about soldiers slaughtering scores of the enemy, but of individual men – and women – putting their lives at risk to rescue or help fellow human beings, regardless of their sex.

If anything, the argument had got the genders wrong when it came to people forming attachments. Sonja found herself right now unable to concentrate on her mission because of the man she was now fairly sure she loved, Hudson Brand.

The very thought of being in love again scared her, and she hated to admit that a very small part of her might be pleased that he was gone. Nevertheless, in her mind she composed the explanation she would have given to him, if he had listened, and if she had been brave enough to say it to him.

Believe it or not, she might have said, *there is a nice, soft, gooey part inside of me that makes me human and makes me able to love.* She would have had to pause there, she was fairly sure, to wait for his laughter to subside. She was well aware of how she presented to others, how most people only ever saw her tough exterior and the work she did rather than the person inside the uniform.

Hudson Brand had seen all of her, laid bare, had touched every part of her, kissed every part. *But that part of me*, she thought, trying hard to find the words for herself, even if he would never hear them, *gets bruised very easily and can't deal with anything that looks like abandonment.*

She had been hurt, in her life, by her alcoholic father, by the mother who had left her, in Africa, to fly back to England where she came from. Sonja had joined her, eventually, after being incapable of dealing with her father's condition. She hadn't understood at the time – she did now – that his problems were a product of his military service in South West Africa, now Namibia, and his exposure to and participation in the worst things soldiers at war could do.

And then there is the strong, hard, mind-over-matter part of me, the soldier in me, that can deal with disappointment, is trained to ignore pain and carry on, but only by shutting down my heart, my feelings, my emotions.

Right now, the hard side of her wanted to do just that, to pull on the armour to protect the vulnerable core. She wondered if that had been part of her foolish motivation for having sex with Mario, to cauterise her feelings for Hudson, whether or not she had truly believed he had been unfaithful. Perhaps, deep down, it didn't matter if Hudson hadn't slept with Rosie, because the tough part of her didn't care; it just wanted to keep him away *in case* her growing love for him didn't work out.

'I am so fucked up,' she whispered to herself in Pesev's bedroom.

She placed a bug behind his bedhead, shifted the bed back into place, and walked through to the lounge area.

Sonja paused and looked around the living room. It was stylish, tasteful and impressive without being ostentatious. It was, she had to admit, better than she could do, despite the wealth she had inherited. She wondered if Pesev had paid a designer, perhaps the same person who had furnished his beachfront lodge, or if he just naturally had good taste.

She started to wonder what a house that she and Hudson Brand shared might look like. But, no, that was never going to happen. She looked out the windows and saw three of Pesev's blue-uniformed maintenance or grounds staff walking towards her, from the direction of the workshops.

As they came closer she recognised one of them as Godwin, the mechanic she had gone to, ostensibly for advice on Hudson's battered Land Rover. Funny, she almost missed the vehicle now, as well as him. Her heart felt empty.

And then it lurched.

Godwin, she now realised, like the other two men, was carrying a green canvas bag. The man just behind him stopped, set his bag down and unzipped it.

The mechanic turned and waved his hand in a frantic, chopping motion, telling him to stop what he was doing, but it was too late. The man, who Sonja now realised was the gardener who had just been tending the lawn, pulled an AK-47 out of the bag and cocked it.

'Shit.' Sonja shrugged off her daypack and took out a walkie-talkie. From under her T-shirt she slid the Makarov pistol from the holster clipped to her belt.

'Cobra, this is Mamba,' Sonja said, calling Paterson using their agreed call-signs. 'I've been compromised, three tangos heading my way, all with long guns.'

She didn't wait for his reply. The men had all unsheathed their weapons now and were moving in on Pesev's chalet at a jog, rifles up. Sonja had all the proof she needed that there was something wrong going on here, but still she had to be sure. She stepped out onto the verandah, in plain sight of all three. The mechanic paused, raised his rifle and fired a burst of three rounds.

'Thank you.' Sonja brought her pistol up and fired a double tap, at the gardener, who was now a few metres ahead of the mechanic. It was long range for a pistol, but she'd been practising all her life. At least one of the rounds found its mark and the man fell. Sonja ducked back inside and dropped beneath the sill of the nearest window.

The phone on Nikola Pesev's desk rang. She ignored it and risked a peep through the window.

The man she had shot was writhing on the ground, calling out in pain. It took her a moment to locate the other two.

One, the mechanic, she thought, had taken cover behind a parked Land Rover Discovery, Pesev's vehicle, or one of them, she assumed. The third man was lying down behind a tree. She fired two shots at the latter as he was closer than the mechanic, who seemed to be in charge, hanging back and directing the others.

The phone on Pesev's antique desk rang out, but a few seconds later it started ringing again.

One of the men was shouting something. She peeked over the windowsill again and saw the mechanic waving his rifle in the air over the bonnet of the Discovery.

'Don't shoot.'

Sonja put two rounds through the truck's side windows. The man placed his AK-47 on the ground in front of the nose of the vehicle, where she could see it.

'Don't shoot!'

'What do you want?' she called.

'Answer the phone.'

'What?'

'The boss's phone, answer it.'

It was still ringing. It could be a simple trick, Sonja thought, designed to give them enough time to close the gap between their isolated places of cover and Pesev's home.

Something had gone terribly wrong here. The phone's chirping grated on her nerves. She moved so that she could see the approach to the chalet, obliquely, out of the window, but without exposing herself to fire from the two men. She picked up the cordless phone, but didn't answer it straight away. She moved so that she could see the Discovery, and the AK-47 still on the ground in front of it.

She lifted the handset. 'Kurtz.'

'Go to my computer and open it. It will connect to the wi-fi immediately and I'm logged into Skype. Turn on the camera.'

'Sure. And then your goons rush me and kill me.'

'No,' Pesev said into her ear. 'I've told them to stay where they are. There are more of them, by the way, ready to come for you in case these first three screwed up, which they did, of course, or we wouldn't be having this conversation. I have Paterson in my custody.'

'What's your password?' Sonja asked.

He laughed. '"Password", of course.'

She scanned the spots where the two able-bodied henchmen were still hiding. The one she had hit was still and quiet, either dead or passed out. 'You're kidding.'

'The obvious is sometimes the best, like hiding in plain view. I'd have thought you would have realised that by now.'

Sonja ended the call and went to the desk. She unplugged the laptop from its power cord and moved back to the window.

She placed the computer on the floor and angled the screen back so she could glance down at it while still keeping the gunmen under observation. She trusted no one any more.

True to his word, the password worked. Sonja clicked on Skype and waited for the connection.

She saw a movement by the tree where one of the men had taken cover so she fired a shot at him, to make him keep his head down.

'Don't kill any more of my men than you have to,' said an accented voice from the computer.

Sonja looked down. There was a lag and the video appeared just after the words were spoken. She gasped. The other computer was angled to show the slender naked body of a black woman, tied down, her legs apart. On the woman's face was a wet towel. There was an agonising, animalistic scream as a bucket of water was poured slowly, mercilessly, onto the towel. The bound woman thrashed like there were thousands of volts of electricity being passed through her.

The bucket and the hands holding it disappeared from the frame for a moment and then the towel was pulled from the woman's face.

Tears streamed down Tema's face as she coughed and spluttered.

The bastard was waterboarding her. Sonja had heard the stories and they had been confirmed, early on during the time she'd spent in Afghanistan, when she had sat in on the interrogation of an al-Qaeda man. She had seen the hardened mujahideen reduced to a screaming, crying mess in what seemed like no time at all.

Sonja hardened her heart, shutting down her emotions. She said nothing.

Pesev changed the direction of the screen until he was looking at her. 'Hey, I'm impressed. She lasted fifteen minutes, more than any man I've ever had to do that to.'

Sonja glared at him.

'It's over,' he said. 'I know everything now.'

'So let her go,' Sonja said at last.

'No, I think I'll kill her, slowly.'

Tema whimpered off screen.

'She knew the risks when she took on the job, took on the likes of you,' Sonja said.

Pesev drew back from the screen. 'My goodness, I heard you were hard, but I didn't think you were such a callous bitch, Sonja.'

'Shut up, Pesev. What do you want from us?'

'Who says I want anything?'

He stood up and walked out of the cabin on to the boat's deck, holding the laptop. There was water all around him, from what she could see; no land.

'You contacted me, you wanted me to see this. Tema is alive. What do you want?'

'Do you want to save Tema?'

'What do you think?'

'You were right; I do want something. Your boss.'

'Paterson? I thought you said you already had him.'

'I do. No, I want Julianne Clyde-Smith.'

Sonja shook her head. 'Are you crazy? After Kim Kardashian she's probably the world's most recognisable woman. What are you going to do, waterboard her, as well, on Skype?'

'No, I just want to blackmail her.'

'Well, I'm sure she'll agree to that.'

Pesev laughed, deep and loud. 'What just happened to Tema is Julianne's fault. This is the price she pays for taking the law into her own hands. I want you to call Julianne, tell her that your operation, your whole team, is compromised, and that I want her to come to my lodge, today, in her own aircraft, and meet me.'

'She's the richest woman in Africa. There'll be a kidnap and ransom team, the bloody British SAS for all I know, here in no time. You don't have a choice.'

'Watch this,' he said.

Sonja could hear Pesev tapping on his keyboard. A minute later a link appeared in the message box on Skype. Sonja clicked on it.

In the video only Tema's tear-streaked face appeared. 'Julianne Clyde-Smith,' she sniffed, 'my employer, has set up an illegal hit squad to carry out assassination missions against poachers and their leaders.'

In the background Sonja heard something indistinct but forceful, as though Pesev was threatening her.

It looked like Tema was reading from a script. Sonja saw her give a little nod to some whispered command.

'Julianne Clyde-Smith ordered the assassination of James "King Jim" Ndlovu and Antonio Cuna at the Sabie River Lodge golf course in South Africa. They tried to kill Nikola Pesev, a respected businessman in Tanzania, because Julianne Clyde-Smith wanted his lakeside beach resort property.'

The video ended.

'Anyone who sees this will know Tema was coerced.'

Pesev came back on the screen. He nodded. 'Yes, any law enforcement people will know that, and some sensible media commentators, but before any voices of reason come to Julianne's defence, or question Tema's words, it will be too late. The families of the dead will force investigations to be carried out. I'm going to make this video public unless Julianne meets with me and agrees to my terms.'

'What are they?'

Pesev shrugged. 'There is some stuff I want to negotiate with Julianne, but that is none of your business. I want your unit disbanded and for Julianne to call off this fatwa she has with the Scorpions. If I ever hear of you, personally, going after any of my people I will take out a worldwide contract against you, and your former lover, Hudson Brand, and Tema, if I spare her.'

'And if Julianne refuses?'

'You've got an hour to get me an answer, Sonja. When you look outside you may or may not see that there are now twelve men surrounding you, from all sides. I know you're good, very good, and you've probably already killed one of my men, but by my man's calculation you don't have many rounds left in the Makarov that Tema says you're carrying and you have just one spare magazine that Paterson issued you with when he gave you and Tema your weapons.'

Sonja exhaled. She didn't blame Tema for revealing the information she had, and she was genuinely impressed by the young woman's ability to withstand as much of the horrific torture as she had. 'What guarantee do I have that you won't kill Tema anyway?'

'None, and if you do manage to shoot your way out of my house now I'll know soon enough, and I'll kill Tema. I've got enough resources to disappear, but I don't want to. I want to stay in business and I want an agreement from Julianne Clyde-Smith to lay off my people and my organisation.'

Sonja thought for a moment. Pesev had said nothing about Mario. As much as she detested him, she wondered where he was right now. It would be best not to mention him. 'So what of Paterson?'

'Oh, he's probably going to die. That's part of my price, and a reasonable one considering how many of my good men he has been responsible for eliminating.'

Sonja felt a chill run through her body. 'All right, I'll call Julianne.'

'Wait.'

'What now?' Sonja asked.

'Tell Ms Clyde-Smith I have a gift for her, one she will thank me for.'

Chapter 27

Julianne Clyde-Smith boarded her private aircraft at the airstrip at Kuria Hills and strapped herself into her seat. The pilot, Doug Pearse, revved the engine to scare off some wildebeest who were grazing on the edge of the runway. They galloped away and the pilot opened the throttle.

She felt the anxiety rising in her chest as the aircraft climbed and set a course for Kipili on the edge of Lake Tanganyika. Normally she would have had her face pressed against the window to take in the sights of the open plains, the picturesque hills and the Mara River, but now she could only concentrate on her hands, clasped tightly in her lap.

This situation was all her fault. There was no escaping it.

James was a hostage under threat of execution and Tema, that lovely, brave, pretty young girl, with a little baby at home in South Africa, was in the clutches of Nikola Pesev. Like Sonja, she wondered where Mario was.

How had it come to this?

It was easy, she knew, to talk tough about crimes, poaching included, but few politicians ever looked past the next news cycle or election to actually do anything about them. Because poaching transgressed international borders it made it that much harder to combat. Memorandums of understanding were laboured over, and even when eventually signed they counted for little. The South African National Defence Force, national parks rangers and police knew exactly where the poachers were in Mozambique, and in many cases who they and their superiors were by name, but they lacked the power to cross the border and hunt them down. Likewise, the rangers in Zimbabwe knew there were Zambians poised across the Zambezi River all too eager to cross and take out the country's elephants. None of them could do anything about it, but Julianne had thought she could.

And she had, damn it.

She raised a knuckle to her mouth. She thought about James. He was handsome, committed to the point of being ruthless, and he had been the right man for her to employ to command this operation that she had concocted. Sure, he had encouraged her, and he had come into her life at exactly the right time, but this had all been her idea.

She'd been interviewed in South Africa's *Sunday Times* and had said she believed that the private sector, safari lodge operators, needed to be more unified, to spend more on the war against rhino poaching. The property owners were well-heeled, successful people, and as such they were strong personalities. It was not easy to get such people to work together, and she had noted on occasion a direct correlation between a person's wealth and the shortness of their arms when it came to reaching into their collective pockets to find more money for anti-poaching teams and equipment.

It was easy for her. While she was no Bill Gates, she could spend the rest of her life, literally, and not run out of money. She had no husband, no children, no siblings. In fact, she had no one.

And then James had come into her life.

She pictured him, but more importantly remembered the feel of him, his smell, his touch. He had the clichéd square-jawed face of a military man, but there was much more to him, a depth of knowledge cultivated through life and education. He had masters degrees in business, criminology, and science, and had earned his stripes many times over in the wars on extremism and terrorism.

She remembered their first meeting. He had been at a conference on rhino conservation; she had been the keynote speaker, and he had been giving a lecture about lessons from Iraq and Afghanistan and how they could be applied in the African context, in the war to protect the continent's wildlife.

She'd wanted to attend his lecture, but after her address she knew that any session she attended would draw attention away from the guest speaker. The media would want to sit and watch her, film her, question her afterwards, rather than pay attention to the person presenting. She didn't need any more of that attention.

Julianne had asked, through the organisers, if she might have a look at James's notes or presentation prior to his delivery. She had a plane to catch back to England the next day and couldn't afford to stick around, nor trust herself to get one of her people to follow up once she was enmeshed in the day-to-day business of running her many companies.

On the first night of the conference she attended a cocktail party. It was as much to ensure media coverage for the organisers as from any desire to mix and mingle. Indeed, she hated doing the latter. She was, socially, a private person, and exposed herself to the bare minimum of functions that her profile demanded.

At the event, which was held in the ballroom of the Table Bay Hotel in Cape Town, she'd found herself chaperoned by the organiser of the conference and engaged in a nonsensical conversation with a government minister who mouthed platitudes from briefing notes and showed no passion for the fight to protect her country's wildlife resources at all.

'Excuse me, you wanted to see me?' a voice had interrupted.

Julianne and her minders had been equally taken aback.

She'd handed her empty champagne glass to a hovering waiter. 'Excuse me?'

'I'm James Paterson. You wanted to see me.'

'No, Mr Paterson, I didn't want to see you.'

'Yes, you did, but you had to leave early.'

'It was your paper I wanted.'

The government minister, used to being feted, not ignored, begged off. Julianne was pleased this handsome, if slightly arrogant stranger had rescued her.

They had talked, too long for the organisers' liking, and she had been fascinated by Paterson's knowledge, his resolve, and his proposal.

'What you need,' he had been bold enough to tell her, 'is a top-class reconnaissance unit, a team of ex–special forces people, or properly trained local operators, who can cross borders legally and gather the intelligence the national police forces and militaries can't. Most importantly, you need someone who can analyse this intelligence and develop courses of action to take the war to the poachers and to cut the heads off their organisations.'

'A hit squad?' she had asked him.

'Most assuredly not. That's too easy, but it's also fraught with danger, for you most of all. No, you need a strategy.'

He had stopped a waiter and taken two glasses from the tray.

'No, thank, you,' she had said. 'I limit myself to one drink at these things.'

'Fine.' He had beckoned the waiter back again. 'Sorry, take these please.'

'Thank you.'

'It's better if we have a drink together, away from this rabble. My place or yours?'

She had thrown her head back and laughed. His direct approach was refreshing, to be sure, but she had no intention of going back to a stranger's room.

'No.'

'Why not?'

'You don't live in the public eye like I do. Right now there are paparazzi –' she had looked around and it took her less than thirty seconds to find three of them conspiring, pretending not to be monitoring her every move, '– who will already be asking each other who you are. Call my office, tomorrow, after you've delivered the presentation you're going to email me tonight.' She had given him her email address and he had nodded, committing it to memory. 'I'll tell reception to accept your call. Do you have the money to fly to England?'

'I do.'

'Then do so. My personal assistant, Audrey Uren, will tell you when I'm free. If you make it to me in London, I'll hear what you have to say about this special unit you want to put together.'

Paterson had sized her up, his eyes all over her, and she had felt at once offended and slightly aroused by his naked appraisal of her. His look had nothing to do with business, and he was doing nothing to disguise that fact. He was an ex-army officer, though clearly not always a gentleman. He had the raw sex appeal of many of the South African male safari guides she had met, and employed, touched up with the veneer of manners and bearing that came from the British Army. His alpha maleness was palpable.

'Very well,' James had said. He had come to her, and into her life.

'Commencing descent, Ms Clyde-Smith,' Doug, the pilot, said over the intercom.

Julianne shook herself out of her reverie. Doug was a good-looking man, but she had no interest in him sexually. She'd had a strict self-imposed policy throughout her business life that she would never sleep with a co-worker or, for the majority of her adult life, a subordinate.

She had broken that rule with James, but she didn't regret it.

The work he had been doing for her in Africa, initially gathering intelligence and building a database of poaching kingpins and, increasingly, a dossier on the Scorpions, had brought them much closer.

She was interested in this work, far more than she was in the day-to-day running of her business empire, which tended to look after itself in the hands of a stable of competent men and women in general management roles. Julianne took a perverse pleasure in immersing herself in the revelations of organised crime's involvement in wildlife poaching in Africa.

As poaching became more businesslike it became an easier target for someone who was an expert at bringing down rival companies, taking them over, dismembering them, and profiting from their demise.

'Ma'am, I'd like to stay with you, that is, by your side, from the time we land,' Doug said from the cockpit.

'Thank you, Doug, but the instructions from Sonja were that I must move alone. I'll be met at the airstrip by her, and some of Pesev's people.'

'Roger that. I still don't like it.'

'I'll be fine,' she said, trying to sound brave. In truth, she was terrified, but she knew she would do anything to save James and Tema.

They had been working late, each having a single malt scotch, at Khaya Ngala in South Africa the first time they'd had sex.

The media loved to speculate about Julianne's love life. She was a single, successful woman approaching middle age who had never been married. Every time she was seen in public with a good-looking male or female – especially female – friend or subordinate, like James, the photographers fired off like the opening barrage of the Battle of the Somme.

The fact was, she chose her partners carefully and rarely, and spent time with them discreetly. It had been that way with James, but he had been different from the others.

He had been quick to accept her ways, her kinks, and to indulge her and complement her. With some of the others she'd been left feeling that they had gone through the motions because of her wealth. That never boded well, but with James she had the feeling that whatever he allowed her to subject him to, or whatever he did to her, it was not about the money, nor the power.

Julianne bit her lower lip. She felt the rising tide of anxiety again, and pictured what might happen to him or what had already been done. Before the day-mare could overwhelm her she used a trick her psychotherapist had taught her. She visualised a 'Stop' traffic sign, big, red and hexagonal with bold white lettering. She mentally held up a hand and mouthed the word. It helped, a little.

James had worked with the Special Forces, including Britain's famed Special Air Service, and he had told her he had gone through brutal 'resistance to interrogation' training as part of his own career development as an intelligence officer. He had learned how to resist torture. He was as tough as he was good-looking.

The aircraft lurched as it hit an updraft rising from the hot African soil. On either side of her she saw dried gold and brown, a few huts, the slash of a red dirt airstrip like a fresh cut, and Lake Tanganyika glittering in the near distance.

The Beechcraft bounced once, no reflection on Doug's skill, and the engines whined as he slowed the aircraft. At the end of the strip he slewed her around and then raced back towards the shack that passed for a terminal. There were two Land Cruisers waiting.

Julianne waited until Doug shut down the engines, then came through the cabin and opened the hatch. Sonja was at the bottom of the fold-out stairs.

'Glad you could make it so quickly.'

'How is . . . how are our people?'

*

Sonja looked at the rich woman. Her face was pale as she gripped the safety cords on either side of the stairs to steady herself.

'Tema is alive. That's all I know. We've got a lot to talk about,' Sonja said, 'but right now my priority is getting Tema off Pesev's boat and out of this country alive. There's been no sign of Mario, and Pesev would have boasted, I'm sure, if he'd killed him. Mario might have run off, though for all his faults he's not one to hide from a fight.'

'And James?' Julianne said as they walked across the strip to a waiting Land Cruiser.

'Fuck James.'

'I beg your pardon,' Julianne said. 'I don't know what's gone on here between you two, but his life is in grave danger, judging by what you told me.'

'He has himself to blame.'

'You're being a little harsh, aren't you?'

Sonja paused before they reached the vehicles. Two of Pesev's men, their escorts, stood by the four-by-four. One had a pistol stuck in the waistband of his jeans. Sonja knew the other had an AK in the vehicle. She was angry enough to kill both of them, but she knew this would result in Paterson's death for sure and most likely Tema's as well. She forced herself to be calm.

'You've been running a black ops hit squad. That's illegal and immoral, but it wouldn't have concerned me at all if you'd told me the truth up-front and given me the opportunity to opt out, and to stop Tema and Ezekial from getting dragged into this dangerous mess.'

'I am doing nothing of the kind. I resent –'

Sonja took a pace closer to the billionaire and poked her in the breastbone with her index finger. 'Shut up.'

'You can't talk that way, and if you touch me again I'll have you arrested and charged with assault.'

Sonja seethed. 'You've been murdering people.'

'And you're a fine one to lecture me. You started a civil war a few years ago. How many innocents were killed in that?'

'None in cold blood, to the best of my knowledge. Your attack dog Paterson's been running his own private Phoenix Program, and when I get back to South Africa I'll do everything I can to help the police with their investigations into the shooting of a man who is most likely innocent.'

'You pulled the trigger on that one, I seem to recall,' Julianne said, not backing down. 'You're a trained killer, a mercenary, persona non grata in your own home country of Namibia. James has a stellar reputation. The media will hang you out to dry.'

Sonja recoiled. 'You think you can scare me? You imagine I'm afraid of some journalists? I'll gut you and make sure your body sinks in Lake Tanganyika if Tema dies.'

Julianne tried to hold Sonja's stare, but her lower lip started to quiver.

'Get in the Land Cruiser.'

Julianne got in, and Sonja climbed in beside her in the rear seat. Pesev's thugs got in the front and they set off down the short but rutted and potholed road to Kipili. Sonja looked at the other woman; they were of similar age, but had lived entirely different lives. Sonja was not poor, but she could not imagine the riches at Julianne Clyde-Smith's disposal. She could have put her money into propping up the various African governments fighting the war on poaching, with varying degrees of commitment and success, but instead she had chosen to go it alone. Sonja didn't know if it was Julianne or James running the assassination program, but Sonja noted that Julianne had not flat-out denied her allegations. She was feeling the guilt, unable to meet her eyes.

'You should prepare yourself for the fact that Pesev has said he will probably kill James, as payback,' Sonja said.

Julianne closed her eyes and swallowed. She gripped the driver's seat in front of her and bowed her head, but said nothing.

Sonja noted, again, the difference in Julianne's reaction to Tema's plight and James's. She knew James much better, of course, but Sonja sensed there was something more. She reached out a hand and placed it on Julianne's.

'Whatever you think of me, I'm a woman, too,' Sonja said.

'He's a friend, as well as an employee.'

'A good friend?'

Julianne nodded. 'Yes. Is it possible to rescue him?'

'I haven't even seen him yet,' Sonja said. 'For all I know he's already dead and Pesev just said he was still alive in order to convince you to come and parlay with him.'

Julianne stared into Sonja's eyes. 'Do you think I would not have come to try and save Tema's life if it was just her in trouble?'

'I think you would have sent people, a kidnap and ransom team, maybe money. I don't think you would have come yourself, alone. That tells me one of two things: either you're in love with James and would do anything to get him back, or you and he are as crooked as I think you are. Perhaps both.'

Julianne sneered. 'You know how many tens of thousands of bunny huggers and vigilantes alike call for the death penalty for wildlife poachers every day on Facebook? You know how many people value a rhino more than a human life?'

'I do, but that doesn't make unsanctioned executions right. There's a difference between a lawful shoot-to-kill policy, like in Botswana and Zimbabwe where rangers can open fire on armed poachers before being shot at, and what you and James have been doing.'

'Yes, the difference is we have targeted the headmen, kingpins, whatever you want to call them, who use poor illiterate people as cannon fodder and get fat on the profits while wiping out entire species. This had to be done, but I have never given an order to assassinate anyone, not ever.'

Sonja shook her head. 'When my partner was killed I wouldn't have argued with you; I might even have volunteered to help, but you've created this mess by your indiscriminate program of killings. You're going to have to be accountable for what you've done at some point in time.'

'Your perspective on this is all wrong. Pesev is the devil. He's the head of the Scorpions.'

'So it would appear.' They crested a hill, and as the Land Cruiser bounced slowly down the access road, Lake Tanganyika danced in the sun, all the way to the horizon. 'And now you've got to sit down with the devil and make a deal, to keep you both in business.'

'I'm not going to let him continue destroying Africa's wildlife.'

'You're going to stop this ridiculous operation of yours and leave it to the legitimate authorities. Pesev thinks he can run rings around them, and in some countries he can, but he's been rattled by what you and James *were* able to achieve, as reprehensible as it was.'

'And if I don't lay off him?'

'He'll release the video of Tema that I emailed you. She spilled enough after being tortured to get you in trouble.'

Julianne sat back in her seat, her customary composure and aloofness returning. 'I'll have a battalion of lawyers and a division of PR people around the world working to counter what she said.'

Sonja nodded. 'I'm sure you will, but if this does just turn out to be a couple of news cycles of bad press, and if you discredit

Tema, or if Pesev kills her because you won't play ball, then I'll come for you.'

Julianne looked her in the eye, but couldn't hold her gaze, because deep down inside she must have known that Sonja meant every word of what she had just said.

Chapter 28

Nikola Pesev's motor cruiser was visible from shore now. Mario sat in the shell of a half-built hut and scanned the area around the bay through binoculars.

In the tiny village of Kipili the heat was keeping most people indoors. A skinny dog chased a goat; three boys kicked a soccer ball made of rags, plastic bags and rubber bands along the rutted dirt road that passed for a main street.

A small green patrol boat, what passed for the Tanzanian navy or coastguard on this part of the lake, was moored in front of two buildings whose drab design and colour definitely marked them as military. A bare-chested sailor in camouflage pants slowly swabbed the deck. It was Sunday and nothing much of anything was happening.

Two Land Cruisers sped through the village, blanketing the playing boys in dust. Mario quickly checked the vehicles and saw they were the same two that had left Pesev's lodge not long ago. Sonja was on board one of them. She, like Mario, had obviously survived the ambush that had netted his boss, James.

Mario had befriended a young girl from the village and offered her fifty US dollars to have sex with him. She had agreed, but would not come to the lodge or his room. Mario had met her in a grove of mango trees just outside of the lodge boundary. He had been with her, in the shade of the trees, when he had heard the gunshots.

It had soon become apparent that Sonja had been in a gunfight with Pesev's men, from Pesev's house, but that she had obviously come to some sort of truce with them as she had gone with them in one of the Land Cruisers. That was odd, as she was not the sort of woman who negotiated.

Mario adjusted his binoculars. Nikola Pesev had a fishing boat as well as his pleasure cruiser, and there was an armed man standing guard on the concrete wharf and breakwater where the fishing boat was tied up. Another man had brought a tray of food from the kitchen earlier and was now alighting from the boat. Mario could see that there were two clean plates and two crushed Coca Cola cans. The men exchanged words and the guard pointed out to Pesev's cruiser, which had dropped anchor in the bay about two hundred metres from shore.

Another armed man was now approaching the fishing boat. He passed the man carrying the empty plates, and then relieved the man who had been standing guard through the long hot morning. From the roster and the crockery, Mario reckoned James Paterson was still alive and being held captive on the fishing boat, with another guard watching him below deck.

Mario focused on Pesev's cruiser out in the bay. He could see Nikola, as he had done before, moving about through the clear vinyl windows in the canvas coverings zipped closed around the boat. He wished he had a sniper rifle, but even if he did he noticed that Pesev never stayed visible for more than a few seconds. There was no sign of Tema, but Mario thought she would still be on board following her daytrip, and was perhaps also a hostage.

Pesev was clearly the head of the Scorpions and needed to be killed; Paterson, Mario's paymaster and commanding officer, had to be rescued. Although the undercover mission had been nothing short of a disaster, even a balls-up of this magnitude provided opportunities.

Mario felt good, despite his broken nose and other cuts and bruises. He felt a clarity of purpose, a freedom to do what needed to be done.

Training his gaze back on the lodge, Mario saw that the Land Cruisers had pulled up outside the reception area. He watched four armed men get out of the first vehicle. From the second vehicle Sonja, two more men and, surprisingly, Julianne Clyde-Smith alighted. They walked into the lodge, out of sight for a few seconds, then out the other side onto the wharf.

The armed men stopped the women about twenty metres short of where the guarded fishing boat was tied up.

Mario focused on Sonja. She held a pistol in her right hand and stayed close to Julianne, acting as her bodyguard. If Pesev had wanted the two women dead it would have been done by now, albeit with some bloodshed. A minute later James Paterson emerged from below decks and was frogmarched onto the rear of the boat. He had his hands tied behind his back and was blindfolded. The man who had been standing guard on the dock also got onto the boat, and disappeared around the far side of the cabin.

Mario saw Julianne raise a hand to her mouth.

She was shocked. The little gesture confirmed what Mario had suspected: that their female supremo was soft on Paterson. She must have come to Kipili, Mario realised, to negotiate Paterson's release.

If he could eliminate Pesev and his men, and free James, Julianne would be saved the ignominy of having to deal with these criminals. Mario would be the hero of the day and Julianne and James would reward him.

The whine of an outboard motor made Mario shift his gaze again. He picked up a Zodiac inflatable boat churning a white arc in the water from the far side of the fishing boat. The guard who had been standing watch was at the controls of the rubber craft, which must have been tied to the other side of the boat on which Paterson was imprisoned.

The armed men who had escorted Sonja and Julianne motioned them towards the Zodiac, which had pulled up at the end of the wharf. As Julianne climbed aboard she looked over her shoulder at the fishing boat, but her lover had already been taken below again.

Mario assessed the situation. The odds against him, one currently unarmed man, were daunting. He needed help, but there was only one gunslinger who was hopefully still close enough to call on. The thought galled him at first, but the more he mulled it over in his mind the less repugnant it became.

He took his mobile out of his shirt pocket and found the number he had saved at Julianne's lodge at Kuria Hills, when James had insisted they all share their contact details before setting out on the mission. Mario hit the call button.

'What the fuck do you want?' Hudson Brand said into his phone.

*

Sonja sat at the rear of the Zodiac as it bounced at high speed across the bay. Julianne was in front of her, an armed man next to her; the driver sat amidships and two more goons sat on the inflated sides of the boat staring back at her. The fourth man from the escorting party had stayed on the dock to relieve the driver, so there were still two armed men guarding James.

Sonja was as tense as a coiled spring, alert for ambush and ready to strike at any moment. Pesev's motor cruiser loomed. The man steering cut the engine to idling speed and they coasted up to the cruiser, which was much more luxuriously appointed than the fishing boat.

A crewman, pistol tucked into his belt, caught a line thrown by the armed man next to Julianne and tied the Zodiac to the larger vessel. The first two gunmen climbed aboard and covered Julianne and Sonja as they made their way past the remaining guard and driver.

Sonja held her pistol in two hands, braced and ready to open fire, as Julianne was helped aboard.

Nikola Pesev came out onto the rear deck, a panama hat shading his face. He smiled and offered Julianne his hand, but she didn't return the greeting.

'Where is Tema?' Julianne asked.

'She's alive, if that's what you're worried about,' Nikola said. He raised his hand to the brim of his hat. 'Ms Kurtz; nice to see you, and thank you for keeping your side of the bargain.'

Sonja raised her pistol and aimed it at Nikola's head. His henchmen all turned their AK-47s on her.

'Show me Tema or I'll shoot.'

'And you'll be dead a split second later.'

Sonja gave a small shrug. 'So?'

Nikola gave a nod and the crewman went below. They waited, all of them silent, until he returned, pushing Tema up the stairs ahead of him. She was handcuffed, but not gagged.

Sonja saw that her eyes were bloodshot from crying and her lip was split. 'Are you all right?'

Tema focused on the deck. 'Yes.'

'Look at me, Tema,' Sonja ordered.

She kept her eyes downcast. 'I told him everything he wanted to know.'

'You held out longer than most men – most people – would. You've done nothing wrong. Did he . . .'

Tema looked up. 'No.'

'I'm not an animal,' Pesev said.

Julianne scoffed. 'That remains to be seen.'

'Take her below again,' Pesev said, and Tema was led away. 'Ms Clyde-Smith, may I call you Jules?'

'No. Julianne if you must.'

'We are here to talk business. My man has prepared lunch. Please join me.'

Julianne looked to Sonja.

'I would prefer it if we ate alone,' Nikola said. 'I am sure there are some things we will discuss that you would not want made public.'

'I have nothing to hide from Sonja. In fact, I want her to know the truth about what I've been doing.'

'You and Paterson,' Nikola said.

'No, me. I take full responsibility for all of the actions carried out by the people who work for me. But Sonja comes into the meeting.'

'Very well, then I will bring my most trusted man with me.'

'Fine.'

'This way, please.' Pesev led them inside the cabin, to the air-conditioned lounge. The polished wood table was set with salads and cold meats. There was French champagne and South African white wine on ice.

A crewman in a starched white uniform pulled out their seats for them.

'Thank you for coming,' Nikola said. 'I must admit, I didn't know if you would, Julianne.'

'You have two of my people hostage.'

'And yet you do not call in the SAS? You, one of the richest women in the world, come alone, as I requested, with just Ms Kurtz, Sonja, your – how shall I put it – "go-between"?'

'I work for Julianne,' Sonja said.

Pesev put his hands together and brought the tips of his fingers up to his lips, then spoke. 'If we are going to have this meeting, this discussion, this negotiation, then we must be honest. Forgive my impertinence, but I do not think you ladies are telling the truth here.'

'How so?' Julianne asked. She declined the offer of wine, as did Sonja, but Nikola took a glass of champagne before dismissing the waiter. His man did not sit at the table but rather in an armchair on the edge of the gathering, his AK-47 on his lap, his hand on the pistol grip.

'You say you have nothing to hide from Sonja,' Pesev said. 'But I think you would not want her to know how you used your anti-poaching operations as a business tool, to protect some areas, yours in particular, but also your allies', and to leave your takeover targets vulnerable to poaching.'

'Rubbish,' Julianne said. 'I did no such thing.'

Sonja looked at her, and wondered if she was telling the truth. Sonja and Hudson had been coming to the same conclusion, but Julianne looked genuinely surprised and shocked at the allegation. Perhaps she was a good actor.

'And you, Sonja, you do not "work" for Julianne, you were trying to undermine her. You believe that Julianne, here, has been running a hit squad, as the Americans would call it. You resent the fact that you were set up to be a hired assassin and that your young protégé, Tema, was corrupted in the process.'

Sonja shifted her glare back to the man at the head of the table. Tema really had told him everything.

'Don't blame poor Tema, Sonja,' Pesev said, reading her thoughts. 'I knew from Julianne's tough talk in the media that she was gunning for us, for me. And a run of operations against my vassals in Hazyview, Zimbabwe and here in Tanzania told me your operation was getting closer and closer to my headquarters. I've been expecting a mission of the type you tried and failed to execute here.'

Pesev paused and all was silent except for the gentle slap of the swell against the hull. Nikola took up a pair of silver salad servers. 'May I serve for us all?'

Julianne and Sonja eyed each other.

He passed the plates around and when he was finished he raised his glass again. 'To honesty, and a new beginning.'

Neither woman raised her glass, but Pesev smiled and took a sip. 'Bon appétit.'

Through a mouthful of food he carried on, punctuating his speech with his fork. 'Julianne, you know that what Tema revealed on the video was said under duress, but it was also true. You have been fighting poaching the way it should be fought, like a war. The enemy's commanders are as legitimate a target as the foot-soldiers in the bush. You are, as the Americans said in Iraq, cutting off the head of the snake. Except the snake is still alive. I am still alive.'

'But you haven't won,' Julianne said. 'We have enough to get you arrested, charged, and put away in any number of jurisdictions.'

Nikola swallowed his mouthful of food and nodded. 'Ditto.'

'You have nothing on me, just, as you say, the word of a woman who would have said anything to stop you from killing her.'

'Yes, enough to have investigations opened in any number of jurisdictions – almost as good as having you put away, and certainly enough to have a number of African governments cancel your safari concessions. Sonja, the South African police are already gunning for you over the shooting of that poor retarded young man who you and Tema filled full of bullets. He was no poacher, he was framed.'

'How do you know?' Sonja asked.

'Because they were my men in the Sabi Sand that night, who ambushed you and your Leopards, Sonja, your all-female anti-poaching patrol, and that boy was not one of them.'

Sonja thought about Hudson's question to her, the information he'd wanted from James, before he'd left in a huff. 'What about the boots he was wearing?'

Nikola nodded again, deep and slow, as if he had been expecting the question. 'Oh, they were worn by the killer all right, but that man was Shadrack's cousin, the other man shot that day. Those boots, in a wonderful piece of irony, were owned by James Paterson. Paterson, knowing that the sole of one of the boots had been split, gave them to Shadrack, who worked as a labourer on the same estate where your friend Hudson Brand lives. Shadrack's cousin took the boots from his simple relative because they were better than his, but he was not a smart operator; he didn't realise the fatal error of taking boots with such a distinctive tread pattern. After the ambush, when it became clear the damaged boots had been worn by the killer of your operatives, the cousin gave the footwear back to Shadrack and paid a local gangster to attack Shadrack, and to slash his back to make it look like he had been injured while scrambling under the razor wire perimeter fence of the game reserve. His plan was to leave town in a stolen vehicle, with his dimwitted cousin in tow, and to abandon the young man, the murder weapon and the vehicle just before the police caught him. As it happened, you people in Julianne's helicopter caught up with them first, and the rest is history.'

'How do you know all this?' Sonja asked.

'The real killer reported to me, after the debacle in the bush, and told me what he was planning to do to save his own skin. I take my hat off to you and your lady leopards – you were worthy opponents to my foot-soldiers.'

Sonja felt the bile rise up but swallowed back the bitterness. The story had the ring of truth about it. She and Tema had killed the man who had murdered their colleagues, but in the process they had also slaughtered an innocent boy.

Julianne reached out a hand and put it on hers. 'You couldn't have known.'

Sonja snatched her hand away. 'Don't touch me.'

'Ladies, please. It's unfortunate an innocent was caught up in all of this, but you exacted your revenge for the loss of the lives of Sonja's shield maidens.'

'So what exactly do you want in exchange for Tema and James?' Julianne asked.

Nikola put down his fork, dabbed his mouth with a linen serviette, put it on the table and spread his hands wide. 'I have to be honest with you, I think James Paterson deserves to die.'

'Why?'

'He has been responsible for the deaths of too many of my business partners, my franchisees, if you will. You know you very nearly put me out of business?'

'I can't say I'm sorry. You're vermin, Pesev.'

'Paterson and that homicidal maniac of yours, Machado, were doing you more harm than good. If I hadn't stopped you then some law enforcement agency somewhere on this corrupt, lawless continent would have finally put two and two together and worked out what you were up to. My foot-soldiers kill wildlife to make me money; your people killed human beings to further your business interests and generate positive PR. You tell me who is more like vermin?'

'I gave no such orders,' Julianne insisted. 'We were only targeting poachers and their leaders.'

'You have a helicopter to transfer your well-heeled guests to your camp in the Kuria Hills, and to assist with anti-poaching when required,' Nikola said.

Julianne stuck her chin out. 'What of it?'

Nikola looked to Sonja. 'Julianne's helicopter was "undergoing maintenance" or too busy to respond to six calls for air support by TANAPA and Helen Mills over her concession on the outskirts of the Serengeti. However, by miraculous good fortune, just a week after Mills agreed to sell her lease to Julianne, her chopper is tracking down and executing my men on Julianne's newest piece of Africa. Coincidence?'

Sonja looked to Julianne. The story tallied with what Helen had told them at Maramboi lodge. Pesev was remarkably well informed about the goings on in Julianne's camp; Sonja wondered if he had a source.

'Preposterous.' Julianne pointed a finger at Pesev. 'You're a butcher of wildlife and a murderer.'

Nikola sighed. 'There is something you don't understand about me, Julianne, nor you, Sonja. I actually do care about Africa's wildlife.'

It was Julianne's turn to laugh now.

Sonja eyed the man with the AK-47. He was getting bored, perhaps not following all of the conversation. The man looked out the window over the lake, but given the close proximity it was too risky for her to try anything. Sonja didn't know what to believe in the conversation playing out in front of her.

'You're joking,' Julianne said to Pesev.

'Oh, it's no laughing matter at all. Tanzania's elephants are on the brink of disappearing and that is not good for anyone, not for me, not for you, not for the government. By my order, there is now a moratorium on organised elephant poaching in this country. There will still be the odd rogue operator, but what I am proposing to you is that with my help you will be able to direct the national parks and police to where those poachers are, and you will be able to ensure they are quickly located and brought to justice.'

'*With my help?*' Julianne said. 'I don't understand.'

'Oh, I think you do, Julianne. You see, I have put the "organised" into the crime of poaching. I want to protect Africa's elephants to ensure a supply of ivory, and the best way I can do that is by killing them – in a controlled manner.'

'You're crazy,' Sonja said.

'Not really, no. Julianne?'

'Yes?'

'You don't have any lodges in Botswana. Do you have plans to spread into Chobe National Park or set up something on its borders?'

'No. I'm looking at property in the Moremi Game Reserve in the Okavango Delta, maybe the neighbouring Khwai Conservancy, but not Chobe.'

'What about Hwange, in Zimbabwe?'

'Not at the moment, no.'

Nikola smiled. 'Perfect. Nearly half of Africa's remaining elephants are concentrated in Chobe National Park and Hwange National Park just across the border in Zimbabwe, perhaps some 300,000 animals in total, moving from one country to the other. In fact, there are too many of them. Their overeating has had a disastrous impact on the natural vegetation and there are constant conflicts between elephants and farmers and villagers along the Chobe River.'

Julianne was open-mouthed. 'Are you saying you're going to contribute to conservation by poaching elephants in Chobe and Hwange?'

He leaned forward, hands clasped, elbows on the table, closing the distance between them. 'Let's call it an unauthorised but much needed elephant *cull*. What I'm saying is that you will have nothing to fear from ivory poachers in or around the Okavango Delta where you might set up a lodge.'

Sonja understood. 'You and your Scorpions want to monopolise the ivory trade. Tanzania's tapped out, so you're going after elephants where they're still plentiful, and you'll take out any small-time operators, competitors, in that area, or around the delta.'

'No comment. What I will tell you, Ms Kurtz, and this is a fact, is that my employees have killed more poachers, rival

353

operators, than you or any of Julianne's people or, for that matter, probably the entire South African National Defence Force in the past year.'

Julianne looked to Sonja. 'James passed on the same information, that the Scorpions were expanding their operations by either absorbing existing small-time poaching groups or, if they resisted, wiping them out.'

'It is possible to sustainably harvest ivory, albeit illegally, without wiping elephants off the face of the earth,' Nikola said.

'And rhinos?' Sonja asked.

He turned his attention to her. 'Haven't you read that there has been a decrease in the number of rhinos killed in South Africa? The year 2015 saw the first decrease in rhinos poached in eight years. Do you think that was solely due to the efforts of soldiers, police and rangers?'

Sonja narrowed her eyes. 'You took enough rhino horn to meet demand, but you took out a bunch of small players at the same time, is that what you're saying?'

He shrugged.

'Enough.' Julianne pushed away her plate of untouched food. 'Tell me what you want.'

Pesev took another mouthful of salad and munched away. 'For you to disband this special unit of yours and stop going after the Scorpions. I never used that name myself in any case.'

'How did you get it then?' Julianne asked.

'There was a man in Mozambique, fancied himself a player. He found himself bound, hands and feet, in a coffin. A dozen highly venomous scorpions were dropped into the box with him to convince him it might be a good idea to cooperate with the organisation that wanted him to join their fold. The shrieking was hard to take, and in the end he had a heart attack and died. That's where the name originated.'

'Are you trying to scare me?'

'I don't think you're easily frightened, Julianne, but I just want to let you know that even if you can't be reached, people close to you can.'

'I've told the press I'm going after the Scorpions.'

He set down his fork and took a sip of wine. 'Then tell the media that you found them and defeated them. The name will not be mentioned again – it was becoming a liability in any case. The figures will show a drop in elephant poaching, very soon, in Tanzania, and in the north of the Kruger Park and the Great Limpopo Transfrontier Park across the border in Mozambique. I've put a stop to elephant poaching in that area as it was starting to get out of hand. The last thing I want is the South African Army and its helicopters, drones, and recce-commandos moving north when rhinos can quietly, selectively be taken when they wander across the border.'

'And you give me your word you will stay away from my lodges and concessions and Tanzania's elephants.'

'Yes, and I give you my word the few rhino in the Okavango Delta will face no threat from my people.'

Sonja leaned back in her chair, taking in this surreal conversation. Here were two businesspeople carving up a large chunk of Africa like a couple of colonial-era monarchs, caring nothing for the lives, animal and human, that their manoeuvring would cost. Julianne may have been negotiating to protect her reserves, people and wildlife, but she was knowingly passing the problem on to someone else.

'And if I agree, what happens to Tema and James?'

Sonja noticed that in front of Pesev she was always mentioning Tema first, whereas when she had arrived her first concern had been for the handsome former army officer.

'You can have the girl as soon as we are done here, but Paterson must pay the price for decimating my business.'

'That's unacceptable.'

'No, that's life,' Pesev said. 'I've seen how Paterson operates. He may be the quiet, backroom manipulator, but if I let him live he will be thirsting for revenge.'

Julianne pushed back her chair and stood. 'Then we have no deal.'

The man with the AK-47 looked up, instantly alert.

'I can't just let you leave, Julianne, without a deal,' Pesev said.

'Then you may as well kill me.' Julianne looked to Sonja. 'Sorry. Take a few of them with you, if you can. I'm not leaving without James and Tema, and if they die, then so do I.'

'Great,' Sonja said to Julianne. 'Are you fucking crazy?'

'What do you mean, Sonja?'

'What do you think you're doing?'

'I *was* negotiating to ensure the safety of two of our people.'

Pesev held up his hands. 'Ladies, please. Sonja, do I take it from your words that you don't wish to go out in a blaze of gunfire?'

Sonja didn't know who of the two she detested more; Pesev for his twisted rationalisations of his crimes, or Julianne, who had been happy to turn a blind eye to a hit squad on one hand, and seemed open to getting into bed with the most serious poaching kingpin in Africa on the other.

'I'm finished with both of you. I want off this boat.' She stood. 'Nikola, you can kill Julianne if you like.'

The man in the cabin with the AK-47 was on his feet now, alert and pointing his rifle at her.

'Please, please,' Pesev said. 'Sonja, you may leave when Julianne does, just as soon as she has seen James.'

'You're bringing him here?'

Julianne had spoken too quickly, too keenly, Sonja thought, betraying, or rather confirming, her particularly personal concern over Paterson's fate.

'Of course, Julianne. As I said, I am not a monster. I know that as your head of security and anti-poaching James must be very *important* to you. I am willing to reconsider executing him.'

'Tema is as important,' Julianne said, but it was obvious the young woman was still little more than an afterthought.

Sonja could understand someone doing something foolish for love; she had almost done the same herself when she'd considered chasing after Hudson instead of staying to finish the mission. Now she wished she'd gone with her heart and hitched out of Kipili, got on the first plane back to South Africa so she could meet Hudson when he returned to Hippo Rock. Julianne was in love, and it was clouding her judgement. If she wanted to do a deal with the devil then she could. Sonja wanted off this boat, but she also wanted to see what Paterson made of the deal that Pesev and Clyde-Smith had hatched or, rather, what Julianne had just sold her soul for.

Pesev spoke to the guard in Swahili and the man, after giving Sonja a wary look, took a handheld radio from his pocket and walked out onto the deck.

'He's getting Tema and calling my other men to bring the fishing boat with James on board. Fear not, ladies,' Pesev said. 'This will all be over soon.'

Somehow, Sonja doubted that.

Chapter 29

Mario swam underwater towards the fishing boat.

With all of Nikola Pesev's staff involved in guarding Paterson or escorting Sonja and Julianne, it had been easy for him to slip unnoticed into the storeroom by the boathouse that contained the diving gear Pesev rented to lodge customers who wanted to explore the clear waters of Lake Tanganyika.

After suiting up Mario had found a wickedly long dive knife, which was now strapped to his right leg. He'd also carried a spear gun in one hand as he waded into the lake.

A shoal of cichlids, brightly coloured tropical fish sought by collectors around the world, parted as Mario glided through the warm water, as silent and deadly as a shark. Mario was getting close and could see the outline of the boat ahead and above him, haloed by the sunlight that penetrated the waters around it.

Mario was ready for the fight, but what he wasn't expecting was for the water aft of the boat to suddenly start churning with millions of bubbles. The growl of twin diesel motors vibrated in his chest. Mario finned as fast as he could, to get to the boat before it slipped its moorings.

He angled up towards the surface, and when he broke the water he could see a crewman pulling in the line that had just been released. Next to his face was another Zodiac, towed behind the fishing and dive boat. It started to move.

Mario unbuckled his dive tank and let it fall from his shoulders to the lake floor. Likewise he had to let the spear gun go as he struck out, swimming overarm as hard as he could as the fishing boat and Zodiac picked up speed. Just when he thought he was too late he redoubled his efforts and managed to slap his right hand onto the transom of the Zodiac.

Arms straining in their sockets, Mario hauled himself closer and up over the rear of the tender. He struggled aboard, panting, and edged his way forward, staying low in the bilge water to keep out of sight of anyone on board the mother ship who might be looking aft.

Mario stopped and rested a moment, water sluicing over his body.

When he had regained his breath and strength he raised his head, looking above the bulbous front of the inflatable. He could see no crewman at the back of the fishing boat. He crawled further forward and reached out for the line tethering the Zodiac. Slowly, hand over hand, he fought the power of the twin diesel engines and the drag of the towed boat to pull the Zodiac closer to the larger boat, one arm length at a time.

As he crossed the wake the little boat bucked and bounced. Mario was able to grab a metal bollard with his left hand, and, holding fast, reached out with his right to grab the safety railing. He was fit for his age, but was panting once he was on board. Water dripped from him onto the sun-bleached deck.

Mario looked up and saw that the man who had been guarding the boat at the dockside was now at the helm on the upper deck, his AK-47 leaning against the control panel next to his right leg. That meant, by Mario's reckoning, that there was now only one man below deck guarding James.

In front of them, a few hundred metres away, was Pesev's luxury motor cruiser. Mario knew he had to act fast. He scaled the ladder to the bridge and when he was at the top rung he lifted his leg and drew the diving knife from its scabbard. His footsteps on the bridge deck were drowned out by the growl of the boat's engines and he was sure no one below heard the thud as the security man fell, blood flowing from his slit throat.

Mario sat in the skipper's chair and kept his head low in case anyone on the other craft was watching their approach through binoculars. He had charge of the fishing boat now, but he still needed to free Paterson.

He rolled the dead man over with his foot and, in doing so, saw the handheld radio clipped to his belt. Mario leaned down, picked up the radio and held it to his mouth. He pushed the transmit button and said a few words of nonsense, deliberately cut short and garbled.

'Say again,' said a voice on the other end.

'Come . . . brid . . . prob . . .' Mario said. For good measure he grabbed the boat's throttle and cut it back to neutral. The bow dropped and then Mario gunned and stopped the throttle again, twice more. He picked up the dead man's AK-47 and cocked it.

'Hell . . . up . . .' he said into the radio again.

Mario looked over his shoulder and saw the top of the head of the other guard emerging from below. Mario dropped the throttle back a little so the boat was moving slower, steadier. He brought the AK-47 up to his shoulder, looked over the edge of the upper deck, and when the man peered over the deck at him, eyes wide with surprise, Mario squeezed the trigger, twice.

*

'Listen to that,' Hudson Brand said to the bare-chested crewman standing on board the green patrol boat moored by Kipili village. 'Gunfire. I told you people were in trouble out there.'

The crewman had steadfastly refused to believe there was danger brewing on the lake, but the faint yet distinctive sound of a rifle being fired had shaken him. He looked to where the noise had come from.

Mario had called Hudson to tell him Sonja was in trouble. Hudson hated Mario, but Machado had told him he needed extra firepower. Even if it was a trap, Hudson reasoned, it would give him another excuse to kill Mario. Every cloud had a silver lining.

'Hudson!'

Brand and the sailor turned at the sound of the voice.

Ezekial was half running, half sliding down the dirt track to the wharf.

'This is my colleague,' Hudson said to the crewman, loud enough for Ezekial to hear. He was relieved that Ezekial had made it; if he was walking into an ambush he'd also need extra firepower. 'Captain Radebe from the South African police.'

'Captain?' said the man.

Ezekial stopped near them and for a moment he looked surprised at being described as a police officer. However, Ezekial was a quick thinker and played along; he pulled out his South African ID book and flashed it at the sailor. 'Yes, that's right. Captain Radebe. We need to commandeer this boat.'

Hudson glanced at Ezekial and nodded. 'I was just explaining, Captain, that you and I are here in Tanzania looking for some terrorists who we believe have hijacked a luxury cruiser from the lodge over the hill.'

'Yes, that's right,' Ezekial said. He lifted the loose shirt he was wearing to show the pistol tucked into his belt. The crewman saw it and looked worried. 'Let's go, sailor!'

Hudson drew his Colt, which he'd kept under wraps until now, and jumped aboard the boat with Ezekial close behind him. The crewman, unused to the presence of armed foreigners and, probably, the prospect of action, said nothing.

'Start the engines,' Ezekial barked.

'Yes, Captain,' said the crewman, and moved to the bridge.

'I got your SMS,' Ezekial said to Hudson in a low voice. 'I was on my way here, anyway. Tema also sent me a message. I wanted to leave her, but I couldn't.'

'I know the feeling,' Hudson said as he let slip the mooring.

'You think they're in real trouble?'

Hudson dropped the rope and clapped him on the arm. 'I know they are, man. Thanks for coming.'

'Do you trust Mario?'

Hudson shook his head. 'Not in a million lifetimes, so watch your back, and mine. But there'll be time for him once we find our women.'

'*Our* women?'

'Yup.'

Ezekial nodded and he and Hudson clasped hands as the patrol boat pulled away from the wharf. 'I like the sound of that.'

*

'Here comes James now, right on time,' Nikola said, pointing out to his other boat, which was approaching from the starboard side.

They all got up from the table and Sonja scanned the oncoming boat. The first thing she noticed was that she could not see who was driving it.

'Get on the radio,' Pesev said to his nearest man. 'Tell Abdul to ease off the throttle, to slow down.'

'Yes, sir,' the man said, then spoke Swahili into his handheld radio.

'He's coming straight for us,' Julianne said.

'There's no answer, sir,' Pesev's man said, panic rising in his voice.

'Start the engines!' Pesev yelled to anyone who would listen. The man relayed the command into his radio, to the skipper.

Sonja could see that the bow wave of the other boat was frothing white, the craft rearing up on its stern.

'Something's wrong, give me your gun.' Pesev snatched the AK-47 from his man's hands, went outside the cabin, took aim and fired a burst of three rounds over the top of the fishing boat's bridge. The warning shots had no effect. 'Open fire on the bridge, stop them!'

A crescendo of fire erupted from the rest of Pesev's armed men and bullets began smashing through the superstructure of the oncoming boat. It held its course, though.

Sonja grabbed Julianne by the arm. 'Quickly, let's get out of here.'

Pesev looked over his shoulder. 'Where are you going?'

Sonja hustled Julianne out of the cabin. 'I'm taking her port side, to the bow. We're going to jump if that thing hits us.'

Nikola turned on them, rifle up. 'Who have you got on that boat?'

Sonja raised her pistol, and pointed it at his head. She pushed Julianne behind her. 'Move.'

The other boat loomed large and the gunmen started to lose their nerve as their fire failed to stop it. Sonja was moving backwards, pistol still up as she shepherded Julianne forward. 'It's going to hit us.'

Sonja turned, grabbed Julianne by the shoulder and propelled her faster.

'You're going to push me overboard!'

'That's the idea.' Sonja ushered Julianne across the bow of the luxury cruiser and when they got to the other side she shoved the other woman in the back. As Julianne hit the water in an ungainly splash Sonja followed her over the side, at exactly the same moment as the fishing boat ploughed into the cruiser.

There was a screech of metal, the splintering of wood and the shattering of fibreglass as the two craft became enmeshed.

Julianne bobbed up, spluttering.

'Swim!' Sonja commanded.

Julianne was floundering so Sonja swam around her and put her left arm around her, holding her head under the chin, above water, as she propelled them backwards with her right arm.

As she swam, she looked up and saw where the fishing boat had carved into the cruiser. Mario emerged from the cover of the fishing boat's cabin and he jumped, like a buccaneer, onto the cruiser. She never thought she would be pleased to see this pig of a man again. He had an AK-47 up and ready and moved confidently, expertly, along the deck of the other vessel. He fired a double tap and killed the first of Pesev's gunmen before the man could even draw a bead on him.

A second man came around the cabin, saw Sonja and Julianne in the water and swung his rifle towards them.

'Dive.' Sonja rolled Julianne over and duck-dived. Underwater, she turned and saw that Julianne was still above her. Sonja grabbed Julianne's arm and pulled her down as bullets started zipping through the lake water around them.

Julianne started to swim, following Sonja down and around the pointed bow of the now stricken cruiser. The keel of the vessel began to fall; the luxury boat was starting to sink. Sonja looked over her shoulder and motioned for Julianne to follow her.

Sonja surfaced on the other side of the cruiser and gasped for breath. Julianne popped up beside her. They saw Mario, feet apart, braced on the deck of the cruiser, water up to his ankles and rising.

'Mario,' Julianne called.

He turned and located them.

Julianne raised a hand and pointed, furiously. 'Look out, behind you!'

Mario spun around and saw the gunman who had fired at Sonja and Julianne, splashing around the superstructure in search of his targets. The man yelled a war cry and opened fire with his AK-47. Mario dived and rolled to one side, avoiding the bullets. His aim was better than the gunman's and when he fired, also on automatic, the three rounds punched into the other man's body, sending him into a dance of death that ended with him flailing and writhing in the water, until he sank beneath the lake's surface.

Mario waded through the reddened water and hoisted himself up onto the deck of the fishing boat, which, though damaged by the ram raid, was still more or less afloat.

'Get James,' Julianne ordered Mario from the water. She started to swim towards the rear of the fishing boat, where she would be able to climb aboard from the diving platform.

Sonja had to get to Tema first. She went in the opposite direction, diving again and swimming underwater back around the front of the cruiser, which had come to rest on the sandy bottom of the lake. The boat was only a few metres below the surface, but it was more than deep enough for Tema to drown in.

Sonja surfaced, took another deep breath and duck-dived again. She made her way down and into the rear of the cabin. Plastic bottles, linen napkins and food scraps floated around her as she navigated her way through the dark interior of the boat. She heard banging and screaming, distorted through the water. She came to a door, heaved on it, but it was locked.

She was running out of breath, but the noise from inside the cabin was getting softer. Sonja rolled and swam back a little. She reached into the waistband of her shorts and pulled out her pistol. She prayed the Makarov would still function, with its wet ammo. Sonja racked the pistol and fired. The lock shattered.

Bracing her feet either side of the door she turned and heaved on the handle. The water pressure was keeping the door closed and she strained. The exertion was threatening to steal the last of her oxygen.

Just when she feared she would be unable to get it open, the door started to move. As Sonja pulled she could feel, now, the thuds of Tema kicking from the other side. Sonja was flung back as the door opened wide. Tema was still in there, though, and when Sonja reached out to grab Tema's hand she snatched it away and moved deeper into the cabin.

Sonja tried hard not to panic, but she could feel herself becoming dizzy. She could not expend more energy than she already had and would be lucky to make it back out the way she'd come in. Her brain was slowing, but through the fog she realised Tema had been underwater for some time now. She drew on the last of her strength and air and swam deeper into the gloom of the flooded cabin. When she was almost blacking out she felt a hand grab her around the wrist and yank her arm upwards.

She surrendered and a second later her head came up out of the water. It was dark; she could barely see.

'Sonja!'

She spluttered, then sucked hard on the warm, wet air in the pocket where Tema had been hiding. Something big was floating and Sonja pushed against it. 'What the –?'

'My guard,' Tema sniffed. 'I feel bad. When we were rammed and started to go down he cut the ropes binding my hands. I repaid him by breaking his nose, taking his knife and then slitting his throat. I got the key to the door and unlocked it, but the water came in before I could open it.'

'Don't worry about him.' Sonja coughed and tried taking more air in. She felt she couldn't fill her lungs. 'Why didn't you get out of here?'

'I can't swim, Sonja. I'm terrified. I can't go under the water. I thought I was going to die in here.'

'You will, unless you come with me. You're running out of air and it'll disappear quicker now I'm here. You have to come with me.'

'I'll drown!'

Sonja reached out for her in the darkness, found her face and stroked it with the backs of her fingers. 'Shush. You'll be fine.'

'It's dangerous out there.'

'It's fine,' Sonja said. 'Pesev's men are dead. As much as I detest Mario, he did save the day and he'll find Nikola and kill him. Mario's a creep, but he's a machine.'

'I don't trust him.'

Sonja was treading water, and while she had regained her composure and some of her strength she knew they could not stay here. 'I don't trust him either, Tema, and that's why we're leaving this place, as soon as we get out of here.'

'What about Julianne and James?'

'I don't care about them,' Sonja said. 'It's just you and me. We'll go to van Rensburg in South Africa and tell her what we know, but that's all we can do. There comes a time in every war, every battle, when you have to cut your losses and run.'

'I can't do this, Sonja, it's dark and it's too far under water. I won't make it.'

'You'll be fine. Just take my hand and kick your legs. I'll get you out.' Sonja put a hand on each of Tema's shoulders. The younger woman was shaking.

'I'm so scared. I shouldn't be here, should never have come to this place. I miss my daughter.'

'Well,' Sonja said, 'then you and I are in exactly the same boat. Take a deep breath.'

'No.'

'Yes.' Sonja pulled down on Tema's shoulders, forcing her head underwater. She felt the girl flailing against her, then brought her up again so her head surfaced.

'No! Don't do that again!'

'Then for fuck's sake, if you want to see your little girl again, take a breath. That's an order.'

Sonja heard the intake of air, drew a lungful of the fetid atmosphere herself, and pulled Tema down.

Tema wriggled and struggled, panicking as Sonja reached for handholds in the cabin interior to help pull them towards the open door. She groped in the greenish darkness and found the entryway and kept pulling. It took twice as much effort, more, maybe, to move the two of them through the interior of the cruiser, but ahead and above her she could see the brighter colours where the sun was streaming through the water.

Sonja pulled Tema over the table where she, Julianne and Pesev had sat. Silhouetted against the sky above them was the spread-eagled form of another of Pesev's dead henchmen.

They were near the open rear deck of the cruiser now. Sonja kicked hard for the surface, but she was anchored. She held Tema's wrist in what must have been a painfully tight grip, but the other woman was not moving.

Sonja looked down at Tema. Her mouth was open. She was trying to say something, but Sonja could see she was taking in water at the same time and starting to convulse. Her foot was trapped. Sonja let go of Tema and dived down. When she got to Tema's foot she saw it had become entwined in a mooring rope. Sonja reached around her belt and found the pouch for her Leatherman. Once more, nearly out of oxygen, she opened the blade and began sawing through the rope.

Tema stopped thrashing and her body floated limply in the water as Sonja finally severed the last few strands. Sonja wrapped an arm around the young woman and kicked for the surface.

When she broke through she breathed in the clean air, but Tema was silent and unresponsive.

'Tema!' Sonja wrapped both her arms around Tema and

squeezed her as hard as she could. Water welled up and out of her lungs and down over her lips.

Sonja searched for help. She heard then saw a Zodiac inflatable boat, but it was racing away from them, towards shore. On board were Mario, Julianne, and James Paterson. *Shit*, she thought. Mario had ignored her and Tema and was looking after his bosses.

Sonja looked back to the wrecked fishing boat and her heart lurched when she saw Nikola Pesev emerge from a hatch. He must have climbed in and hidden when the boat rammed his cruiser. He was holding an AK-47 and his eyes met Sonja's.

'Your friends have left you. How is Tema?'

'She's unconscious, nearly drowned,' Sonja called back to him.

He snorted. 'Well, good for her.'

Sonja stopped swimming. She trod water, supporting Tema, and reached behind her back. 'What do you mean "good for her"?'

Pesev raised the AK-47 and swung the barrel towards Sonja and Tema. 'She won't feel a thing.'

The water slowed her movements, but Sonja was able to get a round off from her Makarov before she even got the pistol clear of the lake's surface. A spout of water erupted and the bullet went close enough to Nikola to snatch the fabric of his shirt. He winced, as if grazed, but when Sonja got the weapon totally clear and pulled the trigger again the mechanism was locked open. The pistol had misfired.

Pesev chuckled.

Sonja couldn't clear the weapon without letting go of Tema, nor could she dive into the water again with the unconscious woman in her arms. The sound of a siren rolled across the lake. Nikola ignored it, but Sonja could see, around the bow of the fishing boat, the low, sleek, green shape of the Tanzanian military patrol boat that had been moored in the inlet by the village of Kipili.

Pesev brought the AK-47 up to his shoulder and took aim.

'I'll make this as quick and clean as I can, Sonja. Any last words?'

'Don't look behind you.'

He laughed, loudly, his muscular body shaking. He steadied his aim. 'OK, I won't.'

Sonja held Tema tight to her body, kissed her on the temple and closed her eyes.

A deafening storm of gunfire was the last thing Sonja heard.

PART 3

The Kill

Three weeks later

She was a hunter.

From her lair, nestled between a smooth pair of granite boulders high atop a koppie she had an almost 360-degree view of her killing fields.

From the dainty klipspringers that hopped nimbly from rock to rock, oblivious of her presence, to the majestic lion who roared to his females and his rivals every evening, to the tourists returning to their lodges from game drives and the staff smoking cigarettes and joints behind the kitchens. She saw them all.

She moved at night, and watched and waited during the day, biding her time, waiting for the kill.

From her place of concealment, she was too high for the hyenas to come nosing about after her, too clever for the lions and too cunning for the humans to have the faintest inkling of her presence.

The only thing that did concern her, made her watch the ground for tracks and sniff the air, were leopards. Specifically, there was a female, as secretive and as nocturnal in her movements as she was, and a big, brash male, the one they called Mbvala, who strode imperiously to the waterhole most nights, broadcasting his rasping, sawing call, defying the other predators and scaring the poor bushback, after whom he was named, half to death. Every now and then he caught one with practised ease.

She watched them, all of them, come and go, noted their routines and learned their secrets.

In the dark she crept below the decks of the suites, waited in the bushes where the people came and went, and she readied herself for the kill.

Chapter 30

Hudson Brand pulled up at the Shaws Gate entrance to the Sabi Sand Game Reserve. A security guard in a smartly starched green uniform and polished boots came up to the Toyota Fortuner and Hudson wound down the electric window.

'*Avuxeni*, Lucas,' Hudson said by way of greeting in xiTsonga.

'*Ayeḥ imjani*, Hudson.'

'*Ndzi kona*.' Hudson motioned to the man and the woman holding hands in the back seat. 'I have two pax, for Khaya Ngala.'

'All right.' Lucas handed Hudson a clipboard, and as he filled out his details and the vehicle's, a female guard with elaborately braided hair opened the rear of the Toyota while another scanned underneath with a mirror attached to a pole. They were looking for weapons, and while the guards were still vigilant it was a fact that in the three weeks since Hudson had been back in South Africa there hadn't been a single rhino killed in the Sabi Sand reserve, nor the south of Kruger. It was no excuse to celebrate, not just yet, but poaching activity had dropped off in the region.

Lucas telephoned Khaya Ngala, giving the names of the guests to the lodge, who confirmed they were booked in. He came back to Hudson, took the money for entry fees into the reserve, went back to the office, then returned with a receipt and permit.

'Mr and Mrs Furey?' Lucas said as he took back the clipboard and leaned into the Fortuner.

'Yes, that's us,' said the man, in an English accent.

Lucas saluted. 'Welcome to the Sabi Sand Game Reserve and enjoy your safari.'

Hudson drove them into the reserve and turned left, following the sign to Julianne Clyde-Smith's flagship safari lodge. On the way they passed a turnoff to Lion Plains, which Julianne also now owned, officially.

He and his passengers said little, and didn't bother to stop for the white rhino and her calf, nor the herd of elephant that they passed. At the final turnoff to Khaya Ngala, Hudson stopped the vehicle. He got out, looked around him in case there were any lions or other dangerous game, then went to the driver's side rear tyre and took off the valve cap. He took out his Leatherman and used the tips of the pliers to depress the tyre's valve until two-thirds of the air inside had escaped. He replaced the cap and got back in.

'Nearly there,' he said to the couple in the back.

'All good,' said Tom. Sannie nodded.

Hudson followed the narrower, winding access road that was, he knew, kept deliberately ungraded to give guests a feeling that they were wending their way into darkest Africa. It made the towering thatch-roofed portico, the smart butler in white offering a silver tray of drinks, and the pretty young woman who opened the door and greeted the Fureys all seem that little bit more impressive.

When his guests had been escorted inside, Hudson went into the cool of the reception area and found the duty manager.

'Say, I've got a slow puncture, mind if I go around to your workshop and put some air in it?'

'Can I take a look?' said the stockily built man in white shirt and khaki trousers.

'Sure.'

He followed Hudson out, inspected the right rear tyre and then nodded. 'Go back to where you came in and take the road marked "Deliveries".'

'Servants' entrance. Gotcha.'

Hudson went back to the Fortuner and retraced his route, slowing for an impressive male nyala that crossed the road in front of him. These normally shy antelopes were congregating around the lodges on the Sabie River, and at Hippo Rock, drawn by the vegetation that still survived among the luxury accommodation units and houses during the drought.

He took the delivery road turnoff, but before he got to the workshop and parking area for the lodge's safari vehicles, Hudson drove off-road, into the bush. He had spied a large termite mound and, weaving in between trees and dying bushes, he managed to park behind the mound, out of sight of the road.

Hudson reached under the driver's seat and took out his 1911 model Colt .45 pistol. He took the map he'd drawn from Tema's instructions out of his pocket and checked it. He pointed his wristwatch at the sun and worked out where north was, halfway between twelve and the hour hand, and set off through the bush to the southwest, back towards the Sabie River.

The whine and screech of a drill and an angle grinder masked any noise he would make walking through the brittle dry bush. Julianne had embarked on a well-publicised upgrade of her lodge. She was renovating and rebuilding her luxury camp, and when it was unveiled in a few months' time it, and its accompanying room rates, would put all the other premier camps in the Sabi Sand Game Reserve to shame. Business was good for Julianne Clyde-Smith.

The other news that had come out in the media following the reporting of Julianne's near-death experience at the hands of the late head of the Scorpions poaching syndicate, whose existence, or former existence, was now common knowledge in Africa, was that Julianne would soon marry her head of security, James Paterson.

Tema was working for Julianne again and was, Hudson calculated as he moved through the bush, somewhere nearby. There was no more elite anti-poaching squad or surveillance unit, or hit squad, or whatever Sonja's unit had been. It seemed there was no need for one any more. Tema had been relegated to walking well-heeled guests to and from their suites to dinner in case they encountered a leopard or buffalo or other dangerous game on the pathways at night.

Ezekial was working for Julianne as well, running tracking and ranger training courses for local youths from the communities near the Sabi Sand Game Reserve. Julianne was publicly channelling her money and efforts into projects designed to improve the lives and futures of people who lived on the border of the reserve and the national park, in the hope that this would stop young people falling into a life of poaching and other crime. Tema and Ezekial were living together, in the staff quarters.

Sonja had been hit by one of Pesev's bullets, which had creased the side of her skull and put her into a coma. Hudson had manned the .50 calibre heavy machine gun on the bow of the Tanzanian patrol boat and had opened up on Pesev at the moment he took aim at Sonja and the unconscious Tema. The heavy slugs had all but cut Nikola Pesev in half, killing him instantly.

Hudson and Ezekial had dived into the water and lifted the women onto the patrol boat. They had revived Tema through CPR, but Sonja was unconscious. Hudson had escorted Sonja back to South Africa on a medical evacuation flight while the others had returned on Julianne's private aircraft.

Sonja had stayed in a coma for three days in the Nelspruit Mediclinic. On the fourth, during the only three hours when Hudson had left her bedside, to drive home and get himself some clothes and to buy some for Sonja, she had come to and discharged herself. Hudson hadn't seen or spoken to Sonja, but she was not far away.

At Hudson's request Tema, now working at Khaya Ngala, had found out the daily routines of James and Julianne, South Africa's newest power couple who were in residence at Julianne's home near her lodge.

Hudson checked his watch. At this time of the day, Julianne would be inspecting the building works at the revamped luxury camp and James would be completing his workout, in their private gym, then swimming fifty laps of the twenty-metre infinity lap pool that ran across the front of the house, overlooking the veld.

Julianne's home sat amid the boulders of a granite koppie overlooking the plain and waterhole below. Hudson skirted the building, keeping off the driveway, circling through the bush until he began to descend. Jumping from rock to rock he moved in front of and below the house, staying out of sight. When he was in line with where he reckoned the gym should be, he started to climb.

It was already hot and Brand was sweating as he climbed until he heard, then saw, the water cascading over the edge of the pool's rim. He crouched behind a boulder, then peered around it.

Paterson was finishing his swim. His last lap was a furious one and when he touched the wall and stood he was panting with the exertion. He walked up the steps, out of the water, and Hudson saw his back. It was striped with fresh horizontal red welts, but another wound slashed the muscles at a 45-degree angle, almost like a perverse 'does not equal' sign.

Hudson came out from behind the rock, his pistol in his hand.

'Nasty cut, James.'

Paterson stepped into a pair of sandals, bent to pick up a snowy white towelling robe and turned, slowly.

'Hudson. Nice to see you again.'

'That back of yours looks like you've been in the wars. Or was it just another Saturday night?'

Paterson pulled on the robe. 'I slipped off the balcony here, fell into a thornbush. Nasty business. What's with the pistol?'

'Oh, I just brought a couple of tourists with me. It's dangerous out here in the bush, in case you haven't heard. I'm working today, James.'

'So am I. In fact, I have a busy day, so get whatever it is that's on your chest off it.'

Hudson kept the .45 trained on him. He knew Paterson would have a weapon, or weapons, somewhere close by. 'Yup, I bet you do. You're the head of a multi-million-dollar business.'

James shook his head. 'No, you've got that wrong. When I marry Jules I'll still be her head of security, nothing more. I'll draw my wage but all of her business interests are in her name only, and that's the way it should be. I can show you our pre-nup if you like. Even if we did get divorced, which I hope will never happen, I'll get nothing. And besides, she's worth billions, Hudson, not millions.'

Hudson smiled. 'Oh, I'm not talking about your fiancée's business, James. I'm talking about yours.'

'I told you, I work for Julianne. I don't have a business. Can we go inside? I'm frying in the sun out here.'

'Sure. You're going to have some visitors soon, so you need to get dressed, but I've got my eye on you.'

Paterson led the way into Julianne's home, and Hudson stayed out of arm's reach, behind him. James went towards a phone on a side table. 'I'm calling the police.'

'Touch that phone and I'll hurt you, James. Besides, no need to call the cops. They're here already – my clients, the Fureys. Tom's actually an ex-policeman, but I think you know his wife, Sannie van Rensburg-Furey. Sannie and Tom don't know I'm here with you right now,' he lied. 'They're getting ready to come and arrest you. I was just the wheelman to get them into the lodge without the Sabi Sand security people letting you know the cops were coming. I took a short cut here, because I wanted a little private chat with you first. We don't have much time.'

Paterson left the phone in its docking station and sat down in a leather armchair. 'I still have no idea what this is all about.'

'Oh, I think you do. The Scorpions.'

'They're out of business. They died along with Nikola Pesev. There's been a marked drop-off in rhino and elephant poaching in most of the areas where they used to operate. The media's been reporting it, especially your friend Rosie Appleton.'

'Yeah, Rosie. Nice girl. Pretty.'

'If you say so.'

'I do. Pretty tenacious.'

'Like other journalists I've met; most of them, in fact.'

Hudson nodded. 'Agreed. Which makes me wonder why a hard-nosed news hound like her would simply disappear from Tanzania and fly back to South Africa just when she knew that we were about to start a surveillance mission on the shores of Lake Tanganyika. She knew we were going after Pesev, pointed us to him, in fact. Did you do a deal with her, James? Did Julianne?'

'As a matter of fact, I did talk to her. I promised her a scoop, if and when we got Pesev, in exchange for her staying out of the way and not following us to Kipili.'

'She sure did run a glowing story – made the national newspapers, radio, television, even CNN and the BBC. You and Julianne were quite the heroes. All thanks to Rosie.'

Paterson started to stand. 'I've had enough of this.'

Hudson closed on him, fast, and rammed the barrel of the pistol into his heart and kept it there, pushing him into a chair.

'Sit down and shut up. Rosie hasn't been returning my calls lately, which is kind of funny because she was all over me when I started an investigation into Shadrack's killing, wanting to know what I had, where I was going, who I was talking to.'

'She got a bigger story,' Paterson countered. 'Lost interest in you. Perhaps she wasn't after your body after all.'

'Yeah. I get that. I'm more interested in her mind than her body. I did a bit of research, looked up some of her older work. You know she caused quite a stir a few years ago, when she was younger, less experienced. Made quite a name for herself, and plenty of enemies in the conservation movement.'

'Really?'

'Don't raise your eyebrow, James, it's too theatrical – gives you away. You're the lord of the files, man. You had one on each of us – me, Sonja, Mario, Tema, Ezekial. You knew who was sleeping with whom, when and where, played us off against each other. You would have had a digital file worth a few gigabytes on Rosie before you let her in for a one-on-one interview with your other girlfriend, Julianne, to talk about taking down the Scorpions.'

'My "other" girlfriend?'

'Rosie was here at the lodge last week, right?'

Paterson shrugged. 'So? It was something of a reunion dinner. Sorry we didn't invite you and Sonja. Oh, no, wait, Sonja's gone missing, hasn't she? Guess you two never kissed and made up.'

'I don't know where Sonja is, and that's the truth,' Hudson said, 'but it doesn't matter. I know where Rosie was, last week, during the day, when you were supposed to be doing your daily workout – you know, the one you never vary?'

Paterson licked his lips, like a snake sensing danger, or prey, and Hudson knew he had him. He backed away from him, giving him a little space. He half wanted Paterson to make a move on him, so he could plug him. Hudson reached into his pocket, took out his phone and tossed it to Paterson, who caught it.

'Push the button. Check the screen.'

Paterson looked down, reluctantly.

'That looks to me like a nice combination of aerobic and weight training, though Rosie's only a little thing, isn't she? Easy enough to lift her up and hold her against the wall like that. 'Course, the fact you're both naked might make the future Mrs Paterson a little dubious.'

'What do you want, Brand? Money?'

'Sure.'

'Really? That's it?'

'Yup. You know me; it's probably all in your files. I'm broke, my rich ex-mercenary girlfriend got it on with Mario, and even if I wanted to forgive her she's up and disappeared. Say, what did ever happen to Mario? I figure a psychotic killer like him probably likes working for you. You using him to rub out rival poaching gangs?'

Paterson simply stared at him.

'Also,' Hudson continued, 'Anna, Shadrack's mom, is not only heartbroken, she's poor, like everyone where she lives, and she's got a daughter in varsity. She needs money; I need money.'

'I've got my wage. It's good, but I'm not rich.'

'Oh, you're plenty wealthy, James. You're the CEO of the Scorpions, Africa's biggest organised crime outfit, and it's going to just keep on getting bigger, isn't it? In fact, it'll probably expand at about the same pace as Julianne's portfolio of safari lodges. I think that maybe an alpha male like you doesn't like the thought of his future wife having bigger assets than him, so you'll start expanding again once things quieten down. This time, though, you'll target your poaching gangs' activities to areas where Julianne doesn't have a presence, so she looks good. I see the number of elephants getting killed in Hwange in Zimbabwe and Chobe in Botswana is on the up again, so maybe you're already back in business, taking up where your partner, Nikola Pesev, left off.'

'You're suggesting . . .'

'I'm suggesting you were the head of the Scorpions all along, and Nikola Pesev was your deputy, or partner, or whatever. I've got a recording Sonja made of Pesev speaking Russian, at his lodge. I'm fairly sure he was talking to you; it was something about "plans being in place for a boat trip".'

'It wasn't me.'

Hudson shrugged. 'Maybe, maybe not, but it was kind of odd how you told us you would email Sonja's recording of Pesev speaking Russian to someone you knew, who could translate it. I was talking to Tom Furey, Sannie van Rensburg's husband, a couple of days ago. Remember him? He remembers you, from that sting operation you were involved with in the UK, where you posed as an arms seller – a Russian arms seller. Seems you learned to speak Russian fluently during your service with the intelligence corps.'

Paterson glared at him. 'It's rusty.'

'Whatever. I figure you told Pesev that you wanted to get your girlfriend, Julianne, to stop her crusade against poaching, but also to compromise her. So, you two cooked up this idea where you'd launch a phony operation against Pesev, he'd get wind of it, and you would be "kidnapped" in inverted commas. Pesev would force Julianne to deal with him, to further his aims and yours, and to secure your freedom. By forcing Julianne into a deal with the devil – Pesev – you'd both have some dirt to use against her in the future if, say, the marriage went sour. She didn't know that you were using your poaching gangs, the bad guys, to help her bottom line as well; she just thought you were targeting bad guys. You're quite a catch, James – a security man with his own private army that can wreak havoc on the legitimate competition to your wife's business interests, and at the same time turn a few million bucks in ivory and rhino horn and whatnot on the side.'

'You can't prove any of this.'

It was Hudson's turn to shrug. 'Probably not, and I know the police will find it hard, too. I figure that things started to go wrong at Kipili when Mario escaped the dragnet that you and Pesev had envisaged. He went rogue, and for you it would work out in your favour whatever went down. Either he'd get caught and killed by Pesev's men or – and here's the interesting part – Mario might come and rescue you and kill Pesev. He got me to help out with that part, and it suited you just fine. When Mario, Ezekial and I got the upper hand, you didn't care if Pesev was killed. Julianne got to claim that she destroyed the Scorpions and she didn't have to make any grubby deals. You got complete control of the Scorpions; win–win.'

Paterson forced a laugh. 'You should write a novel.'

'I wondered,' Hudson said, 'why would you deliberately steer Rosie towards Pesev?'

'It's your fantasy, you tell me.'

'Maybe you were playing Pesev, telling him the media was on to him, and all the while it was you using Rosie to set him up. You told Pesev he was about to be exposed and that made him more willing to try your phony deal with Julianne. Rosie, the South African Police, other enforcement agencies – they were all closing in on the Scorpions and Pesev, your lieutenant or whatever he was, was a perfect lightning rod to keep attention away from you.'

James shook his head. 'You're deluded.'

'I know you're the head of the Scorpions, and Sannie van Rensburg buys my theory as well, even if she can't prove it. She's coming for you anyway,' he checked his watch, 'in about fifteen minutes, for the murders of Goodness and Patience Mdluli.'

'Rubbish.'

'Is it? Sonja and Tema said Patience was hit, but she wasn't in a life-threatening condition when you and Doug Pearse picked her up in Julianne's chopper that night of the ambush. Doug was flying but you were giving combat first aid – that's what Sonja told me during our drive to Tanzania. Patience didn't make it.'

'I did my best. You've been in combat. You know that sometimes you just can't save someone.'

'Yep, I do, but you didn't even try because you weren't on that flight to the hospital. I called the Mediclinic – I used to date a nurse there. She was on duty that night and she told me there was only the pilot, a white man, and another black man on board. Who was the other guy? I figure he was one of your team of poachers who you got Doug to pick up so that it wouldn't look so strange if he arrived at the hospital alone with a dead girl in the back.'

He watched James and waited, but the other man simply shook his head.

Hudson nodded in reply. 'Doug's got a FLIR, a Forward Looking Infra-Red camera on that chopper. You found her, stumbling around in the bush, and he put you down, so you could track her down and kill her. Your other guys you had dismissed, told them to make their way out of the reserve on foot, but you had a job to do and you wanted it done properly, so you did it yourself. You were in charge of the whole operation, leading from the front. You wanted to lead the team that took on the Leopards – Sonja was a worthy adversary for you – and you wanted to be the trigger man on the RPD as well, just like with those IRA guys on the boat off the coast of England, except this time you'd be taking down a national parks helicopter with a machine gun. I know you, James, you're not the backroom guy you pretend to be. You like the killing. Tom Furey told his wife, van Rensburg, all about you. You were on Julianne's chopper after the contact long enough to pick up Patience and then go looking for her sister Goodness while Patience died. Why James? Why didn't you just accept that wounding Patience would have been enough to seal the fate of the Leopards? Did you really have to kill both those poor girls?'

'Doug didn't tell you any of this.' Paterson was looking up now, his eyes defiant. 'Because it's all lies.'

'Y'all got that first part right. Doug got a call from the police yesterday, a simple request asking if he'd mind going through the events of that night, and he didn't show up for work this morning. You can check at the office if you like. He's flown the coop, literally, with Julianne's helicopter. He's left you hanging, James.'

'Nonsense.'

'Yup, deny, deny, deny.' Hudson glanced at his watch again. 'My deal's gonna expire soon, Jimbo.'

'What deal is this exactly? There is no way the police will be able to link me to the killings of either of those two women.'

'You got a point there, James. It's not a slam dunk. Van Rensburg was ready to bring you in to test your DNA against the blood samples the crime scene guys took off the razor wire on the perimeter fence of the Sabi Sand reserve. But, guess what?'

Hudson watched his face carefully.

'What?'

'The samples have gone missing. The police are investigating, but Sannie thinks someone was paid off to get rid of the evidence. That sort of thing happens here, in South Africa, right?'

He shrugged. 'So there is no evidence linking me to the killings.'

'Just your boots. The ones with the slash in the sole.'

'I told you about those boots. I gave them to Shadrack, as a gift.'

'Yeah, I remember, and Julianne told van Rensburg that same bullshit story you fed to Pesev, that Shadrack's cousin was the shooter and he tried to frame Shadrack by giving him back the boots he'd stolen from him. You miscalculated, though, James. You probably thought the South African police would have released the bodies of Shadrack and his cousin by now, but me starting an investigation and Sannie getting on board stalled that process. The cops took a look at the cousin's body and there was no cut on his back, or anywhere else.'

'I *gave* those boots to Shadrack,' said Paterson.

'Somehow, you don't strike me as the altruistic kind, James. You ever given anything to any of the workers at Hippo Rock before?'

Paterson tugged at his right earlobe, looked up, as if trying to recall something. It was a telltale sign of a lie. 'Yes, I'm sure I have.'

'I'm sure you haven't.'

'How would you know?'

'Cameron and Kylie who own the house I live in asked me to thin out their kitchen cupboards, to de-clutter the crockery. The place came fully stacked with old stuff when Cameron inherited it and they got themselves some nice new stuff as gifts when they got married. I gave the old plates and cups and saucers to a couple of the maids. I also gave Shadrack one of my old sweaters when it was really cold, back in July; he was freezing his ass off outside.'

'So?' said Paterson.

'So, you don't know the rules, but Sannie van Rensburg, another generous person, and I do.'

'Rules?'

'James, James, James. It's a shame you're such a tight-ass. What you don't know is that all of the staff from Hippo Rock, even the tried and true, longest serving ones like Shadrack's mom, get searched every day when they leave work. If they are given a gift by an owner, they have to produce a letter from said householder saying what it is they have been given, and that they have permission to take it off the estate.'

Paterson opened his mouth to speak, but couldn't form the words.

'Oh, I know what you're going to say, James. You're about to tell me you did write Shadrack a note, and that it must have got lost. Which is odd, because there's a whole folder of those letters at the Hippo Rock security gate going back at least the last three or four years. Old Solly at the gate is a stickler for that kind of stuff.'

'What do you want?'

'That's the spirit.' Hudson reached into his shirt pocket with his free hand and pulled out a piece of paper. He tossed it to James, who unfolded it and read it.

He looked up at Hudson. 'A printout of a letter from me, to Hippo Rock security, explaining that I gave Shadrack a gift of an old pair of combat boots, one with a damaged sole.'

Hudson nodded. 'I figure an anally retentive ex–British Army officer like you would have made a duplicate, and that if you're asked by, say, a certain blonde detective captain, that you're somehow able to find this in your papers. Of course, I'm sure you actually gave the boots to Shadrack's cousin, and told him to frame Shadrack, but then things went haywire when Tema and the local cops stumbled on the cousin taking his AK-47 around to Shadrack's place. The cousin panicked and shot a policeman, so you then arranged for Sonja and her team to wipe out the pair of them in the heli-borne ambush you staged.'

Paterson stared at him, but said nothing.

'Toss me the phone back.' Paterson complied and Hudson caught it.

'Open your shirt,' Paterson said.

'Want to know if I'm wearing a wire? Sure.' Hudson unbuttoned his safari shirt and showed him his bare chest. He turned, quickly, and flicked up the tail. 'I can drop my shorts for you as well, if you like.'

'No need. How much for the letter?'

Yes, thought Hudson, now they had him. 'A million rand. Half of that will go to Anna, half to me.'

'I don't have that much cash on me.'

'I know you're good for it. And if you don't pay I don't need to go straight to the police. Phase one will be showing Julianne this little pic of you and your workout buddy Rosie.' He waved the phone at James. 'What have you got here?'

'A hundred thousand.'

'Where?'

'In my study.'

'Then let's go have a look-see, nice and slowly. We've still got some time before the cops come calling.'

Hudson backed off as James stood and led the way. Julianne's house was a modern confection of glass and steel, designed to give uninterrupted views across the open grassy plain and water-hole below, and up into the granite koppies that rose behind the building. Those rocks were prime leopard country, Hudson thought as they walked on the polished wooden flooring, the perfect place for a predator to set up her lair.

Paterson entered his personal office area. He pointed to a minibar refrigerator, next to his modern stainless steel writing desk. The office was divided by a row of old-fashioned metal filing cabinets – Paterson was obviously old-school when it came to compiling dossiers on people. On the other side of the cabinets were a low coffee table and two armchairs.

'Cold hard cash, a man after my own heart. Let me see first; I used to keep a .38 special in my fridge.'

Paterson bent, opened the refrigerator door and stepped back.

'Beer, wine, vodka and canned peaches?'

'Money's in the fruit can. I've got a hundred thousand in cash in there. Consider it a down payment.'

'Works for me. Nice and slow, now, take it out.'

Paterson dropped to one knee and reached into the fridge.

'Tell me, what part did Julianne play in all this?' Hudson asked.

'Nothing,' James said, not looking back. 'She was – is – inno-cent. She had nothing to do with the Scorpions. Sure, she was keen for me to set up the special unit to track down the so-called poaching kingpins, and didn't cry when the team starting killing people, but it was never her idea to set up a hit squad. She viewed it all as coincidence, collateral damage.'

Hudson felt his phone vibrate in his free hand. Paterson had the fruit can out and was reaching into it so Hudson risked a quick look at the SMS message on the screen. He saw the sender's name first, Sonja.

Hudson knew she was somewhere close by. She had gone rogue, not answering his calls or messages, but it was Sonja who had taken the pictures of James and Rosie having sex in the gym, which she had emailed Hudson. She could even be watching them right now.

Grenade, said the message.

Hudson heard the click of a spring-loaded lever flying off the hand grenade that James had just slid from the empty fruit can. Paterson's body moved in a blur and there was a crash as he barrelled into one of the upright metal filing cabinets and sent it sprawling.

Hudson fired a double tap, and saw the towelling of Paterson's loose-flowing robe being snatched by the bullet, but the other man was crawling behind the cabinets before Hudson could take aim again. Between him and Paterson, rolling slowly on the floor, was the hand grenade.

*

'Gunfire. Go!' Sannie said.

Julianne Clyde-Smith had been sobbing in her office from the moment it became apparent that Hudson Brand and Captain Sannie van Rensburg had been right about the man she had planned to marry.

Hudson was not wearing a wire, but bugs had been planted under the deck of Julianne's home and in James's office. Julianne had

TONY PARK

just found out that the electricians who had been called to repair faulty wiring in that end of her suite a few days earlier were actually police officers. The problems they had been called to fix were a result of sabotage carried out by Tema Matsebula.

Julianne had immediately denied any involvement with the Scorpions, or with setting up a hit squad, and had threatened to call in her lawyers. However, Sannie had outlined the case they had put together against James and convinced her to listen in to the bugs, to hear what James had to say to Hudson. Sannie had told her she believed James had paid off someone to lose the DNA evidence that would link him to the killing of the woman in the Sabi Sand, and that they had sent Hudson in undercover to try to draw James into a confession.

Now she felt heartbroken, foolish and angry.

The policewoman drew her gun and her husband was on his feet, following her out of the lodge's main office, along the pathway to Julianne's private residence. The officers had a head start on Julianne, and as she came out into the sunshine she heard an explosion.

*

Hudson Brand, ears ringing, back feeling like it was on fire, rolled over, sat up, and raised his Colt .45. He emptied the magazine at the figure in white, who leapt out the gaping opening where a floor-to-ceiling plate-glass window had just disintegrated.

He cursed, slumped back down again and yelped as the glass fragments dug deeper into his skin.

Hudson was aware of footsteps on the floorboards, a shadow passing over him. He blinked and saw through gritty eyes a shaggy green and brown monster, like the Sasquatch or Bigfoot creatures that had been a popular source of myth and speculation during his childhood in the United States in the sixties and seventies.

It leaned over him, its face a mask of mottled camouflage. It smelled pungent, acrid, not totally unpleasant, and not completely unfamiliar.

It slapped his face.

'Hudson?'

If his voice made a sound he couldn't hear it, but the being put a green hand to its head and pushed back its skin, its hood. He saw the auburn hair, the blue eyes through the green and brown makeup, the even white teeth.

'Sheesh, I thought you were dead,' she said.

He could barely hear it, her. Sonja leaned over him, closer, and kissed him. His mouth and tongue searched for her, like a man stranded in the desert licking the last drops of water from a canteen.

She rolled him over, ran her hands over him, and lifted his shirt.

'You're not hit as bad as you look.'

Funny – he felt pretty bad, but at least he could hear her words better. He tried to speak.

'Shush.' She put a finger to his lips, then kissed him again. 'I love you. Goodbye.'

As she moved, her boots crunched scattered diamantes of broken glass. Her ghillie suit, a sniper's one-piece camouflage overall made of scraps of dyed hessian, flapped on her body and he saw the hunting rifle with night sight and silencer held in her right hand.

He closed his eyes, giving in to the pain, and when he opened them again, she was gone.

Chapter 31

Ezekial led the way, scanning the dirt and rocks for spoor and signs of James Paterson. James had been wounded, either by a bullet or flying glass or fragments from the grenade, as every now and then the tracker picked up droplets of blood.

'His stride is long, and he is still strong,' Ezekial said.

'Great,' Sonja muttered. She held her rifle in her right hand, but her left was pressed against the sniper's suit, trying as best as she could to staunch the blood from the wound in the side of her belly.

She had not been far from the house, less than a hundred metres, lying up in the observation post she had created ten days earlier between a pair of granite boulders. All through that time she had watched them, Julianne and James, and all the other staff and guests, from her hide. She hadn't bathed or even brushed her teeth. She had lived like an animal, like the leopards she saw at night, gathering information, and biding her time.

Sonja had seen James's liaison with Rosie and the pieces had fallen more snugly into place. She'd thought, on the boat at Kipili, that Pesev was too smart for his own good, revealing too much inside knowledge. Sonja believed that James and/or Julianne were crooked and she had been watching and listening, waiting for either of them to slip up. Rosie was more than just James's lover or friend with benefits; they had talked about him transferring money to her, and she had made references to him 'doing what needed to be done, especially when it came to elephants'.

Sonja had eavesdropped on phone calls and conversations at night, as she lay beneath the floorboards of the deck on which Julianne and James had their dinner most evenings. She had learned that if Julianne was complicit in any of James's wrongdoing then she was very good at hiding it; more likely, she was innocent.

James, however, spoke Russian into his phone when Julianne was away inspecting the building works at the lodges, and Sonja recorded his conversations on her phone, hiding under his nose, charging her phone with a mini roll-out solar panel she had bought at Outdoor Warehouse after discharging herself from hospital, and then emailing those conversations to a Russian friend she had served with in Afghanistan. She built up her picture of him, which was the same as the one Hudson and Sannie had drawn, clearly. She had watched Hudson sneak up to Julianne's house, and seen Sannie and the man she presumed was Sannie's husband meet with Julianne at the lodge. Through a directional surveillance microphone she had heard Hudson outline the case against Paterson.

While Tema was looking the other way, covering their flank, Sonja took a quick look at her injury, under the voluminous ghillie suit she had bought from a shop specialising in selling paintball guns and imitation military uniforms to weekend warriors in Nelspruit.

A shard of glass had speared into her as she'd jumped from a granite boulder at the moment the grenade had gone off. Through a spotting scope she had seen James plant that grenade in his bar fridge on her second night. She had wondered if he was feeling cornered, like a rat, and was preparing for the day when the authorities might come calling. She had sent the picture of James and Rosie to Hudson from a nondescript email address she had set up, but had had to blow her cover and location by sending him the SMS warning about the grenade.

Sonja had hidden again, after the blast, and watched the police slowly get their act together, calling in reinforcements, but she knew Paterson would be long gone by the time a police helicopter or dog squad arrived. She had snuck off to the staff accommodation, found Tema and dragooned her and Ezekial into action. They were both as keen to bring Paterson to justice as she was, now that they knew he had been giving Mario his assassination orders and that James was responsible for the deaths of Shadrack and their colleagues in the Leopards.

'Are you all right?' Tema whispered to her.

'Fine,' Sonja lied. 'Old age. I've been lying up in that hide too long.'

'Hudson told us that you were hiding somewhere around here. Why don't you take that camo suit off?' Tema said. 'It's crazy hot; you must be cooking in there.'

'Don't worry about me. Keep moving.'

Sonja knew that if Tema saw the gash in her side she would stop and call for help and they would lose Paterson, perhaps forever. The bastard had murdered two of her girls, and for that he would not be allowed to escape.

*

The sun was setting by the time Doug Pearse had picked up the four Scorpions members from across the Mozambican border. That was good, as he needed the long shadows to hide him from sight in case there were any national parks or police aircraft above him.

Doug flew low – NOTE the Americans called it, nap of the earth. He was almost brushing treetops with the skids of Julianne's helicopter. He had to pick up James and he needed his boss and paymaster alive if he was to have any chance of avoiding prison and starting a new life for himself. The hired guns in the back of the chopper would provide the ground security element.

Boarding had been a rushed affair, and Doug had not at first noticed that one of the men who climbed into the helicopter was a white man, his face and hands covered with black camouflage cream. He knew now it was Mario Machado, the latest recruit to James's private army of poachers.

Doug figured that once they were done they would take the helicopter back across the border into Mozambique and get rid of it over there, or maybe even respray and rebirth it, like a stolen car. If the police were on to James, then they would soon learn of his complicity in the death of the female anti-poaching unit member on board this very helicopter en route to hospital in Nelspruit, and how Doug had transported the poachers, with James leading them, on the night of the ambush. There was no going back for any of them.

It had been madness – James was crazy. Far from being the risk-averse backroom staff officer that he liked to portray himself as, James lusted for action and the adrenaline and danger of combat like no one Doug had ever met. He was the head of a major organised crime syndicate, but what gave him the biggest kick was slogging through the bush, carrying an RPD machine gun and trying to shoot down a national parks helicopter, or executing a fleeing female anti-poaching unit member. The madness, and the greed, had been contagious.

'I'm picking up a man, running, on the FLIR,' Doug said to Mario via the intercom. Doug pointed to the ghostly glowing figure making steady progress through the bush below in the now almost-dark bushveld.

'Affirmative,' Mario said. 'That has to be him. Put us down in that clearing over there. We'll get him, you orbit out of visual range.'

'Roger that.' Doug banked, levelled out, flared the nose and put the chopper down in the clearing. As soon as the last man had stepped off he was airborne again.

*

Ezekial stopped. 'Helicopter.'

Sonja, her breathing laboured, caught up to Ezekial and Tema. 'I hear it. Ours or theirs?'

'No lights,' Tema said. 'One of theirs?'

Sonja nodded. She should have thought of that. She was feeling light-headed, probably a combination of blood loss and dehydration from the slog through the bush during the hot afternoon.

'Sonja,' Tema said. 'Let's pull back, call Captain van Rensburg, tell her we've just heard a helicopter.'

'No!'

Tema winced at the retort.

'Sorry,' Sonja said. 'We're so close, Tema. We can get him. Eyes peeled, both of you. That chopper could have been dropping off an extraction team. We know Paterson has an army on the other side of the border. He'll have been calling for help.'

'I'll take point, up the front,' Tema said.

'No,' said Ezekial. 'Let me. I can still track even though the light is low.'

'All right, but look up as well as down,' Sonja said.

Tema moved closer to Ezekial. Sonja was grateful for a moment's rest while the two of them discussed something. Her fingers were still coming away from the wound in her abdomen wet with fresh blood, which was not good. She strained to hear the other two.

'Ezekial, I am just as experienced as you. I can go in front, even if I am a woman.'

'It has nothing to do with you being a woman, Tema. In Tanzania, you thought I was a coward, because I could not kill that man in cold blood.'

'No, not at all,' she said, loud enough for Sonja to hear easily. 'I was undercover; we've been over this before. I had to pretend to be on Mario's side. I hated what he did, executing that man in cold blood.'

'Yes, I know that, but I have to show you that I, too, am a warrior.'

'You don't have to show me anything.'

But it was too late; Ezekial strode off into the darkness. Sonja took a deep, painful breath and followed them.

*

James Paterson allowed himself another stop. He heard it again, on the slight evening breeze, the raised pitch of a person making a point in anger.

That confirmed to him what he believed, that he was still being followed, but the sound of the helicopter ahead of him told him Doug was in the area, and had probably dropped off Mario and the rest of the quick reaction force. He preferred to think of them that way, in military terms, than as a gang of poachers.

It was ironic, James mused, that it was Mario coming to collect him. He had given the order for Mario, Sonja and the others to be killed after they had taken out Obert Mvuu in Zimbabwe. Sonja had been Julianne's pick to head the anti-poaching hit squad and James had known from the start that she would be trouble. He'd achieved most of what he needed, by setting her and the team up to get rid of his last major competitors in South Africa and Zimbabwe, but the team had proven more difficult to eliminate than he had expected. He'd used their survival to his benefit in Tanzania, and Mario had demonstrated that he had no qualms about being employed as an assassin.

James had planned all along to kill Nikola Pesev and Brand was right, he had fed information to Rosie so that Pesev began to feel cornered, therefore making him susceptible to a deal with Julianne to take the heat off him. The plan was that James would 'escape' from the captivity he had never been in and take out Pesev and his bodyguards. As it happened, Mario had beat him to it. Unfortunately, Mario had found James below decks on Pesev's boat, armed and clearly not bound or cuffed. Mario had pretended to believe James had overpowered his guard, but had then got the drop on him and put a gun to his head. Mario had guessed he was not who he pretended, and said he would shoot him so that he, after saving Julianne, could take over as her head of security. Fearing for his life – he had no doubt Mario would kill him – James had let him in on his secret and offered him a place and a share in the Scorpions.

Their war was not over, but now it was definitely time to retreat across the border into Mozambique and lick his wounds on an Indian Ocean island. He was a mess. His skin was covered in scratches from the countless thorns and branches he had run through and his feet were shredded. The sandals he had been wearing when he got out of the pool had been ripped apart on rocks and tree roots. He had ditched the white bathrobe soon after leaping from Julianne's home, and the numerous falls he had taken had covered his body with enough dirt mixed with sweat to camouflage his pale skin. He told himself to ignore the pain. Fortunately Hudson Brand had not had the presence of mind to search him and had missed the phone he had left in his bathrobe pocket. He had been able to contact Doug, who had indeed fled that morning, with Julianne's helicopter, but Doug was still firmly on James's team. Doug had no choice but to stay with James, or else face prison. He was out of mobile phone range now, but he could guess from the direction in which he'd heard the helicopter which way the reaction force would be heading. He assumed Doug had picked him up on the infra-red camera.

James stopped when he heard a bird call.

Ti-ti-ti-tee-teee-toooo, came the call, progressively dropping in speed and pitch. It was the water thick-knee, formerly called a dikkop. In Zimbabwe people called it the Kariba battery bird because the batteries made in that town had a reputation for going flat too soon.

His men had been trained to use bird calls to signal each other in the bush. Mario was close.

*

'Listen,' Ezekial whispered.

'A bird?' Tema said. She did not have anywhere near the knowledge of birds and wildlife that the man she was now sure she loved had.

'Dikkop,' Sonja said.

'It's called a thick-knee these days, but yes,' said Ezekial.

'So?' Sonja asked.

'So this bird lives by rivers, streams, lagoons. There is no water in this part of the reserve.'

They stayed silent and heard the call again.

Ezekial swallowed. 'That is a man. He is good at making the call, but it is definitely not a bird.'

They all raised their weapons, their alertness rising to a new level. Sonja motioned for Ezekial to move forward. After fifty metres she softly snapped her fingers. They stopped and Sonja moved close to Ezekial.

'Can you make that same bird call?'

He nodded.

'Then do it. And be ready.'

Ezekial did as requested and a few seconds later came the same call, in reply, but Sonja's heart skipped. The other man was so close the mournful call sounded like it was being shouted at them.

'*Comandante*, your bird calls are very good.'

The man stepped around a bush. He carried an AK-47, but it was angled downwards. Ezekial, however, had his LM5 up in his shoulder, ready. He pulled the trigger three times, fast. The slugs slammed into the poacher and sent him toppling backwards.

The bush erupted.

Sonja knew there was no option. 'Forward!'

Tema moved up abreast of Ezekial and together they advanced, firing on the move. Bullets whizzed past them and Sonja, who carried a bolt-action hunting rifle, was limited to one shot at a time. She watched for fleeting shadows and fired when she saw movement, or a brief muzzle flash.

Sonja smelled garlic and as she stumbled through a stand of thick bush she almost collided with a man. The long barrel of her weapon clanged against the steel of his. AK-47. Instinctively she brought up her right hand, smashing the wooden butt into the man's face. His finger was on the trigger and he let off a burst of fire, but the bullets went wild. Sonja ignored the cacophony and pressed home her attack. The man stumbled and before he could regain his balance she kicked him in the groin. He gasped and as he tried to bring up his rifle Sonja reversed hers, pressed the tip of the barrel into his heart and pulled the trigger. He was blown away from her.

'Tema!' Ezekial called. 'Behind you.'

Tema, too, was locked in a hand-to-hand struggle twenty metres from both Sonja and Ezekial, but another man had come up behind her and was bringing his rifle to bear to shoot her at point-blank range. Ezekial took aim and Sonja almost couldn't watch. Ezekial fired first and the man behind Tema fell.

Sonja jogged closer, stopped behind a tree and tried to aim at the man Tema was fighting. The two of them were on the ground, fists flailing. There was an AK-47, the poacher's weapon, lying on the ground, but Sonja saw that it had been rendered useless by a lucky shot from one of them. The man had been able to disarm Tema, however, as her LM5 rifle was also discarded. Sonja couldn't fire; the risk of hitting Tema was too great.

The man proved too strong for Tema; he grabbed her in a wrestling hold and rolled onto his back, his arm around her, choking her. With his free hand he managed to pull a pistol from the holster on his belt and held it to Tema's head.

'I'm standing up now,' he called, and as he spoke Sonja could hear then see that it was Mario Machado under the black makeup.

Ezekial was between Sonja and Mario and Tema.

'Stop where you are, Ezekial. Drop your rifle,' Mario said. 'Whoever else is out there, show yourself. If you don't, Tema is dead on the count of one. Five, four, three, two . . .'

Sonja cursed and walked around the tree. 'Don't shoot, Mario.'

He looked to her. 'Put down your weapons, both of you, then walk away from them and kneel down, where I can see.'

'Do as he says, Ezekial,' Sonja said. The young tracker looked to her, his reluctance clear in his scowl, but Sonja nodded and he complied. She laid down her hunting rifle. 'It's all right, Mario, we're not going to try anything. Just let her go and we won't follow you.'

'Don't tell me what to do, woman,' he said.

Sonja cocked her head. 'Listen. The helicopter's coming closer. Do you think James will tell Doug to come for you? Or maybe they'll just fly away and leave you. For all they know you're dead. James would have heard the gunfire. You don't appear to be carrying a radio.'

Mario glanced in the direction of the engine noise. Sonja could see the concern on his face. Even with Tema as a hostage it would be hard for him to escape on foot through the bush.

'Let's stay calm, Mario,' Sonja said. 'You can signal Doug.'

'How?'

'Tema?' Sonja could see the girl was trying to be brave, but she was shaking. None of them underestimated Mario's ruthlessness. 'Yes?'

'Do you still have that torch I gave you?'

Tema's eyes widened slightly. 'Um, yes, I do, it's in my pocket.'

'Mario, is it OK if Tema pulls out a torch and throws it to me? I can signal the helicopter, guide them in; Doug will see I'm unarmed and you're in charge here.'

Mario nodded. 'All right. But try something and I'll pull the trigger. You know I'll do it.'

'Oh yes, I know you very well now, Mario.'

He laughed. 'Maybe I'll take you hostage as well, back to Mozambique, and I can get to know you even better.'

'I'll gladly take Tema's place.'

Mario grabbed Tema tighter. 'No, I think I'll keep the young one instead.'

Tema reached into the side pocket of her uniform trousers.

'Slowly,' Mario said.

She unbuttoned the flap and drew out the torch. As she did so Sonja saw how she flicked a switch on the base.

'Ready?' Sonja said.

Tema nodded.

'OK, do it.'

Tema lifted the torch and drew back her hand, above her shoulder, as if she was about to throw it.

'Hey, watch what you're doing,' Mario said as the tip of the torch touched his neck, lightly.

'Sorry, not sorry,' Tema said as she pushed the torch's 'on' switch. A hundred thousand volts surged through Mario's body and Tema wrenched herself from his grasp. She rolled away as Mario screamed and pulled the trigger, but his shot went into the air as his body convulsed. Sonja and Ezekial both went for their rifles; Ezekial, uninjured, plus younger and faster, got to his weapon first.

'Run, Tema,' Sonja said as she worked the bolt of her rifle, but Tema went back to Mario and zapped him again. Then she leapt away from him, as she would from a dangerous cornered animal. Mario fought through the pain and brought his pistol up.

Ezekial fired first, and didn't stop pulling the trigger until all of the remaining bullets in his magazine had been poured into Mario.

Sonja went to Tema and hugged her. Ezekial got up, dusted himself off and came to them.

'I'm glad you kept that torch,' Sonja said.

'I wish I'd had it in Tanzania when Mario attacked me.'

Sonja smiled. 'Well it was a nice surprise for him now.'

Tema raised her hand. 'Chopper.'

'I hear it,' Sonja said.

The pilot put his landing light on and Sonja saw it, briefly, coming in, not a hundred metres from them. 'Come on . . . let's . . .'

The effort of giving the command was almost too much for her. She tried to run, but her legs felt heavy.

'Let's go, Tema,' said Ezekial. Tema let go of Sonja, retrieved her rifle and she and Ezekial headed into the danger zone.

Through her pain and dizziness Sonja felt something else, a flood of emotion for these two brave young people. She couldn't go on. They wouldn't make it in time. Doug would be on the ground and airborne again in seconds. Not even Usain Bolt could cover that distance in the time they had to do it in.

Sonja slumped against a tree, anger and despair adding to her pain.

With the last of her strength she lifted her rifle, which now seemed impossibly heavy. She didn't even have the power to hold it unsupported. She managed to bring the butt up into her shoulder and then rested the barrel in the crook of a thin branch, and pointed it in the general direction of where the helicopter had landed.

Slowly, and using all her powers of concentration, she worked the bolt and chambered a round.

The helicopter started to lift off. The searchlight under the nose was still on, illuminating Julianne Clyde-Smith's company logo. Sonja tried to steady her aim, but she knew Doug would be climbing away any second now, and she would have no chance to take an aimed shot.

As she expected the aircraft began to climb, but then it slowed.

Sonja blinked away the stinging sweat from her eyes. The rear side door of the helicopter was open and there, with one foot on the skid, was James Paterson, clad only in a pair of swimming trunks, but holding an AK-47. He was taking aim. James had stopped Doug from getting away and, instead, was going to try and finish off her people.

Doug turned the helicopter, no doubt on James's command, so he could get a better shot. The move made James a more difficult target, but the chopper was in a steady hover.

Doug was the pilot who had flown James into the ambush of the Leopards, who had sat by while Patience was killed or allowed to bleed to death on board his aircraft.

Sonja shifted her aim, looked through the telescopic sights and laid the crosshairs over the pilot. He was laughing at something James was saying.

Sonja squeezed the trigger.

Chapter 32

The wrecked helicopter was ablaze on the ground when Tema and Ezekial reached it. The dry bush around it was also starting to catch fire.

Tema held a hand up in front of her face as she approached the crash site. She got as close as she could to the cockpit, but it was clear from the inferno inside that the pilot was already dead and beyond saving.

'Tema?'

She followed the sound of Ezekial's voice.

When she came to Ezekial, twenty metres from the wreckage, his body lit by flames and the heat almost unbearable on their skin, she saw that at his feet was James Paterson. He had been thrown from the dying helicopter, but he was still alive. Paterson turned his head to look at her.

Tema walked up to him, raised her rifle and took aim at the point between his two eyes.

'Go on,' Paterson said to her. 'You'll be doing me a favour. I don't want to see the inside of Pollsmoor Prison.'

'Don't tempt me.'

'Mario told me Ezekial didn't have the balls for the job,' Paterson said, taunting her. 'But he said you were a natural. You had it, Tema; you have it. You're a huntress. You were trained by the best. Do her proud. It's what Sonja would do.'

Tema looked to Ezekial. He met her eyes. 'This man is evil, Tema, evil to people, evil to wildlife, evil to our country.'

She looked at the figure on the ground. He smiled up at her. He was pathetic, and at the same time condescending, the way his eyes mocked her. She took up the slack on the trigger, felt her breathing steady. It would be the easiest thing in the world for her to put a bullet in this man's head.

'Tema?'

She turned and saw Sonja stagger into the cauldron of burning light. She held her rifle by the tip of the barrel, using the weapon as a walking stick. Sonja was older than Tema, almost old enough to be her mother, but she never thought of her in that way. Now she looked frail, as if the light and the fight were gone from her. Tema started to turn.

'No, guard him. Cover him.'

Ezekial went to Sonja instead, and she let him take the rifle and leaned on him for support.

Sonja coughed. She looked down at Paterson. 'Tell me, James, why did you have to kill my Leopards, Patience and Goodness. Like Hudson said, just wounding one of them would have brought enough bad PR for the unit to be closed down. You going after Goodness is what brought you down. Do you kill for fun?'

He shook his head. 'My plan was to be the hero. I left my men in the bush and Doug picked me up. We went to Lion Sands and picked up Patience and stabilised her. We were heading to the Mediclinic when Doug picked up the sister, Goodness, on his FLIR. We hovered over her, and guided her to a clearing where we could land and pick her up as well.'

'What went wrong?' Sonja asked.

'Patience was semi-conscious at first, but she came around and when she did she recognised me. She had seen my face when she ran from the leopard that you people scared out of the tree. As we were coming in to land Patience went for my gun, in the chopper, and screamed to her sister to run for it.'

'So you killed her.'

'I restrained Patience. I needed to get the other sister and told Doug to put me down while he went and collected one of my men – the cousin of the simple boy who you killed – and they flew to Nelspruit. He finished off Patience. As it happened, it took me longer to catch Goodness than I expected. You might have thought those girls were cowards, Sonja, but they both did well, both died well.'

Sonja was speechless. She felt tears well up from deep within her.

Tema looked down at James, along the open sights of her LM5. 'What do you want me to do?' she asked Sonja.

'You know what to do,' Sonja said. 'It's what he deserves, and it's the right thing.'

Tema nodded. 'Roll over, on your belly.'

Paterson laughed. 'Can't bear to look me in the eyes, eh?'

'No.'

'Very well, get on with it,' he said.

Tema set down her rifle, knelt on Paterson's back hard enough to make him flinch, then reached into the pocket of her fatigue trousers and pulled out a plastic zip tie. She fastened his wrists behind his back, nice and tight, and hauled him to his feet.

Above the noise of the buckling, burning wreckage of Julianne's helicopter came the whine of another engine, and the light from above banished the hellish red flickering of the world below. Tema looked up and saw the police helicopter hovering, coming in slowly to land.

Sonja came to her side, and Ezekial covered Paterson as they walked him to the helicopter. Sonja put a hand on Tema's shoulder and gave it a little squeeze; the gesture meant the world to Tema.

Sannie van Rensburg, her husband Tom, and two uniformed police officers jumped out of the chopper and jogged to them.

'We'll take care of this one,' Sannie said. 'Good work. We've got a vehicle coming and we'll take him by road.'

Sonja fell to one knee.

'She's hurt, bad,' Tema said.

'Get her on the chopper,' Sannie said. 'Hudson's on there as well. His wounds from the grenade blast were worse than we thought. A doctor staying at the lodge as a guest is with him; he suspects Hudson may have internal injuries. They can both go to the hospital in Nelspruit, right away.'

Tema draped Sonja's free arm around her shoulder and she and Ezekial linked hands under her to carry her to the waiting aircraft. They loaded her on board and lay her on the floor, next to Hudson.

Sonja had the strength to give a wave as the helicopter lifted off.

Tema turned to Ezekial and he took her in his arms. 'I love you,' he said.

'Same.'

'Let's go home,' he said.

'Yes, let's.'

*

Hudson's eyes swam from the pain and not enough painkillers, but he was aware of the helicopter landing and people getting off.

He turned his head and saw Tema and Ezekial helping Sonja into the chopper. They laid her beside him.

When he tried to speak he found his mouth was dry and he couldn't get the words out. He reached out for her and the movement caused another wave of hurt to wash over him. He didn't care.

Sonja was pale, her grip weak, but she took his hand.

'I . . .' He forced the word out, and it was harder still to make himself heard when the engine noise increased as the aircraft took off again.

The doctor leaned over him. 'Save your strength.'

'No.' He looked her in the eye. 'I came back for you . . . at the lake. I don't care . . .'

'About Mario?' she said.

'Yes.'

'Thank you. I was going to come back to you, Hudson, once this was finished, if you'd have me back. Will you?'

He saw tiny pinpricks of light at the corners of his eyes and the effort of saying a few words had sucked the energy from him. The doctor got between them, placing his ear next to Hudson's mouth.

Hudson felt himself slipping away.

The doctor sat up and looked to Sonja. 'It's the sedative I gave him; it's starting to work.'

'What . . . what did he say?' Sonja asked, unable to hide the hope from her voice.

'He said, "I will".'

Sonja closed her eyes and smiled.

ACKNOWLEDGEMENTS

While this is my fourteenth African novel, with the addition of six biographies that I have co-written for different markets around the world, *The Cull* is actually my twentieth published book.

That landmark warrants some special thanks, not just for this book, but for the many people who have helped me on this wonderful journey I've been on.

My wife, Nicola; mother, Kathy; and mother-in-law, Sheila, have been my unofficial editors on every one of these books. Their feedback, if anything, has become more forthright and valuable with every book. Thank you all for your love and support.

In Africa and elsewhere there have been so many friends and readers over the years who have offered suggestions for stories, logistical help, research assistance and their time as proofreaders that it's impossible to mention them all. Here are a few.

Baie dankie to my friend Annelien Oberholzer who corrects my Afrikaans and Africanisms in every book, and to the rest of her family, Riaan, Adriaan and Leyla, who have looked after my wife and me and our Land Rovers over many years.

Many years on, thank you, again, to my friend John Roberts, who helped with the research for my first book, *Far Horizon*, when he was living and working in Mozambique (where part of the book is set). He remains my go-to guy for all things Mozambican, Portuguese translations, and African politics and history.

Dennis and Liz Lapham, who were shepherding me around Africa twenty years ago, directly helped with *The Cull* by introducing me to the beautiful Chitake Springs in Mana Pools National Park, Zimbabwe, which gets a mention in the book. While I was there, Ashley Lapham gave me a blood curdling demonstration on the use of a cannula while watching a herd of buffalo. Thank you, all, my friends.

It's no accident *The Cull* follows a path from South Africa to Tanzania – my wife and I did this exact trip while I was writing the book. Thanks to my good friends Brett and Claire Martin for being the most low-maintenance travel companions and for putting up with my absences from the conversations while I was writing.

Thank you to Rob Gurr from Ynot Concepts and Veronica Otter and Leanne Haigh from Grumeti Expeditions who organised accommodation for me at three beautiful Lemala camps in Tanzania: Lemala Ngorongoro Camp, Ewanjan Camp in the central Serengeti, and Kuria Hills Camp. Julianne Clyde-Smith's Crossings Camp in this novel is based on Kuria Hills Camp, and it was on a game drive from this stunning location that I witnessed more than three thousand wildebeest and zebra crossing the Mara River, just as Hudson and Sonja do in the book. If you get a chance to visit Tanzania I would have no hesitation recommending these camps.

I met retired South African Police Service detective 'Boats' Botha in the Kruger Park while writing *The Cull* and, like so many other people I've met over the years, he was more than happy to share some of his experiences with me on the spot, and advised me on police investigative procedures. Thank you.

Lion Plains, where Sonja and The Leopards are ambushed, is fictitious, (and, incidentally, also featured in an earlier novel, *The Prey*), but Lion Sands, where they retreat to, is a real place run by friends of mine and it's well worth a visit if you're looking for somewhere to stay in the Sabi Sand Game Reserve. Nikola Pesev's Paradise Bay Lodge is fictitious, but there is a lovely real-life place to stay at Kipili called Lakeshore Lodge. Maramboi Tented Camp in Tanzania is real and it's an excellent base from which to explore Tarangire and Lake Manyara National Parks. In Malawi I stayed at Makuzi Beach Lodge, and used this beautiful spot as the inspiration for Sonja and Hudson's rendezvous. Sonja makes a passing reference to the Blue Canoe Safari Camp, which is located at Matema Beach on the Tanzanian northern shore of Lake Malawi, and it's another wonderful place to stay.

Thanks to all of the staff and my neighbours at the real 'Hippo Rock' (not its real name) in South Africa, where I live part of the year, for your friendship and support.

Thank you, again, to firearms expert Fritz Rabe, who once more made sure my aim was true when it came to gun matters, and to former crime scene investigator Brian Dargie for his information on gunpowder residue. Thanks, also, to Wayne Hamilton from swagmantours.com.au, and Susan Summers and Greg Transell who proofread the manuscript for me; and to Tema Matsebula, whose name I used as a character in recognition of her support and feedback on my recent books.

It's one thing for a writer to research technical facts – such as how to fly a helicopter, fire a gun or track a wild animal – but it's another journey altogether to work out what makes a person act the way he or she does and, for that matter, how and why we do what we do and feel what we feel. I'm extremely grateful to my good friend and guide on this winding, sometimes difficult path, Sydney psychotherapist Charlotte Stapf. Charlotte has acted as a sounding board and given me (full and frank) insights and feedback on my characters. She pointed me in the right direction and supported me when I needed a hand. She also writes a very good blog, charlottestapf.blogspot.com.au. Thank you for everything.

As with previous books, I've surrendered the difficult (for me, at least) task of thinking up names for my characters to a number of worthy charities who have sold or auctioned off the rights for generous people to have their names assigned to the cast of *The Cull* and raised money for many good causes in the process.

Thank you to the following individuals and the organisations they supported: James Paterson (Worldshare International in support of the Heal Africa hospital in the Democratic Republic of Congo); Rosie Appleton and Ian Barton (Juvenile Diabetes Research Foundation); Tim Clyde-Smith on behalf of Julianne Clyde-Smith, and Doug Pearse (Australian Rhino Project); Bishop Barnabas Lekganyane, head of the Zion Christian Church of South Africa on behalf of his son, Ezekial Lekganyane (Limpopo Rhino Security Group); Ken Mills on behalf of Helen Mills (Khowarib Village School, Namibia); Dr Nikola Pesev (Friends of Robins Camp, Hwange National Park); and Donna Machado on behalf of Mario Machado (Breaking the Brand, an NGO tackling demand for rhino horn in Vietnam).

I have taken a voluntary role as a media officer for the UK-based charity Veterans For Wildlife, which pairs former military personnel, who have served in conflicts around the world, with anti-poaching units and conservation projects in Africa on a volunteer basis. Sonja's fictitious unit 'The Leopards' is, in fact, based on the real life Black Mambas, South Africa's first all-woman anti-poaching unit and I was lucky enough to meet this impressive group of people through Veterans For Wildlife. The Mambas are doing inspirational work protecting wildlife, and breaking down gender barriers and empowering African women at the same time. You can read more about the Black Mambas and the real life volunteers who have served in Afghanistan and Iraq and now in the fight against poaching at www.veterans4wildlife.org

I'm often asked if I find the process of editing a book difficult, when I receive feedback on what I've written. I don't. I feel privileged and lucky to be part of the Pan Macmillan family in many parts of the world and when publishing director Cate Paterson, editor Danielle Walker, copy editor Brianne Collins or proofreader Alex Craig point something out to me that I've missed or could have done differently my first reaction, invariably, is 'why didn't I think of that'? Thank you all for your support, guidance, advice, professionalism and friendship since that first book, *Far Horizon*, came out in 2004.

And most of all, if you've made it this far, thank you. I wouldn't be here without you.

Tony Park

AN EMPTY COAST TONY PARK

A body. A cover-up. A buried secret.

Sonja Kurtz – former soldier, supposedly retired mercenary – is in Vietnam carrying out a personal revenge mission when her daughter sends a call for help.

Emma, a student archaeologist on a dig at the edge of Namibia's Etosha National Park, has discovered a body dating back to the country's liberation war of the 1980s. The remains of the airman, identified as Hudson Brand, are a key piece of a puzzle that will reveal the location of a modern-day buried treasure – a find people will kill for.

Sonja returns to the country of her birth to find Emma, who since her call has gone missing.

It turns out that former CIA agent Hudson Brand is very much alive, and is also drawn back to Namibia. Together, they must finally solve a decades-old mystery whose clues are entombed in an empty corner of the desert.

'Tony Park brings Africa to life'
Sunday Telegraph

RED EARTH TONY PARK

On the run, with everything to lose.

On the outskirts of Durban, Suzanne Fessey fights back during a vicious carjacking. She kills one thief but the other, wounded, escapes with her baby strapped into the back seat.

Called in to pursue the missing vehicle are helicopter pilot Nia Carras from the air, and nearby wildlife researcher Mike Dunn from the ground

But South Africa's police have even bigger problems: a suicide bomber has killed the visiting American ambassador, and chaos has descended on KwaZulu-Natal.

As Mike and Nia track the missing baby through wild-game reserves from Zululand to Zimbabwe, they come to realize that the war on terror has well and truly arrived . . .

'Park is now required reading. This is a truly
riveting read you won't want to put down'
Crime Review

extracts reading groups
competitions books new
discounts extracts events
competitions extracts discounts reading groups
books new reading groups
new extracts events
events books extracts reading groups
reading groups books new discounts
extracts books new titles reading groups
new interviews events
events extracts extracts books
discounts interviews new books extracts
new books events events
events new interviews new books
discounts extracts discounts books
www.panmacmillan.com
extracts events reading groups books
competitions books extracts new